Scent of a Rose

Jane Jaffer

Copyright © Jane Jaffer 2006

All rights reserved

No part of this book may be reproduced,
stored in a retrieval system, or transmitted in any
form or by any means, without the prior permission
in writing of the publisher.

Published in Great Britain by
Pen Press Publishers Ltd
39 Chesham Road
Brighton BN2 1NB

ISBN 1-905621-32-9

Acknowledgements

My thanks and gratitude to Lynn Ashman, Grace Rafael and all the staff at Pen Press for showing confidence in my work and enabling me to realize my dream to publish this story. To my editor, Linda Harris, for whipping this novel, *Scent of a Rose*, into shape and finalizing the material. Thanks to Jassim Jaffer for providing the original design for the front cover, along with Jacqueline Abromeit who provided the layout, and to Aymen Jaffer for taking the photograph of the author.

Thanks also, to all my lovely friends for their continued support and encouragement during the fifteen months of this creative process including Lynn Nightingale, Jan Thomas, Roula Harb, Sibella Laing, Caroline Searby, Christianne Mushantef, Misha Daud, Nikki DePodesta, Conny Al Ajjaz, Jane and Rachel Coogan, Sonia Carr, Carol Saker, Frankie Delamain, Amanda Groome, Viv Hicks, Mona Lisa Durr, Bergy Azhari, Salma Schilter, Osvalda Lampertico, Helene Tremblay and Alba Angelaccio. Special thanks go to Cathy Al Delamie for reading the first draft and giving me tips on ways to improve it and to Sue Mullins and Barry and Sue Chapman for their stimulating ideas and comments (many of which I took to heart!).

Above all, I would like to thank my husband, Redha, for believing in me and supporting all my endeavours. And to my three wonderful sons; Sami, Jassim and Aymen. Thank you, boys, for showing an interest in yet another one of your 'mum's projects'. It has been a joy and a privilege to watch the boys grow and develop into three such wonderful human beings.

Jane Jaffer

Chapter One

The significance of the day flooded into their minds as they awoke; today everything would change. They held each other, in an attempt to forget, aware more than ever of the way in which their bodies seemed to merge. Rosie relaxed in the warmth and intimacy of their loving embrace, dreading the thought of his departure. Gazing at her, Stuart knew that each moment now would need to serve as a memory during their imminent separation. Happily wrapped in each other's arms, Stuart tried, without success, to control negative thoughts of the future. Noticing his glum expression, Rosie smiled softly and ran her hands playfully over his smooth, muscular body. "Stu, do we still have time?" she asked invitingly, closing her eyes and leaning back, waiting for his response. He tickled her and she giggled and threw a pillow at him. He bent his head and began to cover her in loving kisses, moving down slowly, an ardent and generous lover, with perfect timing, knowing how and when to bring her the most exquisite pleasure…

Minutes passed. Stuart felt her warm, soft hand on his shoulder, gently shaking him.

"Hey, Stupot, sleepy head. Wake up! We have to get to Heathrow."

He grimaced and slowly reached for his watch on the bedside table.

"It's okay," he yawned sleepily, "as long as we leave by 7.15. I doubt there'll be much traffic at this time on a Sunday."

He watched Rosie begin her daily yoga routine; stretching her lithe body, arching backwards, bending forwards, balancing on one leg. Hearing her slow rhythmic breathing,

2

Stuart envied her calmness. It contrasted sharply with his own agitated state. He did not want to go.

Last year, through his father's contacts, Stuart had applied for a job in Oman. He had received a vague 'don't ring us, we'll ring you' reply, and promptly forgotten all about it. Then, out of the blue, a letter of acceptance had arrived six weeks ago. The job would be challenging, furthering his career and offering him the promise of real experience and an excellent package with plenty of perks and bonus payments. His mother had shown a very mixed reaction to the news. She was delighted. She had always been the driving force behind his success. Throughout his childhood, Stuart remembered his mother always being there, pushing him to achieve. In fact he felt she was probably more ambitious for him than he was for himself. But she also baulked at the idea of him going to live so far from home. It was a two-year contract. Stuart had smiled fondly at his mother and told her that time flies, before promptly accepting the job. But since then he had met Rosie and everything had changed; two years away now seemed like an eternity. He still had half a mind to ring and reject the offer, but felt sure he would live to regret it. He did not want to miss this brilliant opportunity to further his career.

But would Rosie wait for him?

Just five weeks earlier, Stuart had been invited to attend Dan's stag night in Brighton. On the Friday afternoon Stuart and his flat mate, Rob, had joined the massive rush-hour traffic jam and driven down to Brighton, picking up Jimmy in Blackheath on the way. With his usual flair for organizing everybody, Dan had booked them rooms at the Brighton Grand Hotel and worked out an itinerary for the entire weekend: they would enjoy a Chinese meal together and then go clubbing at a club called Creation. Quad biking had been arranged for them all on Saturday afternoon. This was to be followed by a massive pub crawl culminating at the Pussycat Club in Hove on the Saturday night.

Stuart had not seen Dan or Jimmy for about four months, due to a course he had been taking up in Aberdeen, so he was looking forward to catching up with them. When they met in the bar at the Grand Hotel on Friday night Stuart immediately noticed a subtle change in Dan. Stuart found him distracted and unable to concentrate on their conversation. Dan was constantly speaking on the phone or sending text messages to his girlfriend, Kelly. Rob and Jimmy laughed at their friend and began to tease Dan mercilessly, accusing him of becoming an old softy since he had met Kelly. But Stuart thought it was more than that. He thought Dan had lost his sense of humour. He could hardly believe that Dan, a stocky fair-haired, muscular, gym fanatic and one of those eternal bachelors continually intent on his next female conquest, was actually going to tie the knot. As they discussed Dan's future at Jim Thompson's restaurant later that night, Rob and Jimmy continued to ridicule Dan.

"So, Dan, are you really gonna tie the knot, man? You must be mad!" said Jimmy.

"This girl must be something really special," laughed Rob.

Dan just smiled enigmatically and nodded. "Oh she is, mate, she's very special. I've never felt like this before. Wait till you meet her. I really love her," he blurted out.

His mates fell silent.

"Okay, so you love her. Love 'em and leave 'em's what I say," bragged Stuart.

"Yeah, just because you love her, doesn't mean you have to go and get spliced now, does it?" added Jimmy.

"I know it sounds stupid, but I just know that I want to spend the rest of my life with her," Dan announced, staring dreamily into space.

His friends rolled their eyes.

"Oh God, you've got it bad. What you need is a good drink. Come on, let's go over to the club," Jimmy suggested.

They split the bill between them and walked back along the seafront.

Stuart's first glimpse of her affected him deeply. She was standing on her own in the dark nightclub waiting to hang up her coat. She was beautiful. Stuart was absolutely mesmerized. He gazed at her tall slim figure, noticing her flat tanned stomach, her tight blue hipster jeans and the gentle curve of her breasts in a short pink tee shirt. Stuart felt she had an innocence about her that he could not quite define. It was as though she was oblivious to her own beauty. Even in the stroboscopic lights of the club, Stuart was aware that she possessed an inner glow. He was certain this indicated a woman with a kind and generous nature. She had smooth, creamy translucent skin and the longest eyelashes he had ever seen, shading her large violet-blue eyes. Her small feminine nose tilted upwards appealingly.

She moved forward, smiled and spoke to the cloakroom assistant, exchanging her chocolate-coloured suede coat for a small pink ticket. Her movements were fluid and graceful. *Was she a dancer?* he wondered.

As he observed her, a short well-endowed girl with a round face and laughing brandy-ball eyes came towards her. The two girls kissed each other on both cheeks.

"Hey, Rosie! How are you, darling? Good to see you. Come on, the others are waiting for us over by the dance floor."

Soon Stuart lost sight of her in the crowd but he continued to stare after her. *Rosie,* he thought, *what a beautiful name.* Just then, Dan came up behind him. Stuart could smell the alcoholic fumes on his breath and noted his slightly drunken sway. *Perhaps Dan had already had enough to drink,* he thought.

"Hey, what's up?" slurred Dan. "What happened to our drinks, Stu?"

"Oh, yeah, sorry. I was just on my way. There was this girl, I…" he hesitated looking away, "I was just going to the bar, why don't you come with me?" Stuart suggested, taking Dan by the arm and guiding him towards the drinks counter. "Come on, I'll buy you a fruit juice."

"What? A fruit juice? You're joking, man, I need a beer," replied Dan.

With a few drinks inside him, Dan seemed like his old fun-loving self. Laughing, joking and drinking steadily all night, he was clearly intent on having a good time during his last few nights of freedom. But Stuart's mood had been transformed. He was not in the mood for heavy drinking. His mind was in turmoil. *Where had she gone? Had she left already?* He chastised himself; he had just let the most beautiful girl he had ever seen, walk away without even approaching her. *What is wrong with me?* He knew his life had been full of missed opportunities such as this one. He asked himself whether he was going to act this time, or continue to be an observer of his own constant procrastination? Suddenly he realized he could not wait for life to happen to him, it was time to take control and fight for what he wanted. He needed to find her. He left his friends and began searching the club with a sense of urgency.

He scoured the dance floor, but she was nowhere to be seen. He walked all the way around the perimeter of the dance floor, with the music blaring in his ears. Just as he was about to give up hope, he glanced up at the balcony and there she was; coming down the stairs with her hair falling over her face as she laughed. He watched as she and her girlfriends weaved their way onto the dance floor, through the heaving crowd of clubbers. Rosie lifted her arms and began to sway slowly to the beat with her eyes closed. Stuart moved closer so that he could watch her. He noticed a small diamond glinting from her navel. She moved her body sexily.

His mouth felt dry and he swallowed hard. "Hi, do you mind if I dance with you?" he asked, approaching her and hopping from foot to foot awkwardly, in an attempt to dance. She deliberately ignored him, turning her back and continuing to dance with her eyes closed.

"Can I buy you a drink?" he implored.

"No thanks," she answered shyly. Giving him a weak smile, she moved away with her friends. It was not his style to push. Stuart shrugged his shoulders in hopeless acceptance of the obvious. She had made it painfully clear that she was not interested in him. He would have to forget her. Hiding his disappointment, he smiled broadly as he returned to his friends and began asking Dan more details about the wedding arrangements.

However, by the end of the evening, Stuart and Rosie had made eye contact several times. Each time their eyes met, she lowered her gaze and concentrated on sucking on the straw in her drink or she hastily started a conversation with one of her friends. Stuart knew she was aware of him watching her and he convinced himself that the smile she gave him was real and not part of his imagination.

At 3 a.m., as the crowd of clubbers spilled out into the frigid September air, Stuart silently observed her chatting with friends while waiting for a taxi on the side of the road. Stuart noticed a heavily-built man in a black leather jacket, standing directly behind her. She was oblivious to him. Stuart saw the man's body sway under the influence of alcohol, but his eyes were unwavering; he was staring intently at Rosie and muttering under his breath. The man inched forward and with growing alarm, Stuart realized the drunk was about to approach Rosie. Stuart jumped forward, feeling an intense urge to guard and protect her. But at that moment, a white and blue taxi pulled up and Rosie and her friends piled in and left. Stuart walked silently back along the sea front to the hotel, deep in thought. He was hardly aware of Jimmy singing 'My Way' at the top of his voice with true alcoholic bravado.

The next day, the sun shone in a cloudless sky and the sea sparkled with light. Crowds swarmed along the promenade: there were lovers holding hands, pretty girls on rollerblades, young kids on skateboards, seriously helmeted cyclists pedalling furiously along the cycle lane and elderly women walking overweight, short-legged dogs. Market stall holders were absorbed in enticing potential customers to buy Indian cotton tops and silver jewellery inlaid with semi-precious stones. Unshaven hippies sat cross-legged on the pebbled beach, braiding hair and painting henna designs on bare shoulders, backs and tummies to the sound of bongo drums. Dan took his friends to an Italian restaurant for lunch and they took a table on the terrace overlooking the remains of the West Pier and ordered fresh fish, pasta and ice cold Frascati. Dipping chunks of bread into olive oil and balsamic vinegar, the guys talked about quad biking. "It's a real blast, Stu, they've got these gigantic Raptors. You can drive over fields and up and down hills, you know, over rough terrain. The engines are 660 cc's, they're the most powerful quads in the world," Dan boasted, squinting in the sun and struggling with the mother of all hangovers. He rubbed his eyes and replaced his sunglasses.

Stuart peered into the distance.

"Hey, Stuart, what's wrong with you? You don't seem to be listening to a word I'm saying. I was just explaining to you how to get to the quad biking place. The others are meeting us there. Stu, what are you looking at?" He followed Stuart's gaze. "Oh, now I get it," he smirked, "the blonde in the blue bikini, eh?"

"Shut up, Dan!"

"Why, what did I say?" asked Dan, mystified. For the second time, Stuart found himself feeling incredibly protective towards Rosie. He hardly touched his lunch. Drinking his wine thoughtfully, he kept his eyes trained on a certain area of pebble beach. Then, finally plucking up the courage, he told the others he would meet them back at the hotel in an hour's time.

"Why? Where are you going?" There was a pause, while the penny dropped. "Oh I get it, well, don't be late," warned Dan, "I've booked the quad biking for four o'clock and it's at least a twenty minute drive to get there."

"Hi, we met last night," he said, trying to sound nonchalant and relaxed. There was no reply. She was lying on her back, soaking up the sun. He was unable to gauge her response, as she was wearing dark sunglasses, with mirror lenses. She turned her head slightly and he caught sight of himself in her lenses: sandy-coloured curly hair and a mass of freckles. The concave lenses made his nose look enormous. *How ridiculous I look*, he thought. *What am I doing chatting up a girl on the beach, like some seventeen-year-old kid?* He tried in vain to ignore his absurd reflection, as he continued lamely, "Do you live in Brighton?"

She smiled and commented on his extremely poor chat-up line. He laughed and apologized, telling her that he was a bit out of practice, as he had had a steady girlfriend for the past nine months. That is, until she had left him a couple of months ago. He could not tell if this remark provoked her curiosity or her sympathy, but he was infinitely relieved to find that he had finally captured her interest. She turned her lithe body towards him, supporting her head on one hand and smiled shyly up at him.

"So what went wrong? Why did you two split up?" she enquired softly.

"Well," he paused, "she fell in love with my best friend actually."

"Oh, with friends like that, who needs enemies?" she commiserated with a wry smile. He proceeded to embellish the story of his broken romance, intent on keeping the conversation going.

Chatting amiably, Stuart relaxed and found himself laughing out loud for the first time in a long while. There seemed to be a natural rapport between them. She made fun of him playfully and Stuart noticed the way her nose wrinkled when she made a funny remark. He immediately experienced a deep yearning for her, a hunger he had never known. He decided he would die if he did not kiss her sweet pink lips. She was absolutely irresistible, sexy and sensual. He had to fight to control a deep urge to take her in his arms, hold her tight and never let her go. Much to Dan's disgust, Stuart never made it to the quad biking or the pub crawl that night. Walking along the seafront with Rosie, Stuart found himself telling her his life story. Everything just flowed from his lips; facts and feelings pouring out of him. He told Rosie things he had never divulged to another human being; his hopes, his dreams, even his disappointments. She listened intently and nodded with what appeared to be a complete understanding.

Later, the right moment came; they sat in perfect silence on the beach watching the dying sun turn a deep red and he reached towards her, inhaling her sweet fragrance. He tilted her chin and she looked up into his clear green eyes, waiting. Their lips met briefly and they savoured the moment. Then unable to resist, they kissed again with a passion and intensity which surprised them both. He drew her towards him and held her against his broad chest. They parted with a feeling of contentment and watched the flames flickering from a nearby fire, both realizing this moment marked a new beginning, a new era in their lives. Soon, the light failed and they were entertained by a group of foreign students singing Italian love songs, accompanied by the soft chords of an acoustic guitar. The aroma of meat cooking over barbecue coals filled the night air. Suddenly Stuart jumped up. "Wait here! I'll be back in a mo," he said, turning and hurrying away. Rosie was left with a curious feeling of emptiness. Her mind was reeling with the evening's events. *This man makes me feel alive*, she thought. She was totally unaware that she was being watched as she sat quietly waiting for Stuart to return.

Ten minutes later, she laughed, as Stuart returned, panting breathlessly and carrying an opened bottle of Rosé wine and two plastic glasses.

"Oh, Stuart, how romantic! You think of everything!" She smiled, her eyes sparkling as she held out her cup.

"To us!" announced Stuart, touching her cup with his.

"To romance!" she replied.

They talked late into the night and Rosie told him about her life in Brighton and about her sister, Denise: "She's totally different in character from me, but we are really close, there's only two years between us. She's my best friend really," she confided.

Rosie worked as an English language teacher in an institute just off Western Road.

"I just kind of drifted into teaching, though," she admitted. "I mean, I do love teaching, but I know it's not ultimately what I want to do."

"So, what *do* you really want to do?" Stuart enquired with genuine interest.

"Oh, I want to travel, see the world, I suppose. Maybe become a photographer, that's what I really love doing. I love taking pictures."

"Landscapes or people?" he asked.

"Mostly people and situations," she said, turning her head and looking out to sea. "You see, I like to put unusual people together in strange places, you know, sort of out of context. Then, when people see my photos, they have to use their imagination, to really participate in the process. Sometimes people are startled by the juxtaposition of supposedly unconnected people and places. I mean, they have to work out why they are in that situation or place, what's the connection between them or what's about to happen."

Interesting. He figured no two days would be the same with Rosie; he found her exciting and intriguing. He took her in his arms once more and she ran her fingers through his thick, curly hair. They embraced silently and he kissed her lightly on the tip of her nose. They sat holding hands, listening to the sound of the waves breaking on the shore, feeling at one with nature and with each other.

Stuart and Rosie were both unaware of the eyes watching them from afar. The man in the black leather jacket stuffed his red raw hands into his bulging pockets and observed them closely, scowling, as he muttered under his breath.

Chapter Two

Stuart was totally besotted. Rosie possessed a kind of inner wisdom usually only apparent in older women. He had been out with several mature women, much to his mother's disgust. He had tried to explain to her that he usually found young girls boring. He liked women with integrity and a bit of history. Older women had more confidence and experience and they had something to say, which made for far more interesting dates. But he realized there was no future in dating a woman almost old enough to be his mother. He knew he eventually wanted children; a family. It sounded like an old cliché, but Rosie seemed different, unlike any of the other young girls he had met before. She was mature beyond her years. And he could sense that she was immensely talented and creative. He already felt a growing admiration for her liberal attitude and refreshingly honest opinions.

Stuart spent the next five weeks commuting from London to Brighton virtually every day. It cost him a fortune, but there was no way he could stay away from her. They spent most nights wrapped in each other's arms in her small apartment. Then one weekend Rosie had travelled up to London on the train and Stuart had met her at Victoria Station. He had taken her to a tiny French bistro for a romantic candle-lit dinner and later, dancing at the Kasbah. Stuart rarely took girls home to the small terraced house he shared with Rob in Greenwich. But he wanted to share everything with Rosie and that included showing her where he lived. Luckily, Rob and Stuart had an understanding when it came to girlfriends, so Rob had made himself scarce the whole weekend and Rosie and Stuart had had the place to themselves. On Sunday, they had wrapped themselves up in warm coats and hats and taken a walk in Greenwich Park, crunching golden leaves underfoot and watching their breath in the cold morning air. Rosie laughed like a child as they fed the bushy-tailed grey squirrels with nuts. She loved the large brown innocent eyes of the timid, fawn-coloured deer and stood watching them quietly with a rapt expression on her face.

It was at that moment that Stuart realized he was deeply in love with her. Finally, he understood Dan's transformation, realized how Dan had grown willing to commit to a relationship to the point of sacrificing his valuable freedom. Stuart explored his feelings for Rosie. He had always felt a sense of detachment, as if he were looking at life through a plate glass window, but when Rosie was around, he no longer felt that sense of disconnection. She seemed to provide him with the power to make him feel alive. She brought everything into sharp focus for him, making his life real and vibrant. For the first time since he was a small child, he felt really happy to be alive. He remembered his mother once saying:

"When you find your soul mate, nothing else matters. Just being together will be enough."

Oh, God, he thought, *now that I have found the love of my life, how can I possibly think of going away and leaving her?*

His thoughts returned to the present: he was preparing to leave for Muscat, the capital city of Oman. Without her, he would not live, but merely exist.

"Hey come here, you, I want to tell you something," he said.

"I can't stop now, otherwise I lose the flow," she said breathlessly with her eyes closed as she performed the Salute to the Sun. He jumped out of bed and took her forcibly in his arms.

"I love you, Rosie. I'm going to miss you so much, babe."

"Really? How much?" she teased, kissing him on the cheek.

"Promise me you'll think about coming to visit me. I can't wait to see you again, babe. Please say you'll come."

Rosie looked away. "I don't know, Stuart," she faltered. "It seems such a long way to travel."

"Oh come on, it's not that far, really. You said yourself you wanted to see the world. It's actually only six hours away. Listen, we could meet in Dubai. There are loads of cheap flights and package deals to Dubai. Just think, we could book into a posh five-star hotel and stay in bed all day. Please, Rosie, say you'll come," he implored, holding her warm body close to his.

She pushed him away gently.

"Okay, I'll find out. I'll go to the travel agents. Now, come on, let's get ready. I'm going to take a shower."

"I'm coming with you."

"Alright, but Stuart we don't have time for *that*, you can shave while I'm in the shower."

Listening to the forced cheeriness of the DJ on the radio, they drove to the airport without a word, both dreading the final goodbye. After parking the car, they walked hand in hand to the departure lounge and when the last call was announced and he knew he could no longer delay, Stuart held her in his arms, gently pushing her hair back and holding her face between his hands. He kissed her lovingly on the neck, cheeks, forehead and on the tip of her beautiful turned-up nose. Tears were brimming in her violet blue eyes as she rummaged in her bag and produced a small red velvet box containing two halves of a silver heart, each with its own fine silver chain.

"I'll always wear mine and think of you, Stu," she said tearfully, putting the necklace around his neck.

"Oh, Rosie, thanks babe. I'll always wear mine too. Now, promise me that you'll come."

"Okay, I promise," she agreed, and laughed to see Stuart's frown melt into a smile for the first time since their arrival at the airport.

"Goodbye, my wild rose. I love you."

"Have a safe journey. Ring me as soon as you arrive, alright? Love you," she said blowing him a kiss.

She waved as he walked through passport control and watched him move further and further away from her, out of her life, leaving her bereft and alone, with tears streaming down her face.

Stuart had never been so far away from home. He had travelled all over Western Europe, but mostly by train or car. He had flown to Malaga and Corfu, but this British Airways flight to Oman was an entirely different experience. It was really luxurious in comparison to the charter flights he had taken before. He sat in relative comfort, although he thought there was insufficient leg room, considering the amount of time he would have to sit still. He had recently read about the dangers of DVT, so he swallowed an aspirin and kept moving about; lifting his legs and rotating his ankles.

He was amazed at the chap sitting next to him. His neighbour was in his late fifties and had obviously done this trip many times before. As soon as they were airborne, he had ordered a whiskey on the rocks and had drunk it straight down in one gulp. Then, donning earphones and an eye mask, he had gone straight to sleep. His head had tilted backwards and his mouth had dropped open and he was now snoring shamelessly. The stewardess gave Stuart a wide smile as she served him a delicious chicken biriani with a small bottle of ice-cold white wine.

Stuart sipped his wine thoughtfully, realizing how much he was going to miss Rosie and bitterly regretting his decision to leave. But on a more professional level, Stuart had to admit that he was curious and excited at the prospect of working in Oman. He wondered what it would be like.

Apparently, it became unbearably hot in the summer, with temperatures climbing to 120 degrees.

Now it was mid-September, but he had heard it could still be extremely hot until November. His skin was very fair and he burned easily. He wondered how he would adapt to the heat. The recruitment officer had informed him that he would stay in the Intercontinental Hotel in Shatti Al Qurum for the first few nights until his accommodation was sorted out in an apartment block in Madinat Al Sultan Qaboos. The hotel was apparently right on the beach.

Just then, the stewardess announced their arrival in Dubai. There was a flurry of activity, as those disembarking prepared to leave. Once they had landed, a trail of businessman carrying briefcases, smart women carrying designer handbags and scruffy backpackers left the plane. Only a handful of people waited on board to fly on to Oman. Soon, a whole troupe of Indian cleaners boarded the plane and began to pile rubbish into giant plastic bags. Even though night had fallen and it was already dark outside, Stuart could feel the heat rushing in from the open door. Fatigue suddenly overwhelmed him and he longed to arrive in Muscat and get some sleep.

When the plane finally touched down at Seeb International Airport nearly forty-five minutes later, Stuart looked out of the window with curiosity. He could see several low white buildings and a few planes on the tarmac; Gulf Air, Emirates and Oman Air. A mobile flight of steps was pulled into position and, as he descended, the heat engulfed him. His thoughts turned to cold, wet blustery days spent in England and he imagined Rosie dressed in her suede coat with a long woollen scarf wrapped around her beautiful neck. He loved to see her wearing mini skirts with thick tights and boots and his body tingled at the thought of her. What time would it be in England now? Six thirty on a Sunday evening. Rosie had probably been out for a walk, braving the wind and rain. She loved to walk along the promenade when the sea was rough and powerful and always returned with rosy cheeks and sparkling eyes. It would be getting dark there now and Rosie would be opening the door to an empty flat... Stuart's heart ached at the thought.

He boarded the bus with the other passengers and carried his briefcase and laptop into the terminal building, where he was directed to join a long queue to obtain a visa. After an interminable wait, he showed his passport to the policeman in a khaki uniform and was ushered through to the carousel to collect his luggage. Stuart was astonished at the sight he encountered as he wheeled his trolley through the automatic doors and into the terminal; a sea of floating white dishdashas worn by dark-haired men, with small embroidered pillbox hats on their heads. He stood still, watching two men rub noses in a respectful greeting. The swarthy young boy in front of him, wearing a baseball cap, jeans and enormous trainers, grinned as a plump elderly woman, covered from head to foot in a black abaya, rushed forward to greet him, copious tears of joy running down her face. She muttered in Arabic and threw her arms up in the air in praise. *"Al hamdu lillah!"*

A tall Indian, in carefully pressed brown trousers and a loose cream short-sleeved shirt, was holding up a piece of torn cardboard with the name 'Cole' written on it.

"That's me: Stuart Cole," he said, smiling and holding out his hand. The Indian's head wobbled from side to side and he grinned broadly. "Oh yes, sa'ab, Mr Cole come, I take you to the InterCon, I get vehicle in parking. I come, wait here," he gabbled, rushing off towards the car park.

Fifteen minutes later, Sabir, the driver, drove along the dual carriageway with the air conditioning blasting out cold air and an Indian love song blaring out from the car radio. Stuart was relieved to find that Oman was much more developed than he had anticipated. The tree-lined roads were wide and modern and looked almost unnaturally clean. They drove over several fly-over bridges and Stuart noticed huge white buildings, each with their own unique architectural features. Sabir informed him that they were government buildings. Eventually the car pulled up outside a large cube-shaped grey building with a multitude of windows. The doorman at the Intercontinental Hotel removed Stuart's luggage from the boot and placed it on a trolley. A pretty young girl with a blue scarf covering her head and a huge set of pearl-white teeth, smiled and welcomed him at reception. Stuart felt like laughing out loud as he rode a great glass elevator up to the third floor, half expecting to see a man in a top hat open the door. The solemn faced bellboy studied Stuart with some degree of curiosity. He showed Stuart to his room, deposited his luggage and grunted his thanks for the tip Stuart pushed into his hand.

Stuart looked around; double bed, en suite bathroom, TV, mini bar. *Um, I could get used to this*, he thought. He unpacked the bare essentials, while watching news about Iraq on BBC World. He quickly switched off the TV, too tired to think about current affairs. Although he usually took a shower, he decided to unwind in a warm relaxing bath. He ran the water and climbed in, feeling the tension in his body melt away. Twenty minutes later he woke suddenly. He had been dozing and the water had turned cold. Wearily, he pulled himself up, dried off and put on some soft shorts. Even with the central air conditioning, it seemed too hot to wear a tee shirt. He sat down on the bed and ate the small square of chocolate he found on his pillow, then he eased himself in between the starched white sheets, reached for the telephone and dialled Rosie's number.

*

When Rosie drove away from the airport, she wiped away her tears. He was gone. Taking a deep inhalation, she felt like she was coming up for air after being immersed in a deep pool of passion. She knew she was going to miss Stuart terribly, it felt strange to be alone. She recalled so many happy memories. They had had a lot of fun together. *Stuart makes me feel good about myself,* she thought. Her analytical mind began to kick in; *was it love, though?* she asked herself. Or was he just a mirror, in which she saw herself reflected so favourably? In a way, she admitted to herself that it was quite liberating to be alone again. She wondered how she would spend the day and decided she quite liked the delicious thought of being totally on her own, pleasing herself. When Rosie was with Stuart, they usually ended up doing whatever *he* wanted to do. Not that she minded, but it was somehow a luxury to know she could now selfishly plan the entire day around her own needs and desires. When she reached Brighton, she had to drive around for twenty minutes looking for a parking space. It was always difficult on Sundays. She eventually squeezed the car in between a Mercedes and a Honda Concerto and ran towards her block of flats in the cold morning air. As she pushed the key into the lock, she thought she saw a man's reflection in the glass door, but when she turned, there was no one there. She closed the door behind her and took the small lift to the third floor. Rosie opened the door, threw down her keys and bag and went straight to her stereo. She put on some jazz, changed into an old pair of jeans and a soft warm sweatshirt and happily curled up on the sofa with *The Sunday Times* and a boiling cup of orange spiced tea.

Around 8.30 p.m. that evening, the phone rang.
"Hi, Rosie, it's me."
"Oh hi, how was your flight? You sound so close, are you in Oman already? What's it like? Is it hot?"
"You wouldn't believe it, Rosie, it's boiling, but it's beautiful and the hotel's right on the beach." He lowered his voice, "I miss you," he whispered.
"I miss you too, babe. It's lonely here without you," she added mournfully.

"What did you do today?" he asked.

"Oh nothing, really. I just roamed around, read the papers and went for a walk. I thought about you all day though," she crooned, knowing that was exactly what he wanted to hear.

"Did you? I wish you were here with me right now," he murmured.

"Why? What would you do to me?" she asked playfully.

"Mmm, you know," he answered.

"Really? Mmm I can imagine that," she replied suggestively.

"You're so naughty!" he said sternly and laughed. "Hey, I'd better go, babe. It costs a fortune to ring from the hotel. I'll try and organize a mobile phone tomorrow an' I'll give you a ring. Now be good, don't forget me and, Rosie – send me an email."

"Okay, I will. I love you," she replied simply. She put the phone down and smiled. *Dear Stuart*, she thought, *he's such a nice guy*. She ran herself a warm bubble bath and added a few drops of relaxing essential oil, before climbing in, laying back and thinking of all the happy moments she had shared with Stuart. She made up her mind to telephone the travel agent the next day.

On Monday morning Rosie had an argument with the director of studies at the Brink School of English where she worked. Andrew Barker was a complete moron. How he had ever become a Director of Studies she could not imagine, he was so completely dictatorial and incompetent. *He couldn't direct traffic, let alone a team of twenty staff*, she thought. He never considered anyone else's opinion and was useless at resolving issues between staff members. He did not have a clue how to talk to the students either; his patronizing manner had annoyed many of them, and they often claimed that he treated them more like children than young adults. Before the holidays, Rosie had put in a request to teach the intermediate classes this term. Teaching the beginners classes over and over again had become a chore. She knew that if she did not have a change soon, she would be bored out of her mind. Now she discovered that Andrew had totally disregarded her request and he had put her down for six beginners classes each week. To add insult to injury, he had also assigned her the late shift four days a week, which meant working really unsociable hours: from 4 p.m. till 9 p.m. *Well, forget it.* As Rosie walked along Western Road, to meet her sister at Barney's restaurant, she resolved to look for another job as soon as possible. She wondered how easily she could extract herself from her contract at Brink.

Denise stood up as she came in. "Hey, what's wrong with you? You've got a face like thunder," she said, her brown eyes laughing. "Are you missing Stupot?"

"Yes of course, but it's not that. It's that bloody Andrew again."

"Why, what's he done this time?" enquired Denise, rolling her eyes.

"Oh well, he's just so damned annoying. Anyway, I'll spare you the gory details, but suffice to say that I'm looking for another job," she said, throwing her bag down on the chair and removing her chocolate-coloured suede coat.

"What? You don't mean to say he's given you the sack, do you?" asked Denise wide-eyed.

"No, no nothing like that, but I've just about had enough of him. Now I've got to work four evenings a week."

"Well, you shouldn't mind that, now that Romeo has left the scene," said Denise, her eyes glinting mischievously.

"I'll treat that remark with the contempt it deserves," Rosie answered in mock annoyance. "It's the principle that counts. Andrew is just so uncooperative and anyway, I think it's time I moved on," she announced.

"Well then, go for it," replied Denise encouragingly.

Rosie and Denise drank a bottle of Montes between them and ate Caesar salad with grilled prawns. As usual whenever the two girls got together, Denise started telling jokes and making funny remarks about all their mutual friends. Rosie was soon laughing uncontrollably.

"Hey don't look now, but you've got a secret admirer," said Denise looking across the room.

"Oh really, what's he like?" asked Rosie giggling, trying to keep her eyes on Denise.

"Oh he's gorgeous," Denise laughed.

Rosie turned around slowly and saw an ugly looking man in a shabby black leather jacket sitting at the far table. He was blatantly staring at her.

Rosie smiled at him politely before turning back to Denise and nearly snorting with restrained laughter. "Oh God, give me a break!" she laughed.

As they left the restaurant, Rosie was aware of the man's eyes following her out the door. She shivered involuntarily. "Yuk! What a creep!" she said when they stepped outside.

"Yeah, I know and all the good men are gay in this town!" Denise laughed. She changed the subject as they walked slowly up the high street together. "Rosie, you haven't been to see Mum lately."

"No. Why? She's okay isn't she?"

"Yes, yes, she's fine. It's just that well, she does miss you when you don't pop in regularly, you know."

Rosie had to admit she had been pretty tied up with Stuart over the last few weeks. She felt somehow angry with Denise for bringing up the subject, but at the same time, wracked with guilt. *Why does mum always make me feel guilty?* She decided not to make an issue of it and just simply promised her sister that she would go and see her parents at the weekend.

Chapter Three

When Elizabeth opened the door of their house in Woodingdean, Rosie knew immediately that something was wrong.

"Hey, Mum, how are you? What's the matter? You don't look too happy, are you feeling alright?" asked Rosie, noting her mother's anxious expression. Sheba, the golden retriever, jumped up and licked her hand. She stroked him as her mother replied, "Oh, Rosie, it's so good to see you dear," she said, kissing her on both cheeks. "No I'm fine, darling, it's Dad, he's not feeling too well today."

She led Rosie down the narrow hallway, with its cream flecked wallpaper and red patterned carpet, into the living room. Sheba padded along behind her, wagging his tail from side to side. Flashing bright images from the television screen reflected on the far wall. Her father was lying on the green floral sofa with a blanket over his legs and a pillow behind his head. His face looked pale and drawn.

"Hi, Daddy, what's wrong?" she exclaimed, shocked at his appearance. *He looks so old and grey.*

"Hello, my love! This is a nice surprise! How are you? Oh, it's nothing, just me old ticker playing up a bit, I'll be right as rain in a day or two. Now, tell me all your news, dear. How's the old car?" he asked pulling himself up into a seated position and resting his hand on hers.

Rosie smiled and told him that the car was in the garage, yet again. Then she told her father about Stuart's new job in Oman.

"You'll be feeling lonely then, love."

She nodded and smiled. Her father always seemed to know just how she felt, as though there was some kind of mental telepathy between them. She loved him so much. Her mother was fussing around in the kitchen, making her a cup of tea. *She still doesn't remember I prefer coffee*, she thought. As soon as that spiteful thought crossed her mind, she regretted it and told herself not to be judgmental and ungrateful. Her mother always meant well and tried hard to please her.

"So when are you going to visit him?" asked her father, more as a prediction than a question.

"Oh, I don't know, we'll see, maybe I will. I'm not sure yet."

Her dad chuckled.

"What's so funny?" she asked.

"Nothing, it's just the thought of you wearing a billowing black abaya."

"Oman is not like Saudi Arabia, Dad," she replied defensively. "It's much more liberal. I wouldn't have to wear an abaya at all, women are very liberated there, they work and have equal rights…"

"Alright, alright, keep your hat on. I was only joking, I just think a face mask might be an improvement!" he joked.

"Dad, you're incorrigible," she answered sternly, feigning annoyance. They both laughed.

Elizabeth returned with the tea pot on a tray, together with three of their best china cups and saucers and a plateful of flapjacks and digestive biscuits. *I always gain weight when I come home*, Rosie thought. Her mother started making conversation.

"Do you remember Tony Jarrow? You know, the tall good-looking boy you went to school with. I think he was in the year above you, Geraldine Jarrow's son, they live in Harringtom Road?" her mother asked.

"Vaguely. Why? What's he done?" Rosie and her dad exchanged glances and smiled. They both knew exactly where this was leading.

"Well, he's done very well for himself, he's been promoted to top management at Americanex. Geraldine says he's earning a fortune." She paused, treading carefully, "apparently he's coming home for the weekend."

Rosie watched as her mother fell silent and carefully poured the tea into the cups. The china clinked as she handed Rosie a cup with shaky hands. Elizabeth continued, "By the way, Rosie, what are you doing on Sunday? Only, I thought I might do a lunch and invite some people over. You know, Aunty Joyce and the Smiths and well, we haven't seen the Jarrows for ages and I—"

Rosie could feel her hackles rising and her face flushing as she immediately interrupted, "Mum! Dad's not well enough for dinner parties, he's ill, can't you see? And anyway, I can't come. I've promised Denise I'll help her decorate the new flat."

"Well, I was going to ask Denise as well, of course. I—"

Rosie interrupted, "Mum look, just forget it," her voice rising, "stop trying to organize my life!" Rosie was almost shouting now, "I'll find my own dates, thank you very much and anyway, as you are well aware, I already *have* a boyfriend," she added abruptly. There was a painful silence.

Elizabeth bit her lip, tears pricking her eyes. Peter shook his head.

"Just drop it, Elizabeth," he implored as Rosie jumped up, collected the cups and disappeared into the kitchen. Peter could hear his daughter washing up and scrubbing the crockery with an unnecessary furiosity.

"You know she hates it when you try to organise her, love," Peter whispered.

"I'm only trying to help," replied Elizabeth emphatically. "I know she'd like him, but she never gives anyone a chance."

"She told you, she's already got a boyfriend," Peter added.

She glared at her husband and replied, "Yes, but he's thousands of miles away now, isn't he?" Elizabeth tossed her permed head of hair, stormed into the kitchen, picked up a tea towel and started drying the dishes. Her pursed lips turned pale as she fought back the tears. *Why does Peter always have to side with Rosie? He never supports my position.* Sometimes it felt as if Rosie and Peter were ganging up against her.

The stony silence between mother and daughter became unbearable. Rosie dried her hands and returned to the living room without a word. The concerned expression on her father's face made her feel incredibly guilty. She had upset her mother again.

"Have you been to see the doctor, Dad?" Rosie asked, smiling weakly.

"Yes, love, he's given me some tablets and told me to take it easy for a bit. It's nothing to worry about. I'm fine, really," he said breezily, trying to reassure her. He patted her knee and smiled sympathetically. Elizabeth came in, smoothed her apron down and sat on the edge of her seat, with a pained expression of self pity on her worn face.

"So dear, how's work?" she asked stiffly, trying to regain control. When Rosie told her she was thinking of looking for another job, Elizabeth's face brightened.

"Oh, good, I think you've been wasted in that place. You need to find a job where you'll be more appreciated. Why don't you apply to that nice big language school near Brighton College? Or you could work in an office for a change. I'll buy the *Argus* and have a look in the employment pages for you if you like, dear."

Rosie nodded, immediately feeling defensive but made a conscious decision not to rise to the bait.

Changing the subject, Rosie turned the conversation to Aunty Joyce, her eighty-three year old, fiercely independent aunt who lived alone in a bungalow two streets away. Things were beginning to prove difficult as her health deteriorated.

Rosie thought her mother was really an angel, popping in to see her on a regular basis. Elizabeth began to give Rosie an overly detailed update:

"Well, I had a bit of a cold last week and your dad was under the weather so I could not get in to see her. So when I went to see her yesterday I said to her, 'What did you have for lunch yesterday, Aunty?' and she said, 'I had a cheese sandwich.' Then I looked in her fridge and you wouldn't believe it, Rosie, there was nothing in there! I said to her, Aunty, how did you eat lunch when you haven't got any food in the house!' She's not eating properly these days, Rosie. So I made a shopping list and went to take some money from her purse and I found she had no money, so she obviously hadn't even cashed her pension. So off I go to the post office and then they asked to see me identification, oh, it was such a to-do, I tell you. When I got back, I had to clean all her cupboards before I could put everything away. I don't know, Rosie, I'm worried sick about her, really I am. I'm afraid she'll leave the cooker on and burn the house down or something, she's getting so forgetful. She's a danger to herself really, something'll have to be done soon, or I don't know what will happen. She can't cope on her own, but you know what's she's like."

Rosie nodded. She suggested her mother should call the social services and ask for their advice, to see if Aunty Joyce was eligible for a home help.

"Yeah, but she'd never agree to having strangers in the house, now would she?" replied Elizabeth looking at Peter for confirmation. He raised his eyebrows and shrugged. It was going to be a long battle persuading Aunty Joyce to accept the inevitable.

During the journey home on the bus, Rosie sat thinking about her parents; she loved them both dearly. She frowned, anxiously thinking about her father's failing health, he did not look well. She decided to do some nutritional research into dietary suggestions for heart patients. *He should be on a cholesterol-free diet.* But Rosie knew it would be nigh on impossible to change her parent's diet. Meat, potatoes, white flour and refined sugar in the form of bread, cakes and biscuits had been their staple diet for as long as she could remember. Rosie's thoughts turned to the friction that was always present between her and her mother. *Mum's such a control freak. Why does she always have to organize everybody?* Rosie was aware that she herself shared her mother's tendency to take control, but she did her best to reject that side to her own character, always fighting her instinctive desire to dominate others. Rosie could not understand why her father put up with it. He just seemed to accept everything her mother said and rarely argued with her. His whole life seemed to revolve around *her* family, *her* friends and *her* interests. Rosie decided *she* would marry a man with a much stronger character than her father's, someone who would *never* allow her to boss him around. She wondered if Stuart would be strong enough to handle her. It was not until much later that Rosie realized her father's ability to accept and love Elizabeth unconditionally, was actually one of his greatest strengths.

The bus dropped her off in Western Road and she popped into Waitrose and picked up some rocket leaves, two soft avocados and a chunk of parmigiano cheese, intent on making a delicious salad for one for her evening meal. Rosie was painfully aware that her life had gradually begun to revolve solely around food. She lived to eat, rather than eating to live. Her only remaining pleasure in life gleaned from culinary delights. *What else do I have to look forward to?* she thought glumly. As she walked along the dark deserted streets, carrying her shopping bag, her thoughts inevitably turned to Stuart. She had not heard from him for four days now. *Is he missing me? Has he already found someone else?* she wondered, feeling more and more despondent and convinced that he no longer loved her.

Loneliness seeped into her bones and she could feel the tears blurring her vision, a lump of thick emotion forming in her throat. She took out a tissue from her coat pocket and wiped away her tears.

So pre-occupied with her own thoughts, she failed to realize that she was not alone. For even the most casual observer, it was obvious that the pretty young girl with the long blonde hair was being followed. It was only eight o'clock in the evening, but it had already been dark for hours and the side streets running off the main road were quiet and empty. Rosie suddenly heard footsteps behind her. She turned her head and innocently glanced over her shoulder and was startled to find an ugly man with bulging eyes and an unkempt appearance, bearing down on her. Rosie gave a shout as he grabbed her by the shoulders and pushed her hard with the full force of his weight. She gasped and fell backwards into the dark bushes, her shopping bag spilling its contents onto the pavement.

"Just shut up, keep quiet and you won't get hurt. Lie down!" he muttered darkly, swaying, a crazed look in his dark piercing eyes. She lay on the cold pavement shocked and dazed. Then, finding her voice, she began to scream with fear. She struggled to get up, scratching her arms and tearing her tights on the bushes, but it was too late. Her assailant swiftly came up behind her, grabbed her by the arms and yanked her further into the dark undergrowth, his face contorted with desire and lust.

"Leave me alone! F*** off!" she yelled at the top of her voice.

"Come here!" he demanded angrily, turning to face her and dropping to his knees. He grabbed her by the shoulders and pinned her to the ground. The smell of stale alcohol on his breath was overpowering. She kicked out at him and one of her shoes went flying off into the dark air, as she struggled to break free. But she was no match for his physical strength.

"Help me! Somebody please help me!" she screamed.

He covered her mouth with his large rough hand, muffling her screams. As he ripped open her blouse, blue buttons scattered randomly to the ground. She inhaled sharply through her nostrils and moved to retaliate; scratching his forehead with her long nails and frantically pulling at his shaggy dark hair.

"Leave me alone!" she wailed desperately, but very little sound escaped from her mouth.

Disgusted and angry, she found an unknown strength; biting at his hand and lashing out furiously with all her might, her fists banging against his chest. He frowned and swore at her loudly, reaching out to grab her hands and stop the constant onslaught. Swiftly, she darted out from under him, proving to be far more agile than her attacker. She scrambled onto her hands and knees, breaking free and randomly kicking out at him as she stumbled onto her feet, bent double in sheer panic and terror. He was still on the ground and he lurched forward on his knees and grabbed her slim ankle, but she screamed and kicked him hard in the shoulder. She broke free, then turned and ran, sobbing, into the desolate black night.

She could hear him in hot pursuit, cursing and shouting behind her as she ran blindly along the road, one shoe on, one shoe off, holding her coat and ripped blouse around her. "Help me, help me! Please God, somebody help me!" she screamed.

Rosie had the presence of mind to push open a gate and stagger up the garden path of the first house she could find with lights in the window. Too frightened to look behind her, she knocked frantically on the door and rang the bell continuously, horrifyingly conscious of her assailant's dark shadow passing over her, moving away into the night.

"Please open the door!" she yelled, "open the door!" She shouted, banging her fists on the door.

Suddenly, light flooded into the dark street. The door opened and a elderly woman with grey hair and pink glasses, stood blinking, puzzled and alarmed at the sight of the young girl before her; wide-eyed, confused and in obvious distress. The woman quickly assessed the situation, noting Rosie's dishevelled clothing, torn tights and tear-stained face. She peered anxiously into the street, reached out and swiftly pulled Rosie into the house before closing and bolting the door quickly behind her.

"What ever is the matter, dear? What's happened? Are you alright? Come in, come in," she said, ushering her into the living room. The woman walked unsteadily into the kitchen and bolted the back door before returning to the living room and staring at Rosie.

Rosie sat down and tried to talk but she was too breathless and could not stop shaking.

"I... there was this man," she panted, "he followed me... he... he tried to rape me!" she let out a sob and burst into tears.

"Oh, my goodness, how awful, you poor thing. There now, it's alright, dear, he's gone, it's alright now," she quivered.

Rosie was shivering and clearly in shock. The woman rushed into the hallway and picked up a chunky yellow woollen cardigan and carefully draped it around Rosie's hunched shoulders.

"Now, you just sit there while I call the police and then I'll make us a nice cup of tea, alright, dear? Shall I ring your mother, does she live near here, dear?" she asked.

"No, no! Please don't ring my mother," she pleaded, "she'll get in a terrible state and my Dad... well he's got a heart condition."

Rosie looked towards the red and green floral curtains at the window.

"Are you sure he's gone? I think he's still outside, waiting for me. Oh God! It was so horrible! Why did it have to happen to me?" she wailed, clutching her stomach and moaning.

The woman's lined face was reflected in the dark bay window as she lifted the net curtain and peered outside.

"I can't see him, dear, I think he's gone," she said, walking shakily into the hallway. She dialled the emergency services and gave her name, address and telephone number in a trembling voice. "Hello, yes, could you please send an officer over here right away? There's a young girl... I don't know... I'm not sure... yes... something has happened... there's been an incident. Can you hurry please? Thank you very much."

The woman replaced the receiver heavily and disappeared into the kitchen. Rosie could hear her running the water, filling the kettle and preparing the tea; *such a normal, routine activity*, thought Rosie. Yet she knew that for her, nothing would ever be normal and routine again after tonight. Horrifying images replayed in her mind: the bulging crazed eyes and alcoholic breath of her assailant, the awful feeling of being overpowered and pinned to the ground. The mere thought of his hand over her mouth caused her breathing to become laboured. She felt a tight constriction in her chest. Suddenly bile rose in her throat and she clutched at her stomach, reliving the moment his hand groped at her body, tearing at her blouse.

"Where's the bathroom? I think I'm going to be sick," she announced, cupping her hand over her mouth and staggering out into the hall.

With a startled expression on her face, the woman pointed to a white door and Rosie rushed into the bathroom and threw up.

Rosie flushed the toilet. Tears flowed relentlessly and she found herself sinking down onto the tiled floor and sobbing her heart out. She gazed with disbelief at her torn tights and visualized her missing shoe lying somewhere outside in the shadows.

He's waiting for me, she thought, *Oh God I hope they catch the bastard.*

The ensuing nightmare loomed large in her mind; *what would happen now*? Would she have to go to court and recount the sordid details of the attack in front of her parents? How could she endure the embarrassment and put her father through the humiliation? Then an even worse scenario occurred to her: what if they did *not* catch him? She would never know if he was out there somewhere in the shadows, watching and waiting for her. Thank God she had not succumbed to him, but perhaps he would try again, to take his revenge. A sickening thought came into her mind; she would be able to identify him. Would he now want to silence her, maybe even kill her? Fear gnawed at her stomach. She felt dirty and defiled and longed to go home and take a shower.

But I can't go home, she suddenly realized, shivering uncontrollably. How could she ever feel safe at home on her own again? *Perhaps he knows where I live.*

At that moment a gentle knocking on the door brought her back to the present.

"I've made you a cup of tea, dear. Do you take milk and sugar?"

"Oh, thank you, I'll be out in a minute, just milk please."

Rosie splashed her face with cold water and dried herself on the small white embroidered hand towel. The reflection in the mirror seemed unfamiliar; her eyes had a haunted look she had never seen in them before. She wiped runaway mascara from her face and tried to compose herself. The door bell rang just as Rosie came out into the hall. She quickly ran back into the bathroom and locked herself in, listening intently at the door and sweating nervously.

Was the man insane? Would he break the door down?

The woman looked through a spyhole set in her shiny brown wooden front door and then unbolted it. Two tall uniformed police officers, one male, one female, stood on the doorstep.

"Good evening. We received a call from a Mrs Thomas, at this address. What seems to be the trouble?" enquired the policeman.

"Yes... yes... that was me... I phoned you. Come in. There's a young girl in there," she said pointing towards the bathroom, "There's been an incident."

The woman coughed and knocked gently on the bathroom door and called out in a quivering voice, "Hello, dear. Can you come out now please? The police are here."

Rosie opened the door. A pitiful sight met their eyes. The girl looked shaken and tearful. The short-haired policewoman came towards Rosie and immediately put an arm around her shoulders.

"My goodness, what happened to you? Come on now, let's go and sit down, shall we? Then you can tell us all about it."

They moved forward, the policewoman guiding Rosie towards the living room. But Rosie hesitated, looking at the cream telephone on the hall table.

"Do you think I could just ring my sister and tell her to come over?" she asked in a small shaky voice.

"Why, yes of course, dear," Mrs Thomas replied.

Rosie dialled the number. The two officers accepted a cup of tea and asked the woman a few questions while Rosie waited for her sister to pick up the phone.

"Hello, Denise, it's Rosie," she said, trembling, "listen, something's happened. No.... no... I'm alright. I just wondered, could you come over? I need you to be here with me and I need a lift. I... well... I'm in someone's house... a lady... she's been very kind... oh, hold on, I don't know the address, I'll just find out, no, it's okay, I'll tell you when you get here, don't speak to Mum or anything, will you? Just come, okay?"

She called out to Mrs Thomas and asked for the house number.

"It's 65, D... Street, yes, that's right. I'll see you then."

There was a pause in the conversation as Rosie re-entered the room and sat down. "Now then, let's start at the beginning, shall we? What's your name?"

Rosie took a deep breath and began to answer their questions. Sometimes she stopped and stared vacantly into space, reliving the trauma in her head. The policewoman gently coaxed her to continue, making notes on her writing pad.

"Had you ever seen the man before?"

"What?"

"The man who attacked you – had you ever seen him before?" she asked.

Rosie frowned. Maybe she had seen him before. There was something familiar about him. "No, I don't think so."

Once he had the basic details, the tall policeman rose and leaving his colleague with Rosie, he strode out into the street to investigate. He found the scene of the crime without difficulty, as Rosie's shopping was still strewn all over the pavement. He spoke into his radio, calling for forensic support and began sealing off the area with white ribbon and searching through the undergrowth. He found Rosie's red leather purse and saw her brown shoe lying in the gutter. Fifteen minutes later a small grey car pulled up, and a short balding man with rimless glasses got out and shook hands with the police officer and immediately began examining the area. He opened a large leather bag and took out some enormous tongs and several transparent plastic bags. Holding the tongs, he carefully lifted Rosie's shoe out of the gutter. Wet mud dripped from the shoe as he placed it in a plastic bag.

"Obvious signs of a struggle," he commented, inspecting the depression in the privet and the broken twigs and leaves.

"Anything stolen or was it a sexual attack?"

The policeman pointed to the purse. "Looks like it was sexual."

The short man opened Rosie's purse with his gloved hands. Cash and cards were still in place.

At that moment, Denise drew up behind the police car with a feeling of growing alarm, her stomach churning. She looked across at the two men and pointed to number 65. The policeman nodded and she hurried up the garden path and rang the bell. The policewoman opened the door and immediately led her into the living room, where Rosie sat huddled in an unfamiliar yellow cardigan. Her sister rose and stumbled into her arms, almost collapsing with relief. Denise hugged her for a full minute, feeling Rosie's chest heaving and shuddering with emotion.

"What happened, tell me, Rosie, are you alright? Sit down, sit down."

The woman came over and handed her a box of tissues and Rosie took a handful and blew her nose noisily. "Oh, Denise, it was so horrible, this disgusting bloke attacked me, ripped my clothes and everything, it was just so gross, I feel so dirty," she cried bitterly.

"Rosie, oh my poor darling, tell me the truth now Rosie," she paused, looking deep into Rosie's eyes, "did he rape you?" she asked.

"No... well... he nearly did... he would have, if I hadn't managed to fight him off, I mean, I was able to slip out from under him. Oh God, Denise, what am I going to do? I can't go home. Maybe he knows where I live." She was shaking like a leaf.

"It's okay, babe," her sister soothed, "you're coming home with me."

Chapter Four

The call came through when she was at her lowest ebb. In the aftermath of the attack, Rosie had gone through a whole range of emotions. She had felt disgusted and degraded at the thought of being touched by a stranger. The attack had been so intrusive, encroaching on her own personal space and so aggressive. She was angry with herself for taking the unnecessary risk of walking home alone at night. If only she had had the car, none of this would have happened. She felt incredible rage towards the man and imagined herself swearing at him, striking out at him and even stabbing him with a knife. Rosie was horrified at herself and shocked that she could feel so much hatred. She tried to control these powerful feelings and hoped that in reality, she would never resort to violence. Rosie had always tried to see the best in others and had great empathy and understanding for those less fortunate than herself. However, now she could feel nothing but hatred and contempt for her attacker even though, on an intellectual level, she could reason that he was probably one of the world's sexual deviants because of his own bad experiences or inadequacies.

People who have never been shown love are incapable of showing love to others.

The whole experience had revealed a different aspect of her own personality and she decided she did not like this new venomous monster rearing its ugly head inside her.

Rosie was virtually living at Denise's flat now, as the mere thought of being in the flat on her own at night, freaked her out. She felt physically sick with fear whenever she went out, continually looking over her shoulder, expecting to see her attacker around every corner. She knew this situation could not continue, her mother was starting to ask questions and she felt like an intruder at Denise and Tony's place. Rosie had gone back to work two days after the attack and had decided not to mention the incident to anyone, not even her friend, Jan. Rosie just wanted to forget the whole thing, to bury it in the depths of her mind. However, that had been virtually impossible, as she had been required to report to the police station twice; once to give a statement, describing her attacker to help them build a picture of him and once to try and identify him from a line of suspects. That had been a really nerve-racking experience, even though she knew the suspects could not see her through the one-way glass. She had scrutinized every one of the men lined up against the wall. They all shared a similar build and had that same unkempt appearance as her attacker, but she could not positively identify any one of them as the man who had made her life a misery. Unless her assailant made another appearance, Rosie doubted he would ever be found. She found it impossible to put the incident behind her knowing that he was still on the loose.

Although Rosie had seen a counsellor twice, she battled alone with severe depression. Work was horrible, she hated the late hours and had to park her car on the expensive meter right outside the Institute now, to avoid walking anywhere in the dark. Her relationship with Andrew had not improved even though she avoided him as much as possible. Inevitably they sometimes found themselves in the staff room at the same time. Everyone had noted the tension between them. One day, Andrew made a sarcastic remark and Rosie had run into the ladies room and cried her eyes out. It seemed she had no resistance and had become extremely sensitive and tearful at the slightest provocation. Her colleague, Jan, had asked several times why she seemed so tense and nervous and Rosie was finding it increasingly difficult not to divulge her true state of mind. The whole thing was getting her down.

Usually, when she felt down, Denise would be there to cheer her up; they would go Salsa dancing and have a real laugh. But now Rosie did not feel like going out in the evenings and Denise had a serious relationship with Tony and could not be parted from him. Rosie found Tony irritating. He was constantly whispering sweet nothings into Denise's ear and performing other romantic gestures. *He's such a smooth operator*, thought Rosie. Rosie gradually became convinced that his actions were all part of an act, performed especially for her benefit, which she found sickening. Denise seemed to be completely taken in. Rosie could not help asking herself if her impressions of Tony were not coloured by her own recent trauma. She decided not to get involved. But seeing Denise and Tony kissing and cuddling all the time just made her feel more lonely and excluded.

A vicious cycle began to ensue; Rosie started eating for comfort, which resulted in serious weight gain and an even deeper, darker depression. Now, when she looked at herself in the full length bedroom mirror, she began to despise herself. Her stomach protruded. *I look about four months pregnant.* A roll of fat hung around her midriff and her thighs were beginning to look decidedly chubby. Depression sent her running back to the kitchen for more comfort foods: nachos and guacamole, roasted salty nuts, toast with lashings of butter and Marmite, bars of chocolate, strawberry ice cream and chocolate chip cookies. Once she started eating, she just could not seem to stop. Her skin had broken out and she was spotty and constipated from constantly over-loading her system. *Oh God, I've got to do something*, she thought. *I feel as though I'm descending into a deep dark hole.*

When she answered her mobile phone and heard his voice, all the misery of the last week rose to the surface.

"Stuart! Oh, darling, how are you? I miss you so much."

Stuart heard a stifled sob at the other end of the phone.

"I need to see you, Stuart. I'm so lonely and fed up without you. Can't you come home?" Rosie pleaded.

Stuart's heart ached to hear her trembling voice. She sounded so weak and vulnerable. "Hey babe, what's wrong? Are you okay? Has something happened? Tell me darling, what is it?"

"Oh no, it's nothing... no... I... I just miss you, that's all. I hate being here on my own. Can't you come home for a while?" she begged.

Stuart explained that it was impossible for him to leave. He had only just settled in and had been given tons of work to do. That was why he had not had a chance to ring her. He went on to tell her that the job was all absorbing, challenging and interesting, but he found the very apparent office politics totally incomprehensible. There were so many nationalities with different cultural implications and petty jealousies between staff members that he just could not fathom.

Rosie tried to concentrate on what he was saying, desperately trying not to pour out her heart and tell Stuart about the attack. She asked him about the heat.

"Oh, it doesn't really bother me anymore," he told her. "There's air conditioning wherever you go; in the car, the office, the house, the pub..."

"The pub?" Rosie was incredulous to hear there were pubs in Muscat.

" Yes there are. Oh and I meant to tell you, I met this mad Scottish chap at the pub the other night. He runs a training institute here and I mentioned your name and told him you were a TEFL teacher. He said they were always looking for English language teachers, especially good looking ones!"

"Stuart!" she said sternly in mock annoyance. "Hey, did you take his number? Only I might be interested."

"Oh, Rosie, really? I know you would love it here, babe, and it would be so cool to be together wouldn't it? Oh and guess what? There's no tax, so whatever you earn, you keep. Let me investigate a bit more and I'll let you know. Hey, I've got a good joke for you, listen to this: a guy goes into a bar and he brings out a tiny little man in a dress suit, who starts playing a tiny grand piano. Everyone is amazed. The guy explains he had rescued an old woman from a mugging and she had gratefully granted him one wish. But she was hard of hearing, so he had ended up with a twelve inch 'pianist'! Do you get it?" asked Stuart, laughing.

"Oh, is it something to do with the word 'pianist' sounding like something else?" she answered, giggling. By the time she put down the receiver, she was feeling much better. *Dear Stuart*, she thought, *he always makes me laugh. Maybe I will go to Oman*, she thought. *Anything to get away from these awful memories.*

Rosie found the thought of starting a new life in a completely different country very exhilarating. There were bound to be so many interesting places and people to photograph. She knew that leaving her family would be the hardest part, but she decided that if she was able to get a one-year contract, the time would fly. Even if things did not work out and she hated every minute of it, she would at least be able to put this traumatic experience behind her. It was time to re-invent herself and she sat down and wrote an email to Stuart, reminding him to speak to the Scot again, to ascertain the seriousness of his job proposal. For the first time in weeks, Rosie went to sleep feeling full of hope. If she could find a way of extricating herself from her existing contract and get a job in Muscat, then maybe she really had an exciting future ahead of her instead of an awful past to contend with.

Rosie had never missed a Christmas at home with her family. It was a family ritual: they would gather around the fire on Christmas Eve, drinking warm, dark red mulled wine, flavoured with oranges, cinnamon and cloves. She and Denise would spend the rest of the evening wrapping up presents, while her parents attended midnight communion.

On Christmas morning the girls would wake to the rich aroma of turkey roasting in the oven and the whole family would prepare lunch together. Rosie had not eaten meat for years, so her father always prepared a grilled trout with almonds, especially for her. This year Rosie found herself wishing that Stuart was going to be with her. Not that he ever had been there for Christmas before, but she was sure he would fit in very well. She imagined him chatting with her dad about cars and football, while she helped her mother in the kitchen. Rosie was particularly looking forward to this Christmas, as she was planning to leave soon after.

In early November, Rosie had held a letter of application in one hand and an umbrella in the other, hesitating. As the rain fell gently on the wet pavement, she inhaled the fresh damp air and made a decision, dropping the letter into the bright red post box. *I have nothing to lose*, she thought. Three weeks later, she had received a reply thanking her for the application and offering her a job as an English language teacher in the Finja Training Institute in Oman.

When Rosie broke the news to her boss, Andrew had been surprisingly accommodating, allowing her to extricate herself from her existing contract without disadvantage. He had agreed to release her from the beginning of January.

Now, her entire body yearned for Stuart and she found herself smiling involuntarily, filled with a delicious anticipation at the thought of seeing him again. She longed to be held in his arms and rest her head against his broad chest. She loved the way he massaged her back when she felt tense. He was so loving and giving.

Rosie wondered if she would be able to maintain her silence about the attack once she saw Stuart in person. She felt that telling him would serve no purpose and might actually affect their relationship adversely. She was determined to bury it and pretend it never happened. To think she would be in Oman by the middle of January was both thrilling and unsettling. Taking a step into the unknown was both nerve-racking and exciting. She told herself she had been in a rut, playing it safe for far too long. This was the opportunity she had been dreaming of in all those quiet moments in her lonely bed at night. *But what would Oman be like?* she wondered, envisaging hump-backed camels swaying over endless sand dunes and young girls dancing in exotic dresses to the sound of beating drums. She imagined Arabian horses galloping over burning sands and bearded men with silver daggers in their belts. In anticipation, Rosie had already bought herself a new digital camera, so that she could send photos back to Denise by email.

On the more practical subject of accommodation, Rosie had contemplated living with Stuart in Oman, but after some deliberation, she had decided against the idea. She would stay with him just for the first couple of weeks after her arrival and then go flat-hunting for her own place or perhaps share with another girl, if she could find someone she liked. Thankfully, the Institute's housing allowance would allow her some freedom and independence. Stuart, of course, had tried to pressurize her into staying with him and in a way, she was tempted. Since the attack, she hated being on her own, especially at night, but she still felt living with Stuart would be a mistake. It was far too early in their relationship to make that kind of commitment. Rosie valued her freedom and was really not ready to make a long-term commitment to their relationship. Communicating by email on an almost daily basis, Rosie had implored Stuart to take things slowly, saying that they had all the time in the world to develop their relationship. If it was meant to be, everything would work out. Eventually, after hours of internet discussions, Stuart had relented and agreed with her decision.

Even so, Rosie was still a little concerned about how things would be in the first couple of weeks in Oman. She knew she would be totally reliant on Stuart. She would not know a soul. That could be extremely dangerous, because she knew Stuart well enough to know he liked her to rely on him.

It was as if he wanted to prove himself indispensable. In the five weeks they had spent together, she had already felt slightly suffocated by his possessive nature.

Rosie's thoughts returned to the present as she entered the dingy multi-storey car park in Brighton and carefully drove up and round and up again until she found a parking space. She made a mental note of the car's position and took the lift to the shopping mall. As Rosie always worked better under pressure, she had left most of her shopping to the last minute and was now going to have to rush around the Churchill Square Shopping Centre buying gifts at five o'clock on Christmas Eve. Time was of the essence, as she had promised to be home by nine for dinner with her parents, before they went to church. She ticked off the list with each purchase she made: Mum, a gold cross and chain; Dad; a dark-blue dressing gown and a grey leather belt, (Dad loved belts for some reason!). Aunty Joyce would be joining them for Christmas lunch, so she had bought her a pink cardigan. Denise was always fairly easy to buy for, as they had similar taste. She chose her a new Dido CD, a wine rack for the flat and some of her favourite perfume.

Rosie was secretly pleased that Tony would not be joining them for Christmas lunch. He would be coming over after having lunch with his own parents in Shoreham. Somehow, Rosie felt that she had lost her sister since Tony came on the scene. *Crazy to be jealous of my sister's boyfriend,* she thought. But she really could not warm to his character and could not work out what made him tick. Rosie had always prided herself on being a good judge of character, but she found Tony complex and difficult to read. She could never really tell what he was thinking. Rosie had been staying at Denise and Tony's for weeks now, since the attack, and on more than one occasion Rosie had been unnerved to find Tony standing absolutely still, watching her with a strange expression on his face.

Now Rosie reluctantly put her mind to choosing a present for him. Rosie wandered around aimlessly searching for something that she thought he would appreciate, but could find nothing appropriate. She left the shopping centre and walked briskly against the bitterly cold sea breeze until she came to Market Square. A busker was standing in a doorway with a guitar on his hip, singing 'American Pie'. He sounded so much like Don Maclean, it was uncanny. His warm breath was clearly visible, as he sang out into the cold night air. A sad looking girl, with a roll-up hanging out of the side of her mouth, accosted Rosie: "*Big Issue*! Buy me last copy, love, so I can get a cup o' tea."

Rosie had nothing but admiration for the creator of *The Big Issue* magazine. It gave homeless people an opportunity to earn some money and self-respect. There seemed to be so many young homeless people living in Brighton. She could not imagine how awful it must be to be living on the streets at Christmas. *I'm so lucky to have a loving family*, she thought. She wondered if some of the homeless just lacked a sense of belonging in their own homes and preferred the camaraderie on the streets. Perhaps she was naïve. She looked closely at the girl. Was she a drug addict? Rosie decided that even if she was, she did not deserve to be alone on the streets at Christmas. Dropping a pound into the busker's hat, she went over to the shaggy-haired girl and bought a copy of *Big Issue*, even though she had already read it.

"Thanks, love. Merry Christmas!" The girl dug her rough, cold hands into her pockets and stumbled off down the road.

Rosie sauntered into a bookshop and began browsing through the books. Whenever she was surrounded by books, she found she became absorbed and time became irrelevant. Eventually she decided on a golfing book, as Tony had recently taken up golf and joined the Devil's Dyke golf club. The book was full of tips on improving one's game. Something caught her eye: a Dubai travel guide. A pang of excitement and a sense of longing for Stuart brought her out in a sweat. She had booked an Emirates flight to Dubai, as she and Stuart planned to spend a few days in the Jumeirah Beach Hotel, before flying on to Oman together. She hurriedly bought the two books, realizing the time. Her shopping bags banged heavily against her legs, as she ran back to the car park and drove at breakneck speed back to Denise's flat to collect some presents. Packing her clothes into a small overnight bag she raced out of the flat and locked the door behind her. Luckily her mother always kept scissors and wrapping paper in the spare bedroom for last minute wrapping, so she knew she could wrap her presents while her parents were at midnight communion.

Rosie finally arrived at her parent's home at 9.15 p.m. She was greeted at the door by Denise and her mother. Her father's face lit up when he saw Rosie. They drank each other's health with warm mulled wine and in the warm soft glow of the fire in the fireplace, Peter watched his two daughters, giggling like schoolgirls, while they decorated the tree with golden baubles, silver lametta and candles. It was his favourite time of year and he was pleased to see the girls still shared the same feeling of excitement they had always felt as children the night before Christmas.

When she awoke on Christmas morning, Rosie felt nostalgic, recalling all the happy Christmases of her childhood. She remembered how she would stand on tip toe, trying to peer through the keyhole at the presents under the tree in the living room. One year Father Christmas had given her a beautiful doll nearly as tall as her tiny four-year-old self. Rosie made a mental note to ask her mother if her dolls were still in the loft. She had loved her dolls and spent many happy hours dressing them and feeding them and pushing them around in a life-size pram. Now, as she lay in her little single bed in her parents' house, she smiled to see her little teddy, still sitting on the shelf wearing yellow polka dot pyjamas and a comical expression on his dear little face.

Whenever Rosie came home, it felt as if time slowed down, grinding almost to a halt. She turned over in bed and stretched languorously, feeling warm, safe and totally secure. She could hear the murmur of voices; probably her father listening to the radio, moving about downstairs, basting the turkey and covering it with rashers of bacon to prevent it from burning. He always took charge of the kitchen on Christmas day. Suddenly there was a knock on the door and before she had time to answer, Denise came into the room and jumped onto her bed.

"Merry Christmas, Rosie! Did you sleep well?" she said, bouncing up and down.

"Mm, like a log." Rosie replied, yawning.

"D'you know I can't believe it, I've put on weight already and I've only been home for twelve hours!" moaned Denise, laughing.

"Me too, I think it's inevitable. Let's just enjoy it, eat whatever we want today and eat nothing tomorrow!" suggested Rosie.

The girls talked about their new year's resolutions. Finally, the conversation turned to Rosie's departure. "I can hardly believe you're going away. It'll be so strange without you," Denise admitted.

Rosie could not help making a cutting remark: "Oh, I'm sure you won't notice my absence – you are so absorbed in loverboy Tony."

"Hey, that's not true! Oh, Rosie, you're not jealous are you?" she laughed. Her eyes were full of love and tenderness for her kid sister.

"Of course not, but I hardly ever see you alone these days cos loverboy's always in tow…"

Denise frowned and looked down.

"You don't know what you're talking about, things are not what they seem, Rosie."

"Uh, what's that supposed to mean?"

"The people who have the most to teach us are not necessarily the people we love," said Denise enigmatically.

"Uh? That's a bit profound for first thing in the morning. What on earth are you talking about?" Rosie asked.

"Nothing. Some other time. But, Rosie, you know I'll miss you and I'm never gonna let Tony come between us. Anyway, you know that after what happened, it's important for you to make a fresh start," she paused. "My only real concern is Mum. She'll find it difficult when you're gone, but don't worry about her, I'll look after her."

"I'm not worried about *Mum*, I'm worried about Dad, he's the one who's not well." Rosie retorted. Suddenly she felt overwhelmed with mixed emotions. "Oh, Denise," she said, "I hope I'm doing the right thing. What if anything should happen to Dad while I'm away?" Her face contorted with pain.

"Hey… come on… buck up! It's Christmas day, don't cry for God's sake. Dad is fine, he has his medication. You know he always wants us to follow our dreams. Come on, girl! Let's go and make some coffee, I brought some filtered coffee on the way over yesterday." Denise gave her a hug and dashed out to take a shower.

After breakfast the whole family congregated in the living room and Denise appointed herself Mother Christmas, handing out presents. Dad poured them all a glass of sherry and they laughed, kissed each other and Rosie took photos of everyone receiving their new gifts. Rosie was thrilled. Her parents had bought her a platinum gold necklace with matching earrings. It was beautiful and must have cost a fortune. She bent to kiss them both. "Thanks, Mum; thanks, Dad," she choked, her voice full of emotion.

Her father smiled and patted her on the head, saying she deserved it. Later Rosie helped her mother prepare the vegetables: roast potatoes and parsnips, Brussel sprouts and carrots, while Denise made the bread sauce and brandy butter for the rich Christmas pudding which would be set on fire before being eaten. Then her father drove over to pick up Aunty Joyce.

Elizabeth tried not to think about Rosie leaving. She found it difficult to come to terms with the idea of her little girl flying away to live in a foreign country. *One reads so much in the Daily Mail about terrorism in the Middle East.* How could she be certain Rosie would be safe? She had met Stuart and thought he was a nice boy, but would he be able to look after Rosie? She had voiced her fears to Aunty Joyce, her only confidante. Aunty Joyce had responded firmly telling Elizabeth that Rosie must be allowed to make her own mistakes and that parental interference would only make Rosie more stubbornly committed to leaving. Aunty Joyce thought her niece had a marvellous adventurous spirit. She imagined Rosie as a pioneering woman, like Freya Stark and Gertrude Bell and others that she had read about in books from the library. She felt immensely proud of her niece.

Peter held up his glass and made a toast as they sat around the dining room table.

"To health and happiness!" he announced.

Then Denise added, "To Rosie's new life in Oman!"

Tension filled the air, as everyone around the table began thinking their own thoughts about Rosie's departure. Her mother struggled to stay calm and turned the conversation to Denise's new flat. Denise and Tony were having problems with the landlord. They had broken a mirror while decorating and were fighting over the enormous cost of replacing it. But Denise seemed reluctant to discuss the issue. After a huge lunch the girls felt absolutely stuffed and decided to take Sheba for a walk, while Aunty Joyce and Peter dozed in front of an old film on the television and Elizabeth pottered around in the kitchen, putting leftovers into Tupperware boxes. The sisters let themselves out of the house and walked towards St Ann's Well Gardens.

Grey squirrels with bushy tails scampered over the hard frosty ground and ran nimbly up dark tree trunks in the failing light. A bitterly cold northerly wind blew strands of Rosie's long blonde hair over her face. She took a green beanie from her pocket and pulled it down over her head and ears. *I won't miss these arctic conditions, that's for sure. I can't wait to feel the sun on my face*, she thought.

Out of the blue she asked, "Do you think you and Tony will get married?"

Denise looked startled. She did not answer immediately. "I'd like to... I mean I do love him... but something happened the other day that really made think carefully about our relationship."

Rosie stood still. "Yeah? What happened?" she asked quietly.

"I found a list."

"What do you mean, a list? What kind of list?" Rosie enquired with rising curiosity.

"Oh, I don't know for sure, but I think it's a list of all the girls Tony's been with. I... I don't know." Denise was looking down, brooding.

Rosie laughed. "You mean he keeps a record? Does he give them points out of ten as well?" she giggled, trying to catch Denise's eye.

"It's not funny, Rosie," Denise shouted angrily, turning to face her. "I mean there are literally about sixty names on that list! It's like they're all his conquests or something. It's so immature. I'm still in shock," Denise admitted.

Rosie could see how upset Denise was becoming and she tried to comfort her by making light of it. "Oh Denny... I don't suppose it means anything. I mean, all young guys do that kind of thing. Maybe he wrote it when he was seventeen, or maybe they're just the names of girls he only wished he could have gone out with. Have you questioned him about it?"

"No."

"Why not?" asked Rosie in amazement.

"Because it would mean admitting that I'd searched through his closet. I can't do that," Denise confided.

"Well, you're going to have to, Denny, otherwise it's going to become an issue that'll come between you. Deal with it, Denise!" Rosie implored. "Don't let it spoil your relationship, it could be nothing, you don't know. Find out! You have to ask him."

"Oh, yeah, and how do I know I'm not just one more name on the list? How do I know if he'll be happy to live exclusively with me for the rest of his life and not get roving eyes and want to start adding a few more names to the list again? Maybe it's his ambition to increase its length! I don't know what to think, Rosie, I'm so confused. I thought I knew him so well and now I'm not sure about him at all. I think he must have incredibly low self-esteem to act like that, don't you? He's like a stranger to me now. I lie awake watching him sleep and wondering who he is. This just changes everything for me." A tear rolled slowly down her pale cheek.

Rosie nodded, feeling a mixture of sympathy and indignation. Tony was the love of her sister's life. How dare he jeopardize Denise's happiness! What an idiot he must be. She had a good mind to confront him, but she knew Denise would go mad if she interfered. They walked back to the house in silence with Sheba pulling on the lead. Rosie put a comforting arm around her sister's shoulders and gave her a hug.

"Come on, cheer up! You just have to talk to him, Denise," said Rosie, looking deep into her eyes.

Denise nodded and smiled faintly as Rosie handed her a tissue.

"Now come on, Denny. We can't go into the house while you're looking so miserable. Questions will be asked. Cheer up. Maybe you've completely misinterpreted the whole thing... Oh!"

Just then Rosie heard an engine roar around the corner and saw a bright red BMW convertible coming down the road. "Oh, talk of the devil and he's bound to appear! Here comes Tony now. Quick, go inside, wash your face and put on some lippo Denny, while I stall him."

Denise hurried inside and Rosie waved her hand as Tony pulled up and parked. He jumped out with a grin on his face and kissed her on both cheeks.

"Merry Christmas, Rosie!"

"Hi, Tony, Merry Christmas. Hey, aren't you forgetting something?"

"No, what?" asked Tony, mystified.

"My present, of course!" Rosie said sternly with her hands on her hips and a smile on her lips.

"What makes you think I'd give you a present?" replied Tony, playfully. He found Rosie very sexually appealing and sometimes he really wished he had met her first. *She's got a great body,* he thought, as he put his arm around her waist and they walked slowly up the drive together.

"Well of course you should, because I've bought one for you!" she laughed. "How are your parents?"

Maybe one day I'll come on to her, Tony thought, mesmerized by the sight of Rosie's beautiful full glossy pink lips.

"Oh they're fine. Some of their friends just came over, so I was able to slip away," he answered.

I would love to see her naked, he thought.

"Denise and I have just been for a walk. We ate so much," she said patting her protruding stomach, "we thought we'd better go and work some of it off."

Rosie felt Tony's hand squeeze her waist. *He's not listening to me.* Suddenly she realized what was going on in his head and finally she understood why she could not warm to him. Instinctively, she had known Tony's true nature. Now she could see Tony for what he really was: *a womanizer. Oh my God, poor Denise,* she thought. *I hope she doesn't marry him.*

The following weeks were spent in preparation for Rosie's departure. When she left the Institute, the staff gave her a little party in the staff room. Andrew made a speech of thanks for her time and efforts but Rosie could not help wondering whether he was really being sincere. She was totally bowled over by the staff's generosity. Her colleagues beamed at her, as Jan placed a beautifully wrapped gift, tied with a purple shiny ribbon, on her lap.

"This is from all of us. We're going to miss your smile, Rosie," said Jan quietly.

Inside was an elegant slim leather brief case.

"Oh wow!" she gasped.

She lifted it up by the handle and instinctively inhaled the wonderful rich smell of leather. Everyone laughed as Jan informed her that its value was not to be sniffed at. Rosie felt quite overwhelmed as she mumbled her thanks, looking around at each of their smiling faces. However, she knew she would not really miss any of them, except Jan, who she had grown quite close to.

During her last classes, she relaxed informally with the students and there was a real party atmosphere. The students performed a little spoof on life in the language school, with one of them sending up Andrew's patronizing attitude and another student imitating her teaching methods and exaggerating her mannerisms such as flicking her hair back repeatedly and saying 'good, well done!' over and over again. It was so funny and really made her laugh at herself. She was touched to find that they had all clubbed together and bought her a pair of dangly silver earrings. Before the end of class, she exchanged addresses with many of the students and eventually she left the Institute full of promises to visit students if she ever she found herself in Italy, France, Sweden or Holland.

Rosie was now staying at home, much to her mother's delight. Denny wanted her to stay on with them but Rosie felt awkward with Tony; she did not trust him. *Anyway, it's nice to spend some time with dad*, she thought. One day, towards the middle of January, Rosie agreed, after some persuasion, to go shopping with her mother for the first time in years. If they had had more money, Rosie was convinced her mother would have become a shopaholic. Elizabeth loved any excuse for a bit of retail therapy.

"Now you'll need lots of cool cotton dresses and underwear. You won't be able to wear synthetic fibres as they'll make you sweat too much," her mother advised. "And don't forget it's a Muslim country, so you'll have to be careful about what you wear, I mean, no mini-skirts and plunging necklines, dear."

"Oh, Mother, don't fuss please. I've told you, Oman's nothing like Saudi Arabia. Stuart says I can wear what I like, within reason."

"I know, but you won't be able to go around showing off your midriff like that," she responded, pointing at Rosie's tanned diamond studded navel. Her mother waltzed into a department store and Rosie groaned. She would not be seen dead in the dreary clothes on display.

"I don't mind looking for underwear in here, Mum, but don't start looking at clothes because these are just sad, they're not my style at all," she commented, waving her arm vaguely at the drab clothes on the faceless dummies. Her mother ignored her and headed straight for the fashion rails.

"Oh look! This is nice, dear, what do you think?" she asked, holding up a gross green and yellow floral dress on its hanger.

"No, Mum, I don't think so," replied Rosie, shaking her head, "please, let's just go to the lingerie department."

But her mother was absorbed in scouring the rails. Soon Elizabeth began to feel exasperated by Rosie's lack of enthusiasm. "But it's cotton, it's perfect for the heat and look, dear, it's reduced! It's in the sale! It's such a bargain at that price," her mother said, inspecting it carefully.

"Mum, I said no, now please let's forget it, I don't like it!" she said her voice rising with indignation.

Her mother looked aghast at her daughter. "You're making a scene, Rose!" she replied in strangled hushed tones, looking around and hoping that no one she knew was in earshot. Her mother noisily returned the dress to the rail and stormed out of the shop, muttering about Rosie's ungrateful nature.

Rosie watched her mother walk away. Her mother was so infuriating. But Rosie's anger soon turned to pity. *In a few weeks time we'll be missing each other*, she thought.

"Mum!" Rosie shouted, hurrying after her mother, "Alright, Mum, I'm sorry I shouted. It's just that sometimes you don't seem to listen to me. I've told you so many times, I don't like the clothes in that shop, so why d'you have to ignore me and just keep pushing them down my throat?"

Elizabeth twirled around to face her daughter, with an angry frown.

"Rose! I wasn't 'pushing the clothes down your throat'. I was just trying to spend some time and money on equipping my daughter for the future. Pardon me if I did the wrong thing." Elizabeth was deeply hurt by Rosie's churlish attitude. Her eyes pricked with tears. *Why does Rose always treat me so badly? I am only trying to help.*

Rosie rolled her eyes. "Oh come on, Mum, let's go and have a coffee," she said, trying to make amends. They stepped onto the escalator and stood still as it moved upwards.

Rosie was trying to soothe her mother's hurt feelings, when suddenly she froze. Coming down the opposite escalator, she saw a sight that almost made her heart stop beating and turned her stomach to jelly. It was *him*. She was sure of it. The man who had attacked her and destroyed her innocent belief in human goodness was coming towards her.

Rosie was stunned. She did not know how to react. She quickly turned her back on him and bent down, as if to search through her shopping bag, as the escalator continued upwards. She could feel her face burning with embarrassment.

"Rose, listen, I think it'll be a good idea to buy a vanity case with a combination lock..." her mother rambled on, unaware of any sudden change in her daughter.

Rosie struggled to overcome her desire to vomit. Fear gripped at her stomach. *Has he seen me? Should I call the police? If I do, then mum will find out what happened. No, I have to ignore him.*

The moment passed, and as she glanced behind her, she could see his wide body and head of thinning hair descending. She felt weak with relief and her legs wobbled as they walked towards the café. Rosie tried to breathe deeply, to calm her beating heart. She peered carefully over the railings and saw the man disappear into Virgin Records.

Oh my God! Rosie thought, clutching her mouth, *I have to get away from here. Thank God I am leaving soon.* She tried to compose herself and focus on her mother's conversation. She saw a tall security guy prowling around in thick-soled shoes, holding a two-way radio attached to his ear. *Should I alert security? Have a quiet word in his ear?* she asked herself.

"Two cappuccinos please," said her mother, "and excuse me but can I have mine with decaf coffee please and one of those nice croissants with chocolate inside?"

"Mum, I... I'm not feeling well," she said, rubbing her forehead and squinting. "I think I'm getting a headache. Do you think we could go home now?" asked Rosie quietly.

"Well of course, dear, but just let's go and take a look at some swimming costumes in M&S. They've got some very nice feminine ones and I think you'll be needing a good quality costume in a modest style that won't perish and lose its colour too quickly."

Rosie did not have the strength to argue. She shrugged her shoulders. The fight had gone out of her, all she longed to do was get home to her parents' house as quickly as possible and bolt the door behind her.

She meekly followed her mother around the shops, with her head down, furtively looking for her attacker around every corner, expecting to see him exiting a shop at any moment. Supposing she came face to face with him, what would she do? Many nights she had lain in her bed and imagined herself screaming, kicking and punching her assailant. The whole nightmare of the attack came back into her mind, as though it had happened just yesterday, instead of months before. She felt herself shaking and went into automatic pilot, following her mother around the shops and nodding like one of those dogs in the back of car windows. Rosie tried on dozens of swimming costumes in the changing room at M&S, waiting for her mother's approval. Eventually she allowed her mother to talk her into buying an old-fashioned all-in-one costume in a dark maroon colour with fake lime green and yellow flowers attached to it. Rosie hated it and quietly vowed that she would never wear it. She sighed deeply with relief when they finally left the shopping centre and made their way home to Woodingdean. Rosie silently told herself she would never feel safe in Brighton again.

Chapter Five

Her mother announced she would not be coming to the airport. She said she could not face it. Rosie pursed her lips, feeling it was a bit of a cop-out but then told herself to refrain from passing any judgement. She realized how difficult things would be for her mother when she left. Denise helped Rosie load the car with large suitcases and bags, while her mother hovered, repeating items from a checklist that she had painstakingly written many days before. Sheba ran around the car, wagging his tail, convinced that he was about to go for a ride. Her father rubbed his chest, disappeared into the kitchen and swallowed his medication with a glass of water. He sighed. *Will Rosie be alright? A single girl in an Arab country; will she be harassed? There were so many imponderables. One thing was for sure; life at home without Rosie would be dull.* He would miss her more than she would ever know. He climbed slowly into the back seat of the car and Denise closed the door behind him. Sadly, he watched Rosie and Elizabeth saying goodbye to each other. He knew Elizabeth would be worried sick about Rosie and it would be up to him to reassure her, by hiding his own concerns.

Denise reversed out of the drive and Rosie waved to her mother from the window. She suddenly felt an overwhelming desire to rush back and hug her mother and to apologize for being mean and ask her forgiveness. But instead, she just sat there, tears streaming down her face, as the car moved off down the road. She already felt guilty for putting her mother through so much pain and anxiety. Rosie looked out of the back window. Her mother looked so small and lonely as she stood at the front door, waving goodbye. Rosie felt exasperated. *Why do I always have to feel responsible for mum's happiness?* She told herself firmly: *I have to get on with my life, I can't hang around forever. I need to get away.*

The A23 was shiny and wet with a continual rainy drizzle. They drove in silence, listening to the regular squeaking swish of the windscreen wipers. Gatwick was confusing, as Rosie could not work out from her ticket whether the Emirates flight was leaving from the North or the South terminal. Finally, they parked in the multi-storey car park and made their way to the correct terminal, Denise wheeling one heavy suitcase and Rosie pulling the other. Her father walked slightly behind them both and he was struck once again, by the marked difference between his two daughters: one short, dark and curly-haired, the other tall with straight blonde hair. He was happy that they both got along so well and knew Denise would miss her sister. *Just as well she has Tony to keep her busy*, he thought. They walked though the crowded terminal and found the check-in desk.

"Now then," said her dad as they reached passport control, "be sure to ring as soon as you get there and remember if you don't like it, love, just jump on a plane and come home, alright? Keep us posted," he added, giving her a hug and patting her on the head.

"Yes, Dad, don't worry I'll be fine. Look after yourself and… and look after Mum," she blurted out with tears in her eyes. Rosie took a deep breath and bit her lip as she turned to Denise. They looked deep into each other's eyes with love and understanding. Rosie hugged Denise and whispered quietly in her ear: "Maybe you're right about Tony. Talk to him, Denise, you have to get to the bottom of it. Listen, there are plenty more fish in the sea, you know."

Denise was surprised at the comment but nodded and held her sister's hands at arm's length.

"Now let me look at you. It's not fair, you know," she laughed, "next time I see you, you'll be all tanned and healthy looking, while I'll *still* be all spotty and white!"

Typical of Denise to lighten the atmosphere with humour, even when she's feeling so low, thought Rosie.

The aerial view of London was amazing; watching the Thames snaking its way through the huge city with its thousands of roads and tiny cars, made her feel incredibly small and insignificant. It seemed to put her own life, with all its worries and problems, into perspective. She sat back in her seat and thought about her life in a more objective light than ever before. At last, she felt she could relegate her traumatic experience to her dim and distant past. The attack was just something that had happened and now she could move on and learn from it. In future she would try to be more aware of her vulnerability and not put herself in dangerous situations. She was certain that nothing came by chance in this life. The people we meet and the situations we experience are all carefully designed to give us opportunities for growth and development. She believed that if we fail to learn these lessons, the situations and patterns of behaviour will be repeated again and again in one form or another until we at last understand and grasp what we need to know.

A certain excitement began to grow inside her as she thought about her future in a strange country. She was itching to take photographs of new and exotic locations and imagined herself talking to the local people in Oman. Each night before going to sleep, Rosie had been listening to a taped Arabic course and she now tried to recall some of the phrases which she would need to know:

"Salam alaikum. Keef halick? Ana esmi Rosie." (Peace be with you. How are you? My name is Rosie.)

She was looking forward to practising Arabic with the shopkeepers:

"Bikam hatha?" (How much is this?) She had read that bargaining and haggling over prices was de rigeur in the souq and she was determined to try it out. She intended to buy some of the beautiful antique silver jewellery that had been

hand-made in Oman. Much of the silver had come from melted-down Maria Teresa coins which had been used as currency during the spice trading days. Apparently the women wore huge, heavy silver necklaces and thick bangles around their ankles and wrists. It really was going to be fascinating to find out more about Oman's culture and people.

As Rosie imagined seeing Stuart at the airport in Dubai, she found herself getting hot with anticipation. They were going to stay in the Jumeirah Beach Hotel. She rummaged around in her bag and brought out the Dubai guide book and sat back in her seat to devour its contents. Forty-five minutes before landing, Rosie rushed to the toilets and inspected herself in the mirror. *Yuk!* The flight had dehydrated her skin and her eyes were puffy, where she had inadvertently slept in her make-up. She removed her mascara and splashed her face with cold water. She bent forward to brush her hair and nearly hit her head on the door the toilet was so cramped. She reapplied some make-up and changed into her new pink tee shirt and squirted some perfume behind her ears and on her wrists, to freshen up and get into the holiday mood. She smiled at herself in the mirror and pinched her cheeks to make them red. Several men looked up at the attractive girl with flowing hair and sparkling eyes, as she weaved her way back to her seat, to wait for touch down.

Chapter Six

Stuart grinned from ear to ear, when he caught sight of her. Leaving her trolley in the middle of the walkway, she rushed into his arms. Tears of relief and joy fell as she smothered him with kisses. He held her tight and gently massaged her back. They swayed to and fro, unable to tear themselves apart.

"Missed you so much, babe," he murmured into her hair.

"Oh, Stuart, I've missed you too! Hey, you look different somehow, what have you done? Oh, you have a moustache now, umm... very distinguished!" she laughed, stroking his moustache with her fingers. "And you're so tanned."

Stuart put his arm around her shoulders and taking control of the trolley, led her out into the bright Dubai sunshine.

"Wow, it's so lovely and warm!" she exclaimed. "I can't wait to get to the beach!" Stuart hailed a taxi and they sat in the back with their arms around each other. Rosie tried to kiss him.

"Hey, hold on sexy lady, not here, or we'll get arrested!" he chuckled. "Just wait till I get you to the hotel," he added, tapping her gently on the tip of her beautiful upturned nose. She smiled and sat quietly snuggled up in Stuart's arms as he told her about their plans for the day.

"First, we'll go and chill out at the hotel, order room service for breakfast and then take a swim. They have this amazing pool with a bar in the middle and there are sun loungers and parasols and even a hammock on the beach. The sea is crystal clear and so lovely and warm. Yesterday when I arrived here, I took a swim and there were all these little fish swimming along beside me. It was so cool. You'll love it, Rosie. We'll have a siesta after lunch and then take a walk along the beach to watch the sunset. Did you bring your camera?"

"Yes of course; in fact, I've bought a new digital one."

"Oh, great, then you can print them off yourself."

"Is there somewhere I can buy a printer?" she asked.

"Rosie, we're in Dubai, you can buy anything you want here, it's a shopper's paradise! Oh, we're going to have a great time. It's so good to see you, babe," he said, pulling her towards him. She rested her head on his broad shoulder.

The wave-like structure of the Jumeirah Beach Hotel appeared to be made almost entirely of glass. It stood shimmering in the heat as they drove up to the entrance and made their way into the foyer. Rosie was immediately impressed. The interior appealed to her love of dramatic colours and seemed to combine all the elements of earth, wind, fire and water. It was so refreshingly different to stuffy, dark and formal hotels she had stayed in before. Here, Rosie felt a mixture of luxury, indulgence and relaxed holiday fun. The staff at reception wore brightly coloured uniforms and smiled at her as they went to check in. Looking up, Rosie saw the most amazing three dimensional map of the Arabian peninsular covering the entire ten story high wall, stretching right up to the roof of the hotel. A red light showed Dubai at its core.

Later, Rosie stood on the balcony overlooking the sea and felt herself unwind. She closed her eyes and felt the gentle breeze play on her face. She jumped as Stuart came up behind her. He put his arms around her waist and gently blew into her ear.

"Hey, why are you so jumpy?" he enquired.

"Oh it's nothing, you just startled me, that's all," she said defensively.

He laughed, bent down and lifted her up in his arms and carried her towards the enormous king sized bed. Initially, Rosie giggled, wrapped her arms around his neck and held

Stuart tight but as he lowered her onto the bed and started pressing himself up against her, memories of the past surfaced and she let out a gasp and shouted,

"No Stuart! Stop it! Get off me!" She pushed him away roughly.

Stuart rolled to one side and looked at her, puzzled. "Hey, what's wrong? What did I do? I only want to kiss you, babe," said Stuart innocently.

"Well I know… I know… I'm sorry," she frowned. "It's just that I… I feel I need to freshen up first, after the flight, I mean." She leapt off the bed and opened her suitcase. "I'll just take a quick shower and brush my teeth. I won't be long" she said placatingly, aware that she had hurt his feelings. She disappeared into the bathroom and bolted the door behind her.

She leaned against the back of the door, breathing hard. *I've got to clear my mind, I mustn't over react,* she thought. *I don't want him to suspect anything. I can't bear the thought of having to tell him all the sordid details.* Vivid memories of the attack replayed in her mind. She bit her finger and closed her eyes tight, trying to focus and stop her heart from beating so fast. As she calmed down, she told herself that the attack had happened in another time and place. Here she was, thousands of miles away, at the start of a new beginning, a new era in her life. She repeated affirmations to herself while she stood under the shower: Release the past! Think positive! Control the mind! She tried visualizing herself standing under a waterfall of cool, invigorating, cleansing spray. She imagined all the dross, tension and negative impressions being washed away, leaving her purified and at peace. She regarded herself in the mirror. She could do with a good sleep, but she decided she did not look too bad. A siesta after lunch would set her up for the night ahead. She smiled at herself and tried to look breezy, relaxed and sexy, as she opened the door, wearing her new red silk and lace underwear.

Stuart was lying on the bed reading the guide book. Rosie clambered on to the bed and kneeled in front of Stuart. "So, have you missed me?" she enquired in a lazy, husky voice. She reached out and ran her fingers through the few sparse hairs on his chest, hoping that things would be okay. As long as she could initiate things and keep control of the situation, everything would be fine. She moved forward and planted a kiss on his forehead. He dropped the book and turned to her, smiling. He put his hand on the back of her neck and drew her towards him. Rosie tensed her body and closed her eyes, desperately trying to block out painful memories. She willed herself to submit to Stuart's passion with a growing sense of alarm. Rosie lay back and gritted her teeth, believing stoicism was the only way to deal with the situation, being totally unwilling to share the pain that was eating away inside of her.

Stuart frowned. It was so good to hold Rosie in his arms again. He loved making love to her. But somehow, this time he still felt frustrated. He held Rosie close and kissed her gently on the top of her head. "Are you okay, Rosie?" he asked, lifting her chin and looking deep into her eyes.

Rosie nodded vigorously. "Yes, I'm fine. Why?" she asked, with innocent violet blue eyes.

Stuart searched for the right words. "Nothing. It's just that you... seem a bit tense."

"No, I'm fine, really I am."

"Okay, good."

Rosie was having fun with her new camera. She had already taken photos of Stuart lying on a sun lounger, dozing and sitting at the bar on an underwater seat. Stuart made her pose coming out of the sea in her bikini, like Halle Berry in *Die Another Day*. She laughed and splashed him and he chased her along the beach. Rosie took a whole stream of pictures as the golden sun sat on the water and gradually sunk down beyond the horizon, turning the sky red hot and smoky purple. Now they were sitting at the beach bar in the soft evening light, and she felt herself blushing as she ordered a cocktail entitled 'Sex on the Beach'. "How embarrassing!" she laughed.

It was awesome. Rising out of the sea on a man-made island in front of them, was the most amazing sight; the Burj Al Arab; a seven-star hotel built in the tall, gentle curving shape of a sail. Soaring 321 metres above the Arabian Sea, the tallest hotel in the world flashed its lights to warn aircraft of its enormous height. It towered above them and as Rosie looked up, she could just see the circular disc shaped helipad, jutting out. As Rosie and Stuart sipped their drinks, they watched the hotel's facade gradually transform itself in a whole spectrum of soft coloured light, changing from soft blue, to pink, purple and then a deep sea green.

Rosie and Stuart showered and dressed for dinner and forty-five minutes later they were ushered into the shuttle limo with its padded white leather seats for a visit to the Burj Al Arab.

"I feel like a superstar in this thing," exclaimed Rosie with excitement.

The limo had tinted windows, a bar, a TV and a fantastic sound system, which was playing loud belly-dancing music, as they drove along the causeway towards the hotel. The doorman opened the door and ushered them inside. As they mounted the escalator, they felt as if they were entering another world. A world full of opulence, where no expense had been spared; shining marble floors, sparkling fountains, crystal chandeliers, golden columns and huge vertical fish tanks, alive with an array of brightly coloured fish. It was unbelievable. They had read that the royal suites had gold-plated palatial fittings with rotating beds, jacuzzis and even private cinema screens.

Rubbing shoulders with the rich and famous, they drank a glass of rich mellow red wine in the bar on the top floor looking out over the sprawling city with its twinkling lights. Reluctantly, they decided to head for a restaurant that was a little more within their price range. They left the Burj Al Arab and took a taxi to a Cuban restaurant, but after watching a breathtakingly passionate couple dance the tango, they finally decided to eat at the nearby Italian restaurant, as Rosie wanted to sit outside under the stars.

"Oh, Stuart, life in Brighton seems a million miles away. It's January and it's late at night, yet here we are sitting outside and it's so warm and I feel so relaxed, I absolutely love it here. I'm so happy, Stu. Thanks for giving me the push I needed to move on with my life," she said, placing her hand in his.

Stuart grinned. He responded by delving into his pocket and bringing out a small dark blue box with a ribbon on top. He leaned towards her. "Here, babe, I bought you this the other day, it's only something small, I hope you like it."

Rosie lifted her eyebrows in surprise. She carefully opened the box and took out a beautiful sparkling white gold bracelet.

"Oh, Stuart, you shouldn't have! It's beautiful, oh darling, I love it, it's perfect," she said putting it around her wrist. Stuart beamed to see her looking so happy and she leant right across the table and gave him a big kiss on the lips. "That was so thoughtful of you," she crooned.

"You're welcome. Okay, so what shall we do now?"

"I don't know. Is there some place we can dance, Stu? I'd really love to go dancing."

They paid the bill and climbed the stairs to a nearby nightclub. It was nearly midnight and just beginning to fill up. Rosie pulled Stuart onto the dance floor and they danced together slowly, holding each other tight, heads touching, hips gyrating. When the slow song ended she kissed him lovingly again and felt she could not wait to get back to the hotel. Then Stuart went to get them some drinks and Rosie looked around for somewhere to sit. She soon started talking to an English girl called Hannah, who had been living in Dubai for two years.

"It's a great life here, we go out nearly every night and really have a blast. Are you just visiting or intending to stay?" Hannah asked, dragging on her cigarette.

"No, I've got a job in Muscat," Rosie explained.

"Oh have you? Lucky you! I've never been there, but friends of mine say the beaches are beautiful and that the place is really so clean and unspoilt. The locals are supposed to be very friendly. I wouldn't mind coming down to take a look some time," said Hannah, casting a glance at Rosie and waiting for a response.

"Oh well sure. I'll give you Stuart's address, you'd be welcome to come and stay with us anytime."

"Really? That's kind of you, thanks a lot, maybe I will. Do you have an email address? Let's keep in touch, then." They were exchanging telephone numbers when Stuart returned with their drinks.

"Hi, I'm Stuart, pleased to meet you," he said, holding out his hand.

"This is Hannah," said Rosie, "She works for a courier service here."

"You must be busy then, we call the normal post 'snail mail' out here," he joked.

He sat down next to Hannah and was soon deep in conversation with her. Rosie could not hear what was being said, but as she watched him lean towards Hannah, she felt a stab of jealousy. Hannah's green eyes sparkled and she tossed her long, thick chestnut brown hair, laughing out loud at one of Stuart's jokes. *She's flirting with him*, Rosie thought. Just then she heard the dreamy voice of Amy Lee and Rosie pulled Stuart to his feet, shouting, "Hey this is a good song, come on babe, let's dance!"

She attached herself to Stuart and danced holding on to him as though her life depended on it.

Rosie was shaking like a leaf, lying flat on her back with her arms crossed. She could feel cold water flowing down her back and told herself that what she was about to do was sheer madness. She pushed herself forward and felt a rush as she began a terrifying and thrilling descent down the highest water slide in the Wild Wadi aqua park. She hated feeling so out of control, unable to stop, going faster and faster. Suddenly, there was a swooshing sound as she hit the water and found herself submerged. She could no longer hear herself screaming. As she surfaced, gasping for air, she found Stuart standing on the edge of the pool laughing at the startled expression on her face. Rosie was so completely stunned, she hardly knew whether to laugh or cry. She frowned, she pouted, but then the tension left her body and she dissolved into a fit of giggles and sat down in the water.

"Wow, that was cool!" she announced.

They returned to the sun loungers to dry off and warm up in the sun. "Hey, can you put some cream on my back, babe?" Stuart requested.

"Sure, you're beginning to burn," Rosie warned, rubbing cream into his freckly red skin. "You'd better cover up, put a tee shirt on."

"Alright, mum!" he laughed.

She smacked him on the back.

"Ouch, that hurt!" he shouted.

Rosie and Stuart had spent the morning in the City Centre. Although Rosie had been to Bluewater Shopping Centre in Kent, one of the largest shopping centres in Europe, she was totally amazed at the size, variety and quality of shops in the City Centre. She bought herself a beautiful thin cotton pinstripe pencil skirt and a white blouse for work. She knew she would need to make a good impression with the staff at the Institute. Stuart convinced her to buy the matching jacket because he said it made her look businesslike and mature. She would have to give the appearance of being a strict authoritarian with the students. Any unprofessional behaviour and familiarity with the students would mean the end of her authority in the classroom. She had learnt that lesson the hard way years ago when she had first started teaching. *Familiarity breeds contempt. Keeping a professional distance earns respect.*

As Wednesday night was their last evening in Dubai, before flying on to Muscat, Stuart took her for dinner on a traditional wooden dhow as it sailed down the Creek. The boat gently swayed to and fro as the couple shared a traditional Arabic meal of hummus, tabouleh, Lebanese bread, white cheese and olives, falafel, biryani and kebabs. Rosie watched the silvery moon's reflection playing on the dark water and sighed with pleasure. It was all so romantic. Later, they sat in a small cafe at the water's edge and she and Stuart sucked and blew and choked as they tried smoking apple-flavoured tobacco though a long shisha pipe. Once they learnt the technique, they sat in silence happily listening to the soothing sound of the water bubbling as it filtered the tobacco. Rosie felt her spirits lifting as they watched the world go by and she felt sure that she would blossom and grow from the experience of living in the Middle East.

Chapter Seven

After a short forty-five minute flight, Rosie and Stuart finally arrived in Muscat. Rosie stood blinking in the brilliant sunshine while Stuart went to collect the car. *The atmosphere is different here*, she thought as they drove along the highway and turned off at the Al Khuweir roundabout. *It's peaceful and calm.* At last, she sank down into the deep blue cushions of the sofa in Stuart's Madinat Al Sultan Qaboos apartment and found herself feeling almost overwhelmed by all the different sights and sounds she had experienced over the past three days. She yawned, closed her eyes and drifted gently into relaxed state of consciousness.

"Oh no you don't!" said Stuart, gently lifting her up in his strong arms and carrying her through to the bedroom. Rosie smiled and feigned sleep, silently submitting to Stuart's task of undressing her. He unzipped her dress and pulled it over her head and honey-coloured arms. She immediately curled up into a foetal position, her palms joined near her cheek. Stuart pulled the sheet up over her lightly tanned body and stroked her hair lovingly. She purred like a contented cat and allowed exhaustion to carry her into a deep sleep. Stuart whispered softly in her ear, "Sleep, my sleeping beauty, and I will awaken you with a kiss on my return."

He tiptoed out of the bedroom and gently closed the door. He picked up his car keys, put on his sandals and let himself out of the flat without making a sound. As he drove to the supermarket, he whistled a tune and made a mental list of all the foods that he knew Rosie liked. He envisaged a romantic candlelit supper and was intending to prepare a delicious stir fry with prawns, noodles and cashew nuts, served with a cool white wine. *I'll buy a dozen red roses for my beautiful wild rose.* He was suddenly struck by his transformed circumstances. Rosie's arrival changed everything. He visualized the two of them doing everything together; camping under the stars, going to wild parties, dining in smart restaurants, swimming in the ocean and sailing and diving together. He had so many plans. They would never be apart. They would eat, sleep and plan every moment of their lives together. He smiled as he thought, *she will always be there when I come home*, realizing he would never feel lonely again. She had talked of getting her own apartment, but he had no intention of letting her do that.

Now that she is finally here, I will never let her go.

Rosie woke at dawn the next day to the sound of the muezzin calling the faithful to prayer. *"Allah Akhbar!"* Friday was a holiday and Rosie lay in bed watching Stuart sleep. She sighed. *Dear Stuart*, she thought, *he looks so angelic. He's been so good to me, so thoughtful and caring. He deserves better*. She knew she could not want for a more loving and attentive guy. *I've got to get a grip*, she told herself. They had hardly made love since her arrival. Every time Stuart became amorous, Rosie tensed up and made some excuse; saying she felt too tired, or she had a headache or a pain in her stomach. Sometimes she succumbed out of necessity, just to keep him happy. But when it was over, Rosie could hear Stuart's silent thoughts, wondering why she had been so passive and cool towards him. Rosie could see the effect her aversion to sex was having on their relationship. Stuart was trying to be patient but without any knowledge of the attack he was unable to comprehend the true nature of the problem.

She looked around her. Everything seemed a bit strange and unfamiliar, but she knew Stuart would help guide her through, help her to find her feet. She jumped out of bed and stretched. Despite the curtains being drawn at the window, the bright sunlight was seeping through, filling the room with a warm yellow glow. She took a shower and went into the kitchen to make some coffee.

Yikes! What's that? Something darted quickly across the kitchen wall.

"Stuart! Come quickly! Stuart!" she shouted, walking backwards out of the kitchen, closing the door and running back to the bedroom. She shook him. "Wake up, Stuart!"

"Um? What's wrong? What happened?" Stuart asked groggily.

"There's an animal in the kitchen. Come on, Stuart! Please, come on! You have to do something," she pleaded.

Stuart swung his legs off the bed and pulled on a sleeveless tee shirt. He walked bleary-eyed into the kitchen. Rosie stood behind him, looking at the stark white wall over his shoulder. "What is it?" she asked.

He grinned. "Oh, Rosie, it's nothing, it's just a lizard, it won't hurt you," he laughed walking back towards the bedroom.

"But… but what's it doing in the kitchen? It's unhygienic. Please, Stuart, you have to get rid of it."

"On the contrary, lizards eat the flies, so they actually keep the place clean," he explained.

"Well, I'm not having it in my kitchen. I'm not going in there until you deal with it," she announced peremptorily, putting her hands on her slim hips and waiting for Stuart to act.

Stuart frowned. He stormed back into the kitchen and closed the door. After several bangs and crashes, Stuart emerged and announced the kitchen was now an animal-free zone.

"You didn't kill it though, did you? I didn't want you to kill it."

"No, no, I just shooed it out of the window," Stuart replied as he stumbled towards the bathroom.

"Shall I make you some eggs?" she asked gratefully.

"Mm, yes please, with tomatoes, toast, butter and a cup of tea," he added, disappearing into the bathroom.

Coming right up, sir. Who does he think I am, a waitress?

Later, Rosie folded her clothes carefully and put them in the drawers and cupboards Stuart had designated for her use. She hung up her suits and jeans and then decided to iron her white shirt ready for the next day. She wanted to be totally prepared for this new challenge. She wondered what it would be like. Would she like the students? Would the staff be friendly and show her how things were done?

Stuart could see Rosie was deep in thought. "Hey, babe, what's on your mind?"

She explained her concerns as she ran the iron up and down. Stuart came over and put his arms around her waist. "Everything will be fine, you'll see," he said. She turned around and Stuart held her head between his hands and kissed her gently. "Now, grab your bikini, we're going swimming."

Rosie smiled, turned off the iron and went to get her things. When she opened the drawer, the awful maroon swimsuit her mother had bought for her, lay on the top of the pile of swimwear. Rosie remembered the argument she had had with her mother in the shopping centre. *Dear Mum, I hope she's alright.* She felt a pang of homesickness. Her parents' home seemed a million miles away. *I'm living in a different world.*

Ten minutes later they drove into the Intercontinental Hotel car park. It was packed. A live band was playing salsa music. They found a table by the leisure pool and ate some delicious seared tuna steaks with green salad. Several people came over to say hello to Stuart.

"How come you know so many people, Stu? Everyone seems incredibly friendly." Stuart explained that in a small expatriate community, friends were more like family. "There's an intensity to friendships here, friends are really important. We all live in such close proximity, we attend the same parties, meet in the supermarket and generally entertain more often than we would do at home. We're not preoccupied with commuting, shopping and doing DIY on our homes and we have more time and money to see friends on a regular basis. And the local people work hard at maintaining their family ties. They are really friendly and hospitable. When I first arrived here, one of the guys from work took me wadi-bashing into the interior and the locals invited us into their home for coffee and dates. Even though they had never met us before, they treated us like long lost friends. They even invited us to stay for lunch!"

Later, when Stuart showed her the health club facilities, Rosie decided there and then that she wanted to become a member. Stuart suggested she look around first before making any snap decisions. After lazing by the pool, they wandered down to the sea shore and walked right along the beach to the Grand Hyatt Hotel. Rosie breathed in the fresh sea air, finding it all so invigorating. She loved being in a natural environment and envisioned herself walking along the beach each day. How brilliant it would be to work in such a holiday atmosphere: sun, sea and sand. What more could she want?

Chapter Eight

On Saturday morning, the first day of the week in Oman, Rosie climbed out of Stuart's car, smoothed down her pinstripe skirt and looked up at the imposing white building in front of her. *Well, this is it; new job, new life.* She waved goodbye to Stuart and pushed open the door. She was greeted by a thin, swarthy-faced young receptionist wearing a black headscarf. After waiting for a few minutes while the girl contacted the director, Rosie was escorted to the elevator and told to take the penthouse floor. She quickly ran a comb through her hair, as she looked up at the changing numbers on the elevator control panel and prayed silently that the director would be nothing like Andrew from Brink. The doors opened and she was met by a tall, elderly man with pince-nez perched on the end of his nose. He looked down at her over the top of his glasses and smiled kindly. He immediately reminded her of all the benevolent teachers she had known, who had conscientiously guided her through her education, encouraging her to reach her true potential. She knew at that moment that she was going to like working at the Finja Institute.

Thomas MacKay had made up his mind long ago to relax and enjoy life. He had been running language schools in the Middle East for longer than he cared to remember. He liked his job and he liked his social life. *Work hard, play hard*, had always been his motto and his lined and craggy face seemed to prove the point. With years of experience, he was able to run the Institute without exerting any real effort at all. He had taught more classes than most people had had hot dinners and could teach a class standing on his head. In fact he had actually done just that, once when he was teaching a health education class and introducing the students to yoga and karate. He had been a keen fitness freak in his younger days, but now the only regular exercise he managed entailed propping up the bar and lifting a drink to his lips. His wife, Deidre, had given him an ultimatum: if he did not stop drinking, she would leave him. She was tired of him coming home legless from the bar, tired of him crashing out on the sofa fully dressed, tired of having to nurse him through almighty hangovers and angry each time he spent their hard earned cash on drink. *Good money down the drain*, she had said. She had had enough. In retrospect, Thomas realized he had made the wrong decision at that point. He had been defensive and unwilling to change. He hated the way Deidre always tried to dominate him. He was adamant that no one was going to tell him how to live his life. He was too long in the tooth to change his ways. *She could take him or leave him.* So Deidre had left. Thomas had now been on his own for the past ten years, drinking away his loneliness every night. Predictions for the future appeared grim: he saw himself being drawn into a deep, dark tunnel which stretched out endlessly in front of him. He had no idea how he could ever emerge into the sunshine again. Was it too late for him to change? Would he ever find happiness again?

Thomas welcomed Rosie with a warm handshake and then proceeded to show her around the Institute. He introduced her to an extremely tall, broad, dark woman with a huge turban of brightly coloured cotton wound around her head. She was busy in the staffroom, photocopying from a text book. "Hello," she said brightly, displaying a huge set of gold and white teeth. "My name is Laila, pleased to meet you," she added, holding out her hand. "Where are you from?" she asked.

"I come from Brighton, a seaside resort about seventy kilometres from London," Rosie replied.

"Oh, my brother lives in Manchester. I hope to visit him this summer," said Laila. She told Rosie she had a Masters in English from Khartoum University in Sudan.

Thomas asked Laila to supply Rosie with files and timetables and then he guided Rosie down a long corridor to take a look at a few classes. They peered through the windows inset in each of the classroom doors. It was strange to see a class of Omani men wearing dishdashas with kummars on their heads and women wrapped in abayas and head scarves. Most of Rosie's classes in the UK had been a mixture of Europeans, Russians and Far Eastern nationalities. Rosie supposed it would be easier to work with a class where everyone shared a common cultural and linguistic background.

When they returned to the director's office, Thomas leaned back in his black leather swivel chair and decided to impart a few home truths. "Now, Rosemary," he said, using her full name earnestly, a smile dying on his lips, "life in Muscat can be a lot of fun, but you must always remember two things. Number one, we are guests in this beautiful country and as visitors, we must always respect the culture and the people. So keep your skirts below the knee and your cleavage inside your blouse. No messing with the locals and keep a businesslike relationship with all the students. Give 'em an inch and they'll want to take a mile, if you get my drift. So, look after your reputation." He looked at Rosie sternly over his pince-nez and continued, "Number two, work hard and you will go far in this institute, so don't screw up by being late for work. Reliability is the key. Always keep up to date with your lesson plans and marking. Keep on top of the job! Oh and as you're now on our sponsorship, that means no working for anyone else and no private lessons without asking my permission first. And don't go thinking you can change jobs whenever you feel like it, because if you leave the Finja Institute, you'll have to leave the country."

Rosie was speechless. She was more than a little taken aback by his manner. *He is like Andrew after all*, she thought. All the rules and regulations he had outlined sounded like a clear contravening of her basic human rights. She immediately felt herself bristling. Ever since she was a little girl, Rosie had hated being told what she could or could not do. Surely it was up to *her* to choose what she would wear and who she would work for? *Give me some credit. I'm not a child who needs to be told what to do,* she thought to herself.

Thomas stood up, went over to a filing cabinet and took out a timetable for Rosie. He could see that she was a little put out by his pep talk. *Never mind. It needs to be said,* he thought. He handed her the timetable. "We work to a five-week schedule here and then we have a week off. Many of the lessons are in the afternoon and evenings because a lot of the companies send their employees along to us after work. The government offices work from 7.30 until 2.30, so they're free after that. The private sector tends to work from 8 a.m. until 1 p.m. and then from 4 p.m. until 7 or 8 p.m. So they have a nice siesta in the afternoons. We have kids' classes too from 5 p.m."

Rosie was aghast as she scrutinized her timetable. She had had no idea she would have to work so many evenings. *Not again!* she thought drearily. Stuart would not be impressed. He finished at 5 p.m. most days, seven at the latest. Now she realized she would not be home until gone 9 p.m. three nights a week. *Think positive*, she thought, *starting work late means I'll be able to go for a swim and a walk on the beach each morning, or even have a lie in, if I want to.* She smiled brightly, trying to hide her disappointment as she stood up.

Thomas rose and shook her hand. "Rosemary, it's a pleasure to meet you. I hope you'll be very happy here. Why don't you go down to the staffroom and make yourself at home, have a coffee and prepare your lessons etc?" He looked at his watch. "You have approximately two hours before your first lesson. Laila will help you get sorted out.

Now remember, my door is always open, so don't hesitate to come and see me, if you need anything or have any problems. Maybe I'll see you and Stuart in the pub later tonight?"

Rosie mumbled uncertainly, making a mental note to avoid the pub at all costs. She thanked him for his help and headed out of the door. Thomas waited for the door to close before quietly opening a drawer and unscrewing the lid on his little silver flask. He held the flask to his lips and put his head back, taking a quick swig of the warming liquid inside. *She'll do very nicely*, he thought.

Two hours later, Rosie walked into her first class with some degree of trepidation. *Come on, Rosie, don't be nervous. You've taught the simple and continuous past tense dozens of times. You can do this*! She put her files down on the desk and looked up to see twelve beaming faces looking up at her with interest. "Good morning!" she announced "My name is Miss Rosie and I am going to be your teacher for the next five weeks."

"We are very lucky!" one tall male student shouted out, grinning.

Was he being sarcastic? Rosie smiled and thanked him, but requested that in future, he put his hand up if he had something to say. Rosie proceeded to hand out small pieces of folded card and asked the students to write their names in English on the card and display it on their desks. She always liked to get to know the students' names as soon as possible, believing that building a relationship with each student usually helped them commit to the learning process. Rosie turned and picked up a whiteboard marker and began to draw a time-line on the board as a way of explaining the past tenses.

"Here, Miss Rosie, jou need dis?" A short, rotund youth was standing next to her, holding out a clear perspex ruler.

"Thank you. What is your name?" she asked.

"My name Mohammed. Jou married, Miss?" he asked grinning from ear to ear. The whole class collapsed into a fit of giggles and Mohammed bowed to his audience, lifting his hat and doing a funny little dance before returning to his seat to the sound of loud handclapping applause.

Well, at least they're not hostile, she thought. She tried not to react and calmly ignoring his question, requested the students to write down a few sentences about themselves, realizing that she needed to assess their ability before wading in to tenses. "I want to know who you are, where you live, where you are working and what you are hoping to gain from these English classes."

Rosie moved around the class peering over the students' shoulders to examine their writing skills. Many of them were shy and hesitant and most wrote from right to left in their own Arabic script, which she really could not make head or tail of. "Please write in English. Put your pen down when you are finished. Now then, who will go first?"

No one answered.

"Sara," she announced, turning to a wiry, fine-boned girl and reading the card on her desk, "Could you please stand up and tell us about yourself?"

Sara, wearing a black headscarf and a pained expression, shook her head and smiled weakly. "Now come on, Sara, just tell us a bit about yourself."

Sara refused to budge. She stared at Rosie with her big brown eyes, as she cringed and sank further down in her chair.

"No? Okay, well, who would like to tell us about themselves?"

No one answered. *Oh dear,* she thought, *this isn't going too well.* "Right, I want you to find a partner and talk to each other, tell your partner about yourself," she instructed.

No one made a move. Everyone looked warily at each other.

It seemed Mohammed had been an exception. Her students were extremely reserved. *They even seem reserved with each other. I wonder why they are so shy? Were they frightened of making fools of themselves?* she wondered. *Perhaps they have insufficient vocabulary. Strange. I thought this class had reached intermediate level.* Then, just as she was despairing, a thin Omani boy with glasses and a very serious look on his face, rose to his feet.

"My name is Essam. I come from Sinaw. I work HSBC. I come, learn English, make more money." He quickly sat down. There was a pause. The class made no response.

"Well done, Essam." She looked around the room. "Anyone else?" she asked in anticipation. A youth with typically African features stood up slowly with a frown on his face and said, "My name Gameel. Me no job, no money. I need learn English. I want job in hotel."

Rosie had heard that many hotels were under construction in Oman and she could understand why. *It's a tourist's paradise.* Stuart had explained that the government were wisely diversifying the economy. The oil would not last forever. By the end of the lesson Rosie felt she had finally broken the ice. She laughed when one boy came up to her and asked if she knew his brother because he was studying in London.

"London is a very big place, Saif. I don't actually live in London anyway, I come from Brighton, on the south coast," she explained.

"You come my house for dinner? My mother cook for you," asked Saif, smiling broadly.

Rosie was startled by this great show of generosity and hospitality. "That's very kind of you, Saif, but I have plans for dinner. Perhaps another day. Thank you, anyway." She beamed.

Her first day was exhausting. She was surprised to find that most of her students could get by reasonably well in spoken English, but there was a marked discrepancy between their written and oral ability. She realized after questioning staff over a sandwich at lunch, that many Omanis are multilingual, due to the country's seafaring historic links with India and Africa and the large expatriate community that exists in Muscat. *Necessity is the mother of invention. It's amazing what we can learn when we have to,* she thought. She wondered when she would get the opportunity to speak Arabic here. She was hoping to visit the souq on Thursday morning.

Stuart picked her up at 4 p.m. and she stretched out and yawned as they drove home to the apartment. She could not wait to kick off her high-heeled shoes, take a bath and relax.
"So, how was it? " Stuart enquired.

"Oh, it was good. Very different, I mean not what I'd expected, but I think I'm going to enjoy working there. The students are great. It's just a case of getting used to everything, keeping an open mind. It's such a different culture, it's so fascinating and even the staff are a real mixture: Sudanese, Russian, Egyptian, Australian, I feel I've got so much to learn from them and the students. Thomas is a bit of a case isn't he?"

"Yeah. Why? What did he say?"

"Oh, well, he read me the riot act about what I could and couldn't do, looking after my reputation etc. Is he serious?" she asked.

"'Fraid so, this is a very conservative country," Stuart replied. "By the way, I've invited my friends Sam and Laura over for dinner."

"Oh great. When?" She asked with growing alarm at the thought of having to do a dinner party.

"Tonight."

"Tonight? Are you serious? Stuart, I've just had an exhausting day! All I want to do is curl up with a good book. The last thing I want to do is start organizing a dinner party for people I've never even met before!" She spoke with growing anger at Stuart's total lack of empathy. How could he ask friends over without consulting her? She sat in stony silence.

Stuart just laughed at her. "Alright, keep you hat on. It's really no big deal. We'll get a takeaway. I thought you'd like to meet some of my friends. We could go out for a drink with them instead, if you like. Sorry if I did the wrong thing." He glanced over at her, smiled and rubbed her knee.

She thought of Thomas suggesting they meet for a drink. "No, I don't want to go out either. I just want to relax. Anyway, I've got lesson plans to do for tomorrow." Rosie sat in a sulk until they reached home. She immediately disappeared into the bathroom and bolted the door behind her. *How could he be so thoughtless?*

Stuart sighed, smoothed down his red hair and rubbed his freckly neck, in an attempt to release the build-up of tension caused by a day's work and an argument with Rosie. *She is so easily irritated*, he thought. Stuart decided it was just a little tiff and she would get over it soon enough, especially when she met his friends. He was looking forward to seeing Sam and Laura. *I'm not gonna cancel. It's my home and if I want to invite friends over, I will. It's her loss if she decides to hide away in the bedroom,* he thought. He went to the store room and pulled out some cans of beer and a couple of bottles of wine, placing them in the fridge to cool down. He could hear Rosie running a bath. He opened a can of beer and switched on the TV and watched *Eastenders* on BBC Prime, enjoying the pure escapism of immersing himself in life on the Square.

Twenty minutes later, Rosie emerged in a towelling bath robe and came silently over to the sofa and ruffled Stuart's hair. She knew she had upset him and was determined to make amends. "Sorry I was angry, babe. But you do understand, don't you? You must ask me first before you include me in your plans," she said soothingly, putting her arms around his neck.

"Okay, I said I was sorry." Stuart replied, with hurt in his voice. He pulled her towards him and they kissed lovingly. "Hey, what are you wearing under that bath robe?" Stuart enquired.

Rosie laughed "Why don't you come and find out?" she replied suggestively as she ran towards the bedroom. Stuart rose and leapt over the sofa, bounding after her. They fell on the bed and kissed. He stroked her cheek and looked longingly into her eyes.

"I love you, Rosie. Promise you'll never leave me."

Rosie responded by kissing him on the lips and instructing him to lie on his stomach and offering to give him a massage.

"Oh yeah, oh, that feels good," he groaned, as she pummelled his shoulders and massaged his neck with tiny circular movements. She moved down his back and began slapping his skin with her cupped hands.

"Mmm."

Stuart purred contentedly and then slowly turned over and put his hands on Rosie's hips, looking up into her eyes. Rosie held her breath, willing herself to accept his advances but feeling as if her body was being violated all over again. She closed her eyes as they began to move rhythmically as one, until the bed creaked and Rosie let out a deep sigh of relief.

An hour and a half later Sam and Laura arrived. They were both of Italian descent and certainly appeared to be a very stylish couple. Sam was in his early thirties. He was of medium height with shiny black curly hair and he had a slightly dark, sullen look on his face. *Lip curling, smoulderingly good looks*. Rosie figured he was one of those strong silent types who rarely said a word but was seething with inner turmoil and passion. The type who was always holding an inner dialogue with himself which often drowned out any one else's voice. His entire demeanour changed however, when he gave Rosie a disarming smile and handed her a bottle of wine.

"Pleased to meet you, Rosie," he said warmly and then quickly made himself right at home on the sofa. Laura was sweet and feminine, as her name suggested. She had a beautiful Mediterranean olive complexion. Her deep brown, orange flecked eyes were warm and laughing. She was fine-boned and slightly built with medium-length dark shiny straight hair. *Her short floral dress looks about a size eight*, thought Rosie, enviously admiring her smooth tanned legs and feet with their carefully manicured toenails in their diamante sandals.

Laura sat next to Rosie and asked her how she liked Oman. The two girls immediately hit it off and their conversation quickly became intimate. "Do you miss your family?" Laura asked.

"Not yet, well sometimes, but I think in a few months' time I will begin to," Rosie predicted.

"The key is to keep yourself really busy, especially at weekends. Then the time will just fly past. Have you got a year's contract?"

Rosie nodded.

"Well, as you've arrived in January, I guess that means you'll have to stay here during the long hot summer, when most people leave. You'll need to join a club or take up painting or something, otherwise you'll get really bored. Actually, that's the time to visit Salalah, because it is much cooler down south in summer. It gets the khareef…"

Rosie was not listening. She was wondering if Stuart would go on leave without her. How would she manage in Oman on her own? She realized she would have to make lots of friends. *I must not rely totally on Stuart.*

Sam and Laura had lived in Muscat for almost five years and they were both camping fanatics. "There are so many beautiful places to camp in Oman. Can you imagine a thousand kilometre coastline with so many unspoilt beaches?" suggested Sam.

"Yes, and we think the beach is crowded, if there's one other person on it! Then, there are wadis and mountains to explore as well," Laura added.

"What's a wadi?" Rosie questioned.

"Oh it's a dried-up riverbed. But some have beautiful deep pools of crystal clear water to swim in. We'll take you to Wadi Shaab and Wadi Bini Khaled, they're really amazing places. Hey, do you guys want to come camping with us next weekend? We're going with our friends Penny and Shabib to the Wahiba Sands. You'd love it, Rosie. We've been several times before and we go dune driving and camel riding. Once we took a ride in a hot air balloon over the desert. It was incredible."

Rosie found Laura's enthusiasm infectious. "Wow!" exclaimed Rosie. "What do you think, Stuart? Shall we go to the Wahiba next weekend?" asked Rosie.

"Well, we don't have any camping gear. I mean we're not exactly equipped for it," Stuart replied cautiously.

"Oh, come on, Stu, you can buy everything you need from the shops here. They've got tents and sleeping bags etc and they're much cheaper than you would find them at home." Sam advised. "Anyway, you won't need tents for the Wahiba trip. We're going to stay in a camp, it takes all the hassle out of camping. They've got these barasti huts made from palm fronds with little beds and there's even a proper loo and running water. The guys that run the camp provide all the meals and guide you to the best dunes for dune driving and take you to visit a Bedu village and stuff like that. It's great. Why don't you come?" Sam suggested.

Stuart looked at Rosie. "Okay, cool, yeah, I think that would be great," Stuart responded.

"Okay, I'll have to check with the others and make sure there are enough beds available, but it shouldn't be a problem. I'll let you know on Monday," Sam promised.

Stuart picked up his car keys and headed for the door. "I'm going to get some Chinese food. What are you guys having?"

Stuart soon returned heavily laden with everything including the chopsticks. The rest of the evening was spent discussing their imminent trip to the desert. By the end of the evening Rosie's head was buzzing with all the exciting possibilities Oman seemed to offer. Sam was apparently a keen diver and he told them some amazing stories about sea creatures and dolphins. It made Rosie think about the possibility of buying an underwater camera. Maybe she would even overcome her fear and learn to dive while she was here.

When Sam and Laura finally left, Rosie frowned as she suddenly remembered she had work tomorrow morning and still had unfinished lesson plans to write. She yawned as she began to clear the table and load the dishwasher with Stuart.

"So, are you pleased I invited them?" Stuart said, fishing for a compliment.

Rosie straightened up and looked at Stuart. "Of course I enjoyed meeting Sam and Laura, but you are missing the point." She looked Stuart straight in the eye. "Let's get one thing straight, shall we? Don't make plans without consulting me first, that's all I ask, okay?"

Stuart glared at Rosie and decided not to talk anymore. They carried on clearing up in stony silence until Rosie could stand it no more. "Oh, don't sulk, grow up! Yes, I had a great evening. It's just that now I'm really tired and I've still got work to do. I want to be fresh for tomorrow morning, I'm on early again."

"What do you mean, 'again'?" Stuart demanded.

"Well, Thomas told me today that I'll have to work three evenings a week."

"What does that mean exactly?"

"It means I won't get home until 9 p.m. on Saturday, Monday and Wednesday night," she admitted.

"Oh sh*t! Well, that's gonna mess up everything, isn't it? How can we go to the Wahiba Sands if you're still working on Wednesday night?" Stuart replied angrily.

"Well, don't shout at me, it's not my fault. You got me the job, remember!" she retorted.

"Oh yes, that's right, blame me! I thought I was doing you a favour!" Stuart shouted. Rosie calmly walked away. *I'm not gonna listen to him ranting and raving.*

"Hey, don't walk away from me when I'm talking to you!" he responded angrily.

"Goodnight, Stuart. I cannot talk to you when you are shouting at me. Please try to be civil. I'm going to bed now. I'll have to get up at 6 a.m. to write my lesson plans, so please stop shouting. Goodnight," she said, slamming the bathroom door behind her.

Rosie could feel the tears welling up inside her. She removed her make-up and splashed her face with cold water. Later, she climbed quietly into bed and pretended to be asleep when Stuart came in. *Oh God,* Rosie thought, *I need to find myself an apartment.*

Chapter Nine

Thomas had proved to be the kind, fatherly type, despite his initial sternness. He had readily agreed to let Rosie change shifts the following Wednesday, so that she could go to the Wahiba Sands with Stuart. Now, feeling the need to disconnect with the group, Rosie stood alone in the vast desert, feeling incredibly alive, her senses tingling with the experience. She was acutely aware of the enormous space surrounding her, but she felt no fear, just a sense of her own insignificance in the face of such an amazingly daunting landscape. The barren desert stretched endlessly out in front of her and as she turned her head, she realized the horizon was almost identical in every direction. A slight breeze lifted the shifting sands and the towering, undulating, burnt ochre dunes changed shape and form before her very eyes.

It was so still and quiet. Never before had she experienced this almost deafening silence. She closed her eyes and breathed deeply, communing with nature. The sun was beating down mercilessly on her bare head and the sand underfoot yielded as she shifted her weight. Minute grains of sand clung to her skin and hair. Suddenly Rosie heard distant laughter. She looked down from the crest of the dune and saw Stuart and the others eating breakfast in the camp far below.

When they had arrived at the camp of barasti huts the day before, Stuart had swiftly pulled her into their designated hut, taken her in his arms and kissed her urgently, his hands beginning to explore her warm body.

"Hey, Stuart, not now, wait until tonight," she responded, firmly pushing him away. "Oh, come on Rosie," he pleaded.

"We're in the desert, it's a perfect setting for 'lurve'," he joked.

Rosie had laughed as he had bent down on one knee and kissed her hand, but she frowned with a sudden dread, thinking that he was going to ask her a serious question. Luckily, at that very moment they both heard a scream. Emerging from the hut, they found Laura sitting astride a camel. Laura swore out loud, lurching forward as the camel raised its hind legs. Rosie and Stuart had nearly cried with laughter, as they watched Laura hold on for dear life. The camel straightened his front legs and Laura was tipped sharply backwards. "Don't laugh, you two, it's your turn now!" Laura shouted, without turning her head, her knuckles white as she gripped the reins tightly. Five more camels were waiting quietly with bored, haughty expressions on their faces. A young Omani boy in a white dishdasha, casually held onto the master lead which attached each camel to the next. "You come now, ride 'gamal'," he said, beckoning them with a wide grin on his young face. Rosie immediately ran back into the hut and picked up a checked Arabian headdress, winding it around her head and face in Bedouin style.

Stuart and Rosie had mounted the dromedary camels and headed off through the desert. *It's like entering another era, travelling back in time, to the age of Wilfred Thesiger and Lawrence of Arabia*, she thought. Rosie liked the slow languid movements of the camel and quickly adjusted to the camel's rhythm and pace.

Up ahead, camouflaged against a backdrop of dunes, they had seen a small encampment of arish huts made from palm fronds and tents of woven goat hair. The camel's neck stooped down as it lowered its front legs. Rosie slipped forward and nearly fell off. They dismounted with growing curiosity and followed Ali into an arish. Inside, the hut was simply furnished with brightly coloured woven mats and cushions made from dyed goat hair and sheep's wool. An

Omani Bedu with chiselled features and a very weathered dark skin welcomed them into his home. "*Al Salam alaikum*! Sit down," he entreated. His broad smile revealed several missing teeth. Everyone sat quietly, absorbing the unique atmosphere of this Bedouin encampment. Kneeling in front of them, the Bedu poured thick black coffee, flavoured with cardamom pods, into small 'finjan' cups and handed them around. Flies were swished away as the Bedu offered them a plateful of dark, sticky dates and a bowl of halwa – a sweet dish consisting of starch, ghee and sugar. They gratefully accepted. "You like Oman?" the Bedu asked.

"Oh, yes, '*na'am*' we love it," they replied, almost in unison.

"You, first time in Wahiba?" he asked, looking straight at Rosie, then lowering his eyes politely.

"*Na'am* (yes) first time, but I am definitely coming back again!" she laughed. "*Ana ahab al sahara*, I like the desert."

The Bedu nodded and smiled. "You speak Arabi? *Zen, zen*," (good), he cackled.

"*Ana ataulam*, I'm learning," she replied modestly.

Ali led them over to a group of Bedu women in burka masks who were sitting cross-legged on the ground under a makeshift shade. Some women were busily spinning wool with wooden spindles, while others were dying the white skeins of wool a deep ruby-red with a root called madder in a boiling vat of water. "What are those round brown things floating in the vat?" Rosie enquired.

"Oh, those are dried limes."

How hard these women work, Rosie thought, sweating in the heat. Ali showed them into a tented area where two women were weaving on simple ground looms, made of wood. Rosie could see the rich red, black and white designs taking shape on the looms.

"What will the cloth be used for?" asked Laura, smiling and shaking hands with one of the women. Ali told them much of the cloth would be made into camel bags and rugs and sold in souqs and heritage shops to local people and tourists.

"You want buy some?" he asked. He took them to meet a young girl called Sulayma, who showed them a selection of items made by the Bedouin. Rosie chose a wall hanging for the apartment she had yet to find. *My first purchase.* She suddenly thought of her mother and decided to buy her a bookmark. *I'll post it with a letter tomorrow.*

Rosie asked if she could take some photographs of the women working. She had been warned that some Arab women did not like to have their photos taken even if they were completely covered. Many were anxious that no man should see their faces. It was '*haram*' (forbidden) to show your face to any man other than one's husband or close male relatives. Some also believed a photo represented an image or extension of themselves which could possibly be used against them, like an effigy. The elderly woman who appeared to have authority over the women nodded in assent. Rosie was in her element as she happily snapped away, taking pictures of their incredibly dignified faces and their gnarled hands busily working on the loom. She found the Bedu extremely hospitable. Ali told her that hospitality was customary in the desert, even enemies can claim shelter and protection for three days.

As they rode their camels back to the camp, Rosie's head was teeming with thoughts of the past. She imagined she was treading the same overland routes of camel caravans throughout the ages, transporting frankincense, copper, indigo and spices across the desert seas.

Later that night, they had shared a beautiful night under a midnight blue canopy of a million twinkling stars. Rosie was amazed and enthralled by the sheer number of stars visible to the naked eye. She was also surprised by Sam. He was usually a man of few words, but that night he talked with great knowledge and enthusiasm about astronomy. It seemed he loved astronomy with a passion and as the friends lay on their backs in the cold dark sand, he pointed out some of the main constellations. He talked about the Greek astronomer Ptolemy, who in 150AD listed constellations represented by mythological beasts and heroes such as Pegasus and Heracles. He pointed out the Plough, the Bear and Sirius; the brightest star in the sky, apart from the Sun, informing them that it is 8.7 light years away from earth. "Did you know that there is a star called Betelgeux, which is 10,000 times brighter than the Sun? It appears dimmer though, because it is 650 light years away."

Wow. Rosie was staggered by Sam's breadth of knowledgeable about the universe. *I could listen to him all night*, she thought, turning her head to look at his profile in the light of the moon. Stuart followed her gaze and anxiously reached for her hand.

"Hey, let's go to bed," Stuart whispered softly in her ear.

"No. Not yet. Let's stay a while, Stuart, I want to hear more about the stars. Sam knows so much, it's fascinating."

Stuart pulled a face, shrugged his shoulders and jumped to his feet, digging his hands into his pockets as he headed for the huts. *Oh no,* she thought, *he's in a sulk again.* Sam continued to talk of astronomy until late into the night. Rosie listened with a rapt expression on her face and by the time she climbed into the small iron bed, Stuart was already snoring.

Now, in the morning light, Rosie stood alone on the crest of the great dune and she could hear Stuart calling her from the camp far below. The cloudless sky above was a brilliant shade of blue and Rosie felt truly happy to be alive. She took a last look all around, breathing in the stillness and shouted "Coming!" as she raced down the dune, nearly falling in the soft, deep sand. Rosie had just enough time to gulp down some tea before the friends piled into the Land Cruiser and their guide, Ali, drove them over the sands to the highest dunes. The six of them crammed into the four-wheel drive together, and their heads were in danger of hitting the roof as they bumped up and down over the sand. Then the car started slowly climbing upwards and Rosie put a hand over her eyes. "Oh my God! This is scary!" she exclaimed anxiously, as the car reached the peak and began to tip over. The others laughed. Perched on the top of a massive dune, they peered over the edge. "Hey, let me out!" screamed Rosie, panicking with a sudden fear of heights, "I'm not going down *that* in the car, please, no seriously, let me run down," she pleaded. Rosie opened the car door, jumped out quickly and ran at full speed down the enormous dune. Soon, the momentum made her lose her footing and she fell, tumbling over and over until she arrived at the bottom. She stood up slowly, breathlessly spitting the sand out of her mouth and laughing.

Following her lead, Stuart jumped out too; he walked backwards and then took a running leap, launching himself into thin air. He flew forward until gravity took hold and sent him plunging sharply downwards. He landed in the soft sand with a muffled cry. He ran down and joined Rosie.

"I wish I had taken a picture, Stu. You were suspended in mid air!" Rosie laughed. Rosie and Stuart squinted in the bright sunshine. The Land Cruiser looked so small.

They watched the car tilt and begin its descent. Sam, Laura and their friends, Penny and Shabib, screamed with exhilaration as the car zoomed down the dune and came to a stop beside them.

"Wow! That was so cool. Let's do it again!" said Laura.

Ali nodded and they all piled back into the vehicle and went in search of another thrilling dune ride. Later, Rosie managed to catch them all on film, leaping into mid air together and tumbling down the dunes. Sam showed them how to sandboard and Rosie took a great photo of Stuart balancing before he fell head first into the fine, deep orange sand.

At about one, Ali parked the vehicle and attached a woven cloth to the car door. Everyone helped dig poles into the sand

and soon they were sitting on mats under a large shade, eating rolled-up Lebanese bread filled with goat's cheese and mint leaves. The friends chatted quietly, aware of the echo they were creating with every sound they made. Strange, thought Rosie, how a person could have such an impact on a place and yet at the same time feel completely dwarfed by the desolate and remote environment. It reminded Rosie of the sea. *You can have fun splashing around in it, but you must never underestimate its power.*

Ali talked to them about the nomadic lives of the Bedouin. It was a life lived on the edge, devoid of excess and comfort, with one incident or event perhaps meaning the difference between prosperity and hardship: a dried-up well, the death of a camel, a single rainfall, could have a devastating impact on a Bedouin family. Rosie learnt that the Bedu women were fiercely independent, as they often had to assume total responsibility for the running of the camp, when the men were travelling in search of fresh grazing land, hunting, or transporting dried fish and other goods between the coast and the interior market towns.

Rosie asked how the Bedouin tribesman could survive the harshness of the desert, incredulous that they could tolerate living in such incredible heat in this barren land. Ali explained that the tribes' livestock provided the Bedouin with food and drink. "Did you know that camel's milk is a rich source of vitamin C?" he volunteered. "Dried dates are the Bedus' staple diet. They're highly nutritious." He explained how the Bedu make baskets from palm fronds and weave rugs and trappings to sell or trade in the markets for the other goods they require. They follow seasonal migration patterns, leaving the desert and its coastal regions in May, when fishing for kingfish, tuna and sardines becomes impossible and the heat is incredibly intense. At that time they travel to some of the market towns, arriving in time for the annual date harvest and living in arish huts just outside the towns. Ali told them the dates are harvested, sun-dried and packed tightly into bags of woven palm. Sam suggested they should take a trip to Sinaw, one of the market towns, so that Rosie could experience the hustle and bustle of market day and see these amazingly hardy people trading their animals and goods in this fascinating country.

Soon they packed up their makeshift tent and piled back into the car to return to the camp. On the way, they passed a Toyota pickup truck, loaded with women and children. A camel wearing a haughty expression sat in the back of the truck. Rosie reached for her camera and asked Ali to slow down so she could take some photos.

The women in the truck smiled and waved at her. *The Toyota and the camel*, she thought. *Will cars eventually replace the work of camels in the desert?* Rosie hoped not and decided that camels were far more practical for the terrain. *Wheels get stuck in the sand and cars guzzle expensive, polluting fuels which harm the environment. The camel is more than just a transporter of people and goods, it also provides sustenance for the people.*

They left the camp at about three and started the long journey home. Rosie suggested the girls travel together, so Stuart reluctantly jumped into Sam's car with Shabib and Laura drove the girls. They all agreed that the trip to the desert had been a great success. Rosie really wanted to get to know Laura and Penny and suggested they all meet up for a girly night at a local Italian Restaurant the following week.

"Apparently they do Salsa dancing there. Have you ever tried it? It's really a blast."

Rosie turned to Penny and asked her about her boyfriend, Shabib.

"Is Shabib Omani? How come he has such a cockney accent?"

"Well, he was apparently brought up in South London and only came back to live in Oman to kind of find his roots," Penny explained.

"Oh, do his parents still live in England, then?"

"Well no, they all live here now. I think his family returned to Oman a few years ago but Shabib decided to stay in UK. He only came back here about eighteen months ago."

"He seems like a nice guy," Rosie commented.

"Oh, he's the coolest guy I've ever been out with, he really treats me like a lady. He's so loving and generous. I think I'm falling in love with him," Penny declared.

"Really, Pen? What do you think your parents would say about that? I mean, if you decide to marry him, do you think they'd be happy about it?" asked Laura.

"I don't know if they would like it or not. I mean, they've never met him, but I think if they could see how happy he makes me, they probably wouldn't mind. I don't know, let's wait and see. It's a bit early to think of settling down, I've only been going out with him for about three months!" Penny admitted.

"Yeah, but some people say they know straight away whether he's 'the one'. Do you think he's the one for you, Penny?" Rosie enquired.

"Well, I do think he's my soul mate, we fit, if you know what I mean. But I don't know what he'd be like to live with."

The conversation subsequently turned to Stuart and it was Rosie's turn to open up and talk on an intimate level. *You would never get a group of men talking so openly about their feelings to new friends. Men are always on the defensive, never wanting to show their vulnerability*, thought Rosie. "Well, I really get on well with Stuart, I mean he's a great guy and a very generous lover, if you know what I mean! He always puts my own needs first. But the problem is, he's very possessive and gets jealous if I even look at another guy. He wants to know where I am and what I'm doing all the time. And he wants to do everything with me. I was flattered at first but quite honestly, I find it a bit suffocating. I mean, sometimes I like to do things on my own," Rosie admitted.

Penny said she had had a boyfriend like that once and she just felt like running away from him all the time. "Are you guys living together?" Penny enquired.

"Well, yes and no, I'm staying with Stuart right now, but only until I find my own place. I'm going to start looking around tomorrow. I just need to find myself a nice little flat and then I'll move in and have my own space. I don't want to hurt Stuart's feelings, but I think Stuart is getting too serious too quickly and I'm just not ready for that kind of commitment," she admitted.

"I'll give you the name of an estate agent. Some of the flats are fully furnished, so you don't have to spend a fortune on furniture," Penny suggested.

"Really? Oh great. Thanks. I'll give them a ring tomorrow."

When they reached Madinat Al Sultan Qaboos, they kissed and hugged like old friends and arranged to meet at the Italian restaurant the following Thursday night. Rosie could not wait to take a refreshing shower and hit the sack. She was secretly pleased to find the flat empty when Laura dropped her off and she dashed into the shower and let the water run over her body. She groaned at the thought of work the next day. As she lay in bed that night, she thought: *this time last night I was lying under the stars in the desert*. She had loved the experience and promised herself she would return to the desert at the earliest opportunity. Rosie heard the key in the door and quickly turned out the lights and pretended to be asleep.

Chapter Ten

"It's perfect!" Rosie announced to the estate agent, looking around the large sunny room. So many of the flats Rosie had viewed were dark and dingy and she knew she could not live in a place where there was no natural light. Rosie fervently believed that walls could absorb the emotions. Unhappiness, friction, negativity (and even death on one occasion), could still be felt in some of the empty houses and apartments she had visited. This flat in Shatti Al Qurum was small, but it had a sunny atmosphere and best of all, it had a terrace overlooking the sea, something she had always dreamed of. "How much is it?" she asked, confident that the Institute's housing allowance would be sufficient. The pretty dark-haired estate agent smiled and muttered an exorbitant figure.

"Oh, wow, I don't know if I can afford that! Can't you bring it down a little?" replied Rosie, clearly horrified at the price. The estate agent shook her head.

"Anyway, I'll talk to my boss and see if he'll agree. I'll get back to you in a day or two, is that okay?" said Rosie.

"That's fine, Rosemary, but don't leave it too long, these new flats are going like hot cakes!" the estate agent warned.

When Rosie told Stuart she had found her dream home, Stuart had been less than delighted. "It doesn't make sense for you to spend all that money, when you could stay here with me, for nothing. Look, if you stay here, you can pocket the housing allowance and save a good bit of cash for our holidays."

Rosie shook her head. "It's not about the money."

Stuart sulked miserably.

"Stuart, look, we've been over this so many times. I need my space. Please try to understand, babe. It's not that I don't love you," Rosie explained.

"Oh, isn't it? Well, I think it's *exactly* that. You don't love me and you still want your freedom. You've made that perfectly clear. You tense up every time I come near you. You never seem to want to make love, never take the initiative. You've changed, Rosie, you're not the girl I met in Brighton. Anyway, if that's what you want, then go, I don't care! You can have all the freedom you want," Stuart shouted, slamming the door behind him as he stormed into the bedroom.

Rosie sat quietly on the sofa. *Poor Stuart. Why does he always see everything in black and white. It isn't that simple. There are always shades of grey; complexities to any given situation.* She did love him and she knew she was being unfair to him by deliberately keeping mum about the attack. But she just could not open up to him. She was convinced that even if she told him, it would not change how she felt about living together. She did not want to live with him. Living with Stuart would be all about compromise and Rosie did not feel like compromising, always having to explain her actions or give in to him, just to keep the peace. If their relationship stood any chance of surviving, Stuart would have to change.

Rosie knocked softly on the bedroom door, wanting to reassure Stuart and tell him not to confuse issues. She just needed more time, before settling down. She opened the door quietly and stumbled in the dark towards the en suite bathroom. She could see Stuart lying on the bed with the covers pulled right up over his head. Rosie sighed and began removing her clothes. She took a shower, slowly massaging her skin with olive soap. When she finally lifted the sheets and climbed into the double bed, she reached towards Stuart. He was lying on his stomach, feigning sleep. "Stuart, hey babe, don't be angry with me," she soothed, stroking his back. "Come on, Stu, don't take things the wrong way. I still love you."

"Sure you do, that's why you're moving out, very logical," he snapped, without turning to look at her.

Rosie gave up, turned over and curled up into the foetal position. She sighed deeply and decided to let him sulk until morning.

Over the next two weeks, Rosie and Stuart hardly spoke. They avoided each other most of the day and at night mindlessly watched television together in stony silence. Rosie was finally relieved to move into her beautiful little flat the following Thursday afternoon. Stuart had made himself scarce and Rosie was very grateful to Laura for kindly helping her to move all her belongings. When Laura left at around five, Rosie was sweating. She felt completely wiped out. She took a shower and then sat down on the sofa and listened to some sitar music. Moving house in the heat of the day had been exhausting. But thinking things through, Rosie knew she had made the right decision, even though she felt a pang of loneliness. She settled back on the cushions with a long cool glass of lime juice and decided she was going to be very happy in her own little apartment.

The door bell rang later that evening. Rosie jumped up from unpacking books, to find Stuart grinning awkwardly on the doorstep, holding an enormous potted rubber plant in one hand and a bottle of wine in the other. "Just thought I'd come and see if you're okay," he mumbled, swallowing hard.

Rosie beamed. "Yes, I'm okay," she paused. "But I'm all the better for seeing you, babe." She reached forward and melted into his arms.

He put the plant down and lifted her up, carrying her through the apartment. She giggled, wrapped her arms around Stuart's neck and pointed to the window. "Take me outside onto the terrace, quick, let's watch the sunset. It's so beautiful, look!" she sighed. They stood on the balcony looking out to sea and watched mesmerized, as the huge red ball of light made its descent, sinking slowly down, filling the sky with warm orange and candyfloss pink hues. In its wake, the sun left streaks of red and smoky purple across the sky, before it finally disappeared from view.

"If an artist were to paint a picture using those colours, we'd say it was unrealistic," Stuart remarked. "It's breathtaking, isn't it?"

Rosie smiled. *Dear Stuart, he's so romantic*, she thought. She turned towards him and kissed him passionately on the lips. When they finally parted, the bare shoulders of the sky were wrapped in a deep blue velvet cloak and their feelings for each other were revived and seemed to be stronger than ever.

"This is such a calm, peaceful place to live isn't it, Stuart?" she said, looking up into his eyes. And Stuart had to admit that she was absolutely right, as he took her by the hand and led her into the bedroom, murmuring that it was time for them to christen the new bed. Rosie frowned. She was determined to overcome her aversion to making love. She lay back on the bed and closed her eyes, allowing Stuart to take her body and fill her senses.

An hour later Rosie went into the kitchen and poured herself a glass of red wine, troubled by the realization that, even though she had managed to overcome her dread, she had felt absolutely nothing during their lovemaking. It was as though she were dead inside. She suddenly heard Stuart call out, "Oh by the way, Rosie, some guy from the Brink Institute rang about your last pay cheque."

"My pay cheque? What, from December? Are you sure?"

Stuart shrugged, "Well, I don't know. That's what he said. Anyway, I gave him your new number, so I guess he'll give you a ring tomorrow. Maybe they owe you some money."

"Ah, you must be joking! Getting money out of Brink was like getting water out of a stone! I can't see them volunteering any more. I'm surprised they even bothered to make an overseas call," she answered with a laugh.

"Hey by the way, Rosie, I've bought us tickets for the comedy store next Thursday night at the Plaza."

Rosie raised her eyebrows, "Really, so are we still going out together then?" she asked playfully.

Stuart grinned, took her in his arms and kissed her on the tip of her nose. "I guess so, you can't get rid of me that easily," Stuart laughed.

Chapter Eleven

The next day, Rosie came home from work carrying two heavy bags of shopping. As she fumbled for her keys, she noticed a tall young woman wearing an elegant black chiffon abaya with flared sleeves. She cast a glance in Rosie's direction and gave her a wide smile as she unlocked the door of her own apartment. Rosie returned the smile and said *"Salam Alaikum."* Five minutes later there was a knock at the door. Rosie was surprised to see the woman in black holding out a plate of home-made date cakes for Rosie. "Oh, how kind of you. *Shukran*," said Rosie. Salma was newly married and had lived in the apartment for just three months. She was a science lecturer at the university and spoke perfect English. Salma was very curious to hear all about Rosie's job at the Institute and wanted to know if Rosie liked Oman. She asked Rosie to come and visit her whenever she was free Rosie promised she would. Rosie felt deeply honoured to have been invited and saw this as a great opportunity to really get to know the local people.

Two weeks later, Sam invited Rosie and Stuart for lunch at the dive club. Stuart accelerated, changing gear, as the four-wheel drive ascended the steep road through the mountains. Rosie was in awe of the stark, jagged mountain peaks on either side of the road and as they reached the crest of the hill and turned to descend, the view took Rosie's breath away. Beyond the harsh mountains, lay a beautiful sandy cove and a sparkling, crystal clear blue sea. *God, that is so idyllic.*

They parked the car and walked past a deep diving pool towards a large tiled terrace overlooking the sea. Sam rose and greeted them and the waiter immediately came over to take their order for drinks. "I'd like a fresh lime juice with a little sugar, please," Rosie requested.

"Where's Laura?" Stuart enquired, looking around.

"She's gone to change into her bikini, she'll be back in a sec. So how are you, Rosie? How are you enjoying the job?" Sam asked.

Rosie nodded and launched into a story about two of her students. "You'll never guess what happened. Fathima and Hamed have fallen in love and are planning to get married. And they met in my class! Can you believe that?" Rosie laughed.

"Love in the classroom! How romantic," Sam agreed, grinning.

"So the whole class are invited to the wedding in a few weeks' time."

Just then, Laura returned and the two girls hugged and kissed each other.

"Wow, Laura, you look great," Stuart said admiringly, as Laura sat down. Her slim body was lightly tanned, smooth and hairless and her eyes sparkled with health.

"Thanks, Stu, yeah, I've been on a detox diet, cutting out coffee and alcohol, junk food and wheat and stuff like that."

"Isn't it hard, though? I mean, I can't imagine eating a sandwich without bread!" Rosie declared.

"Well, it's surprising how quickly your body adjusts, you just get used to it and I've found it's really made a difference to how I feel. I used to feel stiff and tired at lot of the time."

After lunch, Rosie and Laura went for a swim and Sam took Stuart to sign up for a diving course. "Why don't you do the course with me, Rosie," Stuart suggested.

"No thanks. I think I'd really panic under the water, I don't think I could do it," she replied honestly. Stuart shrugged and went off with Sam. As they swam, Rosie told Laura all about the classroom romance and asked her if she'd like to go to the wedding with her. "Have you ever been to a Omani wedding before?" Rosie enquired.

"Oh yes, they're incredible, totally different from our weddings," Laura explained.

"Really? Tell me, I don't know what to expect. What should I wear? Should I take a gift?" asked Rosie.

Laura told Rosie that usually the wedding parties are segregated and held in two different locations. The men have their own celebrations and then accompany the groom to the women's party.

"I always feel sorry for the groom having to enter the women's party, virtually on his own. Imagine the poor guy being faced by seven hundred women all staring at him."

"Seven hundred?" Rosie asked, incredulous.

"Yes, sometimes they announce the wedding in the mosque for the whole community to attend. It's a nightmare for the organizers because they never know exactly how many people will turn up. Maybe you'll be invited to the henna party as well," Laura added.

"What's that?" Rosie asked. Laura explained that Omani weddings often last a full week and usually start with a henna party to prepare the bride for her wedding night. Intricate designs are applied to the hands and feet of the bride. "Henna is used all the time by the women in the Gulf. It softens the skin and the designs last weeks, depending on how long the henna is left on before washing it off. Henna is not considered a barrier to cleanliness, as it goes deep into the skin. Modern make-up and nail varnish would ideally have to be removed every time one prays and that would be difficult as a good Moslem prays five times a day!"

Rosie and Laura emerged from the sea and dried off. They applied lashings of sunblock and pulled their sunloungers under the shade of an enormous coconut palm tree. Laura continued: "Traditionally a bride from Mutrah will wear a green and red tunic and trousers with a matching headscarf. She'll sit on a stage quite passively and probably listen to advice given by her elders. Various symbolic objects will be displayed in front of her such as a mirror, a cup and a plant, which perhaps represent hopes for a happy marriage. The sheikh and her male relatives enter the room and all the women cover themselves. The sheikh asks the bride if she agrees to marry the groom. This ceremony is like a betrothal or engagement. The 'white' wedding could take place the next day or weeks, months or even years later. It depends on their circumstances and agreement. Maybe the couple are still studying or cannot afford to set up home yet. Anyway, after the white wedding, the marriage is consummated and the couple can start living together as man and wife. Mind you, Oman is so culturally rich and diverse because of its historical ties with Zanzibar, Baluchistan, Iran and India, that the wedding you attend might be quite different. I can only tell you about the ones that I've been to."

"Well, however it turns out to be, I'm sure it will be a fascinating experience." Rosie replied.

Two weeks later Stuart told Rosie that he would have to go to England for a week. He had to attend an oil and gas conference and then spend some time in Aberdeen. Rosie's thoughts immediately turned to home and tears pricked her eyes as she thought of her family. Stuart agreed to take some post and parcels for her. Stuart ended up staying the night in her apartment. The thought of him leaving, made Rosie realize how much he meant to her. They held each other in a loving embrace and Stuart stroked her forehead until she finally drifted into sleep.

Chapter Twelve

Two days later, Rosie got an overseas call on her mobile phone.

"Hello? Oh yes, of course I remember you. Hi, Hannah! Oh, it's great to hear from you. How are you?" she exclaimed.

"I'm fine, how are you? Are you enjoying Muscat?"

Rosie was quick to enthuse about her new life and told Hannah about all the exciting things she'd been up to in the last few weeks. There was a pause.

"Listen, Rosie, I'm really fed up with Dubai, work is getting me down. I think I need a break from this place, I want to ask you a favour. Please say no if it's inconvenient, but I wondered if I could come down and stay with you for a few days?" Hannah asked shyly.

Rosie did not hesitate. "Sure you can, it would be great to see you. Oh and guess what? I've just moved into a lovely little flat on my own."

"Why, have you broken up with Stuart?"

"Well no, not really, I just felt I needed my own space. So when can you come?" Rosie enquired with growing excitement.

"How about next weekend? I could come down when I finish work on Wednesday evening and maybe stay until the following Monday. Would that be okay?" Hannah asked hesitantly.

"Of course it would. In fact it will work out perfectly, as Stuart is going away on a course, so we can have some girly nights out," Rosie responded happily.

"Hey, that's great. Rosie, I'm going to ask you something else too, I hope you don't mind. After your last email about the desert, it's made me think I'd really like to go there. Do you think we could go to the Wahiba for a night or two?" Hannah requested.

"Oh, Hannah! That's a great idea, I'm dying to go back there. It's so beautiful, you'll love it, Hannah. I'll try and set it up. Let me know your flight details and I'll come and pick you up. Hey, look forward to seeing you, then. Don't let work get you down. See you on Wednesday then, bye."

Oh it would be great to see Hannah. Rosie didn't really know Hannah at all, but she already felt they shared an affinity. They had been emailing each other regularly since the night they had first met in the nightclub in Dubai. Rosie remembered what Stuart had said: *Friendships are really quite intense out here. Your friends become your family.*

Rosie jumped when the phone rang again.

"Hello? Oh hi, Denise, how are you, sis?" Rosie asked with surprise.

Denise sobbed and answered in a small, shaky voice.

"We've broken up, Rosie. It's over."

"Oh no, what happened, babe, tell me," said Rosie sitting down.

"Well I saw Tony in a bar with another girl. How could he do this to me, Rosie?" Denise cried. "He knows how much I love him, now he's ruined everything."

"Well, it's his loss, Denny. You are better off without him. Actually, I never really liked him, I think he's a womanizer. But listen, Denny, are you sure there isn't some perfectly reasonable explanation? Maybe the girl was a colleague from work or something," Rosie suggested.

Denise replied, "No. They were kissing, Rosie, *kissing* in public. I couldn't believe it. I walked over to them and calmly poured my drink over Tony's head. I told him it was all over between us," Denise recounted, sobbing.

"You did what? Oh my God Denny!" Rosie was shocked. She had never known Denise to do anything remotely rude or impolite to anyone before. "What did he do?"

"Oh he reacted badly, of course. He was angry with me, he felt humiliated. The bastard, he showed no remorse whatsoever, though. I loved him so much, Rosie, now I just hate his guts," Denise sobbed.

"So what are you going to do now? What's gonna happen about the flat, Denny?" Rosie asked gently.

"I don't know, Rosie. When he came back home, I wouldn't let him in. I threw all his clothes out onto the landing. That's the end of it. But I can't afford to keep the flat going by myself, so I don't know what I'm gonna do," Denise sobbed.

It broke Rosie's heart to hear her sister crying. "Come on, Denny, you can advertise, find a new flatmate."

"What and invite a complete stranger into my home? No thanks, I don't think so," she said sadly.

"Why not? People do it all the time. Trust me, Denny, it might be the best thing that's ever happened and in years to come, you'll be so grateful you found out about Tony now, before you signed on the dotted line. Suppose you'd married him and then found out? Come on, Den, open yourself to something new and forget him," Rosie suggested.

"Sound advice, I'm sure, but it's not that easy, I still love him, Rosie," Denise said, hopelessly sobbing.

"I know, I know, babe." Rosie replied soothingly. "Hey, why don't you book yourself into a health farm for a couple of days? It would do you the world of good and help you see things more objectively. Or go and stay with Mum and Dad, give the flat up, make a fresh start?" Rosie advised.

"Maybe. I'll see," sniffed Denise.

"Hey, I've just thought of something!" Rosie paused. "Why don't you take a holiday and come out and see me? Think about it, Denise. You'd really like it here, lots of sunshine and fresh air."

"Are you enjoying yourself, Rosie?" Denise mumbled softly.

Rosie proceeded to tell Denise about all the interesting places she had visited and made Denise laugh when she told her about the couple who had found love in the classroom. The conversation then turned to her parents and Rosie was surprised to hear that her parents had taken up sequence dancing and were out at least three nights a week, dancing in different locations, with a whole new group of friends.

"Dad really loves it, he keeps talking about it and showing me all the steps he's learned. You should see them, Rosie, dancing around the living room and laughing and joking. I think it's given them both a new lease of life."

"Unbelievable! I'm so pleased to hear that, it's just what they needed; learning something new, keeping fit and making new friends," Rosie replied. When Rosie hung up she smiled at the thought of her parents dancing, but frowned as she sat pensively thinking how she could help Denise recover from her loss of not only her boyfriend, but also her self-esteem. *I'll make it up to you Denny, just wait and see.*

Wednesday came at last and after her classes, Rosie zoomed around the supermarket, not knowing quite what to buy, as she had no idea about Hannah's likes and dislikes. *Anyway, I think we'll eat out,* she decided. Rosie was planning to take Hannah to a Mexican restaurant for dinner that night. They did line dancing there once a week. It seemed strange to Rosie, to wear boots and a cowboy hat and line dance in Muscat. She realized that expatriates always try to keep their culture alive when they are living abroad. She supposed it was a natural instinct to try to hold on to one's roots. That was presumably why there was a strong Caledonian society and an American Women's group and one could even take up cultural classes like Indian, Irish or Scottish country dancing. *There were so many surprises in this place,* thought Rosie.

She had recently discovered that there was even an ice skating rink and an ice hockey team in Muscat.

Oman was proving far more diverse than she had ever expected.

Rosie saw Hannah's tall, slim figure approaching as she pulled up outside the arrivals hall at Seeb International Airport. *The plane must have come in early*, Rosie thought Hannah looked decidedly glum, but Hannah immediately brightened up and waved when she saw Rosie. She struggled over to the car pulling an enormous suitcase, a bulging holdall and a rucksack on her back. *Wow, that's a lot of luggage for a few nights' stay*, thought Rosie. Hannah climbed in to the car and Rosie gave her a warm hug, getting the distinct impression that Hannah really needed it. Hannah clung to Rosie as if she had known her for years and murmured "It's so good to see you, Rosie." As she pulled away from her, Rosie noticed tears brimming in Hannah's green eyes. "Hey, what's wrong, Hannah?"

"Oh, it's nothing, I'll tell you later," Hannah replied, blowing her nose. "Hey, so this is Muscat. Yippee! I'm so happy to be here."

They drove back to the flat and sat together on the terrace chatting like old friends. "It's strange, I feel as if I've known you for ages, Hannah," Rosie remarked.

"Yeah, me too. Maybe we met in a previous life!" Hannah joked.

"So tell me, why are you so miserable, Hannah? What happened?" Rosie questioned.

Hannah's dark chestnut hair fell forward as she bent her head. She took a pack of cigarettes out of her bag and lit up. "Oh is it that obvious? It's nothing, it's just work. You see, I really thought I was going to get promotion and then I couldn't believe it when the management gave the job to a new guy, who'd only just joined the company three months ago. It's so unfair. I mean, I taught that guy everything about the job and he leaned on me quite heavily at first and now, he's my bloody boss! I don't understand why the company didn't have the confidence in me to do the job," Hannah confided, her voice quivering with emotion.

Rosie did not know all the circumstances but she felt Hannah ought not to take it too personally. "Perhaps they wrongly assume that a man will be more reliable, you know, not go off and get married and have kids etc. Did you go and ask for an explanation?" asked Rosie.

Hannah inhaled deeply and flicked the ash off the end of her cigarette onto the balcony floor. She explained that she had gone in good faith to see the GM and he had told her that in his opinion, she had not taken enough initiative and shown that she possessed the required leadership qualities to do the job.

At this point Hannah's voice became hard and angry as she said she had not been given sufficient opportunity to shine. "The GM really shattered my confidence and I was so incensed, that I told him where to get off. Needless to say, I am now looking for another job." Hannah paused before adding, "Maybe I'll take a look around here, what do you think?"

Rosie said she thought it was a great idea and that she would ask Stuart to put out some feelers, but explained it was not always easy for expatriates to find work in Muscat, as there were plenty of local people looking for work. Rosie told Hannah she would take her to the Mexican later, where they would meet up with Stuart, Laura, Sam, Penny and Shabib. "Stuart is leaving for UK tomorrow, so this is our last night before he leaves."

"Oh, sorry, did you two want to have a romantic tête-à-tête? Have I ruined your plans?" asked Hannah, apologetically.

"No, not at all, we're gonna have some fun together with our friends tonight. Maybe we'll go dancing afterwards," Rosie said they would go to the Al Bustan Palace Hotel for the day on Thursday and just relax and chill out on the beach. She planned to take Hannah to the desert on Friday and had requested a day off on Saturday, so they could stay over night in the Wahiba Sands. Rosie showed Hannah to her bedroom and while her new friend took a shower and settled in, Rosie rang Stuart to arrange the evening.

After some delicious steaming vegetable fajitas, Rosie, Hannah, Laura and Penny joined in the line dancing and Hannah got hopelessly confused trying to follow the steps. They all collapsed in a fit of giggles at the end of the song. Then they split the bill and drove over to Shatti Al Qurum and parked outside the nightclub. As usual on a Wednesday night, the club was noisy and crowded. After ten minutes, Laura was complaining about the smoke and the heat. "I can hardly breathe, it's too smoky," Laura commented, coughing.

"That's a joke, coming from you," laughed Sam. "Laura used to smoke like a chimney," he explained.

Stuart asked Rosie to dance and she stood up and asked Hannah to join them. The dance floor seemed hardly bigger than a postage stamp and they could barely move without bumping into somebody. Then the MC played some Arabic music and a very large girl with dyed blonde hair and dimples in her cheeks, tied a long scarf around her hips and started belly dancing. Soon, several people formed a circle around her and clapped in time to the music.

"Music is in their blood," Sam said, watching the girl move her hips suggestively. "Come on, it's your turn!" Laura laughed, pushing Rosie into the middle of the circle. She danced around the space shyly moving her hips, while everyone cheered.

Stuart placed another round of drinks on the table in front of them. "Eh, that's not water," said Penny, choking on her drink.

"Oh, you've got my drink by mistake," said Hannah, drawing on her cigarette, "it's a double vodka."

Hannah took a giant swig of vodka, stubbed out her cigarette and grabbed Stuart by the hand. Rosie watched in surprise as Hannah pulled Stuart onto the dance floor and started dancing. Laura looked at Rosie and raised her eyebrows. "Hannah's a good dancer, isn't she?"

Rosie nodded and tried to ignore Stuart and Hannah by turning her back to the dance floor. The next song was a slow smoochy number and Rosie was convinced Stuart would come and ask her to dance. But he did not. He merely glanced in her direction, smiled weakly and shrugged his shoulders. Hannah's long arms were wrapped around Stuart's neck as she moved suggestively to the beat. Rosie saw her lean towards Stuart and whisper in his ear. He laughed. Rosie pursed her lips and looked away from the dance floor, determined to act cool.

Later that night, Stuart held Rosie in his arms and kissed her gently on the tip of her nose. They were standing on the terrace of her apartment, in the light of a full moon. Hannah had removed her shoes and she padded through the living room, complaining of sheer exhaustion after their hectic night out. "You guys really know how to party!" she commented.

"So do you," Rosie mumbled under her breath.

"I'm bushed. See you in the morning," Hannah called, leaving them alone. Stuart pushed Rosie's hair back and asked, "will you miss me, babe?"

"Of course I will, silly," she replied, kissing him on the lips and exploring his mouth with her tongue. Let's go to bed, Stu," she whispered, suddenly feeling electrified by his touch and wanting to claim him as her own. They moved to the bedroom and undressed each other slowly, savouring every moment.

"I love you, Rosie," Stuart murmured, kissing her smooth shoulder as he removed her dress. "I will love you forever," he announced, pulling her down onto the bed and caressing her gently. Rosie struggled against the negative thoughts that suddenly crowded her mind. She closed her eyes and tried to surrender to Stuart's touch, desperate for his affection and determined to let go of the past. But as Stuart moved with a growing intensity, Rosie could only close her eyes tight and hold her breath, waiting for it all to be over. At last, Stuart sighed contentedly and lay back on the pillow and immediately drifted into a deep sleep. Rosie turned onto her side and stared into her dark past, unable to flee the shadows that continued to haunt her.

Chapter Thirteen

After their heavy night out, Rosie and Hannah lay comatose on the blue sunloungers at the Al Bustan Palace Hotel. "I feel like I've died and gone to heaven. This is bliss," Hannah murmured.

"I know. It's my favourite place, it feels so indulgent to do nothing but chill, doesn't it?" Rosie answered. She watched Hannah spray herself with suntan oil and suddenly frowned as she noticed many raised red scars running across her wrists.

Hannah added, "I think we need it after last night, that was wild. Did you see that guy who came up and asked me to dance? He looked a bit of a nerd, but actually he was a real gentleman. It's so nice to be treated like a lady sometimes, isn't it?" Hannah commented.

"Yeah, I guess so, what's his name? Did he ask you out?" Rosie probed.

"His name's Dave and yeah, he did, actually. He wants to see me on Saturday night, will that be alright? Do you think we'll be back from the desert by then? I gave him my number, he's going to ring me on Saturday evening at 6 p.m. to confirm," Hannah announced.

"Well, you don't waste much time, do you?" laughed Rosie, relieved that Hannah was pursuing love elsewhere. "You've hardly been in the country twenty-four hours and you've already got yourself a hot date!"

Hannah laughed, "Well, it's about time something went right in my life. Anyway, I don't know how 'hot' it will be, I don't really fancy him, but I'm sure it will be a lot of fun. He drives a Porsche and has promised to take me for a drive."

Rosie frowned. *Why would she want to go out with someone she is not attracted to?* She implored Hannah to be careful, getting into cars with total strangers. "Some men can't be trusted," Rosie stated.

Hannah laughed and told Rosie that statement applied to *all* men. For some reason, Rosie suddenly felt the need to confide in Hannah. She started recounting details of her traumatic experience in Brighton. Tears welled up in her eyes. The attack had really had such a profound effect on her. She did not think she would ever be able to heal the emotional scar it had left on her.

"I'm so sorry, Rosie, that must have been gross. What a bastard."

Rosie nodded. "I feel so angry with him for taking away my faith in human nature." Rosie looked far away out to sea. She told Hannah that she had read somewhere that the way forward for victims of rape was to hold the image of the rapist in their heads and offer him forgiveness. "Forgiveness is the key to healing the wounds of the past and moving on. Holding anger and hatred in our hearts means we are never free of the pain."

"Yeah well, I don't know about that. If it had happened to me, I'd have killed the bastard!"

Rosie was shocked. She replied, "Well, I'm sure the guy had a lot of problems. I feel sorry for him in a way—"

Hannah interrupted, "What? After what he did to you? How can you feel sorry for him? You must be crazy," Hannah commented.

"Well, I do. But I can't forget and I don't feel safe anymore, at least not in Brighton. I'm far more wary of men now. I was always so trusting before. It's changed my whole perception. The world is not the safe place I once thought it was."

"Too bloody right," said Hannah. "But, you know, I do know a bit about dealing with anger, I went through a stage of feeling an all consuming hatred towards my father," Hannah said.

"Why? What had he done?" Rosie asked aghast.

"Well, it was more what he hadn't done, actually," Hannah replied. She explained that her father had left her mother when she was only eighteen months old. "I never really knew him. I spent my childhood feeling like I'd been abandoned. Everyone else at school had a mother and a father but I only had a mother. I felt different, like something was always missing in my life. Look, I know relationships don't always work out, but it took me years and years to be able to forgive him for not staying with my mum. She was always very bitter about it too. Imagine being left to support a kid on your own? She was only eighteen years old herself." Hannah went on, "He never came to see me, never sent me any letters or presents, never phoned to find out how I was. I haven't seen him since I was two," she shrugged. "That hurts so much. It made me start believing that there was something wrong with me, something unlovable about me. I know it sounds crazy, but when you're a kid you get all mixed up about people's motives. I thought it was my own fault somehow."

Rosie put her arm around Hannah's bare shoulders. "That must have been dreadful. But you mustn't think like that. It was his loss. I bet he's a lonely old so-and-so now. Did your mum ever marry again?" Rosie asked.

Hannah nodded and talked a bit about Stan, who had met and married her mother when she was ten. "He was a great guy and all that and at first he really tried to get along with me, but somehow, I just felt pushed out. I lost my sense of belonging. You know, when it was just Mum and me, it was okay, we looked after each other. But when Stan came into our lives, I just felt like I was in the way all the time," Hannah admitted.

Rosie nodded in understanding. She had felt a bit like that with Denny and Tony.

Hannah shrugged. "Anyway, Stan and me mum went out on a pub crawl two years ago and never came back."

"What do you mean?"

Hannah lit another cigarette before replying. Her voice was choked with emotion. "They crashed into a tree and that was that."

Rosie stared. "Oh God, how awful."

Hannah sniffed, holding back the tears. She said she was over it. That was the reason she had left UK. She felt there was nothing left to keep her there anymore. Rosie did not know how to react. Hannah shrugged her shoulders and went back to talking about her father. She felt she had come a long way towards forgiving him, "but I still wish I could talk to him and find out why he treated me so bad."

"Have you ever thought of looking for him? I have a friend who did that. There's this organization that can run a search for you. They set up a meeting if both parties agree. It helped my friend deal with a lot of emotional baggage she was holding on to," Rosie said. Hannah nodded and said she had considered it but never plucked up the courage to do it.

Chapter Fourteen

Hannah and Rosie spent the evening preparing for their trip to the Wahiba Sands. Laura had tried to book the girls into the camp they had stayed in before, but it was apparently full. Undeterred at the prospect of going it alone, Rosie had bought a large tent, a lantern, two mattresses, some sleeping bags and chairs. It was quite a lot of money to spend on one night in the desert, but Rosie loved camping and intended to see as much of Oman as she possibly could over the next few months, so figured she would get a lot of use out of her new camping gear. The girls shopped together for a readymade barbecue tray and a cold box with blue ice packs. Rosie decided they would barbecue kingfish, Halloumi cheese and vegetable kebabs.

They packed everything except the cold box into the car before going to bed and at eight the next morning, Rosie and Hannah worked together in the kitchen; chopping salads and cooking pasta to eat with the barbecue. There were so many things to remember; matches for the barbecue, drinks, food for breakfast and lunch the next day, water for washing, sunblock, hats and a change of clothes. Finally they finished packing the car and picking up some take-away cups of coffee, they drove to the nearest petrol station to fill up. Hannah rubbed her stomach and lit a cigarette.

"Are you okay, Hannah?" Rosie enquired, drinking her cappuccino.

"Yeah, I'm fine. It's just excitement. Are you sure you know where we're going?" asked Hannah.

'Yeah, we'll pitch our tent right next to the tourist camp. Then we can visit the Bedouin camp in the morning. The tracks are clearly marked, so we'll just stick to the tried and trusted paths," she said, reassuringly patting Hannah's leg.

"Hannah, you'd better put your cigarette out, while we fill up."

Exasperated, Hannah rolled her eyes and pulled a face. Rosie was always trying to tell her what to do. It was getting on her nerves. She stubbed out her cigarette and stared through the window. Her stomach continued to churn.

When they reached the Al Kabil Guest House, they decided to stop and have lunch. They had been driving for about three hours and were both feeling tired. The restaurant was totally deserted. Thin rays of brilliant sunlight escaped the blinds at the windows and fell across the empty tables. They ordered dhal, rice and a salad of tomatoes, onions and limes. An hour later, they climbed back into the car and soon left the tarmac road and drove off-road towards the Wahiba Sands. As they approached the desert, several huge dunes appeared through the haze of the late afternoon sun. Rosie stopped the car and took a few photographs of the dunes. She liked the way the light affected the colour of the sand.

Some local youths were tinkering with an old car, trying to get it started. "It's amazing how they manage to drive normal cars in such deep sand," commented Rosie. The boys came over and stood watching the two girls, as they let the air out of their tyres. "You go sahara?" asked a tall, swarthy youth in a dishdasha. Hannah looked closely at the dark-haired youth, her stomach churning with a combination of fear and excitement.

"Sahara?" Hannah looked confused.

"Yes," answered Rosie abruptly, jumping back into the car.

"We're going to the Sahara?" asked Hannah.

Rosie laughed and explained it was the Arabic word for desert.

"Fee hawa ilyom!" one of the boys shouted.

"What did he say?" Hannah enquired, looking back at him through the rear view mirror.

"I don't know, probably something rude! Come on let's get going, we've got to pitch our tent before it gets dark."

The boys were waving and calling. Rosie waved back at them and then focused on the track ahead. She failed to notice the wind rustling the leaves of the few remaining trees.

Rosie changed the CD. Pink Floyd's 'Dark Side Of The Moon' seemed entirely appropriate for the surrounding lunar-like landscape. They bumped along the track with the sand swirling all around them. Despite the windows being closed, Rosie could feel the acrid taste of sand hitting the back of her throat. "Yuk! Have you got any polo mints in your bag, Hannah? I've got this horrible taste of sand in my mouth."

Hannah nodded, fumbled in her bag and handed Rosie a sweet.

"The sand is really red, isn't it? But over there," Hannah pointed, "the dunes are completely different, all orange and brown."

"Yeah, the different colours give the dunes such depth, it's like they are alive. I suppose the desert is alive in a way. Apparently, there are more than two hundred species of animal and plant life living in the Wahiba. I just hope we don't meet too many of them tonight!"

"Yeah, me too. No close encounters with scorpions and camel spiders, thank you very much. I heard a story about a guy who was bitten by a camel spider when he was asleep. The thing anaesthetised his skin. When he woke up, half his ear was gone!" said Hannah.

"Eh, is that true? How disgusting!" Rosie replied.

The girls stopped talking and listened to Pink Floyd. "I think this place is beautiful in a stark kind of way, don't you? But imagine this desert was once fertile land, though. Makes you think, doesn't it?" Rosie announced

"The desert is encroaching miles per day all over the world, as we cut down trees and strip the land of its fertility," Hannah said, trying to make light conversation, to calm and distract herself from a tangible feeling of fear and unease in the pit of her stomach.

The rising dunes on either side of the track seemed huge and desolate. It was daunting. They drove on for hours without seeing any signs of life. Hannah turned the music up to block out her mounting fear. *We are all alone in this vast desert.*

Hannah coughed nervously and said, "Looks like it's getting a bit windy." She noticed the air was turning white with small particles of sand.

"Oh, I think that's just the effect of the car, disturbing the sand," said Rosie, peering out through the windscreen, "Now, the camp we stayed in before should be just a bit further up here. I seem to remember we had to turn left somewhere."

There was no sign of any track, but the road seemed to be getting bumpier. They drove on in silence, straining to see through the haze. Forty-five minutes later, there was still no sign of the camp.

"It *is* getting windy, Rosie." Her friend nodded but remained silent.

"It's like one of those old London pea-soup fogs!" Hannah commented, laughing just a little too loudly, trying to hide her nerves. She lit a cigarette. Rosie grimaced.

"Do you have to smoke, Hannah? It makes me feel sick," said Rosie.

"Yes I do actually. It calms my nerves," Hannah replied abruptly drawing deeply on her cigarette.

Visibility was growing steadily worse and Rosie's nerves were on edge. She found Hannah pretty exasperating at times. The girls drove on for another half an hour, getting deeper and deeper into the desert without seeing any signs of life. Rosie slowed the car to a snail's pace.

"I can't see where I'm going," she said, rubbing the windscreen with a cloth.

"Put your headlights on," Hannah suggested. The lights showed a heavy white haze of sand all around the car.

"Well," Rosie coughed. The combination of sand in her throat and nerves in her stomach was making her feel nauseous. She admitted defeat, "I'm sorry, Hannah, but I think we might have gone in the wrong direction, it's so difficult to see where we're going. Maybe we'd better just set up camp along here? What do you think? In the morning we'll be able to find our way."

"Yeah, good idea, I think we'd better stop. If we carry on like this, we'll just get hopelessly lost," Hannah said with a feeling of dread. She lit another cigarette and inhaled deeply.

Rosie pulled a face, coughed and retched, sand and smoke mingling in her throat. She turned the steering wheel and stopped the car abruptly. When she opened the door, the wind blew the swirling sands inside the car. Rosie jumped out quickly and bent over, with the feeling she was about to be sick.

"You okay?" Hannah asked from her seat.

Rosie made no comment. She held on to the open door for support.

"What's wrong?"

Recovering, Rosie looked up at Hannah and decided to say what was on her mind, "It's you."

"Me? What have I done?" Hannah demanded angrily.

"How on earth can you think of smoking at a time like this?" Rosie asked, trying to control the urge to vomit.

Hannah pulled a face. She opened her door and slipped out of her seat. She took a last puff of her cigarette before flinging it to the wind. The girls worked silently together. Rosie opened the back door to search for the tent. In seconds, everything in the car was literally covered with a thick layer of red sand. Rosie felt the grit of sand between her teeth, even though her mouth was closed.

Hannah shouted, turning away, "Ouch, I've got sand in my eyes!" Her eyes were smarting and she closed her eyelids tight. Rosie groped her way towards Hannah and put an arm around her, leading her back to the passenger seat. She shouted above the roar of the wind. "You just sit here and wash your eyes out with water from this bottle. Here, take some tissues. I'll try and get the tent up," Rosie volunteered, wishing she had not been foolhardy enough to come to the desert alone. She unrolled the tent and immediately lost sight of three pins as they fell into the deep sand. The tent flapped high into the air and the wind howled around her. Rosie had difficulty anchoring the tent to the ground. It blew sideways, flapping in every direction and momentarily escaped her grasp completely. She clambered over the mounds of sand and grabbed hold of it. Hannah's eyes were burning and watering as she watched Rosie's futile attempts to erect the tent. She reluctantly climbed out of the car and offered to help.

Shouting over the howling wind, Hannah suggested they unzip the entrance to the tent and just dive in, using their weight to keep it in place. Rosie nodded and took the torch and the pole attached to the parasol out of the car, intending to prop up the ceiling of the tent with it. She unzipped the tent and put her head inside, kneeling on the sand and clambering in with difficulty. Hannah crawled in behind her, turned over and sat down. Before Hannah could close the entrance, small piles of sand had gathered on the floor. They sat in the dark, breathing hard and trying to calm themselves. The roof of the tent rested uncomfortably on their heads. Suddenly Hannah gave a manic laugh.

"What's so funny?" asked Rosie.

Hannah shrugged, "Well, you've gotta see the funny side of it, haven't you?"

Rosie did not answer. She pushed the pole into the floor and wedged it into the top of the tent. "Oh my God, this is awful!" Rosie said apologetically, looking at her friend in the eerie light of the torch. "Hannah, I'm so sorry I got you into this mess."

Hannah smiled, "Oh come on, Rosie. Don't take everything so seriously. You've got to laugh, haven't you? It's not exactly a romantic night in the desert, is it? There's never a dull moment with you, Rosie, is there?"

Rosie laughed weakly. She could not see what they had to laugh about.

"Yuk, I've got sand everywhere, it feels gross," Rosie remarked, running her hands through her dry, matted hair. "We'll need to get some water and the sandwiches, if we're gonna spend the night like this. I'll go. I'd better lock the car door as well."

Rosie felt for the keys in her pocket. "Sh*t! Where are the keys?" Rosie felt in her other pocket and groped the dark sandy floor in vain. No keys.

"Now, don't panic, Rosie, they must be here somewhere," said Hannah joining in the search.

"Oh Hannah," Rosie moaned, beginning to feel hysterical, "supposing the keys fell out of my pocket into the sand! We'll never find them!" She bit into her knuckle, rising panic constricting her lungs.

"Of course we will, they can't have gone far, let's just wait until morning. Once the wind has died down and it's light, we'll find them. Don't panic," Hannah said firmly, almost shouting at her friend.

Rosie stumbled out of the tent with the torch and could barely see the car through the haze of sand and the failing light. Soon it would be pitch black. They were stranded in the middle of nowhere. Rosie's legs started wobbling. *Where are the bloody keys?* She could hardly see the ground. She made her way slowly towards the car. Luckily, it was not locked. She struggled against the wind to open the door and was thankful that the light came on as she climbed in. Looking out of the window, all she could see through the haze, was the dark mound of Hannah's body huddling inside the semi-erected tent. Rosie clambered into the back seat and searched for the sandwiches in the small lunch box. *Oh my God, this is awful.* Rosie turned and saw that the keys were still in the ignition. *Al Hamdu lillah!* Rosie sighed with relief. She quickly picked up the bottle of water and the lunch box, found some towels and took the keys out of the ignition. She locked the door and made her way carefully back to the tent, holding everything in her arms. The wind blew her hair over her face and sand worked its way into her eyes. She squinted and fell to her knees, calling Hannah's name to the wind. Hannah unzipped the flap and Rosie handed her the items before she clambered back inside. The effort had been exhausting.

Rosie sat cross-legged opposite Hannah, breathing hard after the exertion. They looked at each other over the spooky light of the upturned torch.

"I found the keys," Rosie announced breathlessly and taking a sip of water from the bottle.

"Oh thank God, losing them would have been a disaster," Hannah agreed.

"Give me the bottle. I must wash my eyes out, they're so gritty. I don't want to get trachoma or something."

"What's that?"

"It's an eye disease. It used to be very common here," Rosie explained, splashing her face with water and groping for a towel.

"Oh, nice of you to mention it, just when I was beginning to calm down," Hannah giggled.

The girls laughed together with relief and ate the sand-filled sandwiches. Hannah suggested they tell each other stories to take their minds off their predicament. They started talking of childhood memories, school pranks, old boyfriends and weird experiences that they had had in their lives.

"I remember when I was at school, we had a teacher called Mrs Gomm. We used to call her Gomm, Gomm, the atom bomb. She kept a massive hammer in her desk drawer and if we made too much noise, she would bring out the hammer and bang it on the table. There were all these round pock marks on the desk, where she'd banged the hammer."

"Are you serious? She'd be imprisoned for that, these days," Hannah laughed.

"Yeah, well anyway, one day I remember we glued her coffee cup to the desk. It was so funny, watching her try to lift it. We were all sniggering. She nearly flipped. She took the hammer out of the drawer and banged it on the desk, demanding to know who was the culprit. No one owned up of course, so we all got detention that day."

Hannah laughed and told Rosie about her first job. "I had the most amazing job when I was at college. You'll never guess what I did."

"Worked as a masseuse for the local football team?"

Hannah laughed. She told Rosie that her mother had worked for a private detective agency and one summer, the agency asked Hannah to do an undercover job for them. It involved masquerading as a young student doing a summer job, but the real work entailed investigating a huge multi-million dollar pilfering operation taking place in the large depot of a giant stationary company. It was Hannah's job to find out who was masterminding the theft and to name those involved in the scam.

"Wow, that sounds like a fascinating job. You were a spy! Was it well paid?" Rosie asked.

"Oh, I got paid a fortune, well, as a poor impoverished student, it seemed like one hell of a lot of money to me. But it was a horrible job, really. Imagine making friends with everyone and then having to grass on them. I felt really bad, even though they were the guilty ones," Hannah admitted.

"Yeah, I know what you mean, it must have been difficult," Rosie agreed.

"To be a spy, you need to have utter conviction, or be extremely well paid!" Hannah concluded.

The wind continued to howl and the flimsy walls of the tent flapped incessantly. The temperature dropped sharply in the twilight and Rosie and Hannah shivered. The girls decided not to leave the torch on indefinitely, but to save its dying batteries for emergencies only. Lying down on the plastic floor of the tent, Rosie put her arm around Hannah and they huddled up close together for warmth. The ground was hard and uncomfortable. They lay in the cold, staring up into the dark and listening intently to the sound of the howling wind. Soon, Rosie heard Hannah's deep and rhythmic breathing and she realized with dread that she was very much alone with her bleak thoughts. Fear and anxiety quickly filled the darkness and Rosie prayed that everything would be back to normal by morning.

Chapter Fifteen

Rosie was shivering uncontrollably. It was far too cold to sleep. She felt extremely uncomfortable and continually changed position to relieve the pressure on her hips, shoulders, knees and head. She silently rubbed the small silver heart on its chain around her neck, thinking of the day she had given the identical one to Stuart. *Is he still wearing his?* she wondered, negative thoughts running through her head. *If only Stuart were here*, she thought, *he would know what to do.* By the time it grew light, Rosie's whole body was aching. Suddenly she tensed every muscle, as she heard a loud screeching sound. She grabbed Hannah's arm in fear.

"Eh? What the hell was that?" stuttered Hannah, trying to open her sore, puffy eyes as she sat up.

"I don't know, but it sounded like a fox to me. I've heard that sound before, when I stayed with my cousin Ann in Kent," Rosie said, trying to stay calm.

"Do they have foxes in the desert?" Hannah scratched her arms and legs furiously. "Oh God, Rosie, I'm itching all over. I think I've been bitten alive by mosquitoes," she complained.

Rosie yawned, "Yeah me too, but *you* managed to sleep through everything. I hardly slept a wink," Rosie lamented.

"Did I? I still feel tired though." Hannah cocked her head, listening hard, "At least the wind has died down. Hey, listen, there's that screeching sound again. I'm going to take a look." Hannah courageously unzipped the tent and peeked out. "Oh God!" she said in a flat voice.

"What? What can you see? Is it a fox?" Rosie asked anxiously.

Hannah paused before replying. "No, there's no sign of any fox, but you'd better come and take a look at this," she said slowly, crawling out of the tent on her hands and knees. Rosie followed, dreading what she would see.

There were deep paw prints all around the tent. Looking carefully all around, Rosie could see nothing but an uninterrupted desolate landscape, stretching out endlessly in every direction. Then she saw it. The car was half buried under a huge mound of course red sand. "Oh no! How are we gonna get in the car?" she asked.

"We'll have to dig it out. Did we bring a shovel?"

"No."

"Oh, great. What do we do now? Sh*t!" Hannah cursed, scowling angrily and stomping around, kicking the sand. She tried to open the car door. It was impossible. She banged her fists on the roof of the car. "Bloody hell! I can't even have a fag!" she moaned, seeing her pack of cigarettes lying on the dashboard.

"Hannah, there's no point in getting angry, you'd better save your energy. Come on, let's get digging," Rosie said, using practical common sense.

"Oh yeah, piece of cake," Hannah responded bitterly.

Rosie was shocked at her sarcasm. "Look Hannah, let's just try, shall we? Unless you've got a better idea."

The sun rose high in the sky as the girls painstakingly worked with their bare hands to remove the enormous drifts of sand which had half covered the car.

"God, I'm so thirsty," Hannah croaked, wiping the sweat off her face and feeling a thin layer of sand all over her skin. She wandered back to the tent and took out the half bottle of water. She took a swig. The water was warm. She looked around at the huge emptiness, wishing she had never come. Suddenly she screamed. Rosie turned towards her and saw a thin white snake slithering swiftly across the sand, just inches from Hannah's right foot. Hannah yelled and ran towards Rosie, clutching her arm and shaking like a leaf.

"Oh, God! I'm petrified of snakes. Has it gone?" she asked, peering cautiously over her shoulder.

Rosie nodded, holding onto Hannah and watching the snake disappear behind a gorse bush. Now Hannah's fear turned to anger. "Bloody hell! Just think," she said, "that snake could have been under the sand as I was digging with my bare hands. My God! I could have been bitten!" she exclaimed in alarm. Rosie tried to reassure Hannah by saying she was sure there weren't any poisonous snakes in Oman.

"How do you know that? Since when are you an expert on wildlife?" Hannah asked nastily.

"I'm not. I just remember reading an article somewhere."

"Well, I'm not convinced. And I'm not going to risk my life," Hannah announced, storming off towards the tent. Rosie's jaw dropped open. Refraining from passing comment, Rosie pursed her lips and calmly knelt down in the sand once more and began unearthing the car, while Hannah stood around, her arms folded over her chest. Fifteen minutes later, Rosie stood up wearily. With two gritty hands she pressed the door handle, pulled hard and managed to prize open the door.

"Oh, thank God!" she cried. "Hannah, come and get in this side and climb over to the passenger seat."

Hannah shrugged her shoulders and pouted, clambering in without a word. Rosie climbed in and turned the key in the ignition. They both felt a sudden blast of hot air coming out of the air conditioning vent. The two girls sat with their eyes closed, exhausted, covered in sweat and sand and waited for the air to cool their faces.

Hannah lit a cigarette and sighed with relief. Rosie closed her eyes, determined not to comment on the smoke. After a few moments of recovery, Hannah, acting like some kind of scavenging animal, climbed into the back seat and rummaged around in the boot for food and water. They shared a litre bottle of water to quench their thirst and hungrily devoured an entire Tupperware box full of potato salad between them, using pitta bread to scoop it up, in the absence cutlery. Without voicing their fears, Rosie's eyes met Hannah's and she announced, "Okay, let's get going."

"Yep," Hannah nodded, attempting to sound nonchalant and casual. Rosie hummed tunelessly as she turned the key in the ignition and pressed the brake pedal, putting the car into gear. She accelerated and the wheels turned slowly, sending up a spray of sand. But instead of moving forward, the wheels just spun deeper and deeper into the sand. "Oh sh*t! Stop, Rosie! We're stuck, it won't move," Hannah shouted.

Rosie turned the engine off, then tried again. She could feel the wheels churning up sand and boring deeper into the soft sand. Rosie yelled, almost becoming hysterical.

"Oh no, oh God, please. What are we gonna do? We're stranded," she cried. She was breathing fast, almost panting with fear.

"Okay, shut up! Get a grip, Rosie!" Hannah said firmly. "We just need two planks of wood to put under the front wheels. Maybe if you change the car's resolution it would help. Put it into low gear," Hannah suggested, trying to take control of the situation.

"I already did that when we let the tyres down."

Rosie accelerated again. Once more the wheels spun deeper into the sand.

"Oh, what are we gonna do, Hannah? Where are we gonna find two planks of wood? I'm so sorry for getting you into this mess, Hannah," Rosie shouted, biting her nails in anguish and beginning to cry.

Hannah shrugged her shoulders. "Look, Rosie, have you got the number of the guide from the camp you stayed in last time you were here? Maybe he could come and help us pull the car out with a tow rope."

Rosie hesitated. "I don't know, maybe." She took out her address book and flipped through but found nothing. She scrolled through her cell phone directory without really expecting to find Ali's number. She stared at the names coming up on the screen: Jan, Jane, Jass, Karim, Ken, Laura... "Laura! That's it! Laura was the one who booked the camp, she'll have Ali's number!" Rosie said hopefully. She rang Laura's number and waited. There was no network. "Oh God, it's not connecting," she said desperately pressing buttons.

Hannah suggested they climb up one of the sand dunes.

"We might get a connection up there and at least we'll get an idea of where we are."

Rosie nodded and turned off the engine. There was silence all around. The door creaked open and Hannah took a bottle of water from the cool box and climbed out of the car. The sand was burning hot. Rosie hopped from foot to foot to relieve the blistering heat coming up through the soles of her shoes.

"Those sandals are too flimsy, put your trainers on," Hannah advised.

Rosie nodded and searched for her running shoes. She pushed her sandy feet into her grubby white trainers, realizing that she would soon get blisters. But there was no time to start searching for socks. Hannah walked briskly away from the car towards the giant sand dune in front of them. Rosie followed. Soon the intense heat forced them to slow their pace and progress almost ground to a halt. Their feet sank ankle deep into the soft sand and they slid backwards with every step forwards. Sharp thorns attached themselves to their trouser legs and the particles of sand inside Rosie's shoes began to rub her feet raw.

"This is a nightmare, I'm so sorry, Hannah," Rosie apologized breathlessly, shaking her head. Tears pricked her increasingly dry eyes.

Hannah was having difficulty breathing as the hot air seared her lungs. She coughed and spluttered but pushed herself forward, refusing to accept that she was unfit. "Oh come on, like I said, it's not your fault. You can't control the weather, can you? Anyway, it was my idea to come to the desert in the first place," Hannah admitted, trying to relieve Rosie's guilt. She stood still, panting and sweating. Rosie noticed Hannah's face had turned bright red with the exertion.

The sight which met their eyes when they at last reached the peak was depressing. They were faced with a completely bleak, featureless landscape, a vast empty desert. Rosie fell to her knees, sobbing. "We're lost, Hannah, we're hopelessly lost!" she cried, covering her face with her hands, her shoulders heaving. Hannah bent down and pulled Rosie to her feet and held her. "Come on, it'll be okay, Rosie," she said breathlessly, "we'll find a way out, don't worry. Try the phone again," she said pointing to Rosie's silver Nokia. Rosie rang Laura's number. The screen displayed the dreaded words: No Network. The girls looked at one another with sheer desperation on their faces. *What are we going to do?* The two friends slowly made their way back down to their makeshift camp wondering how they were ever going to get home.

*

On Sunday morning, Laura rang Rosie's number to find out how she and Hannah had enjoyed their desert experience. She was not unduly worried when she found Rosie's phone was switched off. She assumed Rosie was back in the classroom, teaching. It was not until later that evening, when Laura rang Rosie's home number several times and got no reply, that she became a little concerned. *Maybe she's working the late shift,* she thought. She rang The Finja Institute and asked to speak to Rosie. The receptionist told her Rosie had not been in all day. On Monday morning, Rosie's phone was still switched off and Laura became increasingly convinced that there was something seriously wrong. She sat in her office, biting her nails and wondering what to do. She had tried Rosie at home and at work.

Something's happened. I know it, thought Laura. She told herself not to exaggerate. Sam was always telling her that she overreacted. Maybe Rosie and Hannah had just decided to stay for an extra night or two. That was no big deal. They were probably having a blast. But what if they *did* have a problem?

Laura decided to ring Thomas MacKay's direct number. When he answered the phone and told her that Rosie had not informed him of any delay, Laura's fears were confirmed. Thomas complained, "I've had to find cover for all her classes, which hasn't been easy, as we're extremely busy these days. I'm telling you, I'm quite surprised at Rosie letting me down like this…"

Laura interrupted him, saying that she was sure there was a perfectly good reason for Rosie's absence. She promised Thomas she would ring him when she had some news.

Now Laura hurriedly searched for Ali's number and dialled it, only to find that it, too, was switched off. She decided to ring Sam. He was in the field and not easy to locate. The office agreed to page him urgently and ten minutes later, he called back. When Laura explained her concerns, Sam listened carefully. Then he said he was sure there was some reasonable explanation for the girls' delay. He suggested they wait until the next day before raising the alarm. Laura disagreed with him. "I know there's something wrong, Sam. I can feel it in my bones. We have to do something," Laura implored. Finally, Sam caved in under pressure and agreed that if they still had no news by evening, he would investigate. Laura spent the day waiting and worrying. She had an uneasy feeling in the pit of her stomach. At 5 p.m. Laura rang Rosie's number again. The annoying female voice on the recorded message told her, "It is not possible to get in touch with the called subscriber, please try later."

Laura jumped up when Sam finally walked through the door. He dumped his tatty brown briefcase on the armchair and stretched out on the sofa. It had been a long day. They briefly embraced and he ruffled Laura's shiny dark hair.

"Hey, what's wrong with you? You look stressed out," Sam said with his usual lack of perception.

"Have you forgotten? I told you, Sam, I'm worried about Rosie and Hannah. They're out there alone in the desert somewhere. They should have been back days ago."

Sam told her she was worrying unnecessarily. But Laura insisted Sam call his friend Steve. She knew that Steve had good contacts with several Wahiba Sands guides, as he regularly travelled across the desert on exploration tours. Steve was one of those laid-back guys, nothing seemed to faze him. However, when he heard about the girls, he immediately agreed to help. He got in touch with the man he considered to be one of the best guides in Oman.

*

Hilal was taking a shower when the call came through. He had planned a relaxing couple of days with his family after a particularly strenuous and eventful seven-day crossing of the Wahiba with a group of Italian tourists. They had been very demanding, wanting to travel miles each day in search of wildlife to photograph and insisting on dune driving at every opportunity. He had also had to learn to cook Italian food as the group seemed unable to survive without their daily dose of pasta. Hilal was pretty exhausted. His initial reaction to the news had been one of exasperation. Why had two young inexperienced girls taken it into their heads to go out into the desert alone? Their stupidity could be costly, not only in time and effort, but in terms of lives being put at risk. At that moment, his tall voluptuous wife came into the room and started laying the table, her long dark plait swinging from side to side as she moved silently. Hilal came up behind her and held her in his arms, mumbling into her ear. She laughed and leaned her head back on Hilal's shoulder. But her smile soon faded when he told her he would have to leave again, straight away. The whites of her eyes flashed daggers at him. She pursed her lips and returned to the kitchen. Minutes later, he winced as he heard her banging about in the kitchen, muttering under her breath, closing drawers and dropping plates in anger. Hilal sighed as he quietly made his preparations to leave. He had upset her again. She still had not forgiven him for being away during a family wedding.

Hilal rang his colleagues, Ali and Mohammed, and asked them to meet him in Al Kabil Guest House. It was already late in the day to launch a search party and without some idea of where the girls were heading, finding them in the vast desert would be like searching for two needles in a haystack.

Chapter Sixteen

The chrome door handle was burning hot. Rosie used the hem of her tee shirt as a kind of oven glove, to protect her hand from the burning handle. She climbed into the car, leaned over into the back and pulled out the tent groundsheet. "We can make a shade by securing one end to the car door frame and the other to the cold box on the sand. At least it'll keep us a bit cooler," Rosie said, holding the dark green sheet in her hand. After some difficulty, they managed to secure it and finally, they both crawled into the tiny shaded area and opened the cool box. Rosie wished she had packed more cooked items and tinned food. All the ice in the cool box had now melted and the raw fish was beginning to smell. They ate salad and hummus and shared another bottle of water. "By the way, how much water do we have left?" Hannah enquired, trying not to sound too anxious.

"We've got another two small bottles in the cold box and a two litre water container, so we should be alright," Rosie said brightly.

"Even so, I think we'd better start rationing ourselves. We don't want to run out."

Rosie frowned and nodded.

The brilliant blue sky was completely cloudless. Rosie heard a sound and looked up to see the huge wingspan of a large dark bird, circling overhead. *Is that a vulture?* Even with her sunglasses on, her eyes were struggling to deal with the relentless glare of the sun. The searing heat and nervous exhaustion forced the girls to lie down and rest under their makeshift shade. They dozed off and when Rosie woke up, her entire body was stiff and sore. A thin layer of red dust covered her face, neck and arms and as she wiped her face with the back of her hand, she felt the sand scratching her skin. Large red patches appeared on her arms and chest. There was no sign of Hannah.

As Rosie struggled to her feet, the blood seemed to drain from her head. Steadying herself, she looked up to see her friend standing on the top of a sand dune. Rosie could see the quiet desperation in Hannah's movements as she struggled to get a connection on Rosie's phone. Things did not look good. Rosie's chest felt tight and constricted. *We'll never get out of here. I'll never see my family again. I'm going to die here.* Hannah came down the dune to join her. She was sweating profusely. "Did you get through?" Rosie asked, already knowing the answer.

Hannah's expression said it all. "No," she said despondently.

"Oh, Hannah, what are we gonna do?" Rosie cried, wringing her hands.

"I'll tell you what we're not going to do," Hannah said emphatically, "We're not going to get melodramatic, we're not gonna overreact. We'll set up the tent properly now, before it gets dark and cook ourselves some supper. We've got enough food and drink for now, and Laura is bound to realize there's something wrong if we don't show up, isn't she? So everything will be alright. Trust me, Rosie, don't give up hope. It's just a minor incident, something for us to tell our grandchildren about in the years to come. We'll be laughing about this by next week," Hannah continued, dragging on her cigarette, as she tried to convince herself Rosie thought about work and wondered how Thomas would react when she failed to show up for work. *Maybe Thomas will raise the alarm.*

Rosie and Hannah worked together to erect the tent properly, piling up sand over the pins in the hope that it would keep the tent in place. Then they decided to climb up another dune to see what lay beyond. An hour and a half later, they neared the crest of the dune and suddenly heard the distinct and unmistakable sound of a car's engine. Hope gave them both a fresh spurt of energy and Rosie struggled to the top and caught a glimpse of a pickup truck travelling across a vast plain. Hannah shouted out, raising her arms in the air and waving frantically. "Hey, over here! Come back!" Hannah cried. Without a moment's hesitation, she raced down the dune at breakneck speed, shouting and waving her arms, in an attempt to catch up with the vehicle. Rosie shook her head and called out, "Hannah! Come back! It's hopeless, they didn't see us."

But Hannah just shook her head and continued – running, walking and hobbling over the burning hot sand, ignoring Rosie's shouts. She ran until all Rosie could see of her was a mere dot on the horizon. And then, to Rosie's dismay, Hannah disappeared completely.

Rosie could smell fear. Suddenly she was alone in the vast, empty desert. *Oh my God, please hurry back Hannah,* she prayed silently. Two lonely, blisteringly hot hours elapsed, with the tyranny of the sun beating down on her head. She scanned the horizon, worried that Hannah had perhaps become disorientated and unable to find her way back. But there was a faint glimmer of hope. Perhaps Hannah had managed to find help. Rosie bit her nails to the quick wondering what had happened. Finally, she saw Hannah's tall, slim figure slowly returning. She looked tired, hunched and dejected. Rosie came down the dune to meet her and the two girls hugged despondently. "I could see the truck in the distance, but the driver couldn't see me, then I lost it," Hannah panted, her mouth dry and her lips cracking. She fell to her knees under the shade and cried pitifully. She was completely wiped out.

Rosie tried to be optimistic. She suggested they climb a dune to the west of their makeshift camp, to find out where the car was heading. "I can't," Hannah replied listlessly, "I'm too tired, I need to rest. We have to conserve our energy now, Rosie, take it in turns. You go. I'll wait here." Hannah lit her cigarette with shaking hands and lay back on the mat with the back of her arm shading her eyes. Rosie nodded. She offered Hannah a bottle of water from the cool box, trying to delay the inevitable. How could she muster sufficient courage to face the desert alone?

At last, Rosie stood up, took a deep breath and told Hannah she would be right back. She took a bottle of their precious water and walked away on wobbly legs, with a growing sense of panic in her stomach. She took a last look at Hannah, lying under the green shade and then turned away with determination. Petrified at the thought of spending another night lost in the desert, Rosie fervently hoped that she would see a settlement from the top of the dune.

The sun burnt her scalp and drained her energy, as she slowly moved towards the giant dune. Eventually she began her ascent, feeling spaced out and dizzy with heat and exhaustion. Her heart sank. On the crest of the dune, she stared out over a sea of silent, endless rippling sand. There was no sign of an oasis. No signs of life. A vast barren plain stretched away to the right with nothing to show but a few sparse gorse bushes. The heat rippled up from the earth's core, distorting her vision. She turned and peered to the left. Something came into soft focus. *Is it water? No, it can't be. It's just a mirage,* she told herself. But there was something, she was sure of it. Half camouflaged against the dust, Rosie could see a indistinct white blur on the horizon. She squinted and shaded her eyes with her hands to see more clearly.

"Hannah! Hey! I think I've found something! I don't know what it is, but I can see something white over there." She pointed her finger in the direction of the blur, suddenly aware that she was talking to herself.

Rosie looked back towards their makeshift camp in the distance. She could not see Hannah at all. She turned and hurried down the dune, slipping and sliding in an effort to return to the camp and give Hannah the news. She called out as she drew near but Hannah did not answer. She waved and shouted in a croaky voice. Hannah was lying down and appeared to be asleep. Rosie began to run, stumbling forward as fast as she could, keeping her eyes trained on Hannah's lifeless form. "Hey, Hannah! Wake up! I think I've found something. Come and take a look," she shouted at the top of her parched voice. But Hannah did not move. *Oh, my God, there's something wrong with Hannah.* Rosie now ran at full speed, falling and rolling over, shouting. "Hannah, wake up, are you alright?" There was no response. As Rosie came closer, she saw that the makeshift shade had turned Hannah's face a ghostly green. *Oh God, what's wrong with Hannah?*

At last she reached the camp and knelt down beside Hannah. She lifted Hannah's head and cradled it in her arms. "Hannah! Wake up!" she screamed, slapping Hannah's cheek and pouring the contents of a Tanuf bottle of water over her friend's face. Hannah spluttered and coughed as she slowly came round. She opened her eyes, dreamily. "What happened?" Hannah said softly. She looked around, wide eyed, unseeing.

"It's okay Hannah, you're alright. The heat's affecting you, you're dehydrated. I'll get you some water. Listen, Hannah, there's good news, I think I've found something."

"Oh, that's great," she paused, "but I've just got this thumping headache and my legs are aching so much. I think I'll just lie here for a while…" her words trailed off, as she lapsed into sleep again.

"Hannah, don't go to sleep, please," Rosie implored, slapping her face again. But it was no use. Hannah did not respond. As the sun moved its position, the harsh sunlight began to play down on Hannah's sunburnt face. Using enormous amounts of her own failing energy reserves, Rosie pulled Hannah out of the sun then sat back on the mat, breathing hard and crying softly to herself. But no tears emerged. With her last remaining strength, she pulled out a bottle of water from the cool box and drank a few sips. She put her finger into the water and then, holding Hannah's head up, she dabbed her wet finger over Hannah's parched lips. *She's got to drink.* Rosie went to the car and found a small plastic teaspoon. For half an hour she painstakingly dribbled tiny spoonfuls of water into Hannah's dry mouth. Hannah slowly opened her eyes and smiled gratefully at Rosie. "Are you okay now, Hannah?" Rosie asked with concern.

"Mm, I'm alright, I just feel so incredibly tired," Hannah replied sleepily.

"Now listen, Hannah, I'm going to make us something to eat. You just rest here in the shade and I'll cook us some food, okay?"

Hannah nodded, too tired to open her eyes and reply.

Rosie pulled herself up, black spots playing before her eyes. She held her head until her vision cleared and drank a few more sips of their diminishing water supply. She remembered she had packed some Isostar to replenish the mineral salts lost in the heat and hunted for them at the bottom of the cool box.

"Hannah," she shouted, shaking her and placing the warm can in Hannah's hand. "This will help to revive you, drink it slowly."

Hannah looked up with a dazed expression on her face and then looked down at the can in her limp hand. She felt as if her hand belonged to someone else. She sat up groggily and struggled to lift the can to her lips. Meanwhile, Rosie lit the readymade barbecue grill using Hannah's lighter. She rummaged around looking for food in the cold box and in the back of the car she found paper plates and cutlery. The sun was low in the sky now and suddenly she remembered it was Saturday night. Hannah was supposed to have a date with the guy she had met last Wednesday. *Oh hell, everything's gone wrong,* she thought. She prayed that Laura would raise the alarm. *Laura is really our only hope.* Would Thomas miss her enough to ask questions? If he did, who would he contact? Stuart was away and to her knowledge, Thomas did not know any of her friends. To Rosie, the situation appeared desperate. If no one came, what would happen to them? If a rescue party *did* start searching, how long would it take for them to be found? Rosie told herself to keep her thoughts in the present. She must not to let fear overwhelm her. Rosie walked over to the car and decided to start the engine again. She pressed the accelerator, willing the car to move forward. But once again, the tyres just sank further and further into the soft deep sand.

Struggling against fatigue and a feeling of hopelessness, Rosie wiped her hands and methodically prepared the barbecue; laying the fish on the grill and carefully slicing the Halloumi cheese. She delved into the cool box and found crudités of carrot and cucumber. Battling against nausea, she tried to eat. The rich aroma of fish filled the emptiness and the azure sky turned a deep shade of orange as the sun sank down behind the dunes. Her spirits lifted and Rosie, intent on acting as if everything was normal, decided to pull out her camera and capture the beautiful sunset on film. She felt nostalgic, recalling all the beautiful sunsets she had shared with Stuart. It was Saturday night and he would be in Aberdeen. *Is he alone?* she wondered, mournfully. Rosie was certain Stuart would not be spending Saturday night by himself. She was instantly overcome with jealousy and regret. She chastised herself. *Why am I such an ungrateful bitch? Why am I so hard to please?* Stuart had made every effort to make her happy. He had so wanted her to be an integral part of his life. Why had she moved out? Why had she rejected his genuine offer of love and commitment? *What is wrong with me?* She cried silently and hoped that she would live to make it up to him. *If only Stuart were here right now, I'd show him how much I care*, she thought. Rosie recognized this longing had much to do with their present predicament and her need for someone to take control of the situation. But she made a silent vow to call him as soon as she returned to Muscat, attempting to bury the thought that she might never return, in the back of her mind.

When the fish and cheese were cooked, she spread the disposable tablecloth on the ground and laid everything out. She nudged Hannah and gently coaxed her to sit up.

Hannah resisted, saying she had no appetite. Rosie persuaded her to at least try and eat, to keep her strength up. Hannah nodded. She bit into a piece of pitta bread.

"I can't eat, my mouth is so dry. I'm sorry, Rosie, but I feel a bit sick, actually."

Rosie insisted, dipping the bread in some yoghurt to soften it.

"Alright, Mum!" said Hannah, smiling weakly, in an attempt to make light of the situation. She took the bread and brought it slowly to her lips. They ate in silence as the night crept in, realizing that this meal constituted about eighty per cent of their remaining supplies. If they were not rescued tomorrow, they would have very little left to eat. The thought did not bear thinking about, but Rosie consoled herself with the knowledge that it was quite possible to go without food for weeks. Surviving without water, however, was quite a different matter.

Night came with an almost equatorial suddenness and Rosie shivered involuntarily at the prospect of another freezing night in their uncomfortable tent. She went to get her jumper from the car to ward of the frigid night air and she sat inside the car with the light on, looking at her own imperfect reflection. She hardly recognized the face staring back at her. A mask of fear and horror had attached itself to her face. Rosie frowned with determination. She had to come to terms with the harsh reality of their situation. They would not be rescued until tomorrow at the earliest. No one would search for them in the dark. Rosie looked across at Hannah sitting under the shade. Thankfully, her friend had revived a little. But Hannah's mouth was so painfully dry, swallowing was becoming a real effort. Rosie took out the two remaining Isostars from the cold box, and looked at them. *I'd better save one for tomorrow*, she thought, putting one back. The two girls shared the warm drink, savouring every mouthful. As the light failed, Rosie cleared away the barbecue, putting the uneaten food back in the cold box and throwing everything else into a large black garbage bag.

"Come on, Hannah, stand up," she said, pulling Hannah to her feet and leaving her briefly behind a mound of sand in order to relieve herself. Five minutes later Hannah walked shakily back to the tent. "I tried to pee, but nothing came out."

She's dehydrated, Rosie thought, with concern. Hannah crawled head first into the tent and collapsed. Rosie followed with the torch. They lay in the darkness, the air thick with anxiety. Rosie prayed and silently promised to live the life of a saint, if God would only help them through this terrible ordeal.

Hannah fell almost immediately into a restless, fitful sleep. Rosie practised deep yogic breathing, determined to fight her mounting fears. When her aching body finally relaxed and she reached the nocturnal landscape of her soul, she visualized she was standing by a beautiful lake of crystal clear water. A smooth petalled, white lotus gently floated over the surface of the water. In her mind's eye, Rosie looked intensely at the flower and saw it magically open its petals, to reveal a perfect golden heart at its centre. As she stared deeply into the flower, she became absorbed into it and she saw her own heart glinting like a jewel, radiating love and light out into the darkness. *Thought, word and deed. Everything starts with a thought.* She tried to imagine a search party making their way towards them now and, holding this reassuring thought in her head, she fell into a deep asleep...

But an hour later she woke with a start. Hannah was moaning softly. Rosie groped in the dark, found the torch and shone it down onto Hannah's face. Rosie put the palm of her hand on Hannah's forehead. Oh, *God! She's burning up!*

What am I supposed to do? Please someone help me, she whispered into the dark night. She poured a few drops of water into the palm of her hand and dabbed Hannah's forehead. Suddenly Hannah's eyes opened wide with terror and she sat bolt upright.

"Hannah, Hannah what's wrong? What is it?" Rosie screamed in alarm. Hannah said nothing, but clutched at Rosie's shoulder, shaking like a leaf. Hannah's eyes were looking right through Rosie, as if she did not exist.

"Hannah, come on! It's okay, look at me! Hannah, calm down," she said soothingly, feeling rising panic tighten her own chest. Seeing Hannah like this, reminded her of the countless times in her childhood when Denise had hallucinated. Whenever Denise had a high fever, she would imagine she could see awful things like toads falling from the ceiling or snakes slithering towards her. It was always a frightening experience to watch and as a child, Rosie had always hidden behind her mother's skirts or held her dad's hand tight until Denise went back to sleep.

Now, there was no one to help Rosie get through this ordeal. Hannah was delirious and Rosie would have to cope alone. "It doesn't matter, it's all gone! Give it back to me!" Hannah rambled incoherently, thrashing about the tent. Rosie held Hannah's head and looked into her eyes.

"Hannah, listen! It's me Rosie, everything's alright, Hannah, come on, have a drink," she coaxed. Hannah shook her head violently from side to side and screamed in fear and panic. Rosie could do nothing but hold Hannah tight and mutter soothing platitudes into her ear. Eventually, Hannah's tense body relaxed and she sunk back down onto the hard floor. Rosie dipped her finger into the water bottle and carefully dabbed drops of water onto Hannah's parched lips. *Oh God, I've got to find help. Hannah needs oral rehydration salts and water, lots of water.*

Rosie lay staring up into the blackness, playing out several possible scenarios in her head. What should she do for the best? She wanted to stay with Hannah, but knew if they did not get help soon, Hannah's life could be in danger. However, if she left and did not find anyone, Hannah's life would still hang in the balance and they would both be alone in the vast desert. Would she have the strength or ability to find her way back to Hannah? She was already feeling extremely weak and muddled. If they stayed together, they would at least have each other. She remembered reading that you should always stay with your vehicle and wait for help. But how long should you wait?

Rosie crawled out of the tent and pointed the torch at the ground. A lizard's yellow eyes were momentarily caught in its bright light. Rosie ignored it. She had no energy left to get upset about a lizard. She shuffled over to the cool box. The few remaining items of food floated in an inch of tepid water. Rosie took some Lebanese bread out of its wet wrapper and tried to eat. She opened the car door and searched in vain for some Panadol. How could she keep Hannah's temperature down without an analgesic? She took out her cell phone and using her last ounce of strength, clambered up a dark dune, in the hope of contacting someone. *Please work*, she prayed. She looked intently at the screen, willing it to work, tapping in her password and then Laura's number. She stared at the message: no network. She stuffed the phone back in her pocket, praying that Laura had already notified the authorities and made arrangements for a search party to comb the desert for them. But when she thought about it logically, she knew everything takes time. It would not be easy to find a tracker. The rescue team would need to be led by an experienced guide, someone who knew the desert like the back of his hand. Rosie suddenly felt optimistic. Perhaps the search party had started out already, at first light. They would be arriving soon. Rosie looked out over the desolate dunes. *But what if no one comes*? *How long can we last out*? Rosie scanned the horizon, her eye instinctively drawn towards the furthest dune. She had definitely seen something out there. *I must go and find help. I can't wait any longer.*

Rosie slid and stumbled down the dune. She felt a new sense of purpose and decided that if she was going to find help, she should go now, at dawn, before the merciless sun rose high in the sky. She told herself to take courage. When she was ready, she clambered into the tent, put her hands under Hannah's arms and dragged her out of the tent. Hannah opened her eyes sleepily and looked at Rosie without any recognition. "Where am I?" she asked in a croaky voice.

"You're here in the desert, Hannah," said Rosie, coaxing her to drink some water. "Now, you just lie here under the shade, while I go and find help. You'll be alright, Hannah, don't move, just stay here. I'm coming back for you, Hannah, I promise. I won't be long," she said reassuringly, trying to hide her own fear. Hannah's eyes opened wide in panic and she clutched Rosie's shoulder.

"Please don't leave me, don't go, stay with me," Hannah implored weakly. Rosie shook her head, as she decanted the last two litres of water into two separate bottles and propped one up by Hannah's side.

"Hannah, I have to go. Here, take a sip," she said encouragingly. Hannah's lips were cracked and bleeding and her face was totally blistered and puffy. Rosie's heart ached to see her friend in such a state. *I'll never forgive myself for this*, she moaned. "Hannah, just hang on, I promise I'll be back as soon as I can."

Rosie cried silently to herself, wrapping a scarf around her head and tucking some glucose biscuits into her pocket. She put the bottle of water into a small rucksack and took a long last look at Hannah, lying prostrate under the shade. Then she turned and walked away.

Chapter Seventeen

There was absolutely nothing to break the monotony of the featureless landscape. With no landmarks, she was frightened she might go round and round in circles. She tried to train her eye on the furthest dune. She had to keep going in that direction. Rosie was parched, but knew she could not afford to take more than a few sips of precious water at a time. The harsh glare of the sun was already beginning to hurt her eyes as it rose in the east. She squinted and strained to see into the distance. Looking over her shoulder she found she had already lost sight of Hannah. Fear clutched at her heart and it began to pound. She was alone. She had abandoned her friend, left her in a terrible state. How would Hannah manage without her? Guilt and anxiety were uppermost in her mind. Was she doing the right thing? After an eternity of endlessly putting one foot in front of the other, Rosie reached the foot of an enormous dune. Her whole body ached unbearably as she made her ascent. Her clothes were dry, hard and caked with sand. Even through her trainers, the fierce heat was burning the soles of her feet. She wiped her sore, blistering forehead. Breathing hard, she reached the crest of the dune and scanned the horizon. Tears pricked at her gritty eyes, as she stared at yet another monotonous waste land. Where was the white object that she had seen yesterday? *It had gone.*

Her disappointment was tangible. *We're never going to get out of here. This is it*, she thought. This time, Rosie was too exhausted to get emotional about it. She tried ringing Laura's number again. The 'No network' message appeared in the window of her cell phone. As Rosie turned, something caught her eye. A white blur, rippling in the heat, against the backdrop of the arid desert landscape. She shielded her eyes and strained to see more clearly.

With a new rush of hope she pushed herself to keep moving forward. Although she was desperate to succumb to the exhaustion she felt, she dragged herself down the dune, her legs buckling under her. Once she had descended, she panicked. The white blur had gone again. Was she still going in the right direction? She told herself to follow her instincts. Suddenly her legs gave way and she found herself on the ground, her body numb with fatigue and her mind closing down. *I can't go on.* But the sand was burning her skin and soon she was forced to rise, breathing hard and swaying like a drunk. Thinking of Hannah, she pulled herself to her feet and shuffled along at a snail's pace. Feeling dazed, light-headed and confused, Rosie felt her surroundings had an unreal quality.

She had been walking for hours. The harsh sun had risen high in the sky and was now on its descent again. With insufficient energy to climb the next dune obstructing her path, she decided to walk around its base. As she stumbled along, the sunlight was suddenly blocked out by the massive dune itself and Rosie fell to her knees and keeled over, lying in the shade. Her throat was on fire with thirst. She brought the water bottle to her lips but only a trickle came out. It was nearly empty. *Please God, let me find help soon. I can't go on anymore.* She crawled on her hands and knees, muttering to herself, aware of the raw fear of death inside her. She came out once more into the blinding heat of the sun and felt her skin burning. She had to stand up. She rose and tottered forward before collapsing in a heap again. She dragged herself to her feet. *I'm going to die. I'm never going to see Dad and Mum and again, never going to see Denny.* Stuart's face suddenly hovered in her mind's eye and she heard him say: "Come on Rosie, get up!" Rosie willed herself to stand and took a few unsteady steps, before falling down again.

At her lowest ebb Rosie lifted her head and tried to focus. Suddenly there it was; the white blur: a Toyota pickup truck. *Oh thank God*! With renewed strength she struggled to her feet and dragged herself towards it. Stumbling forward, she reached the car's door and clutched the handle. It burnt her hand and she cried out in pain. She pulled the door open with her last ounce of strength. It was empty. The disappointment was unbearable. Feeling dizzy, weak and helpless, she dropped to her knees, sobbing. The next moment, the world went black, as she collapsed, falling forward in slow motion, sand rushing up to meet her bare face. Rosie lay totally spent, in a pitiful heap in the shade of the open car door, lifeless and completely alone.

*

Hilal, Ali and Mohammed had finally called off their search as night fell. The sandstorm had caused major shifting sands, totally transforming the whole area, making it difficult to gauge their positions without the use of GPS. The men had spent two futile hours working with torches in the dark until Hilal had taken the decision to halt the search until first light. At 6 a.m. the next day the men resumed their search. The police kept in constant contact with the guides. If the girls were not found within the next few hours, the police had agreed to call in a chopper and do an aerial search of the entire region. Ali and Mohammed had gone in one direction, and Hilal in another. They had arranged to rendezvous at 12 noon. Hilal checked his watch. He scoured the dunes for any clues as to where the girls might have gone, then reluctantly, he turned the car around and drove back to the meeting point. He waited for the others quietly, closing his eyes and trying to use his instincts to work out where the girls might have gone. Five minutes later, the others returned shaking their heads. Hilal suggested they head for the camp four kilometres ahead and then search around it. Although

Hilal had a GPS system installed in the car, he used the sun's position on his arm to plot their course. They bobbed up and down, slowly making their way over the deep sand.

Half an hour later, Hilal heard a car's horn and as he looked in his rear view mirror, he saw that Ali had driven off the track and was flashing his headlights at him. Hilal swerved around in a massive arc, stopped the car and jumped out. "What's up?" he asked, with his hands on his hips. Ali was peering intently through his binoculars.

"Look up there, do you see that piece of red cloth?" asked Ali, pointing half way up a distant dune. Hilal took the binoculars and scanned the area.

Without a word, Hilal nodded and ran back to his car. The two vehicles made their way towards the red blot on the landscape, moving slowly up the dune. Hilal examined the cloth: it was a girl's sleeveless tee-shirt. He looked all around, searching for tracks. Then he beckoned for Ali to drive up to the crest of the dune and jumped back into his own vehicle, to follow. Fifteen minutes later, the search party looked down from the top of the dune and saw the girls' car with its makeshift green shade. *Good work, Ali, I think we've found them,* Hilal said to himself, thinking the sooner they found the girls, the sooner he could go home to his wife. He reached for his walkie-talkie and spoke softly into it.

Hannah heard the sound of an engine and tried to open her eyes and turn in its direction. Her head was spinning. Through blurred vision she saw several pairs of feet running towards her. She was too weak to lift her arm or speak, but she fervently prayed that the guys standing over her at that moment, were part of a rescue party and not some alien tribesmen about to rape her. Hilal carefully lifted Hannah's head and brought a cup of water to her parched lips. "Can you hear me? You okay?" he asked. She nodded slightly and was aware of an unintelligible conversation taking place over her head. *"Ma ashoof thaniah."* (I can't see the other one.) She felt herself being lifted up. Every bone in her body ached. Unable to respond or control her limbs, she lay back in Hilal's arms. She felt an out-of-body sensation, as though she were looking down at herself and her body belonged to someone else. "What is your name?" Hilal asked in English. She tried to speak but no words came out. "Where is your friend?" *My friend.* Hannah's brain did not seem to be functioning. *Friend, what friend?*

The two men ran off to search the area, while Hilal gently wiped the sand away from Hannah's face. He coaxed her to drink minute drops of water.

As Ali returned to the car he could hear Hannah moaning quietly. "It looks like the other one walked away," he said breathlessly. "There are a few footprints over there," he pointed.

Hilal made a decision, "Look, I'll take this girl to the hospital and notify the police, while you stay and follow the other girl's tracks with Mohammed."

Ali nodded grimly. "Okay," he answered. It looked like it was going to be a long day after all. "She can't have gone far," Hilal added, hopefully. Ali nodded and called Mohammed and explained the plan. Hilal covered Hannah with a light sheet and closed the back doors of his vehicle. He figured they could come back and get the girls' belongings later. The girl in the back of his car was extremely dehydrated and getting her to hospital was his top priority. Ali and Mohammed noted their positions on the GPS system and began to follow Rosie's footprints in the sand.

They were experienced trackers and found it easy enough to follow Rosie's tracks. Ali could even see where Rosie had stumbled and fallen over. Mohammed scoured the area with his powerful binoculars. As they came around the base of a dune, Mohammed spotted the white Toyota pickup truck.

"Stop a minute, over there, look!" He shouted. Ali turned sharply and headed towards the white car. They pulled up along side it and jumped out. The vehicle was empty. Was it abandoned? Ali searched the vehicle and found nothing but a few papers and empty onion sacks. He noticed the back tyre had blown and guessed the owner had probably gone to purchase a new one. Just then, Mohammed called him over to the open front passenger's car door. He pointed to the ground.

"Look," he exclaimed. "Something has been dragged along the sand here."

Ali nodded. There was no sign of a struggle, but it was obvious something heavy had been pulled along the ground. The tracks stopped about 30 metres from the car and then wheel marks were clearly visible, moving west. "Interesting," said Ali.

"Yeah, could have been a sack of onions or dates, but there again, it could have been a dead body. Whatever it was," he said, examining the ground closely, "it's long gone."

*

Hours before, time had seemed immeasurable as Rosie lay unconscious on the sand beside the truck. Then, as the sun set in the sky, a tiny rhythmic sound in the distance had began to build and the ground vibrated with the rumblings of a slow moving vehicle. If Rosie had been conscious, she would have heard the car pull up and two doors quickly open. But she was unaware of the deep voices overhead calling urgently to one other in an incomprehensible language. It was only when someone grabbed her ankles and began pulling her across the sand that Rosie swiftly returned from a deep state of consciousness to a feeling of growing alarm. Her limp arms came up above her head as she was dragged along.

"Please! Let go! Don't hurt me! What's happening?" Rosie asked, her voice thin and rasping in her parched mouth. "Who are you?" she croaked, peering up at her captors in the twilight. "Where are you taking me?" she demanded, her head dragging along the ground. She knew she had no strength to fight, as the men lifted her weak body and lay her down in the back of their car. She began to moan. "Oh please God, help me!" she rambled and began to cry silently. *I'm being kidnapped.*

Chapter Eighteen

Dark, curious eyes looked at the blonde-haired girl with interest, through the rear view mirror. A weather-worn hand came down and patted her head. *"Ssh! Khola thamam! Zen, zen,"* (everything's okay, good, good) said a voice in a comforting tone. And as the vehicle bumped along the track to an unknown destination, Rosie passed out.

It was midnight. Rosie awoke, panic stricken and shivering. She tried to open her eyes but her eyelids seemed to have been glued together. Through swollen closed lids, she could sense the flickering light of a candle. Her hands grasped the cloth beneath her in a grip of anxiety. She found herself lying on a thin mattress covered with some kind of woven rug. She moaned and moved restlessly, struggling to lift her hand up to her face. "I can't open my eyes!" she croaked urgently. Her head was pounding.

"Ala kefick! Ala kefick!" (careful, careful) she heard an old woman reply soothingly. And then she nearly jumped out of her skin, as water from a copper pot was dribbled carefully over her face and eyes. *"Khali, khali, zen zen, mafi mushkila"* (leave it, good, no problem).

Rosie blinked several times as the water gradually released her eyelids. Her eyes felt as though they were full of grit and her vision was blurred and hazy. She looked at her surroundings, trying to focus. She saw deep red and black patterned cushions and rugs all around. Clay and copper pots hung from the dark ceiling of the large woven tent. The exotic rich fragrance of frankincense filled the night air. The smiling, weather-beaten face of an old Bedouin woman with several missing teeth, looked down at her kindly and gently pressed her to lie still. Rosie relaxed with relief and gave a weak smile. "Where am I?" she asked quietly. The old woman turned and spoke to someone in the shadows. Then, in an instant, a young guy with shiny black hair and sparkling eyes stood before her. Despite her condition, Rosie shrunk back with alarm as he leant over her. "Please don't hurt me!" she croaked.

The guy laughed gently and stared into her eyes. "It's okay. I am not going to harm you. I will help you," he said softly.

Rosie looked at the old woman for reassurance. She nodded and beamed at her. Rosie exhaled and felt herself blushing. "I'm sorry, I thought you were… going to—"

"Please do not talk. You are very tired," he interrupted. She nodded and smiled up at him. A deep understanding passed between them in that very first moment. It was as if her soul was exposed to him and she experienced the sensation of falling down into his deep, dark eyes. Long lashes swept his high cheekbones and Rosie felt drawn to look at his beautiful mouth as he smiled down at her. He placed an open palm over his heart and replied "You are in my home and you are very welcome, *marhaba!*"

Rosie smiled weakly in spite of herself. "Thank you," she answered gratefully.

"Where is Hannah? Can I see her please?" Rosie asked, closing her eyes.

"Hannah? Who is Hannah?" the man responded with a puzzled expression.

Rosie opened her eyes wide and stared. With growing dismay she realized that Hannah was still lying alone in the dark, empty desert night. "Oh my God!" Rosie cried.

"You've got to help me find her, she's out there in the desert! Please, you have to come with me! She's not well!" she cried, attempting to stand up.

"Whoa! *Alla kefick! Alla kefick!* (Be careful!) You cannot move yet, you are too weak. Lie down, lie down, please." His voice was deep, resonant and masterful. Strong muscular arms held her steady and Rosie felt the surge of desperate energy inside her, die. She lay back at his command. But she lifted her arm again and grabbed at the man's dark blue dishdasha.

"My friend, Hannah, is out there in the desert," she explained, pointing her finger. "We have to go and find her, please, PLEASE help me, please go and look for her," she implored.

The Arab paused before answering. "Your friend, Hannah, where is she? You were alone. There was no friend."

Rosie mustered the energy to explain. "I went to get help. I left her alone... she was ill... I had to go. We must find her, she is not well. She can't be far from where you found me. Please, will you go now and look for her? I don't know if she'll last another night out there on her own," Rosie sobbed.

The young man nodded. He gently lifted her head and helped her to drink some water from a small glass cup. Her lips were dry and cracked. Without a word, he bent down, opened a jar and dipped his finger inside. Slowly he raised his finger to her lips and gently smoothed sweet honey all around her dry, parched lips, constantly holding her gaze. Rosie was mesmerized. She could not look away from him as the thick, sweet liquid dribbled into her mouth. He said, "I will go now, but it is night. I do not know if I can find her in the dark."

Rosie looked so crestfallen that he quickly added, "But do not worry, I will search until I find your friend Hannah."

She clutched his arm and said "Thank you," then added, "I don't even know your name."

The young man smiled enigmatically, "My name is Salim. What is your name?"

"Rosie," she replied softly. He smiled at her. She leaned her head back on the pillow and he was gone.

Chapter Nineteen

Rosie slept fitfully. She moaned softly as images of their ordeal played over in her mind. Each time she woke in the night, the old woman, Amira, miraculously appeared and lifted her head, encouraging her to take small sips of water. As it grew light, Amira lifted and hooked open the flap of the tent and then left. Rosie inhaled the gentle breeze that came wafting in, turning her head to see the brilliant pink sun rising slowly in the sky above the dunes. The sands lightened as the sun grew in intensity. Amira returned, carrying a large clay bowl of water and a cloth. Rosie sat up slowly, feeling dizzy and bleary eyed. She rubbed her aching head. Nodding her gratitude, she leaned forward and cupped her hands, splashing the water over her face and hands. She had never appreciated water so much before in her life. It was so refreshing. As she dried her face she realized how sore and painfully dry her skin had become.

Sights, sounds and smells reached her senses from every direction. She could hear the sounds of movement as the other members of the camp began their day; babies cried, women shouted and goats bleated. She could smell the rich aroma of coffee. Rosie checked her watch. It was 9.30 a.m. She waited with increasing concern. Where was Hannah? Why had Salim not returned? Just then, Amira shouted some words to someone out of sight and within minutes two thin young girls of around eight or ten years old came scurrying into the tent and timidly placed trays piled high with plump, amber coloured mangoes and rich brown dates on the ground in front of her. They lowered their eyes and quickly walked backwards to the edge of the tent before crouching down to the floor. Whispering and giggling, their dark, shiny plaits swinging, they surveyed their strange guest with the yellow hair from a safe distance.

"Eskot!" (silence!) Amira shouted at the girls and then turned to Rosie and commanded *"Ukoli, Ukoli! Lazem takoleen il fotoor!"* (eat! eat! You must eat breakfast!). Rosie could not understand the woman but she smiled and turned towards the trays of food. Amira sat cross-legged in front of her and poured a thick, dark, cardamom-flavoured coffee, coaxing her to eat and drink. The girls brought her cubes of red water melon, white goat's cheese and freshly baked, and paper-thin bread accompanied the meal. Rosie chewed slowly while three pairs of eyes watched her every move. Her stomach churned with anxiety.

Just then, a shout went up as a car approached. Salim jumped out of the vehicle and talked briefly to his mother before entering the tent and kneeling down at Rosie's side.

"Salam Aleikum!" he said, smiling at Rosie. She felt a flutter in her stomach.

"Aleikum asalam," she replied. "What happened? Did you find Hannah?" she asked urgently, trying desperately to read his face for signs of the situation.

"No, I did not find her."

Rosie put her hand to her mouth in panic and alarm. *What had happened to her?*

"But, do not worry, everything is okay. Your friend is in the hospital. I heard the news from a guide in the big camp. He would not lie," Salim answered.

"In hospital! I must go to her now, I must see her, find out if she is alright, it's all my fault," Rosie gabbled.

Salim held up his hand, smiled and she fell silent. At last he spoke. "It is good for you to go to see her. I will take you there."

Rosie sighed with relief. "You're very kind." They both smiled and held each other's gaze, speaking to each other without words, already sharing a deep connection which transcended language and culture.

"But first you must rest a little and then drink some fresh *halib al gamel* to give you strength," he suggested.

"What is that?"

"It is the milk of the camel," he answered.

Rosie nodded in acquiescence. With a smile which showed his perfect white teeth and a swish of cloth, Salim swiftly left the tent, pulling the flap down and leaving her in relative darkness. Rosie's eyes slowly adapted to the lack of light. She smiled to herself, closed her eyes and rested happily, listening to the low tones of men's voices. She imagined them talking, drinking qawah, sitting on their haunches or lounging on huge cushions in the next tent. Suddenly, a bellicose gargle issued from a recumbent camel and made Rosie jump. She lay back and soon fell into a peaceful sleep.

*

At that moment Hannah was lying in a stark, clean hospital bed, attached to a saline drip. An Indian nurse was reading through her notes at the nurses' station when a couple came to the counter.

"Excuse me, we're looking for a girl named Hannah Green who was admitted here this morning," said the girl. The nurse wagged her head from side to side and led the couple down the corridor and opened the door to Room 7.

"Miss Hannah, you are awake? Some visitors have come."

Hannah opened her eyes and saw a man and a woman standing over her bed.

Laura and Sam exchanged glances. "Hi, Hannah, how are you? Are you feeling better, now?" Laura said gently. Hannah stared coldly at Laura and made no answer. "Don't you remember me? I met you with Rosie, in the restaurant. I hear you've had a rough time." Laura watched as Hannah nodded without speaking. A tear slowly rolled down her cheek.

"Now, don't upset yourself, it's okay. Everything's going to be fine. You're on the mend now," Sam said, soothingly.

"Hannah, can you tell us what happened?"

Hannah rolled her head from side to side restlessly and swallowed hard. "I... was... stuck... lost. It was so hot. I was so thirsty. I thought I was going to die." Hannah turned away to hide her emotion, screwing up her face.

Laura tried again. "Hannah, Hannah, I know it's difficult for you to talk, but we need to know." She paused as Hannah turned her head away.

"Listen, Hannah, where is Rosie? Do you know what happened to Rosie?" Laura cupped Hannah's head in her hands, searching her face for answers. Hannah shrugged her shoulders. "She went away... she left me." Hannah's head rolled from side to side as she moaned and cried softly.

Sam and Laura exchanged glances. They left the room and talked quietly. "Oh Sam, what are we gonna do?" Laura implored.

"There's nothing we can do. The police are searching the area, they'll find her. We'll just have to wait and see," Sam replied.

"I can't understand how they could have got separated. Oh, I wish Stuart was here, he'd know what to do. Do you think we should tell Rosie's family that she's missing?" Laura asked.

Sam shook his head emphatically. "No. It's too early for that. We don't want to worry them. Rosie will turn up, you'll see. Anyway, we don't have a contact number for her family, do we?"

Laura said she thought it would be easy to get hold of a number from the Finja Institute. "I could ring Thomas MacKay. I know Rosie always rang her parents every Sunday. They must be wondering why she hasn't called."

They went back to the nurses' station to find out more about Hannah's condition. The nurse spoke to the doctor and informed them that Hannah would need to remain under supervision for at least another twenty-four hours.

Sam and Laura drove back to Muscat in silence.

"I wish we knew who to contact about Hannah. I mean, her next of kin or someone in Dubai who ought to be told. What about her job there?" Sam asked.

"I think Rosie said she was between jobs. That's one of the reasons she came down to Muscat, she was looking for a job."

Chapter Twenty

Rosie slowly drank from the bowl of warm, rich camel's milk. She hoped it would give her the renewed strength she needed to recover. When they were about to leave, Rosie kissed Amira on both cheeks and squeezed her hands, in a gesture to show how grateful she was for all the old woman's kindness. Amira tutted dismissively and waddled outside, embarrassed by all the attention. Rosie patted the young girls on their heads and promised she would come and visit them again soon. Salim carefully lifted Rosie up in his arms and carried her to the waiting car. He wrapped a fine pashmina shawl around her shoulders and put a large blue bottle of mineral water in her lap. He turned to look at her. Time seemed to stand still for both of them. Rosie felt so utterly safe and at home with this man, this stranger she had never known. Her smile radiated the warmth she felt for him, growing deep inside her.

Revving the engine, he announced, "Okay, let's go!" They bounced along the dusty track and the children ran alongside, skipping and shouting and waving. Rosie smiled and waved at them. "You have a lovely family," Rosie said.

Salim nodded.

"How far is the hospital?" she asked.

"Not far. It will take about three hours to get there," he answered.

She nodded and wriggled in her seat. Her body was still aching and sore from the ordeal and she was desperate to have a shower. Her hair was matted and her body rough and grimy with sand. She removed the shawl from her shoulders as the heat grew increasingly intense.

They drove in silence, each thinking their own private thoughts about the last few eventful days of their lives. Rosie prayed that Hannah would be alright. She felt such incredible guilt. She alone was responsible. She had put her friend through an horrendous experience. She would never forgive herself. Rosie started crying involuntarily. Salim stopped the car at the side of the track and looked anxiously at her. "What is wrong? Do you have a pain?" he asked with concern.

"No, no, it's nothing, it's just that I, well, this is all my fault. I am so stupid. I've put my friend in this bad situation. I've made work for you and your family, I've worried everyone." Rosie broke down and cried openly, releasing the tension.

"No, no," he said gently, "do not blame yourself. This could happen to anyone. It is the nature of the desert. We cannot control it. It is God's will," he said, rubbing her back. She smiled through her tears and moved to rest her head lightly on his shoulder. He put his arms around her, feeling slightly awkward. Rosie inhaled the fragrant scent of frankincense permeating his clothes. She nodded and pulled away.

"Yes, I'm sorry. I am so stupid."

Salim interrupted, "You are not stupid. You were very brave to go for help. Do not say sorry!" he said, laughing.

Rosie nodded unhappily. *Guilt achieves nothing. We cannot change the past, only the way we perceive it.* Salim started the engine and drove on. Soon, the rhythmic sound of the engine lulled her to sleep.

As they neared the edge of the desert, Salim's car was flagged down by a policeman. Rosie woke with a start and watched the proceedings with growing alarm. Salim got out of the car and shook hands with the policeman. They exchanged greetings. She looked out of the side window. The policeman was eyeing her closely. He sauntered over to the car and knocked on the window. Rosie looked at Salim. He nodded his head. She wound down her window looking worried and apologetic. The policeman frowned at her. Then his face lit up. He smiled and announced, "So, Salim has found you. We have been looking for you. It is very bad to go to the desert alone."

"Yes, yes, I didn't realize, I'm so sorry, officer, for all the trouble I've caused. It was very stupid of me. Salim is taking me to see my friend in the hospital," Rosie explained. The officer nodded and spoke into his radio. He told Rosie that there would be some paperwork to fill in. She was told to report to the police station as soon as she had visited her friend. Rosie immediately agreed, relieved that the policeman had appeared to be so understanding.

They drove on and Rosie suddenly felt overwhelmed by all the kindness she had received. She became more and more elated with the full realization that she had escaped a terrible fate – a slow death by dehydration. She looked at Salim's aquiline profile. She was so grateful to him. How could she ever repay him? Here was a man who had probably never been in a plane or used a computer before in his life, but it was his time honoured, ancient skills, his knowledge of the desert, that had saved her life. Her own fine education had been of no use at all in the harsh desert environment.

They approached the hospital. "You wait here. I am coming back in one minute," Salim said, parking the car.

"No, no, I want to come..." she began opening the car door. Salim swiftly came round and bent down beside her. "Look, I bring chair, then we go. Okay?" he said.

"Oh yes, I see, okay, thank you."

He closed the door and she watched his tall, graceful figure disappear inside the imposing building. *How thoughtful.*

She looked around her. The hospital seemed to have been built in the middle of nowhere and yet it was huge. Soon,

Salim came hurrying back with a wheelchair. "Your friend is in room 7. Come on, let's go."

Rosie lowered herself into the chair and he wheeled her to the entrance, up the ramp and across the elegant marble foyer. They took the elevator up to the second floor and a nurse showed them the way to Hannah's room. Salim knocked softly on the door. There was no answer. He turned the handle and put his head round the door. Then he wheeled Rosie inside.

Rosie shouted, "Hannah!" and then promptly burst into tears when she saw her poor dear friend lying still, looking so pale and gaunt. Hannah opened her eyes and stared at Rosie without emotion.

Doesn't she recognize me? What's wrong with her? thought Rosie with alarm. "Hannah it's me, Rosie. How are you? I've... I've been so worried about you."

Hannah's green eyes looked coldly up at Rosie. "You made it then," said Hannah, in a harsh, croaky voice.

"Yes, Salim here rescued me," she said, catching his eye. "I'm so lucky," she paused.

"Yes, lucky you," replied Hannah sarcastically.

"Hannah, are you angry with me? I understand, I know I got you into this mess. I'm so sorry, Hannah. I didn't think things would turn out like this, I never meant for any of this to happen. Please believe me, Hannah, I'm so sorry," Rosie answered, taking hold of Hannah's hand and squeezing it. Hannah immediately removed her hand and looked away. "Hannah, please. Please forgive me," Rosie implored.

Rosie waited for forgiveness, tears streaming down her face, but it was not forthcoming. She shuddered and Salim squeezed her shoulder.

Suddenly, Hannah turned on Rosie. "Why did you run out on me? How could you leave me alone in that godforsaken place?" she asked in a low accusing tone. "I was too weak to move and you just left me for dead," Hannah announced, almost spitting the bitter accusation.

"No, no! It was not like that! Please, Hannah, you have to believe me! I went to get help for *you*. I didn't want to go, but I had no choice, I thought if I didn't find help, you would die," Rosie exclaimed.

There was a pause before Hannah answered. "Yeah, well, I very nearly did. Thanks to you," Hannah replied coldly, looking away.

"Please, Hannah, you've got it all wrong. I walked for hours and then I passed out. I didn't regain consciousness until I was rescued by Salim. When I realized Salim hadn't found you, I begged him to go and look for you. He searched for you all through the night, until dawn. Then he found out that you'd been taken to hospital. Hannah, you have to believe me," her words trailed off.

"Mmm, well, I'll have to take your word for it, won't I?" Hannah responded.

Rosie stared into space. *This is ridiculous. How could Hannah think that I had deliberately left her to save my own skin? Does Hannah really think I am that selfish?*

"I'll come and see you tomorrow, Hannah," Rosie blurted out.

"Suit yourself," Hannah replied without looking at her. Rosie cried softly as Salim wheeled her back to the car.

"Please do not cry," Salim pleaded quietly, crouching down in front of her. Then he rubbed her back, murmuring, "Hannah does not yet understand. When she is better, she will realize that you were right." He gently wiped away her tears with a tissue and looked deep into her eyes.

"Do you think so?" asked Rosie, recovering her composure. "I hope you're right," she said sadly.

"Yes, yes, you will see. Everything will be alright. Now, we must go to the police." Rosie nodded and they drove on in silence.

Rosie felt extremely uncomfortable having to face the authorities. She knew her actions had caused much inconvenience for everyone concerned. She smoothed down her hair. "When we finish here, Salim, will you take me to the Kabil Guest House?" she asked.

"Of course. Or if you would like, you can stay at my home, you would be most welcome," he added, tentatively.

Rosie felt moved by his kindness, but the last thing she wanted to do was to drive back into the desert again. She wanted to take a long shower and sleep in a proper bed.

"No, no, I couldn't possibly bother you again. You have been so kind. I have caused you enough inconvenience."

Salim looked puzzled.

"What is this word 'inconvenience'?" he questioned. She explained.

"It has been my pleasure," he answered, and then added, "I like to be with you," as he looked deep in her eyes. Rosie blushed involuntarily.

At the police station, Salim shook hands with the officer behind the counter. The policeman looked at Rosie with a stern expression on his face as Salim spoke to him. "What is your name?" he asked without showing any hint of friendliness. Rosie gave her details and apologized for the trouble she had caused everyone.

"Your friend is in hospital. Why you did not stay together with her?" he asked bluntly.

"Well, I... I went to find help," Rosie answered, her voice trailing off. Salim explained her actions and the officer nodded.

"Where is your car?" he asked.

"Oh, my car? I don't know. I guess it is still in the desert," she replied, trying to think straight.

"No, it is not," the officer responded. "Hilal, the guide who found your friend, has parked your car here in the police compound," he said.

"Oh, that's great, I mean thank you. I must thank Mr Hilal," she muttered.

"You can go and collect the keys from room 3," he told her. In a stern voice, he warned her not to go out in the desert alone again.

"The desert is a dangerous place for the inexperienced," he announced. "You have been very lucky."

"Yes, yes, I know that. Thank you, officer. It will never happen again," she promised.

Salim drove Rosie's car to the Al Kabil Guest House. Rosie could hardly believe it was only a few days since she and Hannah had eaten lunch there. So much had happened since then. Salim pulled into the car park and switched off the engine. He sat waiting for Rosie to say something.

"Well," she said, clearing her throat, "thank you, Salim, for everything. How will you get back to the police station to pick up your car?" she queried. Salim said he would take a taxi. Then he shyly reached out and took her hand in his. "I take you to the hospital tomorrow?" he volunteered.

"Oh, that's alright. I have the car now and I…" Her voice trailed off.

"Yes, yes I know, but do you remember the way to the hospital?" he enquired.

"Um, well, can you give me instructions?"

Salim shook his head. "No, I will come. You should not drive alone. I will come and take you there."

Rosie glowed with pleasure. "Are you sure you don't mind?" she asked.

Again he shook his head and grinned.

"Alright then, I'll see you tomorrow. Maybe at about eleven? I think I will sleep well tonight!" she laughed, breaking the tension between them.

Rosie climbed out of the car and waved goodbye. She watched Salim drive away, with a growing awareness that he was taking part of her heart with him.

Chapter Twenty-One

Wearily, Rosie made her way into the small hotel and booked a room. The dark male receptionist behind the desk smiled broadly at her and asked, "You okay now?"

Rosie looked up with surprise from filling in the registration form. She suddenly realized that news travels at the speed of light in such a small community. Everyone within a fifty mile radius had probably heard the news of their ordeal. She smiled broadly, "Yes, I'm fine, thank you."

Rosie walked out to the car again and took out the necessary items she needed. She quickly closed the door on the dusty, tangled mess inside. Everything from their makeshift camp had been hurriedly thrown into the back. When she entered her room, she leaned her head on the door, catching her breath, feeling an enormous sense of relief. Heading straight for the bathroom, she removed her clothes and began washing off four days of sweat, sand and grime. She was filled with mixed emotions as she let the warm water pour over her body: guilt, relief, exhaustion and a warm indefinable feeling for Salim. She sobbed, biting her fist, releasing all the fear, tension and anxiety held inside her body over the past few days.

Catching a glimpse of herself in the mirror, Rosie let out a groan. She was horrified at her reflection. Tears pricked her eyes as she looked at the unfamiliar woman staring back at her. Her face was dry and lobster red. Her cheeks had lost their bloom and dark shadows gave her eyes a haunted look. The blistered sun-burnt skin on her forehead, nose, cheeks and chin produced a tight sensation each time she moved a facial muscle. She ran her fingers over her dry lips, remembering the sensation of honey being dribbled over them and found that she had something to smile about. Rosie climbed into the shower and slowly and gently massaged her sore head and dry lifeless hair, finally managing to get rid of all the sand in her scalp with the use of the three small bottles of shampoo, courtesy of the hotel. *My body will soon heal*, she told herself, trying to develop a positive perspective. She told herself she was extremely lucky to be alive. After rubbing lashings of body lotion into her sore, aching body, she emerged feeling positive and glowing, wearing a bath robe and a towel wound into a turban around her head. She sat down on the edge of the bed, desperate for sleep but determined to make some calls before allowing her head to hit the pillow. But sudden cramps in her stomach sent her rushing to the bathroom instead. *Camel's milk.*

*

Laura's number was engaged.
"Hello?" answered a deep, resonant man's voice answering Laura's phone call.
"Sam, they've found Rosie, I've just had a call from the police," Laura explained.
"Oh, thank God! Where is she?" Sam asked.
"Well, she apparently walked into a police station with a Bedu chap. The police say she's staying at the Al Kabil Guest House. I'm going to give her a call right now," Laura added. "Do you think we should go down there and collect her?" she asked.
"Um, let's wait and see what she decides to do about Hannah. I wonder if she's seen her yet? Let me know what's happening. I'll see you later, babe." Sam rang off.

When Laura rang the guest house, the receptionist told her Rosie's room number was engaged. Rosie was speaking to her boss, Thomas MacKay.
"You had us all worried there, m' dear," said Thomas.

Rosie replied, "I'm so sorry for all the inconvenience I've caused you. I do apologise, I promise I'll make up the time I've lost."

Thomas was not having any of it. "Now, now, don't you go worrying about work, someone's covering for you. The main thing is, you're alright. I think you'd better take the rest of the week off. Give me a ring when you get back to Muscat."

Rosie thanked Thomas, pressed the receiver button and immediately phoned Laura. When she heard Laura's familiar voice, she began to sob. She gulped down the emotions lodged in her throat and poured out her story.

"Was it you that raised the alarm?" Rosie asked, almost sure of the answer.

Laura explained that she had been worried right from Sunday morning when she had been unable to contact her. Rosie was so grateful. She could not thank Laura enough. She wondered what would have happened to Hannah if Laura had not initiated a search. Laura sympathized when Rosie explained Hannah's harsh, unforgiving stance.

"Well, just give her time, Rosie, she'll come round. You've both had a nasty shock. You'll soon be able to iron things out. Thank God you are both alright, that's the main thing. Now, I'm curious, tell me more about this knight in shining armour who rescued you from a fate worse than death?" Laura laughed.

Rosie briefly described Salim and her night with his family. She found herself smiling just at the mere thought of him.

Two days later, Rosie and Hannah were on their way back to Muscat. Salim had filled the petrol tank and pumped up the car's tyres for her. She kissed him on both cheeks and they hugged each other shyly. Somehow, it felt so natural to hold his body next to hers. They both hoped they would see each other again. He waved as they drove away. Rosie was pensive and thoughtful on the journey home. Her mind was teeming with thoughts. She was thinking of Salim and of Stuart, Denny and her mum and dad. This ordeal had somehow changed everything. She also contemplated her relationship with Hannah. *In times of stress*, thought Rosie, *you often see a different side to a person's character*. Hannah was silent, staring out of the side window.

Rosie attempted to break the ice between them, "Are you feeling better, Hannah?"

"I'm fine, thank you." Hannah replied stiffly. They drove in silence, past small villages of sand-coloured houses, shaded by huge date palm trees. Blue domed mosques with tall minarets shone in the bright sunshine. Small children stood by the roadside, selling fragrant jasmine flowers tucked inside giant lush-green banana leaves.

At last Hannah cleared her throat and made an observation. "So, Salim seems very keen on you." The leading question was tinged with jealousy.

Rosie responded carefully. "He saved my life. I'll always be eternally grateful to him, he's been so kind to me."

Hannah scoffed. "Oh, don't be so melodramatic."

Rosie raised her eyebrows. "What do you mean?" she asked, puzzled. Hannah explained that Hilal would have found Rosie, if she had not walked away, leaving her for dead. "But then I forgot, *you* had already been rescued at that point." Hannah's stinging remark cut Rosie to the quick. But she decided not to rise to the bait, calmly explaining her actions for the umpteenth time. "Hannah, I've explained what happened. You know why I left. I was trying to find help. I passed out. As soon as I came to, I sent Salim to find you. Now, let's try and put this whole experience behind us, shall we?"

Hannah frowned, her arms folded over her ample bosom, determined to get mileage out of the situation.

When they reached the apartment, Rosie opened the door. Hannah calmly walked in and locked herself in the bathroom, leaving Rosie to unpack the car on her own. Rosie made excuses for Hannah's thoughtlessness but had to admit that she was beginning to feel resentful towards her. She wondered, not for the first time, when Hannah would be returning to Dubai. Later, Rosie went to do some shopping, while Hannah made endless calls to friends in Dubai, embellishing the story of their traumatic desert experience. *The telephone bill will be enormous*, thought Rosie. She felt lonely, wandering up and down the supermarket aisles pushing a trolley in front of her.

When Rosie arrived home, heavily laden with shopping, Hannah seemed excited and rushed to greet her at the door. "Oh hi, Rosie, let me help you with those," she said breezily, taking the shopping bags. Rosie was amazed at this sudden change of attitude, searching Hannah's face for understanding.

"Guess what?" Hannah could hardly contain her enthusiasm, "There was a message on the answering machine from Dave, you know, the guy I was supposed to go out with on Saturday night? Well, he left his number and I've just called him back. The good news is, not only is he still keen to see me, but he thinks he might have found me a job."

Rosie stared, digesting the news.

"He's coming over to pick me up at eight tonight. Oh, and Rosie, Stuart left a message on the answering machine. He's arriving back in Muscat tomorrow and wants you to pick him up from the airport."

Chapter Twenty-Two

Stuart came sauntering out through the glass doors of the airport into the glaring sunshine. He opened the car door, threw his black leather bags and coat into the back of the car and eased himself into the passenger seat. Rosie moved towards him and he kissed her on the tip of her nose. "Hi, babe, how are you? God, you've caught the sun. Have you been sunbathing?" he asked casually. Rosie smiled. She felt so relieved to see Stuart's familiar face. *Everything will be back to normal now*, she thought. She turned the key in the ignition, wondering where to start with her eventful tale.

Stuart's eyes grew wide and his mouth gaped open as she explained what had happened to her over the last few days.

"Oh my God, Rosie, are you serious? Whatever made you go to the desert on your own? What a crazy thing to do," he said.

Rosie reacted defensively, "Well, we were only supposed to go for one night, just to get a taste of it, I really didn't think we'd have any trouble. Anyway, thanks for your sympathy," she added abruptly.

"What? Oh, come on. You don't expect me to congratulate you for your stupidity, do you?" Stuart replied angrily. "You could have got yourselves killed."

Rosie pursed her lips and replied. "I don't need you to tell me that, thank you."

Rosie was getting upset. Stuart tried to turn the conversation around.

"So, how did you two get out, what happened, were you rescued by the police?" he asked. Rosie described her rescue briefly, breezing over the part about Salim. Somehow she knew Stuart would not understand. She moved on to tell him about Hannah and how the whole experience had affected their relationship badly. Stuart patted her on the head, understanding that Rosie had apparently suffered a really traumatic experience in his absence. "Well, it all goes to show that you cannot manage without me!" Stuart laughed, as they arrived back at his flat.

Rosie cringed, *trust Stuart to say that,* she thought to herself grimly.

Stuart came up behind her while she was preparing tea in the kitchen. He breathed in the sweet fragrance of her hair and sighed deeply. "I missed you so much, babe. Did you miss me?" he asked, running his hand up and down her bare arms and pressing his body up against her. Rosie winced. Her skin was so badly sunburnt and sore to the touch. But she turned and hugged him, burying her face in his chest. "Of course I did. When we were stuck I thought I'd never see you again. I couldn't bear the thought," she said, biting her lower lip. Her words were uttered with absolute conviction, but her mind was thrown into complete turmoil. She cried softly, releasing the tension of the last few days, while Stuart murmured soothing platitudes into her ear. He lifted her up and carried her through to the bedroom.

Rosie lay back on the bed, in a submissive pose, watching, while Stuart removed his shirt. She stroked his broad, smooth shoulders, trying not to tense up as he gently kissed her flat stomach. She closed her eyes to focus on the sensations his touch evoked, willing herself to endure their love making. When he at last claimed her body, they moved together rhythmically. But at the moment of climax, Rosie suddenly opened her eyes and stared straight up at the ceiling. However much she tried, it seemed her mind could not be controlled. Vivid images were playing in her head and she felt a growing confusion. She told herself she had longed for this moment. It was wonderful to be back with Stuart again.

But however much she tried, she could not stop thinking of someone else.

Rosie was greeted like a long lost relative when she finally returned to work the following Saturday morning. Everyone wanted to hear the gory details of her ordeal and each one of them echoed the one central word which described her dramatic rescue – *lucky*. She knew it. She was the luckiest woman alive. The relief at getting back to normal, acted like some kind of drug on her. She felt high and totally elated. Being conscientious by nature, Rosie could not shake the guilty feelings she possessed at taking so much time off work. She vowed to work as hard as she possibly could, and began to throw all her energies into the classroom. Secretly, she knew there was another reason for wanting to focus on work; Rosie needed time to sort out her head, time to think about the growing dilemma she now faced over her relationship with Stuart.

When the telephone rang one morning in early April, Rosie immediately assumed it was Stuart. *Poor Stuart*, she thought. She had been decidedly cool towards him over the past few weeks since her desert experience. Stuart had been grappling with Rosie's lack of sexual libido since her arrival in Muscat. Now things had taken a turn for the worse. He could not understand the change in her. But he loved her. He would not give up. And Rosie was deeply impressed by his persistence. He had been telephoning constantly, wanting to know if he had done something to upset her. But his efforts just made Rosie retreat even further into herself. With growing desperation, Stuart started sending her a dozen red roses every few days with a note proclaiming his undying love for her. He kept coming up with creative ideas for romantic liaisons; he played the guitar beneath her balcony and even bought tickets for them to fly to Paris together for a long weekend. But Rosie had declined the offer. She was flattered, but his actions only served to confuse her further. She needed time and space to explore her feelings for him.

However, if the truth were told, all the exploration had really been focused on her relationship with Salim. He too, had contacted her several times, and Rosie had reluctantly agreed to see him, thinking it might enable her to sort out her feelings for him. She told herself it was the romance of the desert, the exotic nature of the man and the place, which had so enthralled her. If she met him in ordinary surroundings, she was sure to feel differently. Her intense feelings for him were due to the unusual circumstances of their encounter. The desert experience had been highly charged with emotion. And after all, Salim *had* saved her life. It was natural that she should develop feelings for the person who had rescued her. *But how deep were those feelings?*

Rosie thought back to their meeting. Salim had met her on the beach road leading to the Crowne Plaza. He had waved when he saw her car approaching and opened the car door for her. He had stooped to kiss her on both cheeks and she had laughed, turning towards him. Their lips had been just inches apart and a desire and yearning had grown between them. The moment had passed and they had walked slowly along the beach together, watching silently as the enormous orange ball of light sank down over the dark water. They had held hands, listening to the sound of the waves crashing upon the shore, white foam just visible in the fading light and fluorescent plankton glowing green in the dark. Rosie had felt happy and relaxed in his company. She looked up at the darkening sky and saw the silver crescent moon lying on its back, shining down on them. She immediately chastised herself for choosing to meet Salim in such a romantic setting. She had listened attentively as Salim talked softly about his life in the desert. He had such an easy-going, sweet nature. But Rosie had tried to be on her guard. Common sense told her she would be crazy to embark on a relationship with Salim. What did she have in common with him? Her whole lifestyle was completely different from his. Rosie had continued to make light conversation, telling Salim funny stories about her job in the Institute and he had laughed. And it was precisely at that moment when Rosie was trying desperately to assign their relationship to the past, that she knew, without a shadow of a doubt, that she always wanted to be able to hear the sound of his laughter.

But did that mean she loved Stuart any less? She wondered if it was possible to love two men simultaneously. Surely it was unfair to keep both men keen. She would have to kiss goodbye to one. Or the other? Or both? It occurred to her that perhaps she did not really love either of them enough. She thought she loved Stuart, but knew she did not want to live with him. She definitely had growing feelings for Salim. But was it just infatuation? Was she swept off her feet by the romantic notion of an exotic lover? She had never even kissed Salim, but knew in her heart that she very much wanted to.

To complicate things further, Hannah now seemed to be extremely jealous of all the attention Rosie was getting from her two admirers, and this was causing a renewed tension between them. Rosie had tried tactfully to suggest to Hannah that she should move out, now that she had a new job with an oil company and Dave had become her steady boyfriend. But Hannah enjoyed sharing a flat with Rosie and did not want to live on her own or with Dave. And Rosie did not have the heart to force the issue.

Now, as Rosie checked the caller identity on the telephone, she was surprised and relieved to find it was neither Stuart or Salim. She picked up the phone and heard Sam's deep, resonant voice. "Hi Rosie, how are you doing? Hope I'm not disturbing you?" he asked.

Rosie assured him that she was happy to hear from him and had plenty of time to talk as she was on the late shift that day. Rosie was curious. It was not like Sam to ring her at all. Usually their social arrangements were organized by Laura.

"I need your help," he said, candidly.

Rosie murmured encouragingly.

"It's Laura's birthday on Thursday and I want to do a surprise party for her," he explained. Rosie said she would be delighted to help and asked where the party would be held. "Well, that's where you come in, I want to do a sit-down meal, just for the eight of us, with white linen and silver cutlery, champagne and crystal glasses…"

"Wow, that sounds a bit posh!" Rosie announced.

Sam replied, "Well, yes and no, I mean, it does sound grand, but I want to set it all up under the stars."

"Oh, al fresco, how romantic! Where?" she enquired.

"On the beach," he answered.

The next few days were spent busily preparing for Laura's surprise birthday party. Rosie, Hannah and Penny planned to prepare the food between them and ferry it out to the beach near the airport. It was a mammoth task to organize everything and the three girls had a meeting and delegated jobs and wrote long lists of things they would need to take. Keeping Laura in the dark was easy, as Laura was extremely busy at work that week. Sam and Rosie hatched a plan so that Laura would not suspect.

Rosie called Laura on Sunday and invited her and Sam over for dinner on Thursday. Laura hesitated and said she was not sure if Sam had other plans for them that day. Rosie feigned ignorance and asked why. Laura brushed off the question and said she would ring back once she had spoken to Sam. Later that day, Laura rang back and confirmed. "We'd love to come."

On Thursday evening, Sam and Laura arrived. They knocked on Rosie's door and rang the bell several times. "That's strange, there's no one home. I'm sure Rosie said 8 p.m.," said Laura, puzzled. Attempting to keep a straight face, Sam suggested they go for a drive and come back a little later. Laura reluctantly agreed and walked back to the car, hoping everything was alright with Rosie. Sam drove along the beach road, trying to keep up a lively conversation with Laura the whole way. Laura was a bit glum. She was disappointed. Sam had never forgotten her birthday before. She thought back to the previous year, when he had taken her out for a romantic meal for two at the Italian restaurant in the Grand Hyatt Hotel.

Ten minutes later Laura caught sight of a flaming torch in the sand. "Hey, what's that over there?"

Sam stopped the car, "Oh, someone's having a barbecue, I guess."

"Oh, why are we stopping here, we'd better get back now, it's nearly nine o'clock," said Laura, consulting her watch. Then, Sam turned to her, took her in his arms and kissed her lovingly.

"Hey Sam, what are you doing?" she giggled, pulling away. Then she closed her eyes and relaxed, enjoying the sensation of Sam's lips against hers. When Sam finally released her, she nearly jumped out of her skin. All her friends (Rosie, Stuart, Hannah, Dave, Penny and Shabib) were standing around the car, wearing paper hats, blowing whistles and grinning at her.

"Happy Birthday, Laura!" they shouted pulling the door open. Laura was speechless and overcome with emotion. Her mouth fell open as she looked from face to face and then saw the beautiful table heavily laden with silver, crystal and flowers. "Oh, my God! When did you do all this?" she asked, swallowing hard. "It's so beautiful, thank you so much."

She turned to Sam and hit him playfully. "Hey, I thought you'd forgotten. You've been keeping secrets from me!" She laughed and he ran away into the darkness. She chased after him until they were both breathless. Then he took her in his arms and kissed her passionately.

"Hey, you two love birds," Rosie called, "dinner is served." The eight friends sat around the table, talking, laughing and drinking champagne. They took pictures of each other in the candlelight and watched while Laura blew out the candles on her chocolate opera cake. Then Sam made a toast, "Here's to Laura!" They all chinked glasses and enjoyed the last perfect moments of a beautiful night.

Later, Rosie and Laura took a walk along the shore together. Laura was so chuffed at Sam's thoughtfulness. Rosie agreed, "Yeah, Sam must really love you, he made so much effort tonight."

Laura was silent.

Rosie raised her eyebrows. "What's wrong, Laura? Don't you think he loves you?"

Laura shrugged her shoulders and answered. "Maybe he loves me a bit, but not enough."

"What do you mean? Not enough for what?"

"Not enough to marry me."

"Give it time, Laura, you're still young and—"

Laura interrupted, "I'm not so young, I'm thirty-four. I can't wait forever."

Rosie put her arm around Laura as they made their way back to the group.

Why is it we all seem to want different things? Rosie thought. *We are never completely happy with what we have. Why do we always want something more?*

Chapter Twenty-Three

A week later, Rosie and Laura sat waiting patiently in the doctor's surgery for Penny to reappear. Penny already knew the results of the urine test would prove positive. The subtle changes in her body over the last few weeks were enough to convince her: she was pregnant. The girls looked up as Penny emerged from the doctor's surgery and nodded tearfully. The girls hugged her and Rosie drove them straight over to her apartment and made some coffee. They sipped their drinks thoughtfully, giving Penny time to digest the news. Laura finally broke the silence and plucked up the courage to broach the subject. "So, Penny, what are you gonna do?" she asked gently.

Penny shrugged her shoulders, wiping away the tears from her beautiful amber eyes.

"Have you told Shabib?" Rosie probed.

Penny shook her head of short brown hair, her eyes brimming with tears. Laura folded her arms and exchanged looks with Rosie.

"How did it happen? I mean, don't you two use contraception?" Laura asked quietly.

Penny looked up mournfully at Laura. "Usually we do, but you know, just once we didn't. I mean, we got a bit careless. I don't know, I didn't think it would happen, cos of the time of the month."

Rosie could hardly believe Penny was that naïve and ill-informed.

"Are you going to tell him?" Rosie asked.

"I don't know, I mean I suppose I'll have to. I won't make him marry me though, I don't want to force him into anything."

"Would you like to marry him if he agreed?" Laura asked.

"Well, I guess so, I don't know. It's all so sudden. I mean, we don't even know each other that well yet," Penny admitted.

Rosie took a deep breath. "There is another way, you know. You could do something about it, I mean, if you didn't want the baby…" her voice trailed off.

Penny looked aghast. "What are you suggesting, Rosie? No! I could never do that. *No way*! If it's meant to be, it's meant to be. I'm gonna have this baby with or without Shabib," she said bravely.

The girls carried on talking late into the night until Hannah came in from her date with Dave. When she saw the three girls sitting on the sofa together, she immediately felt excluded. *Why didn't they tell me they were having a girly night?* she thought, seething with resentment. She disappeared into her bedroom, slamming the door behind her.

"What's wrong with *her*?" asked Laura. Rosie knew the answer. She was getting used to Hannah's moods and had begun to understand her mentality. She was so insecure, so lacking in confidence that she thought every incident somehow related directly to her. Rosie had never met anyone with such a fragile ego, so easily inflated and yet so easily popped like a balloon. Rosie wondered how she was going to smooth things over with her. Penny had begged the two girls to keep the information about her pregnancy to themselves, until she had decided what to do. Penny certainly did not want Shabib to hear the news from anyone other than herself. Rosie would have to respect her wishes.

Laura offered to drop Penny home. Once they had left, Rosie knocked quietly on Hannah's door. There was no answer. Rosie opened the door slowly and saw Hannah typing away furiously on the computer. Even though Hannah was wearing headphones, Rosie could plainly hear her rock music blaring out. *She'll go deaf one of these days*, Rosie thought. She closed the door quietly and went to get ready for bed.

Brushing her teeth, she thought about Penny and wondered if she would marry Shabib. How would Shabib take the news? Would he stand by her? Or would he turn his back on her? She doubted if he earned sufficient money to support a wife and child. But if they decided not to get married, Penny probably would have to leave Muscat and go back to England. She hoped Penny's parents would support her. All these imponderables got Rosie thinking about Salim. There was a thread of magnetism between them, a strong attraction, a passion, a deep connection, a chemistry that she had rarely felt with anyone else. But they were worlds apart. They were surely totally incompatible as long-term partners. Salim had a different country, religion, language and culture. Could a mixed marriage ever really overcome such enormous differences? Was she crazy to even contemplate such a thing? It was far too early in their relationship to think about marriage, she hardly knew Salim. But should she nip their friendship in the bud now, before it developed into something she could not turn her back on? Her body ached to see him again. And where did that leave her relationship with Stuart? It made good sense to stay with Stuart, he loved her and if she stayed with him, she was sure they would have a wonderful life together, travelling the world. She must forget Salim and be sensible.

Suddenly, there was violent banging on the bathroom door. "Rosie, Rosie, come on out! I've got something really exciting to tell you!" Hannah's bad mood had apparently evaporated and her voice was full of elation.

"Okay, coming! What is it? What's happened?"

Hannah turned from the door and strode into the lounge with Rosie on her tail. "You're never gonna believe it, Rosie, guess what?" she said, pacing the lounge, unable to keep still.

"What?"

"I've found my father."

Rosie sat down on the sofa. She listened intently as Hannah gave her all the details about the agency she had contacted to conduct a search on her behalf. Hannah's father had been found and was apparently willing to get in touch with her. The agency had now given Hannah's email address and phone number to her father and she was waiting for him to contact her.

"Wow, that's brilliant, Hannah. I'm so pleased for you. But Hannah, just be careful. I mean, don't get too excited. Promise me you won't get your hopes up too high. He might turn out to be nothing like the loving father you're hoping for," Rosie warned.

Hannah frowned. She found Rosie's comment so negative and exasperating. *Why can't she just be happy for me?* But Hannah was far too excited at the prospect of corresponding with her father to stay angry with Rosie for long.

"Oh, alright, Mum, I promise," she said, grinning.

Chapter Twenty-Four

The following Thursday night Rosie tried on six different dresses before she finally decided on a long black, slinky halter neck. Regarding herself in the bedroom mirror, she realized she was showing far too much bare flesh for an Omani wedding. This would be an ideal opportunity to wear the beautiful sheer black abaya she had bought in the souq. Rosie really liked the wide chiffon sleeves and the hemline with its hand-embroidered sequins. Now she was totally covered. Wearing the abaya made her think of the puritanical Victorian era, when it was considered improper to show even a glimpse of ankle. *Actually, being completely covered can be very sexy. At least it leaves something to the imagination*, she thought. Taking out her diamond stud earrings from their box and carefully securing them in her ears, she put her driving licence, lipstick and a five rial note into her small evening bag, and walked out into the warm night air, inhaling the sweet fragrant scent of jasmine.

Fathima and Hamed had planned a traditional Omani wedding. The groom and the male guests were to gather in the mosque, while the women would celebrate in style, at the Al Bustan Palace Hotel. Rosie was really looking forward to the experience, although she was a little apprehensive about going on her own. However, many of the staff from the Institute had been invited too, so Rosie had arranged to meet her Sudanese friend, Laila, in the lobby of the hotel. Rosie parked her Land Cruiser in a car park dotted with sleek, expensive cars. A beautiful red Ferrari, parked at the entrance to the ballroom, had been decorated with balloons and streamers and a 'Just Married' sign had been attached to the back bumper. *Lucky Fathima.*

Inside the crowded lobby, scores of glamorous dark-haired ladies were greeting each other with smiles and kisses. Rosie felt decidedly underdressed, noticing their glinting diamonds and heavy, intricate gold jewellery. She glimpsed sparkling sequinned evening gowns beneath voluminous black silk and chiffon abayas. Rosie suddenly felt lonely in the crowd. She did not know a soul. She stood awkwardly scanning the lobby for Laila, willing her to appear. Then out of the corner of her eye, she saw an elegant woman walking shyly towards her.

"You Mees Rozi?" she asked.

"Yes, I am Miss Rosie," she answered, smiling.

"Me, mother, Fathima," said the woman proudly.

"Oh, pleased to meet you. Your daughter is a lovely girl. *Hiya gamila.* Very clever, *hiya shartra.*"

The woman beamed, nodding her head.

"*Marhaba*, (welcome!) Please, you come!" She beckoned Rosie to follow her.

Rosie tried to explain that she was waiting for someone, but Fathima's mother was insistent, already leading the way into a huge sumptuous ballroom, lit by massive crystal chandeliers. Rosie followed, looking behind her for Laila, but there was still no sign of her. The woman ushered her to sit at a large round table for ten, covered in white linen and set with silver cutlery and gleaming white and gold crockery. Small bowls of Arabic mezze (dolmas, hummus and falafel) were already laid out in the centre of the table. As Rosie looked around the enormous ballroom, she could hardly believe her eyes. There were about seventy identical tables, each laid out for ten people. *Goodness me, that's seven hundred!* Then she corrected herself: seven hundred *women.* She had not been in a room full of that many females since she had attended an all girls' school. Rosie thanked Fathima's mother and sat down, feeling decidedly conspicuous, with her fair skin and blonde hair. *No one likes to feel different*, she thought.

Just then, Rosie looked up and saw a tall, familiar figure walking gracefully towards her. It was Laila, wearing a huge grin on her dark face. She seemed even taller than ever. A bright yellow cotton material was wound around her large body and on her head, she wore the typical Sudanese headdress, a turban fashioned from the same yellow fabric. "Wow, Laila, you look fantastic!" Rosie exclaimed, jumping up and kissing her on both cheeks. Lowering herself into the seat next to Rosie's, Laila's gold bracelets jangled together noisily. The tall African giggled and scooped up some hummus with Lebanese bread, popping it into her wide mouth, showing one gold tooth. Later, two Indian girls, Seema and Radhika who also worked at the Institute, joined their table. Rosie was thankful they all spoke perfect English, but was determined to practise her Arabic with some of the other guests.

Suddenly there was a muted hush and all eyes turned to the back of the ballroom. Fathima, wearing an exquisite bridal gown, was slowly making her way down the crimson carpeted aisle. A procession of chanting female relatives followed, showering the bride with hundreds of red and pink rose petals. Rosie stared at Fathima's total transformation. The quiet, plain young girl in the headscarf had become a dazzling bride, resplendent in a cream satin and lace dress with hand-embroidered sequins and pearls sewn on to the bodice and skirt. She wore a diamond tiara on her head, which secured a long cream veil reaching to the floor. The veil only partially covered her glossy black hair; revealing beautiful soft curls. As Fathima neared Rosie's table, she turned her head slightly, batting her long false eyelashes and smiling shyly at Rosie.

The bride carefully climbed up three small steps onto a small erected stage that had been draped with satin material and decorated with huge floral arrangements on free-standing columns. Two deep-blue velvet, brass-studded chairs sat side by side, like thrones set for a king and queen. The bride turned and sat down on one of the chairs, facing the audience. Two sweet young girls, in matching pink dresses, carrying bouquets of small pink roses, sat down nervously on small chairs either side of the bride.

Several close relatives jumped up onto the stage to arrange the bride's dress. They beamed, posing for the female photographer. Rosie looked at the back of the ballroom. Laila followed her gaze. "What are you waiting for?" she asked.

"Where's the groom?"

"The groom?" Laila repeated. She threw back her head and laughed, tapping her forehead. "Don't hold your breath, dear. He's not due until the end of the evening!"

"Oh," Rosie replied in surprise.

The bride's mother addressed the guests, declaring the buffet open. While Fathima sat passively on stage, nervously awaiting her prince, hoards of women swarmed towards the long rows of stainless steel tureens filled with delicious Asian cuisine; fried samosas, fragrant saffron rice, lamb kebabs and chicken curry and dhall. During the meal, two women chanted Koranic verses and young girls swayed, clapping their hands and joining in the repetitive chorus lines. At intervals, several young girls came over to Rosie's table and introduced themselves. Rosie learnt that four of the girls were sisters of the bride, another was a close friend and the rest were all cousins. She particularly like Sara, Fathima's sister. *The extended family is alive and well and living in Oman,* Rosie thought. She could not help comparing Omani family life with the British equivalent. She remembered her grandfather talking of aunts, uncles and grandparents all living in the same street, in close proximity to each other. *Now, even the nuclear family seems to be disintegrating in Britain. People live alone, far from their relatives.* Rosie thought back to the young people living on the streets of

Brighton, with no homes to go to and no sense of belonging; taking drugs to numb their loneliness and pain. Many of her friends, like Hannah, came from single parent families. *It must be difficult both financially and emotionally, to raise a child alone.* Here, Rosie sensed a real interdependency, a caring and sharing between family members and a much slower pace of life. *It must be nice to be a part of such a large family,* she thought. Her eyes pricked with tears, as she thought of her own parents living alone with only Denise popping in now and again. Somehow, she wished her parents had had more children, so that she would not have such a tremendous feeling of guilt about living so far away from them.

Sara took her to meet Khadiga, the matriarchal figure of the family, mother of nine children and already a grandmother to six. The old woman smiled and shook hands with Rosie, patting her on the head. Khadiga's dark hair was streaked with burnished orange where she had applied henna in an attempt to disguise the grey. She looked far too young and glamorous to be a granny. Her face was unlined and her skin soft and clear. *No wrinkles.* Rosie had heard that Omani girls tended to marry young and have lots of children, so it was common for women to become grandmothers even before the age of forty, but Khadiga's granddaughter, Fathima, was at least twenty years old, so Khadiga had to be in her late fifties at least. *Perhaps her secret was a stress-free life.* Rosie guessed that Khadiga had never worked, never taken exams, never had deadlines to meet, trains to catch and progress to make, but she was also sure that life in Oman forty years ago, before the discovery of oil, would not have been easy. Khadiga would have worked hard just to survive. She could not imagine having to wash clothes in a stream, cook over a fire and live without running water or electricity. The thought of no air conditioning in this heat made her feel sick.

Rosie believed there has never been a better time in the history of the world, to be a woman. Education, contraception, labour-saving devices and equal opportunities in employment have given women better health, more money and freedom to enjoy a better standard of living. It occurred to her that perhaps the Omani woman's olive complexion and aversion to the sun explained the lack of wrinkles. Omani women usually avoided exposure to the sun's harmful rays. But Rosie also believed a little sunlight was beneficial. She made a mental note to start using sun block on her face every day.

Rosie stood up and walked towards the stage with her camera. She began taking photographs of the bride and members of her family. Suddenly someone tapped her on the shoulder. A young girl with a severe look in her eye and a particularly drab black scarf wrapped tightly around her head, shouted at her in Arabic. Rosie smiled and shrugged her shoulders. "Motasifa, I'm sorry, I don't understand, what is wrong?" The girl stared at her accusingly, pointing at Rosie's camera with her gloved hand. Sara came rushing over and stood between them. She put her arm around Rosie's shoulders and moved her away from the girl. Sara spoke soothingly in Arabic to the girl. Rosie sat down, looking quite bewildered, unable to understand the flow of conversation between them. The girl scowled and turned on her heel, disappearing back into the crowd. Sara smiled at Rosie and explained. No photographs are to be taken. It is forbidden. Rosie looked at the official photographer and then back at Sara without comprehension.

"Yes, yes, I know we have a photographer, but all of her photos will be given to the bride. No men must see the women uncovered, do you understand? We don't know who might see your photographs. We cannot allow it. Sorry."

Rosie mumbled her apologies and Sara walked away.

Suddenly everyone in the room stood up and hurriedly covered themselves with abayas and head scarves. "What's happening now? Is everyone leaving? The bridegroom hasn't arrived yet," Rosie asked.

"Well, that's just it, Rosie, the bridegroom has arrived and he's coming in now," Seema explained.

A very pale and nervous groom walked slowly down the aisle, followed by his mother and half a dozen chanting female relatives. Hamed looked extremely regal and grand, wearing a golden sheathed sword attached to a belt around his waist, a black cloak (bisht) and turban on his head. *My Goodness, it must take guts for a man to walk into a room full of so many women.* Hamed strode up onto the stage and kissed the bride on the forehead before seating himself on the throne next to her, smiling and nodding to everyone. The newly-weds exchanged gifts and Hamed placed a ring on Fathima's finger to the sound of rippling applause from the crowd. The happy couple raised glasses of apple juice, linked arms and slowly drank from each other's glass. *How romantic.* Rosie really wished she could have taken some photos. The girls from the Institute beckoned for her to follow them up onto the stage to wish the couple a long and happy marriage. They stood around the bride and groom and smiled for the camera. On leaving, Rosie was given a small gift; a small red satin box filled with sugared almonds. Rosie's Arabic was still very shaky but it did not take a linguist to know that the two names written in gold lettering on the top of the box denoted the happy couple: Fathima and Hamed.

Chapter Twenty-Five

It was Friday morning and Rosie lay in her comfy bed, listening to the sound of the muezzin calling the faithful to prayer. She rolled onto her stomach and pulled the pillow over her head, in an attempt to block out the brilliant sunshine pouring into the room through the flimsy pink bedroom curtains. It was no use. She could not get back to sleep. She clambered out of bed, went into the kitchen, made herself some freshly squeezed orange juice, a cup of tea and a piece of wholemeal toast. She put everything on a tray and took it back to bed. She lay back, enjoying the luxury of a day without plans and commitments. At around ten o'clock, she heard a soft knocking on her bedroom door. Hannah poked her head round the door and gave Rosie a dazzling smile. "Can I come in?" she asked.

"Hi, Hannah, sure, come and sit down," Rosie answered, tapping the bed. *I wonder what's happened now?* Hannah's life seemed so full of drama. No day was ever clear of either intense highs or extreme lows. Hannah sat on the bed, adjusting the royal blue tie-dye sarong that she had wrapped around her. Her blue and green bikini top was clearly visible beneath its flimsy material. Her ample breasts rose and fell gently with each breath, lifting the fine gold chain with its letter H.

"How's Dave?" Rosie asked.

"Oh he's great, we're getting on really well. He's such a sweet gut, you know, thoughtful and attentive and he never lets me pay for anything and says I can use his car while he's away next month."

"Oh wow, you mean the Porsche? Lucky you."

"But that's not what I wanted to tell you about," she said, apparently searching for the right words.

"Mm?"

"It's about my dad," Hannah blurted out.

"Go on."

"Well, you know after he phoned me last week I've been emailing him and somehow I feel I'm really getting to know him. I can't wait to meet him," she said, tilting her head to one side, assessing Rosie's reaction, before she continued, "I know what you think, Rosie, but listen, he's explained to me why he couldn't stay with Mum…"

"Oh really? What were his reasons?" Rosie interrupted, full of scepticism.

"Um, well he said when Mum got pregnant, he was just starting out and couldn't afford to be tied down, you know, couldn't take on the responsibility of a child and everything, so he decided he would have to leave. He's not had it easy himself, you know, he's had a difficult time."

Rosie pursed her lips. *I don't want to be judgmental, but it sounds like a cop-out to me. Selfish bastard.*

Hannah drew imaginary pictures on the quilt, waiting for Rosie response. Rosie breathed deeply and replied. "Okay, so well, that's great if he wants to make amends. Maybe you could arrange to meet him when you go to England," she mused.

Hannah suddenly grabbed Rosie's forearm and looked earnestly into her eyes. Rosie saw her lips moving but could not seem to absorb the words issuing from Hannah's mouth.

"Rosie, did you hear what I said? I've invited Dad to come out here and stay with me… us… just for a holiday."

Rosie stared." To stay with… us? Where? Here, in *my* flat?" It took her a moment to gather her thoughts.

"But Hannah, there's not enough room here, I mean, we only have two bedrooms. Where will your father sleep?"

"Oh, don't worry about that. I'll sleep on the couch if I have to, I don't mind, it's no problem, or I could even share your room. I don't mind kipping down anywhere, it's only for a couple o' weeks, it'll be fine, you'll see. Isn't it exciting? I mean, it's amazing to think I'll be meeting me dad for the first time."

Share my room! Rosie smiled weakly and tried to keep things in perspective. *Two weeks*! Rosie sighed. "Um, so when does he want to come?"

"Well, I'll have to organize a visa for him first and than send him a ticket, so it'll take time…"

"Send him a ticket! Why? Can't he afford to buy a ticket to come and see his daughter after all these years?" Rosie was incredulous.

"Well no, he doesn't have a job at the moment. Oh, Rosie, be happy for me, please. I don't mind buying me dad a ticket, for God's sake." Hannah scowled angrily and turned away.

"Oh alright, alright, if that's what you want, then yes, I suppose it's fine with me. As long as it's only for two weeks. You won't have to organize a visa though. He can get a visit visa at the airport when he arrives."

"Really? So it's okay? You don't mind?"

Rosie shrugged and nodded, unable to articulate.

Hannah bounced up and down on the bed yelling "yes! yes!" and then proceeded to do a little dance around the room. Rosie laughed to see Hannah so elated. She was really funny when she was in a good mood. Hannah rushed over to Rosie and started pulling her out of bed. "Oh Rosie, you're a star! I don't know what I'd do without you. You're such a good friend, the sister I never had, really. Now come on, lazy bones, get up! Let's go for a swim."

Reluctantly, Rosie allowed herself to be pulled out of her cosy bed and she went to take a shower.

Chapter Twenty-Six

The two friends sat down at a wooden slatted table shaded by a huge cream parasol in front of the leisure pool. They were just placing their order with the waiter when Rosie saw him. *I might have known he'd be here. This town is too small.* Stuart came hurrying out of the health club wearing khaki shorts, a white sports shirt and a stripy towel around his neck. He immediately grinned when he saw the girls and sauntered over to their table. He was sweating profusely after a strenuous work-out.

"Hi, ladies, mind if I join you?" he asked, taking a seat without waiting for an answer. Rosie felt such mixed emotions. His smile was incredibly disarming. She could feel herself blushing almost in spite of herself. Stuart was so masculine and strong, his body so familiar to her, it was impossible for her not to feel attracted to him. She drank her icy lime juice, looking at him playfully, as she sucked on a straw. Stuart ordered a club sandwich and chatted amiably about work and his new hobby; golf. "How on earth do you play golf on sand?" Rosie asked.

"Well, it's a challenge, but I figure if I can learn to play on sand, a grass course will be a doddle! It's a really sociable game though, and I've met loads of interesting people. A group of us from the golf club are planning to go up and play in Dubai next month. Why don't you come with me, Rosie?"

"Oh, I'd love to, that sounds great," she said, reacting without thinking of the implications, "but I don't play golf. Won't that be a problem?"

"No, not at all, you can still enjoy the club on the Creek and shop until you drop," Stuart replied.

What am I doing? She thought. *Do I still love him?* As an observer, Hannah could see that Stuart was still very keen on Rosie. *Some people have all the luck*, she thought. She thought she was going to have Rosie to herself this afternoon. But now Stuart had spoilt things. She stood up and stretched. "Well, I'm off to take a swim, see you later, Rosie," she said fumbling in her purse to pay her part of the bill.
"Oh now, put your money away, Hannah, this meal's on me," Stuart said, feeling generous and quite chuffed that Rosie had agreed to go to Dubai with him. He had been determined to appear casual and aloof with Rosie, but somehow, he could never put on an act with her, his true feelings always shone through. They wandered over to some sun loungers and relaxed together in the sun. She lay on her stomach with her eyes closed as Stuart pulled down her shoulder straps and rubbed suntan lotion onto her back. She felt so relaxed with Stuart. She knew how his mind worked, knew what to expect from him. They had the same sense of humour and they shared the same hopes and dreams. She knew Stuart was an ambitious guy, a rising star within the company; he was bound to do well. He was reliable and dependable. *He could be my rock.* Rosie was certain that if she chose to make her life with Stuart, he would keep her grounded and give her everything she wanted. They would have a beautiful life together. Rosie screwed up her eyes as if trying to banish an intruding thought which kept recurring in her mind; *but what about Salim?*

The next day Rosie was scheduled to work from 3 p.m. to 8 p.m., so in the morning she was able to meet up with Penny and Laura for a coffee at Costa's on the beach. Penny had phoned to arrange the meeting, so Rosie was convinced Penny had important news to share with them. But when Penny arrived, her expressionless face gave nothing away. Rosie always admired people who had the ability to hide their emotions, never having mastered the skill herself.

People can read me like an open book. The three girls hugged each other and Penny ordered a skinny latte and two cappuccinos while Laura and Rosie found a round table by the window and sat down on the brown leather sofa.

It was May and the temperature had already climbed to more than forty degrees. They could not even enjoy the view of the sea from the window due to the high humidity and condensation on the windows. Both girls looked at Penny, sipping their coffee and eagerly awaiting her news. Her stony expression led Rosie to draw her own negative conclusions. Rosie cleared her throat, "So, Penny, what's going to happen? Are you going to go home to your parents?" she asked, anticipating the most likely outcome.

Penny did not answer immediately. She looked down at her coffee, stirring it slowly. Laura could not bear the uncertainty a moment longer.

"Come on, Penny, tell us what's happening. What are you going to do?"

Penny looked from one to the other. She was touched by their obvious concern. Suddenly Penny clutched their hands and a huge Cheshire grin spread across her face as she calmly announced; "I'll tell you what's going to happen; Shabib and I are getting married!"

Laura and Rosie gasped and exchanged glances.

"Oh wow, Penny, that's great news!" Laura replied, guardedly.

"Yes, wonderful, I mean, that's great… if you are sure that's what you really want," Rosie added, fidgeting uncomfortably in her seat.

"What's that supposed to mean?" Penny asked, frowning.

"Nothing. It's just that, well, it's such a big step, isn't it? I mean, he's from a different culture and religion and everything," Laura explained.

"Yes, Penny, have you thought through all the implications? You might have to become a Moslem, you know," Rosie informed her.

Penny shook her head, "Come on, you guys, it's alright. We're talking about Shabib here, not some stranger who's gonna enforce rules and regulations on me. I thought you'd be happy for me," Penny answered, looking a little crestfallen.

The girls both replied in unison, "We are!"

"Well, you don't sound it. What do you want me to do? Go back to England and become an unmarried mother, a single parent living in a council flat? Or stuck at home with my parents? No thank you very much. Look, Shabib is the father, and he and I have had a long talk and he's willing to support me and the baby. Everything's gonna work out fine. We'll move into a little annexe attached to his mother's house in Ghubra…"

"Whoa, slow down a minute! You're not gonna live with his family, are you?" Rosie interrupted.

"Well, it's only a temporary measure, until Shabib can find a better job and make more money. He said he might do two jobs, you know, one in the morning and another in the evening. Hey, don't look at me like that! It's alright, look, we can't afford anything else at the moment. It's gonna be fine, you'll see."

She looked at Rosie, "The baby's not due until October, so if I'm not too tired, I'll try and continue working until September, then I'll get confinement leave for three months before I have to go back to work."

Laura asked, "Oh, and who'll look after the baby then?"

"Shabib says we're gonna get a housemaid from India or the Philippines. Shabib's mother has already got one housemaid and she said she'd help us find another."

Rosie could not stop herself from asking; "Penny, listen to me, this is not just for a week, a month or even a year, this is *permanent*. How do you feel about living here for the rest of your life? This is Shabib's country, not yours. Won't you miss England?"

Penny laughed. "Like a hole in the head! No seriously, I'm sure I'll miss some things and some people but really, I was fed up with the lifestyle in UK anyway. That's why I came here; to find a better quality of life. I like it here, it's a friendly place. It's calm and peaceful and the people are sweet and genuine. And it's a great environment for bringing up small children. Trust me, I really think I could be very happy living here."

"What do your parents think about it?" Laura asked.

Penny screwed up her face. "I haven't told them yet. They don't even know about Shabib, let alone the baby."

All three girls were silent. They knew it would not be easy for Penny's parents to accept the situation. How would they feel, knowing their daughter would be living thousands of miles away from them, married to a foreigner? The girls offered Penny their emotional support: Rosie raised her coffee cup and smiled saying, "Okay, Penny, you've obviously made your mind up. Let's make a toast. Here's to your new life in Muscat and the new life growing inside you!" The girls laughed and raised their coffee cups and spent the next hour discussing plans for the wedding.

Chapter Twenty-Seven

When Salim rang to invite Rosie to see the greenback turtles in Ras Al Hadd, Rosie did not know whether to accept his invitation or not. She was certain it would be a magical experience and had no doubt she would enjoy Salim's company. But that was the problem. Perhaps she would enjoy herself a little too much. It was all so complicated. Should she tell Stuart of her plans to go away for the weekend with Salim? Stuart only knew the rudimentary details about the Bedu who had rescued her from the desert. He had no idea that her reticence to see him over the past few weeks had been due to the intense attraction she felt towards Salim. She could, of course make light of it. Stuart would never suspect in a million years that she had developed feelings for a nomadic desert inhabitant. But was she being deceitful if she went without telling Stuart? She really wanted to see the turtles and did not know when she would get another opportunity.

After pondering the problem all week, Rosie finally decided the only way she could realistically go, would be if she took a friend along. A chaperone. She wondered who would fit that role? Penny was busy with her wedding plans and Laura and Sam were going diving. That left Hannah. She broached the subject with her one evening and was delighted and relieved when she agreed. In a way, she was surprised, after what had happened during their last disastrous trip together. But Hannah felt she owed Rosie a favour because she had agreed to let her father stay with them in a couple of weeks' time. Hannah also hoped to talk some sense into Rosie. Hannah could not understand how Rosie could ever contemplate having a serious relationship with a Bedu.

Perhaps spending some time with him would help Rosie realize she was just suffering from a ridiculous infatuation.

Early Thursday morning the two girls met Salim on the beach road. Rosie had never shown Salim where she lived, in an attempt to keep her relationship with him at arm's length. Salim bought the girls a coffee and told them about the route they would take to Ras Al Hadd. First, they would drive to Sur, once a major trading port with East Africa and famous for its boat building. Large ocean going dhows had been built there to sail between the Gulf, India and East Africa during the 19th and first half of the 20th century.

Then, he said they would drive on down to Ras Al Hadd and stay in the official camp site, built to ensure the greenback turtles were not disturbed by tourists during their nesting season. It was ten o'clock when Salim and the girls left Qurum and began their five hour journey to Ras Al Hadd. In the car, Salim played them some Arabic music; Fairooz and Um Kholthum. Rosie found their voices very powerful but wished she could understand what they were singing about. Later on, he played them some instrumental belly dancing music. The girls loved it and started clapping their hands, wiggling their hips and laughing. Due to Salim's dark skin, the girls did not realize their hip movements caused him to blush with embarrassment. Rosie asked Salim to stop at intervals along the route so that she could take photographs of interesting sights; dhows in the ancient harbour, a fort and a tomb up on the cliffs overlooking the sea and an amazing mosque which had more than forty domes.

Best of all, Rosie loved taking photos of the children in the villages. As soon as their car went past, small children would immediately appear, waving their hands and shouting; "Hello! How are you?" in their very best (and possibly only) English. The little girls wore brightly coloured satin or cotton tunics over tight-legged trousers and the boys looked like little miniature versions of their fathers; wearing brilliant white dishdashas and embroidered pillbox hats on their heads. Rosie was amazed to see women washing dishes in the streams and balancing huge clay water pots on their heads. *How many people in the world are still living in homes without access to clean, running water?* Rosie could not even begin to imagine living in a house without running water and modern appliances like a washing machine and dishwasher. And yet looking closely at these women, they appeared to be happy; laughing and joking with each other as they went about their work.

Hannah asked Salim why there were so many little walled channels of water running throughout the villages. He told them it was part of the falaj system of irrigation, that the Omanis had devised to make the best use of their very limited water supply. "What kind of plants do they grow?" she enquired.

"Oh, mostly date palms, lime trees, and sometimes mulberries, pomegranates, bananas and water melons. And alfalfa for their goats." They passed sweet young girls calmly walking through the wadis, herding flocks of black long-haired goats. Once they saw a wizened old man carrying a rifle over his shoulder, walking alone across a vast plain dotted with gorse bushes. "What a life," said Hannah, watching him disappear. "The people here must be so hardy and tough."

Suddenly Rosie shouted, "Stop the car!" and Salim pulled over. Rosie jumped out and ran, clutching her camera, towards a small tree with dusty, faded green leaves. Salim looked puzzled; there was nothing to see. Rosie took a couple of photos and clambered back into the car.

"Why were you taking photos of that tree?" Salim asked.

Rosie smiled. "Look," she said, "it's a plastic bag tree."

"What do you mean?" he asked. He looked at the tree again and noticed three plastic bags, one pink and two blue, attached to the tree's thorny branches.

"I think it's quite funny, but it's also a bit sad, I mean, I've seen so many discarded plastic bags blowing around since I arrived here. People don't realize plastic is not biodegradable. Every single plastic bag ever created is still in existence. If the bags blow into the sea, the turtles will eat them, thinking they're jelly fish and then they'll die. Plastic bags block the drains and harm the wildlife. Even if we bury plastic in rubbish pits under the ground, it doesn't solve the problem, because that just poisons the earth. In some countries they've now put a tax on plastic bags, realizing that if people have to pay for bags, they soon learn to be more economical with them. Apparently, it's really cut down the number of plastic bags in circulation, and the money from bags that are sold is being used to fund other environmentally friendly projects."

Salim was silent. He could not understand the problem. He thought plastic bags were great. In the old days, they had only had clay containers and goat-skin bags which were smelly and difficult to keep clean.

They stopped for a picnic lunch on a beautiful deserted beach of soft white sand. Rosie lay down and turned her face to the warm sun, breathing in the fresh sea air. Rosie always enjoyed being in a natural environment. She relaxed, listening to the sound of the waves. But her happiness was not altogether due to her surroundings. Rosie had to admit to herself that she was acutely aware of Salim's presence. Hannah wandered off along the beach, collecting dozens of small pink shells with intricate patterns. Rosie opened her eyes and sat up as she heard the rustle of Salim's dishdasha. He sat down beside her and she could not deny the feeling of agitation caused by his close proximity. She inhaled his fragrance and smiled at him, suddenly feeling awkward and shy. Rosie could not help remembering another time, on another beach with another man. *Stuart.* Pangs of guilt made her turn away from Salim and move to stand up. Salim touched her arm. "Hey, don't run away. Where are you going?" he asked softly.

"Oh nowhere, I'm just... I... I just don't think we should be alone together and..."

"Why not?" he asked, wounded by her words. Then he added tenderly, "Rosie, I would never hurt you." He spoke with incredible passion and sincerity and Rosie immediately felt choked. *Why am I so uptight? Relax*, she told herself. "I know that," she replied simply.

"Then?"

Rosie searched for the right words and decided that honesty had to be the best policy. *Just tell him how you feel.* "Look, Salim, you're a very nice person and... and well, I know I'm deeply attracted to you—"

"So, what's the problem?" Salim interrupted, smiling and reaching out to stroke her long fair hair.

Rosie gazed into his dark eyes and felt herself falling into a mesmerized trance. She tossed her head quickly, to break the growing bond between them, blurting out, "Well, you see... I already have a boyfriend."

Salim's face clouded. Quickly recovering, he cocked his head on one side and answered, "It is not a surprise. You are a very beautiful woman."

Rosie blushed, deeply affected by his sentiments and feeling totally exposed. It felt as though he could see right into the very depths of her soul. He stroked her forearm gently and Rosie felt a wave of goosebumps rush through her entire body. She quickly looked down and drew circles in the sand with her finger, struggling to keep her emotions under control. *It would be so easy to...*

"Rosie," he said, his voice feigning an indifference he did not feel. "it's okay, you know, I do not expect anything. I just like to be with you. Is that wrong? Look at me, Rosie," he pleaded.

She lifted her head, her eyes brimming with tears. Salim searched her face earnestly.

"No, it's not wrong. I mean, I like to be with you too," she swallowed hard, "but it's just that well, our relationship cannot possibly go anywhere. Do you understand what I'm saying?"

Salim paused before nodding sadly, folding his arms. "Yes. I understand. We are too different. We come from different worlds."

"Yes, that's it. We're worlds apart," she said with relief, but was suddenly struck by the finality of the statement, wishing things could be different. She yearned for him, but knew it could never be.

"Salim, I'll always hold you in a very special place in my heart," she declared, her voice thick with emotion.

Salim nodded, taking her in his arms and holding her, while she quietly sobbed.

Hannah had walked further than she had intended. She turned and started walking back. She gasped when she saw the two of them standing together, locked in a lover's embrace. *Oh no,* she thought. *Rosie! Follow your head, you stupid girl!* Hannah strode back along the beach quickly, in some vain attempt to halt the blossoming of an ill-fated romance. Rosie pulled away from Salim and smoothed down her clothes, very aware of Hannah's beady eye, watching them closely. Rosie noted Hannah's expression; furrowed brow, lips pursed. Rosie shook her head. *Hannah has got it all wrong. There is nothing between us. Later I will explain to her that Salim and I have reached an understanding,* Rosie decided. Hannah tried to make light of the situation, sensing their obvious embarrassment and casually announcing that she was eager to arrive at the camp before nightfall. She walked straight past them, towards the car, climbed into the back seat, slammed the door and sat looking straight ahead of her, waiting for the two 'love birds' to join her.

The rest of the journey was spent in relative silence. They arrived in Ras Al Hadd in the late afternoon and the two friends left their belongings in one of the camping huts and went for a swim in the brief twilight. The sun's deep red and golden rays shone down on the wet sand at the water's edge. While Hannah and Rosie splashed each other and screamed with delight like overgrown kids, Salim sat and watched them, feeling somehow bereft. *How can you lose someone who has never belonged to you?* he thought. Deep in his heart he felt he had lost the one thing that had kept him going ever since he had met Rosie: *hope.* And he thought to himself *I will not give up hope so easily. Perhaps it is time for me to meet this man called Stuart.*

Later that night, by the soft silvery light of a full moon, a guide led the three friends down to the beach. They sat down on the cold sand and waited quietly, scanning the breaking waves until suddenly, their patience was rewarded; Salim clutched Rosie's shoulder and silently pointed to a dark shape breaking the white shoreline. Rosie watched enthralled, as a large greenback turtle lumbered slowly up the beach towards them. "Ask the guide to switch on the torch, I can't see properly," she asked Salim.

He shook his head and whispered, "No we must not shine the light, it will confuse the turtle. We must not disturb the process."

Rosie nodded. After some time, the turtle seemed to find just the right spot to lay her eggs in the sand. She slowly began to dig a deep hole, using her flippers. The guide beckoned for them to follow him without making a sound. They moved towards the back of the turtle's bold patterned shell and held their breath when the guide carefully shone the torch down into the hole. They peered over the edge and saw one white egg after the other softly plopping down into the nest. "Wow! How many eggs will she lay?" Rosie whispered, in awe. The guide talked quietly in Arabic and then Salim translated. "A turtle can lay up to 140 eggs in 30 minutes." The friends were showered with sand when the exhausted turtle began to cover the hole, to hide the eggs from view.

The mother turtle then hauled her 150kg bulk back into the dark sea and disappeared. The guide told them that Oman hosts between 6,000 to 13,000 greenback turtles a year, making it one of the major nesting grounds in the Indian Ocean.

Rosie felt deeply privileged to bear witness to this magical event. She scanned the beach for more signs of life. Huge craters had been dug all over the beach by visiting turtles. The guide told them that the turtles return to nest on the very same beach that they themselves were born on. The friends sat quietly on the beach until the first signs of daybreak appeared. Just then Hannah exclaimed, "Hey, look over there!" The guide nodded and the friends followed him. He stooped to pick something up from the sand and held it out in his hand for them to see. "Oh look, how sweet!" Hannah said. A cute baby turtle, no bigger than the guide's hand, lay wriggling its flippers. The girls fell in love with it and watched as the guide put it down gently on the sand again. "Now we have to keep watch for foxes, dogs and crabs. Many baby turtles never make it down to the sea because they are eaten by predators," the guide explained. The tiny turtle ran as fast as its little legs could carry it down the beach and hurled itself into the sea. It was immediately sent sprawling by a huge dark wave and then, less than one hour old, it simply turned and swam out alone, into the vast, turbulent ocean.

The girls ran around the beach with childlike delight, searching for baby turtles. Hannah found one eagerly digging its way out of its nest. She picked it up and stroked its small oval patterned shell. "Oh look, it's so cute. I wish I could take it home," she announced.

"Oh, Hannah, how could you think of doing that? It needs to be free, to swim in the sea. I hate to see animals in captivity," Rosie said.

"Oh I know that, I wouldn't really take it, I just like the idea of looking after it. I mean, it seems so helpless and defenceless, doesn't it?"

"Yeah, I know what you mean, but that's just nature. We mustn't interfere. Let's take it down to the water's edge and let it go."

Hannah held it gently in her clasped hands and kissed it lovingly before placing it on the wet sand. Its little flippers moved quickly across the beach until it met the water. Then it splayed its flippers, letting the water carry it away and swam vigorously towards the deep water.

"Ah, bless," Hannah said.

The next day Salim took the girls to visit an archaeological site where stone bead necklaces, dating back thousands of years, had been found, completely intact. An Italian archaeologist showed them the remains of settlements that they were excavating, including one up high on the cliffs overlooking the sea. "Imagine living here thousands of years ago," Rosie said. The Italian told them about Oman's fascinating history as a seafaring nation, trading in spices and frankincense with other ancient civilizations. Rosie clicked away happily with her camera and before she knew it, she had used up the entire memory card. Later, they walked down to the deserted beach, marvelling at the huge rollers. Being on the very tip of the Arabian Peninsular, the vast Indian Ocean waves crashed down onto the shore with a hugely powerful force. The two girls decided the waves were a bit more than they could handle, so they decided to relax and sunbathe while Salim wondered along the shore by himself.

Rosie followed his white moving silhouette, shading her eyes from the brilliant sunshine. Then she watched enthralled, as he slowly removed his dishdasha, revealing a slim and muscular body. He waded into the rough sea and lifted his strong arms up above his head, leaping forward and disappearing into the ocean's depths. Rosie smiled, waiting for him to surface. Minutes passed. She could not see him. *Where is he?* Rosie gradually became alarmed. She jumped up and ran down to the water's edge, scanning the ocean and shouting Salim's name at the top of her voice. She called out to Hannah who was exploring the rocks along the coastline. Still Salim did not appear, leaving Rosie no choice but to wade into the water, in a complete panic. She took a deep breath and dived in, disappearing beneath the waves. The foaming sea was murky with unsettled sand and Rosie could see nothing. She surfaced, gulping salt water and screamed, "Salim! Where are you?" Hannah came running down the beach to the water's edge, shouting for Rosie to come back. Rosie ignored her and ducked down again, her hair swirling around her face, as she desperately searched for Salim. Her lungs were bursting; she could no longer hold her breath. She pushed herself up and gasped for air, just as an enormous wave arched above her head and came crashing down on her. She was knocked sideways and carried towards the shore. Struggling to the surface, she was instantly drawn back under the murky sea by a massive undertow, which pulled her out to sea. Rosie moved her legs frantically, turning this way and that, unable to breathe.

Then suddenly, strong muscular arms came around her waist and lifted her, pulling her up and out of the water. She coughed and spluttered as Salim took her up in his arms and carried her towards the shore. He lay her down on the wet sand, breathing hard and dripping wet. Rosie opened her eyes and looked up at Salim's beautiful face. With enormous relief, she reached out and smoothed his dark, wet hair, drawing him towards her. They lay still without speaking, soaking wet, panting for breath, wrapped in each other's arms, relieved and totally exhilarated with the knowledge that they had finally found one another. They had rescued each other from a life devoid of passion.

Rosie whispered, "I thought I had lost you."

"I am sorry. It was nothing. I have learnt to hold my breath under the water—"

Rosie put her fingers on Salim's lips to silence him and said quietly, "Promise me you'll never leave me again."

Salim smiled down at her, his hairy chest still heaving from the exertion and replied, "I will never leave you, Rosie. I am yours forever." He kissed each of her fingers lovingly and Rosie lay back, closed her eyes and felt his warm breath on her face as his soft lips found hers.

Hannah looked on in horror. *Oh God, that's it*, she thought.

Chapter Twenty-Eight

Rosie could not concentrate on her lesson. Her mind kept wondering. Tonight she would meet with Stuart to tell him she was formally ending her relationship with him. *Poor Stuart.* She felt such affection for him and hated the idea of hurting him. But she knew she could no longer keep him hanging on, she must tell him now how she felt – before someone else did. She was dreading it. She knew how it would pan out: he would be incredulous to hear she had feelings for Salim. *A Bedu?* A man from a primitive tribe with no education, who had never travelled on a plane or even lived in a city. A man with a different culture, religion and language. Stuart would listen and then he would laugh. She could hear it already; a bitter, horrible laugh, full of hurt, anger and humiliation. How could she give up Stuart for a Bedu? Rosie sighed. It would not be easy to justify. She brought her thoughts back to the present and tried to concentrate on teaching the past perfect tense to a group of bank employees.

At 8 p.m. she was at home, waiting for Stuart to arrive. She paced the floor impatiently, repeating a speech in her head, wanting to get this difficult task over and done with. *Would he be angry?* Rosie had always been a little frightened of Stuart's temper. He could really fly off the handle and shout sometimes. She hated to be on the receiving end of his acerbic tongue. *I must stand my ground. I have to be honest about my feelings. I just don't love him anymore. I love someone else.* This knowledge sent her reeling; could she really make her life with a Bedouin tribesman? She went to look at the pine wall-clock in the hall: *8.30 p.m. It's not like Stuart to be late. Where is he?* The phone rang.

"Hello?"

"Hi, it's me," said Salim, shyly.

"Oh, hi," Rosie answered, feeling a warm heat rising up from the depths of her being, at the sound of his voice.

"How are you?"

"I'm fine," she glowed. "How are you?"

"Good."

The door bell rang and Rosie nearly dropped the phone.

"Look, Salim, can I ring you back in a while? Someone's at the door."

"Yes, fine. I will speak to you later then."

Rosie put the phone down and inhaled deeply, steeling herself to be strong. She opened the door. Stuart was standing there with a huge bunch of beautiful dark red roses. He was looking decidedly awkward. Rosie thanked him for the flowers but wished he had not brought them. It made her feel more guilty than ever about what she was about to do. She kissed him on both cheeks and invited him into the lounge. "I'll just put these in water," she said, escaping into the kitchen and putting them in the sink. *I'll find a vase later*. Instead, she poured two large glasses of red wine for them both, taking a quick gulp of her own drink, to give herself Dutch courage.

When she returned to the lounge, Stuart was standing with his arms behind his back, staring out of the window.

"There you go," she said handing him a glass.

"Thanks," he said, sipping his drink thoughtfully.

"Stuart," she said, taking the plunge, choosing her words carefully, "I know I've been a bit distant recently, but there's been a good reason for all that. Well now, I've invited you over here tonight because I want to—"

Stuart thought he knew what was coming. He raised his hand, interrupting, "No, no, please let me talk first, Rosie. I have something important to tell you."

Startled by this unexpected turn in the conversation, Rosie sat down and looked up at Stuart, watching him pace the floor, a vast torrent of words flowing from his mouth.

"Well, Rosie, you see, it's like this. You've been pretty distant lately, always on your guard, never allowing me to get close to you. I mean, we haven't seen much of each other, have we? Now, since we've had this breathing space, I understand that maybe you're thinking about us getting back together again, and I understand that, but well, quite frankly, I can't." He stopped and turned to look at her intently.

It took a moment for the words to sink in. *What is he saying*? "You can't?" she echoed.

Stuart stopped pacing and smoothed back his sandy coloured hair, leaving his hand on the back of his neck, staring at the rug. He swiftly crossed the room, sat down next to her and took her hand in his.

With great sympathy in his eyes he said, "Rosie, I don't know how to tell you this." His eyes began searching around the room, as if hoping to conjure up the words he needed from thin air.

"You don't know how to tell me what?" Rosie held her breath.

Stuart squirmed in his seat, clutching her hands. "Well, it's not that I don't love you, Rosie, because I do. You're a wonderful girl and I do love you, but it's just that now it's impossible for us to have a relationship because I... I've fallen in love with someone else."

Stuart closed his eyes tight as if expecting Rosie's world to fall apart, down around his ears. The silence was deafening. Rosie gaped, unable to string a sentence together. He opened his eyes and looked at her out of the corner of his eye.

"Rosie, are you alright? Please say something. I know you're upset and it's hard to take. But, please say you'll forgive me, say we'll still be friends. I know how you must be feeling, but I have to be honest with you. I didn't mean it to happen but, well, it just happened and..."

Rosie recovered her composure, controlling an overwhelming urge to burst out laughing. *I've been worrying all this time about hurting Stuart's feelings and all the time he has had someone else.* Rosie strove to hide her elation. This new information carried with it a new sense of freedom, allowing her to be herself and follow her heart, safe in the knowledge that she was not going to hurt anyone else. Rosie pushed the desire to giggle down with a deep breath and endeavoured to play the part of the wounded lover.

Rosie removed her hands from Stuart's sweaty palms and sat back in her seat, feigning disappointment. Then she leaned forward, pressing a finger and thumb into the skin either side of her nose, closing her eyes, as though deep in thought. Stuart took a large gulp of wine, bit his bottom lip, his eyes searching the floor.

"So, who is she?" Rosie asked quietly.

Stuart waved his arms around, trying to be casual, "Oh, no one you know. She's only just arrived—"

Rosie interrupted, "Oh, you didn't waste much time, did you?"

"Oh, Rosie, please don't be like that. I don't know, it was just love at first sight. I met her at a dinner party three weeks ago. Her name's Misha."

"Misha? Is she Russian?"

Stuart was beginning to feel exasperated by Rosie's line of questioning.

"No, of course she's not. She's English. Her mother just happened to like the name," he added lamely.

"Umm, it appears you do too," she replied with an icy tongue. *Don't take this too far. Give him a break,* she thought.

Rosie stood up and wandered aimlessly around the lounge. She opened the glass door and let herself out onto the terrace and stood, looking out to sea, her mind racing; *I can't wait to ring Salim.*

Stuart came up softly behind her, as he had done so many times before, but this time, his hands did not reach out to explore her body. He kept his distance, pleading for her forgiveness. She nodded her head without turning round.

"Rosie, please say you understand."

Rosie shrugged her shoulders. Her mind was running ahead to her rendezvous with Salim.

"I mean, I know we could have had a wonderful life together. It's just that sometimes, fate takes a hand in the proceedings. I didn't mean to fall in love with her, please believe me, Rosie, it just happened. Please say you understand, Rosie."

Rosie turned to look at her tormented ex-lover. She smiled magnanimously and replied, "It's okay, Stuart, I understand, honest I do."

Chapter Twenty-Nine

Three weeks later Rosie, Laura and Hannah walked from Rosie's apartment to the club in the nearby Grand Hyatt Hotel, to join Penny in celebrating her hen night. The wedding was set for the following Thursday night. Rosie and Hannah had spent the afternoon in the City Centre, trying on clothes and desperately searching for something special to wear to the wedding. Rosie had eventually chosen a slinky white halter neck dress and Hannah had found a pair of crimson silk trousers with a matching sequinned top. Laura had bought material to have a dress made up at the tailor's. Laura was describing the dress when Hannah interrupted her.

"But how are you ever going to get a dress made up before Thursday though?" she asked incredulous.

"Oh, in Muscat, it can be done. No problem!"

The conversation was halted as they entered the noisy, crowded bar in search of Penny. Several pairs of men's eyes watched them cross the room. The girls greeted a very radiant Penny with lots of hugs and kisses.

"Gosh, Penny, you look great! I like your hair, it really suits you like that," Hannah said, commenting on Penny's new short punk hairstyle with red streaks.

Penny introduced them to her two friends from work – Sarah, from Kent and Sharon, who was born in Southern Ireland, but had spent most of her life as an expatriate, living abroad.

"I've lived in fourteen houses in nine different countries in twenty-seven years!" she announced proudly.

Rosie wanted to know which country Sharon considered home.

"Well, home is really where I lay my head, I suppose. But I must admit, I do have a soft spot for Muscat. It's certainly one of the most friendliest, safest countries I've ever lived in."

Penny ordered a lime juice for herself and a big pitcher of pale green Margherita's for the girls and they chatted about the wedding, while slowly consuming the thick, icy liquid. Later, they danced to the latest sounds and Rosie weaved her way over to the MC and asked him to mention Penny's forthcoming wedding. Everyone cheered when he announced:

"This one is for Penny and Shabib, who are getting married this Thursday. Another one bites the dust!" he laughed.

Then, Gloria Gaynor's song; 'I will survive', came on and Rosie and Hannah dragged a very reluctant Penny, almost kicking and screaming, onto the dance floor. The girls strutted their stuff around the dance floor, miming to the words and laughing. At the end of the song, they collapsed in fits of giggles and returned to Sarah and Sharon, who were standing around a tall bar table, talking to a tall, blond-haired Scandinavian who introduced himself as an air traffic controller at Seeb International airport. The music was so loud, Rosie could hardly follow the conversation.

"Hey, has anyone seen Laura?" Rosie asked, puzzled by her absence.

"I think she went to the loo," Sharon answered, shouting over the noise.

"I'll go and find her," Rosie volunteered.

"Hold on, I'll come with you, I want to phone Dave and tell him to come down and join us," said Hannah, picking up her silver clutch bag and following Rosie out of the door.

"Hannah, you can't do that. This is supposed to be a ladies night," Rosie said.

"So?"

"Well, you can't invite Dave then, can you?"

Hannah grimaced. "Oh come on, I'm sure Penny won't mind."

Laura was sitting hunched over a small round black leather pouf in the ladies room, staring at her tear-streaked face in the mirror.

"Hey, Laura, what's wrong? Are you feeling ill?" Rosie asked, putting an arm around her and looking at her reflection in the mirror. Laura sniffed and shook her head.

"Come on, Laura, tell us what's wrong,." Hannah added with slight exasperation. Rosie glared at Hannah.

"Well, she can't stay in here all night, can she?" said Hannah, defending herself.

Rosie hoisted herself up onto the counter and sat, swinging her legs, waiting for Laura to reply.

"Have you had a row with Sam?" asked Hannah.

Laura shook her head.

"Well is it something to do with work, then?" Hannah probed, pressurizing her for an answer. Again, Laura shook her head.

"Well what is it, then?" Rosie asked softly.

Laura moaned and started crying again.

Hannah folded her arms and tapped her foot impatiently. "I think she's had too much to drink," she announced, talking to Rosie over Laura's head.

Laura looked appalled. She caught Rosie's eye.

"Hannah look, why don't you go back inside? Or go and ring Dave. There's no sense in us both staying here. I'll bring Laura along in a minute," she said, sensing that what Laura had to say was for her ears only.

Hannah cocked her head on one side, thinking. She wanted to find out what was bugging Laura. She hated to feel excluded and despised anyone who kept secrets from her. On the other hand, she was enjoying herself and she wanted to ring Dave and get him to come and dance with her. She wanted everyone to see that she had a boyfriend. Hannah shrugged her shoulders and turned to leave, without a word.

The loud pulsating music blared in as she opened the door and disappeared.

"Hey, Laura, tell me what's wrong," said Rosie, handing Laura some tissues.

Laura blew her nose noisily. "Sorry, Rosie. Maybe Hannah's right. Perhaps I have had too much to drink. Those margaritas are lethal!" she said, laughing through her tears. She stood up and splashed her face with cold water.

"Rosie, the truth is, I'm jealous as hell and it's killing me. I feel so miserable," she admitted.

"Jealous? Who on earth are you jealous of?" Rosie asked in surprise.

"Penny."

"What? Why, for goodness sake, are you jealous of Penny? I think she's in an awful situation."

"Do you? Well, that's where you and I disagree. I would love to be on the point of getting married and having a baby."

"Oh."

"But Sam won't hear of it. He doesn't want to get tied down and says he's too young to have kids."

"How old is he?"

"Thirty-three."

Rosie did not know what to say. Somehow she sympathized with Sam. Commitment scared the hell out of her, too. It occurred to her that perhaps Laura was with the wrong man. Did Sam really have an aversion to marriage in general or Laura in particular? She wondered if Sam even knew the answer himself. She bent down and looked Laura in the eye.

"Look Laura, there's plenty of time for marriage. You're still young and—"

"No, I'm not! I'm thirty-four and I can hear my biological clock ticking – loudly."

"Yes but, Laura, you mustn't pressurize Sam. It'll put him right off. Just wait and see. Things will work out if they're supposed to, just give it time," Rosie advised.

"But don't you see, Rosie, that's just exactly what I don't have. I don't have time to hang around with someone who's never going to commit. I can't waste my time. I mean, if he loves me, then what's the problem? But if he doesn't love me, then he should let me go, so I can search for someone else."

Rosie nodded.

"Have you told him that?"

"No."

"Then I think you should. Just tell him how you feel. See what he says."

Laura nodded tearfully and the two girls smiled at each other. Laura stood up and gave Rosie a hug. Then she carefully reapplied her lip gloss and the two girls returned to the club's dark, smoky atmosphere. The loud pulsating music vibrated inside their heads as they weaved their way through the crowd and pushed their way onto the dance floor. Forgetting all their inhibitions, the girls bopped wildly to Alice DJ's 'Castles In The Sky'. Just then Dave arrived and Rosie noticed Hannah dash across the room and throw her arms around him. Before long she saw them smooching together in the middle of the dance floor.

At the end of the evening Penny kissed them all and admitted she was suffering from pre-wedding nerves.

"You're not having second thoughts though, are you?" Laura asked inquisitively.

Penny shook her head and rubbed her stomach. She grinned at them and announced;

"No. This marriage is simply meant to be. It's just that I hate to be the centre of attention. You know what I mean; all eyes on me."

The girls nodded.

Chapter Thirty

Hannah put the finishing touches to her bedroom and consulted a mental checklist to ensure she had thought of everything her father might need during his stay: a hand and bath towel, a new pair of men's slippers (she had guessed the size), a radio, a few crime and adventure novels for some bedtime reading and a Men's Health magazine. She went into the kitchen and found a small silver ashtray in the back of the crockery cupboard, placing it carefully on the bedside table in her bedroom. She hoped he would not need it, knowing how much Rosie hated smokers lighting up in her flat. She always banished Hannah to the balcony whenever she needed a fag.

Hannah checked the time on her watch for the fifth time in as many minutes; nine o'clock. The BA flight was due to land at nine thirty. She hurried to the bathroom to check her makeup; bright, excited eyes met hers in the mirror. *I'm going to meet my father*, she said to herself, words that she never thought she would utter. She went into the living room.

"It's gone nine o'clock, Rosie, are you ready? It's time to go," she called.

Rosie emerged from her bedroom, wearing white shorts and a tee-shirt.

"Rosie! You can't go to the airport like that! Come on, hurry up! Get ready!"

Rosie frowned, her index finger lightly stroking her lips.

"Hannah," she paused, "I'm not coming."

"What?" Hannah was incredulous. "Why not?" she asked, with growing anger.

"Well," Rosie replied, searching for the right words, "I just think it's better for you to meet your dad on your own. I mean, it's a private, special moment for you both. I don't want to spoil it."

Hannah's chestnut brown curls bounced, as she shook her head, emphatically,

"Oh, Rosie, what nonsense! Don't be silly! You're my friend and I *want* you to be there, to share my big, special moment. Don't ever think you're in the way, Rosie," she said, giving Rosie a sympathetic smile. She took Rosie by the arm and guided her gently towards the bedroom. But Rosie stood her ground, refusing to budge.

"No, Hannah, I'm serious, I'm not coming."

Bitterness, like bile, rose up in Hannah's mouth, giving her a spiteful tongue.

"Okay, suit yourself!" she responded abruptly, wrenching her hand away from Rosie's arm and turning on her heel. She picked up the car keys, opened the front door and scowling at Rosie over her shoulder, she announced; "I'm really disappointed in you, Rosie. I thought you'd *want* to come with me." She paused and added, "Well, I hope you'll at least join us for a drink when we get back, that's if it's not too much trouble for you."

Rosie winced. *If looks could kill,* she thought.

Hannah slammed the door behind her. *Damn. Bang goes my early night*, thought Rosie. She yawned and looked at her watch and decided that she had just enough time to snooze for an hour before Hannah and her father returned. She felt extremely tired and lethargic these days. Everyone said it was due to the heat. She changed into her burgundy satin nightdress, brushed her hair, settled herself on the bed and started reading Bill Clinton's autobiography.

However, within minutes, Rosie's eyelids grew heavy and she fell into a fitful sleep, dreaming in vivid Technicolor. At first, the trees, the flowers and the people were all violet blue and they appeared to be bouncing up and down. Then without warning, she found herself descending into a tunnel, groping her way in the dark, tasting the fear of the unknown in her dry, parched mouth. Suddenly, she came out into brilliant sunshine and stood in a field of bright red poppies. She felt an indescribable feeling of happiness. But her dream did not end there; her circumstances continued to change with every beat of her heart. She was riding a bicycle. The heat was so intense that the handlebars were burning her hands. She rode in a carefree manner until she arrived at a crossroads, with a glorious red evening sky overhead. She spun around, looking in each direction, wondering which way to go. But before she could move, her bicycle was swallowed up by the melting hot tarmac under her feet. She gasped and looked down to see her legs sinking into a deep green, slimy swamp. Dense foliage sprung up all around her and she shivered in the cold damp air, wrapping a velvet cloak of sapphire blue around her bare shoulders. With every strenuous step forward, she felt in danger of being pulled down into a murky quagmire and entangled in dense underwater creepers.

Rosie heard herself screaming someone's name, but could not make out who she was appealing to. She struggled on, through the dark ominous landscape. A banging sound made her turn and all at once, she saw the smooth languid movement of a bulbous, scaly creature, stealthily gliding towards her through the swamp. She shrieked, her heart thumping hard in her chest. Battling against thick slime, she tried to run, but her legs were immersed in sticky, squelchy brown mud. The thumping of her heart rose to a crescendo and all at once Rosie woke with a start, sweating profusely and breathing hard. But the thumping continued: someone was banging on her bedroom door…

It was Hannah.

"Rosie! Rosie are you in there?" she shouted through the closed door.

Rosie sat up, running her hands over her face, feeling groggy and disorientated. She staggered to the door and leaned against it, her heart still beating fast. She spoke softly to Hannah on the other side of the door.

"Sorry, Hannah, I must have fallen asleep. I'll be with you in a minute or two."

"Okay, I'll get your drink ready, babe. D'you want red wine or a shot of vodka?"

"Oh, nothings thanks, I'll just have water."

"Water! No, come on Rosie you've got to have a proper drink with me and Dad. I'll get you some wine," said Hannah, determined to celebrate.

Rosie stumbled heavily into the bathroom and splashed her face with cold water. Her head felt so muzzy. She rubbed her temples with the towel and opened the pine wardrobe. Balancing on one wobbly leg she pulled on a pair of khaki crop trousers and a blue shirt. She peered at herself in the full length mirror. *Now, try to be polite and not judgmental*, she said to herself. Rosie opened the door, actively arranging a smile on her face, as she prepared to greet Hannah's long lost father.

When Rosie appeared, Hannah jumped up from the sofa, grinning from ear to ear.

"There you are! Rosie, come and meet me dad. Dad, this is Rosie, my best friend that I told you all about, and Rosie, this is me dad – Roger," Hannah said proudly.

Her father extended his hand, smiling awkwardly. Rosie stared at him. She rapidly recoiled in horror, an icy frost starting in the pit of her stomach. It spread upwards, freezing every internal organ in her body.

Hannah made an exasperated tutting sound with her tongue. "Rosie?" Hannah coaxed, glaring at her.

She was falling into a bottomless pit. Her body grew limp and her legs lost their strength. She lifted her arms up to shield her face, as she collapsed. She lay on her stomach, motionless, barely conscious, but acutely aware of Hannah's voice shouting.

"Rosie! Rosie! What's wrong? Look at me Rosie! Are you okay?"

Hannah turned Rosie over and tapped her on the cheek. Rosie slowly came round. She felt as if everything was happening in slow motion. Her jaw was slack and it seemed to take an enormous amount of energy just to close her gaping mouth. Rosie opened her eyes. She shook her head in disbelief. She found herself staring into the eyes of her attacker.

Chapter Thirty-One

Memories of that fateful day in Brighton, sharply outlined yet somehow indistinct, replayed in her mind. Now those same eyes stared down at her. Roger gave her a smile that failed to reach his eyes. Rosie struggled onto her elbows, moving backwards, away from her fear and Hannah's embarrassment. He bent over her, his arms reaching forward to help lift Rosie into a sitting position. Instinctively, Rosie lashed out, pushing him away with a tremendous animal force and grunting, "No!" from the depths of her being.

Thrown off balance, his stout, heavy body toppled backwards and he landed heavily on his buttocks, with a startled expression on his ugly face. Hannah looked from one to the other, in horror.

"Hey, Rosie! Chill out! What the hell did you do that for?" she asked angrily.

Rosie raised her hand to her mouth, suppressing the urge to vomit. She struggled to her feet and made a rush for the bathroom, mumbling her apologies. Totally mystified, Hannah watched Rosie stumble across the living room, her hand gripping her stomach as if she were doubled up in pain. Rosie ran into the bathroom and locked the door behind her.

Trust Rosie to ruin my special moment, I'll never forgive her for this, thought Hannah.

Rosie leaned her back against the bathroom door, her chest heaving and terror in her eyes. Powerful emotions competed for domination; she felt a naked fear for her own safety. But a strong, almost painful desire also rose in her mind. It was a desire to take revenge. A need to make this despicable man suffer and pay for the horror he had inflicted on her. Anxiety surfaced with her next breath; how could she tell Hannah that her father was a rapist? She would never believe her. But he couldn't be her father. It was too unbelievable. He had come to Muscat to find *her*. Rosie made a fist and bit into her white knuckles. *God help me!* Still recovering from shock, Rosie suffered a crisis of doubt. Perhaps she was mistaken. Should she really trust her instincts? Did her memory serve her correctly? *Maybe I'm suffering from paranoia. It's not him. It can't be.*

Rosie opened the door a crack and saw Hannah sitting with her legs curled up on the sofa, knocking back a large glass of red wine, as she chatted amiably to Roger. Hannah's hazel-green eyes were shining and bright. Roger was sitting opposite her, legs apart, with one ankle resting on his knee in a confident pose. Rosie noted his shabby appearance and disheveled hair. His heavy lidded eyes and crooked nose gave him the appearance of a sleazy nightclub bouncer. Whoever he was, he looked disgusting. He wore a continual smirk on his face, as if he had just told a particularly obscene joke.

Could he really be Hannah's father? If he was, then Rosie had nothing but sympathy for Hannah. She watched Roger calmly light a cigarette and toss the match away, over his shoulder. Rosie called out to Hannah in a wobbly voice, her body literally shaking from the shock, anger and fear.

"Hannah, could you come into my bedroom a minute, please?"

Hannah seemed dismissive, ignoring Rosie's request and disappearing into the kitchen. Soon she returned and handed her father a can of beer. Hannah dragged her feet reluctantly towards Rosie's room with a look of considerable annoyance. She continued a conversation with Roger, even as she walked away from him. He frowned and followed her movements with his eyes.

Hannah barged into Rosie's bedroom. "What's wrong with you? Are you ill?" she hissed.

Rosie shook her head.

"Then why can't you be civil? I'm not asking you to like my dad, but at least you could be polite to him, for God's sake," she said in a low rasping voice.

Rosie put her finger to her lips, "Ssh! He might hear you."

"Don't you ssh me! I don't care if my father hears what I have to say," Hannah responded, her voice rising angrily.

Rosie gripped Hannah's shoulders, her fingers digging into Hannah's pale green tee shirt. She looked Hannah in the eye. But Hannah lifted up her arms, in an attempt to break free from Rosie's grip.

"Listen, Hannah. I've got something to tell you," Rosie whispered urgently. She held onto Hannah, who continued to struggle and squirm.

"Look Hannah, you're not going to like what I have to say, but please hear me out and you've got to believe me. It's the God's honest truth, Hannah, I swear it on my life."

Hannah pushed Rosie's hands away and folded her arms.

"Well what is it, then?" she asked with an exasperated look on her face.

Rosie stood with her back to the door, wondering where to start. She decided there was no time to pussyfoot around, so she waded straight in with the naked truth.

"Hannah, this man Roger... who says he's your father."

"What's *that* supposed to mean? He *is* my father! Be careful, Rosie, you're treading on very slippery ground. What are you insinuating? I've just about had it with your snide remarks," said Hannah, turning away.

Rosie brought her face up close to Hannah's.

"You've got to listen to me. You could be in danger—"

Hannah interrupted, "Oh yes, I could be in danger, alright. In danger of losing my best friend, I reckon! Now, get out of my way," she barked, pushing past Rosie.

Rosie shook her head and moved suddenly to bar the door with her body.

"Hannah, there's no easy way to say this, but that man out there, in my living room," she said, keeping her voice low and pointing her thumb at the door behind her, "is the same man who attacked me in Brighton!" Her voice shook with emotion.

Hannah jumped back, as if she had received a blow to the face. Her mouth dropped open and she stared at Rosie, rooted to the spot, unable to speak. The silence was deafening. Rosie waited for a reaction. She came towards Hannah and reached out to put an arm around her shoulders. Immediately Hannah pushed her arm away roughly and through gritted teeth, she quietly replied, "Is this your idea of a joke? You are one sick person, Rosemary. I never thought you'd stoop this low. How dare you accuse my father of something so utterly despicable. You can't be serious. I think you're going mad, Rosie. My Dad would never do anything to hurt anyone—"

"Oh, and what makes you so sure of that? Admit it, Hannah, you know nothing about this guy."

"Shame on you, Rosie," Hannah interrupted, trying in vain to keep her voice low. She paced the room, rubbing her forehead, trying to think straight.

"First of all, Dad doesn't live anywhere near Brighton. He comes from Milton Keynes."

"People do travel around the country, Hannah. There are trains, cars, buses…"

"Alright, alright, don't be sarcastic. But I remember you telling me it was so dark on the night of the attack and you couldn't make a positive identification."

Hannah wagged her index finger at Rosie. "You're just guessing, putting two and two together and making six! Oh, Rosie, I hate you for trying to spoil everything for me. Now you've put this element of doubt in my mind, I won't be able to look him in the eye." Hannah could feel the tears pricking her eyes. *I'm not going to give Rosie the satisfaction of seeing me cry*, she thought.

There was a sudden knock at the door. The two girls jumped and looked towards the closed door. "Is everything alright in there?" Roger asked in a loud, flat voice.

Hannah called back, without taking her eyes off Rosie,

"Yes, sorry, Dad. We're okay. I won't be a minute, I'm just coming."

She pushed Rosie aside and turned the door handle. Rosie grabbed her forearm and swiftly eased herself in between Hannah and the white door.

"Hannah, I know what you think," she whispered, "but what possible motive could I have for lying to you about this? Look, just suppose I *am* telling you the truth. Don't you see? If he's an imposter, you could be in danger. But, even if he really *is* your dad, that doesn't change the fact that he's the man who attacked me. "

Hannah's shoulders drooped. She stepped back, turned and sat down on the bed, covering her face with her hands. It was all too much to take in. *How could Rosie be telling the truth? It was all lies*, she was sure of it. Rosie came towards her. But Hannah immediately rose, avoiding her, tossing her head and wiping away tears with the back of her hand. Hannah continually repeated the same words over and over again as she paced the room. *I don't believe it, it's a lie, it's all lies, it's a lie, I don't believe it.* In an instant she made up her mind and turned towards the door. Rosie jumped forward and thrust her leg out, barring the door with her foot. She pressed her body up against the door and turned the key in the lock.

"Get out of my way, Rosie," said Hannah, her voice cold and harsh. "You've had your say. I don't believe a word of it. You're out of your head. You need to see a shrink. Now get out of my way."

Rosie shook her head and replied firmly, "It's the truth, Hannah. Okay, whether you believe me or not, it's up to you, but I am *not* going to have *that man* staying in my home. You're big enough and silly enough to make up your own mind, but either way, I want him out of my flat right now," Rosie announced, folding her arms and standing her ground.

Hannah was startled. She looked slowly up at the ceiling, trying to take it all in. Then she put her hands on her hips and stared at Rosie.

"What are you saying, Rosie? Are you throwing us out?" She looked at her watch. "It's nearly twelve o'clock at night!" she announced angrily, her eyebrows knitting together.

"I don't care what the bloody time is. I'm not throwing *you* out, but you can't really expect me to sleep with a rapist in my house. He attacked me, for God's sake!"

Then it happened. An anger welled up in Hannah with such a force, that she was unable to control her actions. She let out a grunt and slapped Rosie hard on the cheek. Rosie gasped and impulsively grabbed Hannah's wrist, trying to twist her arm. Hannah cried out in pain. She yanked her arm free and her elbow inadvertently made contact with Rosie's nose. Rosie stumbled backwards, her hip and shoulder slamming against the door. Rosie brought her hand up slowly to her face, stunned by Hannah's outburst. Her nose was numb and her eyes were watering. A small thin line of crimson blood began to trickle down towards her upper lip. The girls stood looking at each other; arch enemies, poised to wound each other further.

Sudden loud, persistent banging reverberated around the room and both girls watched in horror, as the chrome door handle turned and the glossy white door began to shake and vibrate. A deep, flat voice called out, "Hannah, what's going on in there?

"Why've you locked the bloody door? Open up! D'you hear me? I said, open the f***ing door!"

Both girls stared in dismay at the door, locked in a dilemma.

"Just hold on, Dad, I'm coming!" Hannah said feebly. She bit her lip and turned to look at Rosie, confusion and guilt in her eyes. "Are you alright? Your nose is bleeding," Hannah said in a small voice, rushing over to the bedside table and plucking a tissue from the box. She held it out to Rosie, like some kind of white peace offering. Rosie snatched it out of her hand.

"Look, Rosie," she said, her voice quivering. "I'm really sorry I slapped you. I just lost it, okay? I can't believe what you're saying is true. But please, Rosie, don't throw us out in the middle of the night. Let's all get some rest and then I'll try to sort things out in the morning."

Rosie tasted blood on her upper lip. She was shocked with the sudden realization that the woman standing in front of her was a total stranger. She had no clue who she was or how she might react. She could no longer gauge her reactions. She listened to Hannah's apology. But was unable to gauge its sincerity. Was Hannah just trying to secure a bed for the night? Rosie started to argue, but then thought the better of it. A niggling doubt kept coming into her mind. *Maybe Hannah is right. Perhaps I am wrong.* She nodded silently. How could she throw them out into the night with nowhere to go? Surely she could put up with the situation until morning, as long as she kept her bedroom door locked.

Hannah acknowledged Rosie's submission and with a weak smile, she turned away, took a deep breath, wiped her face and unlocked the door. Roger stood menacingly just outside the door, his hands on his hips and an angry expression contorting his ugly features. He looked from one girl to the other.

"Hello, what have you two girls been plotting, then?" he asked, in a condescending tone. Rosie could hear his laboured breath and congested lungs as the stale air left his mouth and polluted the room.

Hannah replied quickly, "Oh nothing, Dad, it's just that Rosie has had a nose bleed, so she's going to bed now, aren't you?" she said, turning to Rosie with a challenging look in her eye.

"Yes, please excuse me," Rosie mumbled, holding the tissue over her nose. She closed the door quickly and heard Hannah and Roger move across the room. With shaking hands, Rosie quietly turned the key in the lock.

Hannah sat down on the sofa, swinging her legs. She started talking breezily about Muscat's various tourist attractions, speaking a little too quickly, her head reeling with Rosie's accusation as she rambled on about vibrant colours and pungent smells in the spice souq and ancient Portuguese forts. All the while, Hannah was watching Roger out of the corner of her eye and holding an inner dialogue with herself.

Is this man really my father? Could he be capable of such violence?

Somehow, Hannah began to feel extremely uncomfortable in his presence, pulling her skirt down over her knees, as he suddenly seemed to have developed a roving eye. *You're imagining things*, Hannah said to herself. Hannah feigned a yawn and said she was feeling tired, desperate now to have some time on her own, to think. Did Roger feel tired after his long journey? she enquired. Roger replied that on the contrary, he felt wide awake and thirsty. He rose from his chair and sauntered into the kitchen, helping himself to another can of beer from the fridge. Hannah followed him, alarmed at his bad manners. He slurped from the can while he searched the kitchen cupboards, leaving the doors hanging open. Eventually he pulled out a packet of nachos. He carelessly split open the packet, dropping several nachos on the kitchen floor without appearing to notice. Hannah took out the red plastic dustpan and brush from the cupboard under the sink and began sweeping up under his feet.

Roger sat down heavily on a kitchen chair and put his feet up on the pine table, munching the nachos loudly. Hannah watched him silently, trying to make excuses for his bad behaviour. She looked at him closely, searching his face for signs of familiarity. Did she look like him? She tried to remember an ancient photograph she had once seen of her mother and father in the early days of their relationship before she was born. Could this ugly man have really been her mother's lover?

"You must be hungry, Dad. Shall I make you something to eat? A sandwich or something?" she asked, half-heartedly, thinking of her mother's words.

He grimaced and shrugged his shoulders. "What have you got?" he asked.

"Sorry?"

He gave an exasperated tut and pointed his thumb at the fridge.

"Got any eggs? Sausages? You can make me a fry-up, if you like."

Hannah took a moment to respond. "Oh, okay. Yes, no problem."

Hannah moved around the kitchen, pulling out cooking utensils and food items from the fridge. While she was busy cooking, Roger roamed around the living room, carefully inspecting photographs and Rosie's collection of Arabian antique silver jewellery. Then Hannah called him into the kitchen.

Chapter Thirty-Two

Rosie could not bring herself to undress. It would make her feel too vulnerable. She lay on the bed with the sheets pulled up high under her chin, watching the shadows on the ceiling. She strained her ears to hear any movement from the living room. Eventually she dozed off, but at four thirty in the morning Rosie jumped and sat bolt upright in bed at the sound of the door handle turning and a soft knocking on her bedroom door. Sweating profusely, she leapt out of bed, grabbed her mobile phone and ran to the door, removing the key from the lock and wondering who she could ring for help.

Surely Roger would not be foolish enough to try anything?

She listened intently, over the sound of her beating heart. Then, she heard Hannah's small trembling voice call out: "Rosie, can you let me in please?"

"Are you alone?" Rosie asked coldly.

"Yes, Roger's asleep."

Rosie quietly unlocked the door and opened it a crack. Hannah pushed the door open with the palm of her hand and came inside. Rosie closed the door silently and locked it again. She turned to face Hannah but could only see her dim outline in the darkness. She moved carefully around the side of the bed and switched on the cream shaded bedside lamp. In the warm glow of light, she saw Hannah in her leopard print dressing gown moving towards the bed. She lay down like a small child, in a foetal position and put her thumb in her mouth. Rosie sat down beside her and rested her head on the pillows. Then, without a word Hannah sat up, turned to

Rosie and the two girls clung to each other, crying softly, both feeling their own personal pain.

"I couldn't sleep. Listen, Rosie, I'm really sorry I hit you," Hannah said, with remorse.

Rosie nodded.

"Rosie, what are we going to do?" Hannah whispered softly.

Rosie pulled away and shrugged. "It's not up to me. Only you can decide."

Hannah sighed and bit the inside of her mouth. "I don't know what to think. I mean, if he *is* my dad, then I can see why my mother left him. He's really crude, ignorant and selfish," her voice was harsh but a slight tremor betrayed her confusion.

"I thought you said *he* left *her*," Rosie answered.

"Yeah well, I always assumed that he did, but I don't really know, do I? I can't ask me mum, can I? She's dead. But I do remember her always saying 'good riddance' whenever I mentioned his name. I think she hated his guts. Me mum and I used to have awful rows when I was a teenager, cos I'd always be questioning her about him. She'd get really livid and never answer me. She'd just frown and say 'let sleeping dogs lie'."

Rosie sighed.

Hannah looked at Rosie with large round puppy dog eyes, "Look, Rosie, isn't there any way you could be mistaken? Please think carefully before you answer me. You know how incredibly important it is to me. Are you absolutely certain he's the same guy who attacked you?"

Rosie rubbed her forehead. "I don't think I'm mistaken, Hannah, I'm pretty sure it's him. I'm really sorry."

Hannah nodded and the two girls sat in silence.

Dawn was breaking, and Rosie stood up and pulled the curtains back. Pale daylight entered the room and Hannah's face turned a ghostly white. Rosie felt nauseous and disappeared into the bathroom. Hannah listened to the muezzin calling the faithful to prayer. She sighed, took a packet of Marlboro Lights from the pocket of her dressing gown and lit up, drawing deeply on the cigarette. A long white trail of smoke came out of her nostrils as she exhaled.

Rosie came back into the room and looked aghast. "Hannah!" she shouted, "what the hell d'you think you're doing smoking in my bedroom? You know I hate the smell of smoke. Go and put it out!" she ordered angrily, amazed at Hannah's lack of sensitivity. Hannah rolled her eyes at Rosie, wearily stood up and dragged her feet to the door, unlocking it with one hand, while holding her cigarette upright in the other, to avoid dropping ash on the carpet. She was startled to find Roger's massively wide figure standing just outside the door. His arms were folded as he stood blocking her path, a blank expression on his ugly face.

"You're up early," Roger commented.

Hannah tried to read his expression.

"Yeah... um... good morning, Dad. Well we were just planning what to do today. Excuse me, I've got to find an ashtray," Hannah stuttered, casting an anxious glance at Rosie, before squeezing past him and rushing into the kitchen, cupping her hand under the cigarette to catch the falling ash.

Roger did not move. He leered at Rosie. She met his gaze defiantly. Then, his eyes flickered and darted around the room, taking everything in. Rosie coughed nervously and went to close the door, but he put his foot out to stop her.

"How'd you get a nose bleed, then?" he asked, staring at her intently.

"What? Oh, sometimes it happens for no apparent reason," she stammered, unnerved by his stare. She felt shivers running down her spine. She slammed the door in his face and locked the door, breathing hard. *I am not mistaken. I am sure it is him.*

She walked into the bathroom to inspect her nose in the mirror. It was swollen, with a faint greenish tinge of bruising around it. She splashed her face with cold water, but felt unable to remove her clothes and take a shower. *Get a grip, Rosie*, she said to herself, imagining the shower scene from *Psycho*.

When Rosie eventually emerged from the bathroom, she changed quickly into jeans and a tee shirt. She listened at the door, heard nothing, then unlocked it and peered out. There was no sign of Hannah or her father. She walked cautiously into the living room and wandered into the kitchen to make some coffee. She found a note on the kitchen table:

Dear Rosie,
We've gone out to look for alternative accommodation.
I'll give you a ring later.
Hugs, Hannah x

Good, she thought. Rosie crumpled the paper and threw it in the bin. Holding her steaming coffee cup in both hands, Rosie walked purposefully towards Hannah's room and opened the door carefully, half expecting Roger to jump out from behind the door. The room was in an almighty mess. Even though her nose was still numb and swollen, a foul smell of stale alcohol and smoke met her nostrils. She retched. A cheap fake leather suitcase lay open on the floor. Clothes were scattered around the room, draped over the backs of chairs and on the unmade bed. She shuddered at the thought of him sleeping between her sheets. *I'll burn those sheets when he's gone*, she thought. A red and white carton of two hundred cigarettes had been torn open and some cigarette packets were strewn all over the floor, together with odd socks and shoes. A half empty bottle of whisky sat on the bedside table with a dirty glass beside it. Her eye was drawn to the chest of drawers, two of which were half open with clothes hanging out of them. A dirty coffee cup, a half eaten biscuit, a set of keys, an airline ticket and a passport lay on top of the chest. She picked up the red document and inspected it:

David Roger Bains, born 16th February 1962.
Next of kin: Sheila Bains, sister, from Saltdean, East Sussex.

David! Saltdean! That's near Brighton! Questions raced through her head. *His name is David. He must be an imposter,* she thought. *But if so, then how did he get Hannah's number? Correction: **my** number.* This was really freaking her out. She turned things over in her mind. *His second name is Roger. He could be Hannah's father. Poor Hannah. How will she ever cope with the knowledge of her father's true nature? Will she reject him or forgive him? One thing is for certain: **I** will never forgive him.* She shuddered.

Rosie went back into the living room and sat on the sofa, drinking her coffee. Her hands were still shaking. Painful memories played over and over in her mind. She saw Roger's eyes; so empty, so full of hatred and anger. She sipped her coffee, trying to calm her nerves and stop shivering. One thing she knew without a doubt; while Roger or David, or whatever his name was, remained in Muscat, she would not feel safe.

She thought of her own loving parents and felt extremely grateful to them. Prisons were full of people who had suffered childhood deprivation. Not that she felt this excused anti-social behaviour, but she could understand how some people tried to block out painful childhood memories with drink and drugs. She wondered what traumatic childhood experiences Roger had suffered. Something must have created his desire to dominate women. His own mother might hold the key to his anger and hatred. Why is it parents get so little training, advice and support for this, the most difficult and important of all tasks?

Her thoughts were interrupted by a phone call. It was Salim. As they spoke, Rosie was overcome with a great need to see him, to pour out her heart to him. She knew she could be totally honest with him and was convinced he would not judge her. She wondered why she had been unable to confide in Stuart. Then she knew. He would have probed, wanting to know all the gory details. He would have been angry, unforgiving and unable to forget. Now Rosie needed Salim's love and protection. She interrupted him, blurting out; "Salim, I really need to see you."

"Mmm, me too. When can we meet?" he asked.

"How about right now?"

"Now?" he answered with surprise.

They both laughed.

Then with a note of seriousness in her voice, Rosie said, "I know it's a lot to ask, Salim, but I have something I really need to discuss with you. Someone is here and I am scared... I..."

"You are scared? Why are you scared? What has happened?"

"Oh, I can't explain now, I'll tell you when I see you."

Salim was silent.

"Salim? Are you there? I can't hear you."

The phone went dead. Rosie anxiously called his number again. It was engaged. She hung up and waited. The phone rang and she pressed it to her ear, desperate to hear his voice once more. "Salim?"

"Yes, I am here. Okay, Rosie I am coming to you. I will ask my brother to do the work for me. I will come, but it will take me two hours to get there, I am still in the desert."

Rosie sighed with relief. "Oh, that's fine, I'll make us some lunch."

"No, please, I will take you out for lunch," he replied.

Rosie grinned and decided this was going to be a good day after all.

Chapter Thirty-Three

Rosie hurried into the bedroom and opened her wardrobe, wandering what to wear. She chose a pale blue shimmering Thai silk dress that she had had made in Ruwi. She hung the dress on the door handle and went to take a shower and shampoo her hair. Looking in the bathroom mirror was depressing. A bluish green bruise had started to appear around her nose. She sighed and hoped that she would be able to cover it up with make-up. After her shower, she smothered her body in rose scented moisturizing lotion and decided to reinvent herself. She parted her wet hair on the side instead of the middle and blow-dried her hair straight. Then she applied a new grey eye shadow with a silvery sheen. She turned on the FM radio and listened to the latest sounds, while she carefully manicured her toe and finger nails and applied some nail varnish. The tension she had felt earlier, was soon replaced by butterflies in her stomach; she was almost weak at the knees at the thought of seeing Salim again.

She stood in her white lacy bra and panties, blowing on her nails, humming to herself and wondering where they would go for lunch. She reached for her blue dress and lifted it over her head, when something made her stop and listen. "Hannah?" she called. She pulled her dress down over her hips and went into the living room. It was empty.

"Hannah, is that you?" she called.

There was no answer.

Get a grip Rosie, you're imagining things. Chill out! she said to herself. *Salim will be here soon.* She began to sing along to the radio. The DJ was playing an old Geri Halliwell number; 'It's raining men'. Rosie moved her hips and soon found herself dancing around the bedroom, singing along with the music. When the song ended, she walked over to her pine-framed mirror, feeling flushed and out of breath. She put her hands up behind her back to finish zipping up her dress.

Suddenly Roger's cold and vacant eyes were staring at her in the mirror. She gasped.

She did not turn quickly enough. Roger grabbed her hands and held them there, up behind her back. Rosie swallowed hard as she saw a flash of steel and felt the cold edge of a knife's blade against her throat. *Oh my God!*

He leered at her reflection in the mirror.

"Hello, Rosie, are you feeling better now?" he asked, feigning concern. "I like the way you dance. Do you do the same thing lying down? Only if I'm not mistaken, we have some unfinished business to attend to."

Rosie screamed and struggled to release her hands, but he held them fast and she felt the sharp point of the blade digging into her throat.

"Now, now, be a good girl and you won't get hurt."

"Let go of me! You vile b*****d! Leave me alone!" she screamed. "Where's Hannah?" she demanded.

"Now, don't you go worrying about Hannah," he said with a sick smile.

Rosie took a sharp intake of breath. "Why? Where is she? What have you done with her?"

Roger only laughed, keeping the point of the knife poised at her throat. Placing mounting pressure on her arms, he pulled her towards the bed and pushed her down onto the quilt. Rosie could hardly breathe, but she felt a flash of anger flare up inside her. She shouted, "You'll never get away with this. Leave me alone! Get out of here now or I'll call the police." She brought her knees up to her chest and pushed him away with her feet.

Roger jumped out of the way, "Oh? Are you threatening me? I'm so scared! Do you know, you're very attractive when you're angry?" Roger answered with a smirk.

"Shut up! Get away from me!" Rosie cried, her legs flailing about in the air. She tried to kick him in the groin, but again he darted out of the way, avoiding her kick and reacting angrily. He swore at her and shoved her back down onto the bed. Then he started to stroke her leg with the cool point of his sharp knife. Rosie cried out and felt a wave of nausea and fear consuming her. She dared not move a muscle, but was unable to control her trembling body. She looked on in horror, as if the whole traumatic experience were happening to someone else.

The door bell rang. Roger frowned. "Are you expecting company?" he asked, suddenly pointing the knife at her stomach.

"No. I mean yes, it'll be my boyfriend," she croaked.

"Oh, your boyfriend, eh? I've seen you two together, canoodling on the beach," he said with disgust.

At first Rosie failed to grasp what this implied, but then the revelation hit her; if there had been any doubt about his true identity, he had now dispelled it. This evil man had been stalking her even before the attack in Brighton. Rosie shivered in fear and revulsion. The bell rang urgently again and she heard Salim call out.

"Hi, Rosie, it's me, let me in."

Roger put his hand over Rosie's mouth, pinning her to the bed, his bulging eyes staring towards the front door, the knife poised in his hand above her head. In utter panic, Rosie pulled at his arm with both hands, struggling to remove his hand from her mouth. She gagged as he moved his hand slowly down, pushing his fingers and thumb into the soft white skin of her neck. He squeezed and Rosie's limbs flailed about helplessly, writhing in agony as she started to choke.

Salim was puzzled. He had driven a long way to see her. She had asked him to come. So where had she gone? Had she forgotten that they had a date for lunch? Perhaps she was intending to cook for them both and had just gone to the shops to buy some food. He yawned and stretched. He had been sitting in the car all morning and felt stiff. He sunk down to the floor in a squat, determined to wait for her return. He closed his eyes and leaned his head on the warm white wall behind him.

It was then that he heard the distinct sound of a muffled cry. He jumped up and rattled the door handle.

"Hey, Rosie! Are you in there? What's going on? Open up!" he shouted.

There was no answer. His instincts told him there was something seriously wrong. He ran his fingers along the door frame looking for a way in. He rummaged in his pocket and took out a small Swiss army knife. Flicking open the knife, he knelt down and looked through the key hole. He could see nothing. He pushed the blade into the hole and heard it connect with the silver key in the dark space. Then Salim let out a soft cry of exasperation as he heard a dull thud. The key in the lock had fallen onto the floor on the other side of the door. He turned the door handle again and shouted; "Rosie, are you there? What is wrong? Please open the door!"

There was no answer.

He had to find a way to get in. He put his shoulder to the door and pushed hard. Nothing happened. He took a run at the door, putting his full weight behind it. It did not budge. Changing tactics, Salim strode down the corridor and pushed open the double doors which led to a stone staircase. His soft white dishdasha rustled and billowed out as he raced up the stairs two at a time. He reached the fire door at the top of the flight of stairs which led out onto the flat roof of the building, his nostrils flaring, panting for breath. The thick white fire door was bolted and stiff.

"*La!*" (No!) Salim cursed in anger, pulling at the bolt with all his might. He turned swiftly and ran all the way back down the stairs to the ground floor.

As Salim's sandals clattered down the stairs, Hannah was going up in the lift, completely oblivious to his presence in the building. She had other things on her mind. She was fed up. Her father was so exasperating. While she had been running around all morning looking at apartments and checking on hotel rates, Roger had been drinking coffee in Starbucks. He had refused to accompany her on her quest to find alternative accommodation, saying, with a smirk, that he was on holiday and preferred to sit and watch the pretty girls go by. He would agree to whatever plans she made. *How convenient*, she thought. *Men! They're so bloody selfish.*

Hannah bit the inside of her mouth. She was worried. Her father did not appear to have any money and she realized he was going to be a huge financial burden on her. How could she possibly afford to pay for them both to stay in a hotel for two weeks? Even renting an apartment was fraught with difficulties. She apparently needed to produce a photocopy of her visa and find a large refundable deposit. She wondered if Rosie would lend her the money. Who else could she ask? She thought of ringing Dave, but he was still in Germany on a business trip and would not be back for three more days. In any case she had had an argument with him before he left. He had broken his promise to her. He had said that she would be able to drive the Porsche in his absence, but just before he left he had deliberately put the car in the garage for a service. *Men are so unreliable.*

I suppose I could ask Stuart, she thought. Even though Rosie had broken up with him, Hannah felt she knew how to sweet-talk him. He had always been really nice to her. She quietly let herself into the flat, wondering how she could ask Rosie for the money. If Rosie would not lend her the money, then she would work on persuading Rosie to let them stay on. *It's only for two weeks, for God's sake. Rosie was being so unreasonable.* Hannah heard voices coming from Rosie's bedroom.

Um, she thought, *who's she got in her bedroom? Stuart?* But then Hannah remembered; Stuart had gone to Dubai with his new girlfriend Misha. Who else could it be? It had to be Salim. Hannah walked into the kitchen feeling envious. She imagined Rosie and Salim kissing. *It's not fair*, she thought. *Men just seemed to drool and dote on Rosie, whereas I always have to work so damned hard to keep a man interested.* She felt tearful thinking of all the men who had walked out on her. *What's wrong with me? Why does Rosie seem to have all the luck?* Somehow, having Dave as a boyfriend was of little consolation.

She pressed the button on the kettle, desperate for a cup of coffee. She wondered how many cups her father had drunk in her absence and hoped he would not get lost finding his way back to the flat. She had given him the address and told him to hail one of the orange and white taxis if he felt too tired to walk home along the beach. As a peace offering, Hannah made three cups of coffee and put them on a tray with a plate of biscuits. She realized she would have to be super kind and nice to Rosie in order to persuade her to let them stay on. She knocked softly on Rosie's door and called out; "Hi, Rosie, I've made you two some coffee. Shall I bring it in?"

She heard movements and then silence.

"Oh alright, suit yourselves. I'll leave it out here on the dining room table, if you're too *busy doing other things,"* she said meaningfully. She turned to put the tray on the table. The next moment the bedroom door creaked opened revealing a sight that made Hannah's blood run cold. She gasped, momentarily losing her balance and the contents of the tray in her hands slid slowly sideways, splashing boiling hot brown coffee down over the edge of the tray. Dark brown spots appeared at random on the floor.

Rosie was standing in front of her, her body rigid with fear. The glinting point of a knife's blade was poking into her throat. Hannah blinked. She could not believe it. Her father was holding the knife at Rosie's throat with a sick smile on his face. He was smirking. He kept his eyes on Hannah whilst he clutched a handful of Rosie's hair in his fist and pulled her head back sharply. Rosie howled.

Hannah's voice trembled with fear. "Dad!" she whispered, "What the hell d'you think you're doing?" Then, with her voice gaining volume, she shouted, "Stop it, Dad! Let go of Rosie right now or else I'll—"

Roger interrupted her, his dark bushy eyebrows knitting together angrily. "Or else you'll what? Are you blind? I don't know if you've noticed but *I'm* the one holding the knife. I'll call the tunes here today, if you don't mind and you'd better not try anything, otherwise I'll slit her throat!"

Hannah swallowed hard. She was close enough to see beads of sweat on Rose's forehead. Hannah searched her father's face. She could smell a faint reek of alcohol. She tried to placate her father with calming words.

"Look, I don't know what's got into you, Dad, but come on, put the knife down. Let's talk about this like civilized people," she said slowly leaning forward to put the tray down on the table, her eyes trained on Roger, aware that she must not make any sudden movements. She stepped sideways slowly, forcing Roger to continuously turn with Rosie, in order to keep Hannah in front of him. He was becoming increasingly agitated. Suddenly, he put his arm around Rosie's waist and his knee between her legs, hoisting her up and lifting her feet off the ground with the knife still trained on her throat. Rosie wailed in desperation as she was pulled this way and that.

"Dad, you're hurting Rosie! Please just put the knife down!" cried Hannah, her breathing uneven and her voice rasping.

Hannah's eyes narrowed, "Stop this nonsense, right now!" she shouted, stepping forward in anger.

"Hannah, please! Be careful!" Rosie muttered in a strained voice.

"Shut up! Who asked you to talk?" Roger shouted, pulling Rosie's hair.

"Ouch!"

He waved the knife at Hannah and told her to move towards the broom cupboard. Hannah shook her head. "I'm not going anywhere. Now put the knife down before someone gets hurt, this has gone far enough," she said quietly, standing her ground.

Roger responded by digging the point of the knife deeper into Rosie's throat.

Hannah gasped in horror. She put the palm of her hand up in the air, in surrender.

"Okay! Don't! Please don't hurt her, Dad," she pleaded, slowly stumbling backwards, keeping her eyes on Rosie. Roger pushed his victim forward with a fist pressed into the small of her back. When Hannah reached the cupboard door, Roger barked at her to remove the key. Hannah turned and took the key out of the lock with shaking fingers. She held it up, her green eyes wide with alarm and naked fear.

"Take it!" Roger said to Rosie, pushing her forward.

"Now, bye bye, Hannah, get inside, there's a good girl."

"Now look Dad, I say we—"

Roger shook his head and barked, "I'm not interested in what you have to say, you've said enough. So, daughter, do as daddy says. Get inside and close the bloody door!"

Hannah responded angrily, "I'm *not* your daughter! You are one despicable sick individual and I wish I'd never set eyes on you!" she screamed with venom.

"Shut up, you bitch!" he shouted, giving Hannah a shove with his free hand.

Hannah fell backwards and caught hold of the door frame with her hands. Shaking like a leaf, she bit into the skin on her thumb, desperately trying to control her anger and wondering how she could diffuse the situation.

"Do as he says, Hannah, please!" implored Rosie, weakly.

Hannah stared pitifully at Rosie, willing her to be strong. Unable to see an alternative, Hannah nodded and reluctantly stepped back inside the cupboard. She closed the door in front of her and stood still, in total darkness. With fumbling hands, Rosie was forced to lock the door.

"Now, gimme the key!" Roger shouted, taking the key and putting it into his trouser pocket. Rosie could feel Roger's body relax slightly.

"Alright, that's taken care of. I'll deal with her later."

Guiding her from behind, Roger and Rosie moved like some ungainly four-legged creature towards the bedroom. Rosie struggled, kicked, leaned backwards and dragged her feet, in a desperate effort to delay the awful and inevitable fate awaiting her. She screamed from the depths of her being. "No! no! Please, let go! Ouch! You're hurting me!"

"Keep still!" Roger instructed, but Rosie was becoming hysterical and could not stop screaming and shaking involuntarily. He yanked her back and suddenly she gave a strangled cry as the knife's blade slowly drew blood from the taut white skin around her throat.

"Rosie! Rosie! Are you alright? Answer me!" Hannah screamed from behind the door, repeatedly turning the handle and pounding on the door with clenched fists.

"Let me out of here, you bastard! I'll kill you if you lay a finger on her!" she screamed, realizing that Rosie was in mortal danger.

Chapter Thirty-Four

Roger pushed her down on the bed and she lay still and terrified, aware that warm blood was seeping from her throat, forming a bright crimson blot on the quilt cover.

I must get up, I must fight, she said feebly to herself. She was on the point of passing out. Somewhere in the distance she could hear Hannah shouting and banging on the door. Roger was leaning over her. With her last ounce of strength, she brought her leg up and attempted to kick him hard in the groin. This time, she managed to make contact and he let out a wail and bent over, bringing his hands up to the affected area, but still clutching the knife in one hand. She quickly dug her weak and shaking hands into the bed's soft mattress and in a second, she managed to push herself up and off the bed. She ran towards the door, with Roger in hot pursuit.

Rosie screamed, "Help me! Oh God, please, somebody help me!"

Roger lashed out and grabbed at the neckline at the back of Rosie's blue dress. She heard a ripping sound. She continued to run, but with her assailant holding onto her dress, she was unable to maintain the pace and her feet were soon pounding the same spot of the colourful kilim beneath her feet. Roger grabbed her arm and twisted it up behind her back, cursing her. Rosie yelled out in agony. He grasped Rosie's shoulders and pushed her hard and she staggered forwards, the side of her body up slamming against the rough cream-coloured wall. She let out an agonized cry as Roger grabbed her shoulders and turned her towards him. He pressed his body up against hers and she could feel his rapid breath blowing onto her chest.

And then, for the second time in less than twelve hours, Rosie received a rough, sharp slap across the face. Rosie's head spun. She looked down through the black spots playing before her eyes and could see a growing bright red stain spreading across the front of her blue dress. Faint and dizzy, Rosie's legs buckled under her and she sank down towards the ground. But Roger yanked her up by the arm, shouting, "Get up, you bitch!" in a harsh and vicious voice. Hardly conscious, Rosie was panic stricken by his seething anger. She could hear him breathing hard, trying to recover from the exertion of the chase.

"So, you think you can run away from me, do you? Well, I've got news for you, little girl. There's nowhere to run, see? So you'd better lie still and be quiet now!" he muttered in a low hiss. He dragged her over to the bed, pulling her by her long fair hair to ensure her compliance.

"Please, please don't! Ouch! You're hurting me!" Rosie cried, lifting her hands up to protect her head. But Roger pushed her onto the bed and began bearing down on her. Rosie could only hit out with her fists, sustaining multiple cuts on her hands and arms from the sharp blade held in her assailant's hand. Blood splattered in all directions.

"What's happening? Open the f****ing door, you bastard!" Hannah screamed in a hoarse voice.

"Get away from me! Leave me alone!" squealed Rosie in fear.

Suddenly there was a loud crash. The knife came down, spearing the quilt and missing Rosie's shoulder by inches. With the full force of his body, Roger fell forwards, right down on top of her. She screamed uncontrollably, thinking that the worst was about to happen.

But Roger lay still and Rosie gradually realized that there was another voice shouting in unison with her own. All at once, Salim came into sharp focus, towering above her, holding the remains of a large, brown shattered clay pot in his hands. Salim stood motionless and petrified, a look of horror on his face. He stared at the man lying in front of him, unable to absorb the reality. In slow motion Salim brought his arms down and released the remaining shards of heavy pot from his grip. They smashed down onto the floor and Salim dropped to his knees, shouting and sobbing, his face turned upward, beseeching Allah's forgiveness.

Rosie could not move. She was pinned down by the enormous dead weight of Roger's body. Whispering "Oh God! Oh God! Salim help me!" she strained to extract herself from under Roger's heavy body.

Salim scrambled to his feet again and lifted Roger's heavy body onto his side. Rosie eased herself out from underneath and rose on shaky legs. She embraced Salim, sobbing and shuddering with shock. He clung to her, tears streaming down his face. They both turned and stared at Roger's lifeless form, lying face down on Rosie's bed. There was a bloody gash on the back of his balding head and the huge swelling surrounding it. Shaking, Rosie leant down and gingerly pressed three fingers into Roger's livid red neck, checking for a pulse. Salim looked at her. Rosie shook her head.

Roger was dead.

Rosie's face crumpled. She moaned softly, putting her hand over her mouth, a morbid fascination making it impossible for her to look away from the corpse slumped on the bed. Roger's lifeless arms hung heavily over the edge of the mattress. Rosie moved her hand down from her mouth to her throat. It quickly became covered in thick, warm blood.

"Oh, Rosie, you are hurt!" Salim yelled, looking in disbelief at the blood pouring from Rosie's throat. The ceramic shards of the clay pot rocked and scrunched noisily under his sandals as he ran for a box of tissues to stem the flow of blood from Rosie's wound. He carefully folded a white Kleenex with shaky fingers and pressed it into her throat.

"Rosie! What's happening?" screamed Hannah with a note of utter desperation in her voice.

"Quick Salim, help me find the key to the cupboard, Hannah is locked inside."

Trying not to vomit, they gingerly rifled through Roger's trouser pockets. Rosie trembled and an icy cold feeling gathered in the pit of her stomach when her hand brushed against Roger's lifeless leg. She quickly pulled the long silver key from his pocket and handed it to Salim. Staggering over to the broom cupboard, Salim unlocked the door and Hannah almost fell out, sweating and breathing hard. She stared at Salim.

"Oh, my God, what's happened?" she yelled in alarm, running past Rosie and into the bedroom. Rosie stood at the door, whimpering in a weak voice.

"He's dead, Hannah! He's dead! I'm so sorry, Hannah. Roger is dead. Oh my God, what have we done?"

Hannah screamed from the top of her voice. "No!" She fell on her father's dead body wailing and gnashing her teeth.

"Daddy! Oh no, Daddy! What have they done to you?" she sobbed.

Rosie clung onto the door handle feeling light-headed. Salim rushed over and picked her up, carrying her over to the sofa. She was weak with shock and the loss of blood. He put her feet up and a pillow under her head. He knelt beside her, his face full of concern. Soon, the blood flow began to slow.

Hannah sat on the bed, cradling her father's head in her lap and rocking to and fro with a dazed expression on her face. Salim looked Hannah in the eye and stated simply; "I have killed him. I had to, Hannah. I had to stop him." He began to gabble hysterically in Arabic, his body shaking uncontrollably.

Hannah nodded, unable to say or do anything. Then without emotion, she announced, "You... you've *killed* my father."

The accusation seemed to gather force within her mind and an explosion erupted inside her. She pushed Roger's body aside and rushed at Salim, screaming and banging her fists against his chest. He put his head down and his arms up to shield his body, unable to stop the onslaught.

"You killed him! You will burn in hell for this!" she screamed, hitting out at him.

Then Salim firmly took control, grabbing hold of her hands and bringing them down to her sides, shouting, "Please Hannah! Calm down, please stop! I had to stop him. I did not mean to kill him. It was an accident."

Hannah glowered, making no attempt to conceal her contempt. "An accident? No Salim, don't give me that, you *meant* to kill him. It was no accident! You and Rosie conspired together, she couldn't bear to see me happy, you deliberately killed my father!" she shouted. Then Hannah gave Salim a massive push and he staggered back out of the door. She promptly slammed the door in his face. Salim stood still, but the room continued to turn.

But Hannah's anger soon dissipated. She slumped to her knees and cried pitifully. Salim listened at the door and knocked gently. "Hannah, I had no choice. I had to stop him. I go to call police now."

"The police?" Hannah cried with alarm, opening the door immediately and changing the tone of her voice," I... I don't think we should call the police, Salim. I mean, not just yet, you must give me some time. I have to sit quietly with my... father and... mourn." Hannah announced.

"Hannah, I do not think we should wait. We have to call police now."

Hannah nodded silently, moving back into the bedroom and sinking down to the floor. She rocked to and fro and began emitting a deafeningly high-pitched wailing sound.

"I call the police," Salim said flatly.

Hannah stopped wailing. "No! I mean, yes, I realize we have to, but... can't you just give me a little time? I need to be alone with… with my… dad." Hannah said tearfully. She rummaged in her pocket and pulled out a packet of cigarettes. She lit up. The flame wavered; her hand shaking violently. Salim nodded silently.

"Okay, Hannah but only ten minutes. We cannot wait longer or the police want to know why we did not ring." He closed the door and went back into the lounge to check on Rosie.

"You need a doctor," Salim advised, inspecting Rosie's knife wound. "It is still bleeding and I think it will need stitches."

Copious tears were streaming untended down Rosie's cheeks. Salim wiped them away and coaxed her to rise to her feet. She wobbled, weak from the shock and loss of blood. He led her into the bathroom, where he carefully removed the tissues at her throat, washed the cut and applied some antiseptic spray that he found in the bathroom cupboard. Rosie winced and moaned in agony.

It was then that they both heard the front door opening. Salim and Rosie looked at each other, alarmed and puzzled. Who was at the door? A nosey neighbour who had heard sounds of a struggle? Had someone already called the police? Salim pressed an index finger to his lips, indicating that Rosie should stay silent. He left her holding onto the sink in the bathroom. He cautiously entered the lounge, looking around anxiously. The net curtains at the window lifted gently in the warm breeze blowing in through the open front door. Salim peered out into the hallway. It was empty. Silently, he closed the door and moved towards the telephone. He should call for an ambulance, call the police. He dialled two digits and then paused with the receiver in his hand. What was he going to tell the police? He did not want to incriminate himself more than necessary. Perhaps the three of them had better sit down together and decide what they were going to say. He put the phone down again and walked to the bedroom door, knocking softly. "Hannah, I call police now, but first we need to talk…"

There was no answer.

Salim opened the door and a puzzled look came over his face. Roger lay spreadeagled on the bed, his unseeing eyes staring up at the ceiling. Salim gave a start and ran back to Rosie, panic stricken. Huddled on the bathroom floor, weak with the loss of blood, Rosie croaked, "What is it, Salim?"

He seemed unable to articulate, his eyes wide with terror as he pointed his thumb behind him. "It's Hannah."

"Why, what's wrong with her?" said Rosie. She staggered to her feet and pushed past him, moving towards the bedroom.

Salim shouted after her, "She's gone, Rosie. Hannah is gone!"

Rosie stopped, swaying to and fro. She looked at him, dumbfounded. Then she stumbled into the bedroom, looking all around, her eyes trying to avoid the horrific sight on her bed. A thought occurred to her and clutching hold of the furniture to steady herself, she weaved her way towards the front door. Salim's brown eyes watched in alarm. "Hey, where you going, Rosie? Come back!" he shouted, following her. Rosie ignored him, stumbling through the open door and down the flight of stairs into the car park, holding the tissue at her throat. Then she stopped and silently pulled at the roots of her hair, screaming, "Sh*t! She's taken my car!"

Chapter Thirty-Five

Rosie and Salim sat by the telephone in the lounge, neither of them wanting to make the first move. Rosie bit her nails, trying to think straight.

How could Hannah just leave like that? Didn't she realize her disappearance would implicate her in the murder, leading the police to form their own obvious conclusions? But Rosie had other things to worry about. She looked across at Salim. He was nervously rubbing his chin and repeatedly removing his kummar and running his hand over his shiny black hair. He stood up, paced the room and then sat down again, unable to conceal his anxiety.

What will happen to him? she wondered.

Salim had killed Roger to save her. He had not meant to kill him. Who would have thought a bang on the head with a pot could cause instant death? Now Salim could rot in a jail for the rest of his life. Because of her. She shivered and wondered, *does Oman still carry out the death penalty?*

Guilt overwhelmed her. She would be eternally grateful to him, but she knew he would receive no thanks or gratitude from anyone else, for saving her. He would be prosecuted and charged with murder. How could she protect him from this injustice? Rosie felt a sudden and intense anger towards Hannah for involving them both in this awful nightmare.

I wish I'd never set eyes on that woman.

She vowed that she would find Hannah and make her pay for this day. A day when three people's lives had been destroyed.

Salim sighed, took off his kummar for the fourth time and rubbed his head.

"Rosie, I cannot believe it. Why did Hannah's father attack you?" He looked at Rosie intently.

Rosie coloured at the insinuation. After a moment's hesitation, she spewed out the grim details of the horrific attack in Brighton. Salim's expression changed from one of dismay to compassion. He shook his head and held her in his arms, listening intently. His deep brown eyes were full of love and tenderness. He stroked her hair as Rosie spoke of Hannah's quest to find her father and of the awful moment when Roger had arrived at the apartment with his excited daughter.

"It's alright, Rosie, it's over now. It's all over now," Salim said, unable to find the words to express his love for her at that moment. He wanted to take away her pain, to love and protect her.

Rosie looked up into Salim's eyes and replied, "No, Salim, it's not over at all. In fact, I think it's only just begun."

Salim knew exactly what she meant. He picked up the telephone receiver. "We have to call now," Salim said softly.

"Are you sure?"

"What you mean?"

"I don't know. Perhaps you should run away, go back to the desert, go somewhere where they cannot find you."

Salim's eyes bore into hers. He shook his head. "No Rosie, I cannot do that. They will find me."

"Maybe not."

"No, Rosie, they will. And it will be worse for me if I run like a chicken."

Rosie nodded. They could choose whether to make the call or not, but running away would change nothing. He could not live like a hunted animal. Sooner or later Salim would have to face charges.

"I know, I know, but what will we tell them?"

"The truth, Rosie. We tell them the truth, that is all we can do," he answered.

"It was self-defence, Salim, maybe they will let you go."
Salim nodded.

Rosie could hardly bear to watch him. He was gesticulating wildly while speaking to his mother on the phone. Rosie wondered how he could ever explain it all to her. The conversation seemed very heated. Rosie quickly dialled Laura on her GSM. She wandered out onto the balcony and looked at the dark blue sea. She watched the waves lapping gently along the shore line and was struck by the realization that whatever happened, it really made little difference in the broad view of things; the sea would always continue its eternal rhythm. Once again, she felt a strange out-of-body sensation, as if she were looking down on herself, watching the whole wretched drama from afar.

Laura answered the phone and Rosie spoke in a flat voice, devoid of emotion, explaining the bare details of the situation, as if she were talking about something that had happened in a movie she had seen. *A murder had been committed. A dead body lay on her bed.* There was silence at the other end of the line, while Laura tried to absorb the unfamiliar words she was hearing, then she replied with a torrent of questions, which Rosie felt unable to answer over the phone. She groaned and replied simply, "I don't know, Laura. I'm so scared and now with Hannah disappearing, I don't know what will happen to us."

"Oh God. Listen, Rosie, I'm coming over," Laura announced.

"No, don't do that!" Rosie said emphatically, "you mustn't come any where near here! I don't want you to be implicated in all this. Listen, I'll ring you later and let you know what's going to happen."

Laura reluctantly agreed, but asked if she could do anything to help. Rosie suggested Laura call Thomas at the Institute on her behalf. Now it was Laura's turn to react negatively, rejecting the idea out of hand.

"No, I can't do that for you, Rosie, you'll have to ring him yourself. The owner of the Institute is your sponsor, so you must let him know what's going on. You'd better ring him right now."

Rosie began to cry softly. "Must I?"

"Yes, you must. Oh, Rosie, I know this is absolutely awful, but hey, come on, it'll be alright in the end. Just thank the Almighty that Salim stopped the bastard. Is Salim there with you right now? Good, okay. Now don't let him leave you alone and promise you'll let me know what's happening."

Rosie agreed, rang off and immediately called Thomas's number. Thomas spluttered down the phone when he heard what had happened.

"Oh no, oh dear no, oh deary me," he said, absolutely astounded. He immediately agreed to call Sami, the Institute's sponsor and told Rosie not to worry. *Fat chance,* she thought.

Chapter Thirty-Six

Forty-five minutes later, the apartment was swarming with uniformed police officers; taking notes, measuring distances and asking probing questions. Salim gesticulated wildly, trying to explain what had happened, but Rosie could sense that the officers were looking at them both with mounting suspicion. It did seem implausible to suggest that Salim had killed Roger in self-defence. Roger's injury was on the back of the head so obviously he had been hit from behind. The cut on Rosie's throat and her torn dress were the only real pieces of evidence to suggest that she was being attacked when Salim struck Roger. Rosie pointed to the blood on the quilt. Surely the police could see what had happened. He was killed in self-defence. But the police were clearly going to take some convincing.

Salim put his arm around Rosie's shoulders. They quietly watched as Roger's body was zipped up in a black body bag and carried out to a police van. Inevitably, Rosie and Salim were asked to accompany the police to the station. First, Rosie was escorted into her bedroom. Averting her eyes, with her heart thumping, she tried not to look at the blood-stained bed, but focused instead on the search for a long loose tee shirt and trousers. Shivering and trembling with shock, Rosie carefully removed her torn blue dress and handed it to the policewoman who informed her that the dress would become an important piece of evidence in the trial.

The trial. Oh my God, thought Rosie.

The silky dress was slipped into the opened transparent bag without a sound and Rosie pulled a brown tee shirt over her head and put on some baggy trousers. She came back into the lounge just in time to see Salim being escorted out of the front door. She rushed down the stairs with the policewoman at her heels, calling his name and sobbing bitterly as she watched him being driven away in the dark blue police car. Its siren wailed. He sat in the back of the car, looking diminished by the events of the day. H*e's being treated like a common criminal,* she thought angrily. She cried out to him: "*Oh Salim, I'm so sorry.*" Then she crumpled like a dried-out leaf and had to be helped back into the apartment to gather her belongings together. A feeling of complete emptiness and helplessness washed over her, leaving her weak and tearful. All her energy was drained, but she could take no rest. The police had other plans for her. Rosie sat dazed and alone in the back of the police car, looking out of the window at the passing motorists and nervously fiddling with her blood-stained handkerchief.

A decision had been taken to escort Rosie straight to hospital for immediate medical attention. The nurse carefully applied an antiseptic liquid and dressed the deep cut on her throat. The intense stinging sensation left her moaning and weeping. A female police officer stood guard outside the curtained cubicle, peering in at regular intervals to watch the proceedings and check on her whereabouts. Rosie found it all so demeaning. She emerged from the hospital with a white bandage around her neck and her head spinning. During the short journey to the police station, Rosie wondered if she was technically under arrest. The thought sent shivers up and down her spine. Once again, she tried to breathe deeply to calm her shattered nerves, but each breath brought intense pain to her throat. She rummaged in her bag and took out her mobile, quickly dialling Laura's number, but the police officer sitting beside her swiftly grabbed the phone from her hand and announced, "*La!* No telephone!"

Rosie stumbled from the car on weak and wobbly legs and the policewoman put a hand under Rosie's forearm to guide her up the stairs. Soon, she was ushered into an interview room, behind the main counter in reception, and told to wait. Left alone, she sat down on a hard, uncomfortable chair and listened to the deafening silence all around her. It occurred to her that the stark white room was probably soundproofed for interrogation purposes. Rosie shivered at the thought and put her head down on the cold grey metal table and quietly sobbed with hopelessness.

Ten minutes later, a short and swarthy uniformed police officer with a head that appeared to be far too large for his stocky body, and shirt buttons about to pop under the pressure of a large paunch, came into the room holding a notepad and pen. He closed the door, nodded politely and sat down opposite her. Smiling briefly, he began to fire questions at Rosie in a harsh voice, showing a total lack of empathy and understanding for the young, tear-stricken girl with the hunched shoulders who sat in front of him.

"Name? Contact address? Labour card number? Sponsor's name and address? Employment details?" he barked in a loud booming voice, which echoed around the bare room.

Rosie answered as best she could, but was unable to think straight. The next question made her gasp: "What was your relationship with the deceased?"

Rosie stuttered, her mind reeling. "The deceased? I... he wasn't... I'm not... I can't answer that. Look, where is Salim? Can I see him please?"

Her request was instantly denied. "Just answer the question," urged the officer.

"Am I under arrest?"

He paused before responding, rubbing his whiskery chin. "Let's just say that you are helping the police with their enquiries, shall we? Now," he coughed, "please answer the question."

"No," Rosie answered bravely.

"What do you mean 'no'?" he replied angrily rising from his seat.

"I mean, if I *am* under arrest, it's my right to have a lawyer present and I should also be able to make one phone call."

A smile spread slowly across the officer's slack features and he replied with sarcasm,

"You think this is television?"

Rosie's failure to laugh, made him snarl in anger. He warned her that any lack of cooperation on her part, would be equated with withholding evidence and criminal complicity. Rosie nodded weakly and swallowed hard, wincing at the accompanying pain. She tried to focus, idly noticing the protruding black hairs sprouting from the officer's large nostrils.

The officer sighed. Rosie followed his feet, in their large black boots, squeaking across the tiled floor and disappearing out of the room. Five minutes later the officer returned, holding a small piece of paper with a name and a number written on it.

"Here, this is lawyer's number. You go with the policewoman now and make the call," he said, gruffly.

"Thank you."

She was led to the phone booth. The lawyer's secretary answered the call and promised to convey her message, but Rosie insisted on speaking personally to the lawyer. She waited, listening to a taped music for five minutes before she was eventually put through to him. He asked her for a few details and then reluctantly agreed to meet her later that day. He was unable to specify a time, so there followed an interminable wait for him to arrive. Rosie filled the time thinking about Salim. She vowed to do everything in her power to extricate him from this awful situation. He had technically saved her life twice and this time, it would cost him dearly. How could she ever repay him?

She thought about her parents and wondered how she was going to tell them the news. She wished to God that Denise could come and help her through the dark days ahead. Finally her thoughts turned to Hannah. She tried to put herself in Hannah's shoes in an attempt to think where she might have gone. Hannah may have already left the country. If she had, then there would be no one to confirm the details of the dramatic events that had taken place in her apartment. Finding Hannah was imperative.

Rosie's thoughts were interrupted by the arrival of a tall, dark thin man in a crumpled brown suit. A large gold Rolex watch hung loosely around his small-boned hairy wrist. He introduced himself as Mohammed, the lawyer, smiling to reveal yellowing teeth and bad breath. Rosie's spirits sank. She had been hoping for someone who would treat her with understanding and compassion. This man seemed to have very little comprehension of the trauma she had so recently suffered. Mohammed sat down and took some documents out of his thin black briefcase. He asked Rosie several questions about the attack in a voice devoid of emotion.

"Were you raped?"

"No."

"Did he injure you?"

"Yes, he..." Rosie had so little energy, she just pointed to her bandaged neck.

He nodded. "What weapon did he use?"

"A knife, he put the knife to my throat." Rosie put her hand over her mouth to stifle a sob. This was not the time for an emotional outburst.

The lawyer continued writing notes. "How did you kill him?"

Rosie stood up with complete indignation, denying the accusation. "I did *not* kill him! I was pinned to the bed with a knife at my throat, for God's sake! How could I have killed him?" Black spots played before her eyes and she swooned. She rubbed her forehead with a shaky hand, clearly distressed.

Mohammed looked up at her, shrugged, sniffed and told her to sit down. "I'm just trying to get the facts. Please try to control yourself, Miss."

Rosie burst into tears and poured out the whole story while Mohammed made a frantic attempt to follow the flow of her words with his pen.

Chapter Thirty-Seven

Hannah could hear the sound of a high pitched wail. It took her some time to realize the sound was coming from deep inside her own body. The whites of her eyes gleamed in the dark like a startled deer's. She had been frantically driving around for hours, unable to clear her head and decide what to do or where to go. Consequently, she was now hopelessly lost in the back streets of Seeb. Neon lights glared at her from small shop fronts selling plastic chairs, cheap suitcases and kids' bicycles. She passed nurseries with black wrought iron gates and rigged up fluorescent green shading, selling plants, statues and hosepipes. A huge fast-food restaurant came into view and she could see small children swarming all over the bright red and yellow play area in the window, like so many colourful giant ants. As Hannah forced herself to calm down, an idea eventually crystallized in her mind. She would drive to Dubai and take a flight to London from there. Suddenly she found herself coming towards the beach road and was able to get her bearings. She swiftly did a U-turn, screeching the brakes, swerving and straightening up on the opposite side of the road.

Sohar. She must drive to Sohar and the Hatta border. She gripped the shiny black steering wheel with her sweaty palms and told herself to keep focused. Twenty minutes later she joined the heavy traffic on the dual carriage way and let out a sigh of relief. *I know where I'm going. I'm on the right track*, she thought. The wide six-lane highway stretched out monotonously in front of her. Peering at her wristwatch, she found it was already five o'clock and she knew it would take her at least another four hours to reach Dubai. Her back was aching and she longed to take a rest. She moved around in her seat, trying to get comfortable for the long journey ahead. But she was unable to calm down. Murderous thoughts kept running through her head. *My father is dead.* The vivid picture of her father's body slumped on Rosie's bed, made her cry out in pain and anguish. She pursed her lips and gripped the steering wheel tightly, her knuckles turning white. An indescribable tightness in her chest provoked a coughing fit. Her body shook and she pounded her breast, tears streaming down her face. So totally incensed and consumed with anger towards Salim, she struggled to breathe. Sub-consciously, Hannah chose to block out parts of the story. She focused exclusively on Rosie and Salim's involvement in her father's demise. Rosie and Salim were responsible for all her pain. *They* had taken away the one person who offered her love and hope for the future. She vowed to make Rosie and Salim pay for what they had done to her. She would make damn sure the police locked them up and threw away the key.

As she drove along the palm tree lined road, feelings of self-pity engulfed her. She could see nothing but a long, blank, empty future in front of her. Her life was meaningless. She sobbed. Potent images of her life, with all its frustrations, played out before her eyes. All the hurts and disappointments she had suffered over the years seemed to come together and merge in her mind, feeding a deep vindictive hatred which smouldered inside her. She muttered to herself, cursing everyone she could think of who had mistreated her; the bosses who had sacked her, the various boyfriends who had dumped her, friends who had become arch enemies, even her mother, who had died on her just when she needed her. She hated them all. There was no one she could rely on, no one who really cared about her. *I don't deserve to be treated like this.* Suddenly she banged the steering wheel and swore out loud, *Rosie's a bloody sh*t! She was going to throw me out, after all I'd done for her. I never hurt her. Why was she so* *mean to me? I thought she loved me, but she's no different from all the rest.*

But the bulk of her hatred was reserved for Salim. It knew no bounds. A globule of bitter spit landed on the windscreen as she swore and screamed and cried and battered the steering wheel, imagining Salim standing there in front of her. The car swerved and a vehicle, coming up from behind in the fast lane, hooted its horn at her. She screamed at the passing motorist, shaking her fist, almost beside herself with rage. *Rose and Salim have taken away my happiness. My father was everything to me.* But in the next moment, as if she were suffering from some form of amnesia, she started cursing her father. He had disappointed her. He had never really been there for her. And now, due to his own stupidity, he had gone and got himself killed. *Stupid idiot.* She ranted and raved until her body slumped in sheer exhaustion. Her emotions were totally spent and she at last felt dead inside.

All at once the sky darkened uncharacteristically and she heard a pattering sound on the roof of the car. It was raining. *Summer rain?* She turned on the windscreen wipers and peered out. Rays of light from the oncoming vehicles' headlights revealed teeming white rain pounding the wet tarmac. *This is weird*, she thought, *it never rains here in summer*. A large illuminated signboard came into view: Welcome to Sohar. *Good. Only an hour to the border,* she thought. She slowed down slightly, breathing hard, beads of perspiration on her upper lip, following her emotional outburst. A flashing orange light appeared on the dashboard; she was running out of gas. She swerved around the large grass covered roundabout and saw a high blue and green signboard advertising a gas station. She indicated and was just pulling in, when she saw a police car waiting at the entrance.

"Sh*t!" She skidded and swerved back onto the highway, frantically looking over her shoulder to make sure she was not being followed and ignoring the hooting horns coming from behind. With shaking hands, she groped for a pack of cigarettes in her brown leather handbag on the passenger seat, keeping her eyes on the road and one hand on the wheel. She lifted the opened pack to her mouth and lifted a cigarette out with her lips. She pushed the car lighter into its socket and waited for the red glowing light to appear, holding the brown section of the cigarette between her pale lips. Finally, she lit up and drew the nicotine into her body with relief, exhaling the smoke through her teeth. She opened the window a little and immediately felt spots of rain land on her bare arm. She shivered in the unseasonably cold damp air and quickly wound her window up again, turning on the fan to dispel the hazy smoke from the car's interior. *This is July, for Christ's sake, how come it's raining?*

Hannah jumped as a flash of lightning lit up the entire area for a split second. She started counting. One... two... three... four... Suddenly a huge clap of thunder rung out across the sky. The few pedestrians on the street ran for cover. *That's all I need*, she thought.

A large yellow shell sign beckoned and she turned onto the forecourt and parked beside a petrol pump. She pressed a button and waited for the passenger window to wind down automatically. An Indian with greasy, wet hair and a large black moustache smiled at her, revealing two gold teeth. The top half of his khaki overalls was saturated.

"Fill her up please," she said peremptorily, rummaging through the glove compartment for music tapes. The man stood watching her, without moving.

She raised her eyebrows.

With a humble bow he whispered, "Madam, please," his head rocking from side to side, raindrops falling on his face.

"What?" she asked, rolling her eyes in impatience.

"Your cigarette, madam."

Hannah sighed in exasperation, turned her head away from him, picked up her bag, noisily lifted the handle and pushed open the car door. She jumped out, drawing deeply on her cigarette and walked purposefully towards the brightly lit service shop as though oblivious to the downpour. She stomped into the shop, tossed her head of wet hair and quickly looked around. Then she strode towards the shelves, picked up two bottles of water, some packet of crisps and sweets, three sticks of chewing gum and a pack of cigarettes. Carrying everything in her arms, with her cigarette lodged between her lips, she deposited the goods on the counter, squinting through the plume of smoke at the young Omani shop assistant. He rang up the items on the till and smiled broadly. "Three rials, seven hundred baizas please."

Hannah did not meet his eyes. She opened her red leather purse and swore under her breath. She recalled that earlier in the day, she had given her father a ten rial note to buy coffee and a brownie. Now she cursed herself for not checking his pockets before she left the flat. She would be totally skint, once she had paid for the petrol. She would have to find an ATM. She emptied all the coins out of her purse, counted them haphazardly and pushed them across the counter together with several green one hundred baiza notes.

Hannah threw her purchases into a plastic bag and ran back to the car. She jumped in and pulled a face as she paid the petrol pump attendant the last of her cash. She put the key in the ignition and started up the engine, pushing a tape into the player. She drove off the forecourt, lit another cigarette and put her foot down hard on the accelerator. She would reach Dubai soon. Then all she had to do was drive to the airport and board the first plane to London she could find She still had a return ticket. She relaxed, turned the volume up and started singing along to the music and moving in her seat to the rhythm of the beat.

She turned left and saw the dark majestic mountains up ahead. Some low sandy coloured buildings came into view as the car climbed up the hill. She turned off the music, combed her hair and looked in her rear view mirror. She quickly applied some glossy orange lipstick to her lips and dabbed a spot on each cheek, rubbing it in to achieve a healthy glow. She stopped beside the window of the border control office and smiled coyly at the man she could see assessing her from his seat. Clutching her red passport, she clambered out of the vehicle, tossing her long chestnut locks and giving a dazzling white smile to the officer on duty. She studied the intricate blue embroidery on the beige mussar covering the officer's bent head as he carefully inspected her passport details. Impervious to her coy smile, he swivelled in his seat and tapped some information into his computer, surveying the screen. Hannah waited, nervously looking at her watch. He frowned and turned to regard her closely, then tapped away on his keyboard again and read some more information. Suddenly he stood up from his seat and told her to wait while he disappeared into an adjoining office.

A tall, heavily built man emerged a few minutes later and came over to the open window to talk to her, smiling broadly.

"Mees Hannah?" he asked, with raised eyebrows, holding her passport in his large brown hand. Hannah nodded.

"Please, you follow me," he announced, coming out of the office through a side door and beckoning for her to follow him, as he walked off across the wide road.

Hannah did not budge. "Why? Is there some kind of problem, officer?" she asked innocently.

"No problem, you come with me."

Hannah's heart pounded in her chest. She quickly assessed the situation, swivelling her eyes around to look at the keys hanging in the ignition of her car and then focusing on the red and white striped barrier at the far end of the checkpoint. The officer was talking into his cell phone but he turned to look at her with an enquiring look on his face. Hannah smiled sweetly at him as she stood rooted to the spot, trying to think what to do. Then she heard voices and saw two uniformed police officers with guns in their holsters coming out of a building at the side of the road. They sauntered towards her.

I'm trapped, she thought.

In a flash, Hannah threw herself into the driver's seat, turned the key in the ignition and pressed the accelerator. With a great skidding of brakes the car lurched forward. She could not hear the shouts and running feet behind her as she hurtled faster and faster towards the barrier, keeping her foot down hard on the accelerator. But glancing in her rear view mirror, she saw a sight that made her gape, then duck and scream out, "No!"

The car was speeding but it all seemed to happen in slow motion; the officer removed his gun and lifted it high above his head. Then holding it steady with both hands, he brought his arms down and aimed the gun straight at her car...

Shots rung out, echoing around the mountains. All at once her back wheel exploded and with a great screech of brakes the car spun out of control. Hannah screamed, "Oh God!" as she turned the steering wheel this way and that, trying in vain to regain control. Then with an enormous crash, the car slid sideways down a gulley at the side of the road and overturned. Hannah cried out into the darkness before everything went black.

There was a moment of near silence when all that could be heard was the rhythmic sound of the wheels continuing to spin on the upturned vehicle. Then all hell let loose. Voices shouted, police sirens wailed, alarm bells rang out and there was the sound of heavy boots running over the hard, wet tarmac. Two officers holding red canisters sprayed the car with white foam and two more men struggled to open the car door. It was jammed. Through cracks in the opaque smashed side window, the policemen could see a young girl suspended upside down in her seat, still gripping the steering wheel. She was completely motionless and her head was held in an unnatural position, pressing down as it was, onto the mangled roof of the car.

Chapter Thirty-Eight

It was late afternoon and Sam, Laura, Shabib and a very obviously pregnant Penny were sitting around the wooden dining table in Stuart's apartment discussing Rosie's predicament. Laura had telephoned Stuart earlier and told him that Rosie and Salim were being held at the police station.

"You're kidding? Why? What's happened? And who the hell is Salim?" he had asked in surprise.

Not wanting to discuss details over the phone, Laura had arranged to meet Sam, Penny and Shabib at Stuart's apartment. Now, listening to Laura explanation, Stuart gave a start and stood up. *Hannah's father had died in Rosie's apartment.* He was incredulous. He began firing questions at Laura as he paced the room. When he thought he was finally in possession of all the facts, he sank down in an armchair and gave a deep sigh, letting the gruesome details of Roger's death sink in. He rubbed his head vigorously, trying to get his head around the unbelievable facts. Beyond the obvious feelings of horror and revulsion, Stuart also found himself wondering how he had been oblivious to the realities of Rosie's life. Why had he not known about this guy Salim? Judging by Laura's explanation, Salim had played an integral part in rescuing Rosie from the desert and now, he appeared to have saved her life again. Stuart felt a twinge of jealousy.

His heart went out to Rosie when he heard of her terrible ordeal. But he could not help wondering why Rosie had chosen not to tell him about the attack in Brighton. He and Rosie had shared a loving intimate relationship. He had been under the impression that their intimacy included telling each other everything. For his part, he had held nothing back. Now he was bitterly disappointed to discover that Rosie had been harbouring a deep dark secret and deliberately keeping it from him, ever since her arrival. Grimly, he recalled their first night in Dubai and suddenly realized why Rosie had been so reluctant to make love. Stuart felt extremely sorry for Rosie, but somehow he also felt a sense of betrayal.

Stuart found the news about Hannah's father incredibly bizarre. How could the same man who had attacked Rosie in Brighton, turn out to be Hannah's father? It was impossible. He voiced his utter disbelief to the others and they all agreed it was hard to accept. But it was Sam, who seemed to have the ability to think laterally, who came up with a new possibility.

"But supposing Roger was only masquerading as Hannah's father."

Penny shook her head. "No, how could that be? I mean, Hannah got Roger's contact details through a missing persons agency."

Sam poured himself another coffee and took a sip before replying, "Yeah that's what she told us, but how do we know she made the first move? Maybe *he* contacted *her*."

Laura put her elbows on the table and covered her face in her hands. It was all too awful to contemplate. "But Sam, if that is the case, how did he get her number?"

Sam shrugged. "It wouldn't have been too difficult, if he had known his victim."

Everyone stared at Sam. It was Shabib's turn to admit he could not follow Sam's argument. "His victim? So Sam, let me get this straight, what you're saying is that Roger came here to find Rosie."

Sam nodded.

"Oh God. This is all so sick," Penny said.

To Stuart, the idea had a dull ring of truth to it. The guy in Brighton was obviously a pervert. Who knows what he would have been capable of? He may have been stalking Rosie and known a great deal about her. He could easily have found out Rosie's contact details in Muscat. But why would Hannah have believed he was her father? Clearly, it was important that they find Hannah and question her about all this. A man who called himself Roger was now lying dead in the mortuary. *Murder had been committed.*

Stuart felt a rising panic in his chest. He coughed, interrupted Laura's explanation and posed a question: "So, is Rosie a suspect in all this?"

The friends all exchanged glances before Penny answered, "We don't know, Stuart. I mean, probably. Until the police can determine exactly what happened, everyone involved is bound to be under suspicion."

"And what about Hannah? You say she's run away?" he asked.

They nodded in unison.

"Well, it doesn't make sense to me," he said, rubbing the back of his red, sunburnt neck, "why on earth would she run off like that?"

Laura explained the little she had learned about Hannah's involvement from her own garbled conversation with Rosie earlier in the day.

"Hannah apparently interrupted the attack but Roger locked her in a room or something. When she was released, it was all over and Roger was lying dead on Rosie's bed."

"God how awful," said Stuart, imagining Hannah's state of mind.

Laura nodded, "Yeah, she must be devastated. But what about Rosie? How she is ever going to recover? You'd think that Hannah would have wanted to stay to support her friend, wouldn't you? God only knows where she's gone."

Penny moved in her hard chair to relieve the pressure on her back, "Yeah it's weird. We've tried phoning and sending her text messages, but she's just not answering."

The rhythmic sound of the revolving fan whipping through the air overhead became apparent, as Stuart paced the living room. He turned to Sam, who was staring into his coffee cup, slowly stirring it contents.

"Sam, why d'you think she ran away? I mean, what has she got to be afraid of?"

Laura answered for him, shrugging her shoulders and suggesting that Hannah was in a such a state and probably did not know what she was doing. Then Sam looked up and surprised them all again. "Maybe… maybe she has something to hide." He tapped the metal spoon on the side of his cup and met Laura's dark hazel eyes defiantly. Everyone looked at him.

"What do you mean, Sam?" Stuart asked.

"Well I don't know, I'm just guessing, but maybe Hannah couldn't afford to get involved. She might have had dealings with the police before." Sam's intense brown eyes looked in turn at each of his friends.

Laura reacted angrily, pushing back her chair and standing up, her head jutting forward in Sam's direction as she shouted at him, "I don't know what you're insinuating Sam, but I don't like it." She put her honey brown hands on her slim hips and addressed everyone, "Come on, guys, be reasonable. The poor girl has just lost her father, she must be beside herself with grief. Don't let's make her into some kind of criminal." She turned and looked coldly at Sam before adding, "I don't think you're being very charitable, Sam."

He shrugged and went back to staring at his coffee cup with a sullen look on his face. Penny's voice was soft but gained strength as she worked to ease the tension between them, "Okay, Laura, calm down, you're right. But listen, Sam could be right too. I mean, it's possible. No, just hear me out," she said raising her hand in front of her, as Laura started to argue.

"When you think about it, Laura, what do we really know about Hannah?"

There was silence while everyone absorbed her words. Laura admitted defeat, pursing her lips and folding her arms. She moved across the room to stare out of the window.

Stuart sat down, stretched out his long legs and crossed his ankles under the table. "Well, whatever her reasons, we really need to focus on getting her back here. Do we have any other contacts we could try ringing? What about that boyfriend of hers and the place where she was working? Does anyone have the number?"

Laura said she had Hannah's office number at work and promised to go and find it. No one had a contact number for Hannah's boyfriend, but Shabib said he might know someone who did. Stuart continued, "Now, Sam, will you come with me to the police station? The way I see it, our first priority is to try and bail Rosie out."

He was surprised when Sam hesitated.

"Um, sure I'll come, but... but wouldn't it be better if Shabib went with you? I mean he'd be able to translate and everything."

Stuart nodded in agreement and looked at Shabib, who seemed to be avoiding his gaze. Shabib and Penny were looking with fascination at Penny's tummy as the baby moved slowly across it. "Hey look, that's magic!" said Shabib with a broad grin on his face. Everyone smiled and Penny said, "Oh he's pretty active, it feels like I'm getting kicked in the ribs!"

Shabib laughed as he squeezed Penny's hand in his dark one and said, "That's my boy, reckon he's gonna be a footballer!"

"Alright with you, Shabib? Can I count on you to come with me?" Stuart asked, refusing to be sidetracked.

Shabib looked up and said "Sorry?" Stuart repeated the request and Shabib immediately agreed. But his furrowed brow and serious expression led Stuart to believe that Shabib was not exactly thrilled by the idea either.

"What's the matter, Shabib? You don't mind coming, do you?"

Shabib stood up quickly, shaking his head emphatically, "No... no, of course not, mate. I'll come," he said, smiling nervously. The whites of his eyes gleamed and Stuart instantly recognized an emotion he had not expected to find there – fear.

Stuart sighed, realizing things were going to be difficult. No one wants to get involved with police enquiries.

While everyone talked amongst themselves about the possible outcome to Rosie's circumstances, Stuart went to his bedroom and changed into a crisp white shirt and some sober black trousers. He chose a subdued grey silk tie, put it around his neck and stood looking at himself in the mirror while he knotted it, trying to gather his thoughts. His freckly face began to colour as something akin to anger took hold of him. He whipped the tie through the air and tugged it into place around his neck. *What a bloody mess*, he thought, not knowing quite who to direct his anger towards.

He returned to the living room and suggested that while he and Shabib were at the police station, the others should continue the search for Hannah. The friends agreed and moved with Stuart and Shabib towards the front door, wishing them both luck. Shabib's tall, wide figure stooped to kiss Penny on the cheek. "See you later *habitbi* (dear). I hope I won't be long."

Penny nodded.

"Please give Rosie our love, tell her we're thinking of her." said Laura with great sympathy in her voice.

Everyone nodded solemnly.

The late afternoon heat was still intense as Stuart and Shabib walked towards the car. Stuart put on his sunglasses and tapped a number into his mobile phone, holding it to his ear as he opened the car door with the remote. "Hi listen, Mish, something's come up," he murmured in a low tone, "I don't think I'll be able to make it in time for dinner. Don't wait for me, okay? No, I can't talk now, I'll explain it all later. I'm sorry, darling. See you later."

Chapter Thirty-Nine

Just two hours later, Laura received a phone call from Stuart with the news that Rosie would soon be released. Her passport would be confiscated and she would have to remain in Oman until further notice.

"How is she?" Laura asked.

"I don't know, I haven't seen her yet. But listen Laura, where is she going to stay? She can't stay at her place cos it's apparently been sealed off by the forensic team." He hesitated, before adding, "I suppose she could stay at mine but, well, you know, I have a new girlfriend and—"

Laura immediately interrupted him, "No... no she can't stay with you, that's not a good idea. She can stay with us, bring her to our house, Stu. Yeah, okay, I'll go home now and meet you there," she said looking at her slim black watch. She put the phone down and turned to Sam and Penny, relief clearly visible on her face. But before she had time to explain, Sam stood up without a word and stormed towards her with an angry scowl on his face. He grabbed her by the wrist and pulled her into the kitchen.

Mystified by his strange behaviour, Laura shouted in surprise "Hey, Sam, what's the matter? You're hurting me! What's wrong?"

"We need to talk," Sam answered abruptly, closing the kitchen door behind them.

Penny rolled her eyes, put her hands, with their swollen fingers, flat on the table top and levered herself up into a standing position. She walked slowly across the room towards the kitchen, hearing the sound of raised voices coming from within. She opened the door and saw Sam gesticulating wildly and shouting at Laura.

"Why did you have to go and invite Rosie to stay with us?" he asked.

"Why d'you think? Rosie's our friend Sam, and we have to help her in her hour of need. What's got into you Sam? Why are you so against having her stay with us?" Laura asked, failing to understand Sam's negative reaction.

"Look, Laura, it's my house as well as yours and you've no right to ask her to stay with us without asking me first," he replied cutting the air with the back of his hand.

"Well, sorreey! Pardon me for breathing! I guess I just naturally assumed you'd want to help Rosie as much as I do. She's been through so much, Sam, I think it's the very least we can do." She folded her arms and looked at her feet.

Sam followed her gaze. He loved her beautiful feet with their carefully manicured nails. "It's not that," he said softly, changing tack, "I *do* want to help her but I just don't think we should get involved, you know with the police and all."

Laura leaned against the cool grey marble kitchen counter.

"Well, a fine friend you're turning out to be! What possible harm can it do to have Rosie stay with us?"

"I don't know… it's just… well, the police…"

"The way you're talking, anyone would think *you'd* had dealings with the police! Have you?"

Sam made a tutting sound with his tongue. "Oh come on, don't be stupid!"

"Don't you call *me* stupid…"

Penny waddled into the kitchen and interrupted them, "It's okay, you two, stop arguing. Rosie can stay with me and Shabib. It's better all round really, because I'll be giving up work soon."

Sam and Laura stopped shouting, looked at Penny and then at each other.

Laura's raised her eyebrows. "Oh, really, Penny? Are you sure?" she asked softly.

"Yeah, actually it will be great for me to have Rosie around and let's face it, she's going to need to do a lot of talking to recover from all of this," said Penny.

The tension subsided. Laura immediately agreed, "Okay, that's very kind of you Penny. Only, before you confirm it with Stuart, maybe *you* had better ask *your* partner first?" she added, glaring at Sam.

Penny nodded solemnly, "Oh yes, don't worry, I'll ask the boss!"

And then she laughed and Sam and Laura smiled at each other for the first time that day.

Chapter Forty

Hannah stared up at the stark white ceiling of the hospital ward. During her short twenty-three years of life she had never heard of the word 'brain stem' before. Now she heard the doctor with heavy black-framed spectacles use the word to describe her condition to the intern at his side. With a stethoscope hanging around his neck he explained that the essential component of Hannah's internal computer, the inseparable link between the brain and the spinal cord, had been damaged during the accident. The doctor continued his conversation with the medical student in a matter of fact voice, as they both moved on to examine the patient in the next bed. End of story.

Hannah lay completely immobilized, paralyzed from head to foot, her brain imprisoned in her inert body. Each time she tried to remember what had happened, her memory seemed to cut out. She had no recollection at all of the recent critical events of her life. Only one recurring thought kept running through her head: *When will they let me go home*? But she could not recall where her home might be. Soon, a nurse in a green and white striped uniform and a medical orderly ambled into the ward and arrived at her bedside, interrupting her only train of thought. The nurse lifted Hannah's limp forearm and checked her pulse, while looking at her watch. Hannah studied the plastic identity badge on the medical orderly's white coat as she leaned over her and adjusted the drip-feed. Hannah could make no sense of the letters: *Fathima*. The two members of staff smoothed down her bed covers and then promptly left without saying a single word to her. Neither member of staff had made eye contact with her. It seemed that the once lively young girl now lying on the regulation hospital bed had been downgraded to a mere patient bed number, a body without a soul. The excruciating and aching pain of loneliness and exclusion seeped into Hannah's bones and lay there, dormant, without any plans to leave. Hannah could not speak. She was totally unable to communicate her thoughts, needs or feelings. A tear rolled down her cheek and plopped onto the starched white pillow case beneath her head.

Then suddenly a familiar face came into view above her. A beautiful young woman with a cream coloured bandage wrapped tightly around her neck and kind, sympathetic eyes was smiling down at her. Hannah thought, *I know this face*, although she was unable to recall her name or remember who she was. In vain, Hannah tried to smile in recognition but she could only manage to blink at her. The woman stroked her hair and Hannah could see the woman's mouth moving but could not understand what she was saying. It was like watching one of those old movies where the sound track is out of sync with the action. The woman's large blue eyes filled with tears and she lowered her head and buried her face in the bedcovers. Hannah could not feel the bed shuddering with the woman's sobs. But Hannah had a deep desire to reach out and stroke the woman's long fair hair, longing to feel its softness under her fingertips.

Suddenly Hannah blinked hard as a strange sensation surged through her head. She felt fuzzy and could hear the sound of running water. But it was not water. It was blood. It flowed around her brain and Hannah panicked, her eyes darting this way and that. The alarm on the machine which regulated her feeding tube, beeped out into the void and the heart monitor gave out a continuous high pitched bleep. Nurses and doctors in white coats came running in, pulling the dull green curtains around her bed and regarding her with concern. Through clouded vision, Hannah observed them all from a distance, almost with amusement, as they performed all sorts of procedures on her numb and lifeless body. It was a body she barely inhabited, one that she no longer felt she had any association with. Then, like a sailor with a heavy heart, watching his home on the land recede, Hannah felt herself slowly slipping away, her life fading into the distance. And even after she had closed her eyes for the last time, somehow she could still see the gentle smile on the face of the beautiful young woman, as the waves of her inevitable fate took her further and further away, towards some distant and unknown shore.

Chapter Forty-One

Seeb airport was packed. Scores of Indians and Pakistanis were on their way home to the Indian sub-continent, weighted down with huge cardboard boxes tied up with bright orange plastic string. Dark-haired men wearing shalwar khamis, carried bulging bags and suitcases full of presents and household goods, high up on their narrow shoulders. Thankfully, Rosie and Laura drove straight past the departure lounge and headed for the arrivals hall. While Laura parked the car, Rosie walked inside and stood by the arrivals door, anxiously watching as each person came out through the automatic sliding doors. She clutched the thick chrome rail with both hands to steady herself, her legs still weak from the traumatic events of the past week. Using sheer will power, Rosie forced herself to concentrate. If her mind started to wander, she knew her body would begin to shake. Laura came up behind her and noticed again how much weight Rosie had lost. She touched Rosie's arm and her friend nearly jumped out of her skin. "Hey, it's only me. Are you okay?" Laura asked soothingly.

Rosie put a hand over her pounding heart and nodded, keeping her eyes on the door. Two minutes later Rosie gave a cry and her frown instantly melted into a smile. With immense relief, Rosie's arms reached forward and she hugged her dear sweet sister, allowing the tears to stream down her face unhindered.

At eleven o'clock the next morning Denise and Rosie left Penny and Shabib's house for a walk along the beach together. Although Rosie and Denise had talked until the early hours of the morning, Denise realized that Rosie still needed to talk. As always, Denise acted as an anchor in turbulent waters, providing a listening ear and a broad shoulder for Rosie to cry on. The two sisters found themselves alone on a beautiful unspoilt beach under the burning hot summer sun. Under different circumstances, Denise would have found it exhilarating. The leaves of giant palm trees swayed gently in the warm sea breeze and at the far end of the beach, Denise could see a lone heron wading through shallow waters, pecking in the sand with its long thin beak. A perfect formation of cormorants flew overhead, dark against the clear blue sky. A fisherman steered his small fishing vessel across the calm blue sea. Denise found it absolutely idyllic. But instead of commenting on the natural beauty all around them, Denise was silent, listening quietly to Rosie, as they walked slowly along, with the harsh sun beating down on their heads.

At one point Rosie could not seem to move. Her voice shook with emotion as she described Hannah's death. The gentle waves lapped at their feet as Rosie sobbed and Denise put her arm around her sister's shoulders and patted her back. Eventually Rosie wiped her eyes and continued, staring at the horizon as though she were lost in the past. Denise did her best to be attentive but she was beginning to sweat profusely in the high humidity. "Sorry, Rosie," she interrupted, "but I just can't take it, this heat's unbearable. I don't know how you can stand it. Can we go back inside now please?"

Rosie nodded and apologized, "Oh I'm sorry, Denny. Um, let's see if Penny's up and ask her to join us. We could drive down to the Hyatt and have a cappuccino."

Rosie parked Penny's car beside the hotel and Denise gave Penny her hand to help ease out of the back seat. Penny waddled slowly up the incline to the door. A cool air conditioned breeze met them at the entrance and with relief, Denise quickly sank down into the sofa with its oversized cushions. "Wow!" Denise exclaimed breathlessly, looking around at the cool marble floors, hand woven Persian rugs, huge brass-studded wooden chests. An enormous domed ceiling and two large richly coloured tents with hanging brass lanterns gave the lobby of the hotel an exotic Middle Eastern ambience. There was a life-sized brass sculpture of an Arab man on horseback holding a falcon at arm's length standing at the hub of a fountain in the centre of the seating area.

Over coffee Rosie told Denise about Salim. He had not been granted bail. He was still being held by the police and would shortly be transferred to prison. "Have you been to see him yet?" Denise asked.

"His mother has seen him, but I haven't." Rosie explained that she had applied for a visitor's permit but was still waiting for it to be granted.

"I'll come with you when you go, Rosie. But tell me, what's he like?"

Rosie smiled weakly and described Salim's beautiful eyes and calm nature.

"Whoa!" Denise interrupted, "Spare me the sordid details! I guess I just want to know… I mean, tell me honestly, Rosie, what do you feel for this guy? I know you must be grateful for all he's done for you. But is there any more to it than that? I mean, are you in love with him?"

Rosie shrugged. "I… I don't know, Denny. I mean, I do feel deeply for him and—"

Denise interrupted again, "And so that's why you broke up with Stupot?"

Rosie nodded. "Kind of. I knew I was developing feelings for Salim. But that's as far as it goes. Look, I might not be alive today if it weren't for Salim, but somehow everything has changed because of… of what happened. I just don't know how I feel about him anymore. I'm all mixed up. I feel so numb inside, Denise."

"That's normal. You've been through so much. Just take it one day at a time, Rose," Denise advised, squeezing Rosie's hand gently.

"Yeah, but Denny, I don't know how long this trial will drag on. What am I gonna do? I don't think I can work. I'm not sure if I can get my act together."

"No, Rosie, you're definitely not going back to work. There's no way. You need to recuperate. Listen," said Denise, stroking Rosie's hand, "I want you to come back home with me. Penny agrees, don't you Penny? It's for the best. You can stay with Mum and Dad if you like. But as I haven't managed to find another flat mate yet, why don't you just come and stay with me?" she suggested.

Rosie stared at them as if they had both lost their senses. "Go home? What do you mean? I can't leave now. How can I leave Salim in jail?"

Penny coughed. "Look, I know how you feel, you want to support him and all that, but honestly, Rosie, what d'you think you can do to help him?"

Rosie was silent. She shrugged her shoulders and replied, "Well, maybe not much. But at least I can visit him, give him my support. Anyway, aren't you forgetting something?"

"What?" asked Denise.

"The police have confiscated my passport."

Denise stirred her coffee slowly and bit into a nutty biscuit, thinking hard. Finally she said, "Look, the police must realize you are the victim in all this, surely we can argue that you need to go home and spend time with your family. As long as you can promise the authorities you'll come back when the trial begins. What d'you say? Shall we at least give it a try?"

Rosie was non-committal. She gave a long sigh and went to pay the bill. She did not say a word as she drove the girls back to the house.

Chapter Forty-Two

The air which hit their nostrils was stagnant and stale. Enormous thick wooden doors rolled open and Rosie and her sister entered in awe of the huge dull grey feeling of misery all around them. The doors closed behind them and Rosie clutched Denise's hand in panic. A sense of hopelessness permeated the air and Rosie had to fight a desire to turn and run. But she was longing to see him, even though she was also dreading it. The two girls sat on a cold stone seat and waited without speaking. At last a surly looking police officer, with cold eyes and a blank expression, beckoned for them to follow him through a series of doors. Metal bars clanged shut behind them and a warden locked the doors with an enormous bunch of keys attached to his thick black belt. Rosie's legs shook and there was a void in her stomach. She turned to Denise and told her in a small shaky voice that she wanted to see Salim on her own. Denise nodded and looked around for somewhere to wait. Rosie walked unsteadily on, steeling herself to follow the warden to a high counter with a glass screen above it.

She waited, anxiously looking through the smeared glass at the door at the far side of the room. Five minutes later the door opened and a gaunt looking man with hollow cheeks, grey skin and a bald head came through the door and shuffled slowly forward. Rosie looked beyond him, hoping that Salim would soon come out through the same door. Then the stooped man with the hollow cheeks stopped in front of the counter, raised his head and looked up into her eyes. Rosie took a sharp intake of breath. This man with a seemingly broken spirit was none other than Salim. Her eyes filled with tears at the pitiful sight. His bare ankles were shackled and his head had been shaved. She struggled to find some signs of familiarity. Was this the man she knew and loved?

Salim reached forward and picked up the telephone receiver on the counter. Rosie followed suit, fumbling for the telephone and holding the receiver up to her ear. She listened, unable to speak.

"Hello," he said in a croaky voice, as if he had not spoken to anyone for days.

"Hello," she repeated.

He smiled, showing that he had not brushed his teeth.

Don't they even allow them toothbrushes? she wondered, instantly angry with herself for thinking such a trivial thought.

"How are you?" she asked quietly.

"I'm fine," he answered bravely.

Fine? How can you be fine? she thought.

"Did you find Hannah?" he asked innocently.

Oh my God, he doesn't know about Hannah. She mouthed the words.

"What? I cannot hear you," he said, shaking the receiver.

Hannah cleared her throat and started again, "Hannah's dead," she said.

Salim swallowed hard, stunned at the news. "What? How? What happened to her?" he finally asked.

Rosie explained briefly about Hannah's desperate bid to leave the country and her subsequent car smash at the border. Salim rubbed his forehead and sighed.

Oh my poor darling, you don't deserve all this, she thought, looking at Salim's beautiful sad face. Rosie tried to comfort him. "Look, Salim, I know what you're thinking; Hannah was the only witness. But I can explain that you acted on my behalf. It was self-defence. You were trying to save me. I'm sure the authorities will take that into consideration."

He nodded and smiled weakly. He replied, without conviction, "Yes, I think you are right."

Oh God! What can I do to make things better for him? Rosie thought, racking her brains.

"I miss you," she said simply, putting the palm of her hand with its slim long fingers flat against the transparent glass screen. He smiled and looked into her eyes, bringing his own large brown hand up to the screen. Their hands met.

"Do you?" he asked earnestly.

"Of course I do," she replied.

He sighed and shrugged his shoulders, looking down at the bare counter.

"What, Salim? What is it?" she asked anxiously, talking into the green receiver and holding it tightly in both hands.

"Nothing. It's nothing." He sighed once more.

"Tell me, please," she implored.

Salim coughed. "When I am leaving here," he cleared his throat, "you will be gone." He searched her face for a reaction.

"Oh, Salim. No I won't. I'll wait for you, I promise," she said, feeling a yearning for him in her stomach. Then her face clouded. "But well, Denise, that's my sister, she wants me to go back to England with her, at least just for a while," she admitted.

Salim ran his hand over his smooth head before replying, "Yes you must go. You will not come back," he predicted.

Rosie shook her head. "I will, Salim! I have to come back for the trial…" her voice trailed off.

Salim grimaced. "That could take a very long time," he said quietly.

Rosie nodded, winding the telephone cord around her index finger. She looked up and saw the sympathy in Salim's eyes. A tear ran down her cheek.

"Oh, Rosie, please do not cry! I am okay. You go. Please," he said, leaning his elbows heavily on the counter top.

She nodded, unable to hinder the copious flow of tears. She wiped them away and tossed her head, biting her bottom lip in an attempt to be brave and controlled.

The tall authoritative figure of the prison warden moved towards Salim and muttered something low in his ear. Salim nodded solemnly.

"Rosie, I have to go now. Promise me something," he said.

"Yes, tell me."

He searched her beautiful face, wanting to remember every detail of it.

"Promise you will not forget me," he said simply.

No longer able to contain her emotions, her chest heaved uncontrollably.

"I'll never forget you, Salim," she trembled, "you will always be in my heart." The receiver hit the side of the counter as it fell from her shaking hand. It hung in mid air, bouncing up and down on its green coiled lead. Rosie turned her head and broke down, crying openly. Watching helplessly, Salim's shoulders sagged and his head drooped. The warden took his cue and beckoned for Salim to return to his cell. Rosie pressed her body against the counter and watched the most courageous man she had ever met, shuffle slowly towards the door. It was no surprise to her at all, that just when Salim had been almost entirely stripped of his human dignity, she found she possessed more love and admiration for him than ever before. It was as if Salim had been given this opportunity to show her what he was made of. The door closed behind him and Rosie found herself alone. And now there was nothing but emptiness and misery stretching out before her.

Chapter Forty-Three

It had taken a week for Rosie's lawyer to obtain her passport. Penny and Shabib had been wonderful hosts, allowing Rosie to sleep whenever she wanted to, cooking her meals (which she sometimes left untouched) and providing a listening ear whenever she felt like talking. But having Denise around was the greatest comfort to Rosie and Penny was convinced that Denise had really helped Rosie avoid sinking into the depths of a dark depression. In fact, all her friends had rallied around offering her support: Laura and Sam had been to visit her three times and Stuart had also come once or twice. Initially Stuart had felt quite awkward with Rosie. He was unable to accept her relationship with Salim, finding it totally distasteful. To think that she had cooled their relationship because of a nomadic tribesman was hurtful as well as downright laughable in Stuart's eyes.

The two of them seemed like strangers as they sat talking politely about irrelevant things in Penny's dark windowless living room. But at the end of his first visit, Stuart had silently pushed an envelope into Rosie's hand, pecked her on the cheek and squeezed her shoulder before leaving. Rosie had gasped when she discovered the envelope contained thirty crisp twenty rial notes. There was a small scribbled note inside the envelope which read: *'Dear Rosie, just a little something to help you through this difficult time. Lots of love Stu x'*. Rosie was touched by his kindness.

Even Thomas from the Institute had dropped by with a huge bunch of red stargazer lilies and her pay cheque. He looked at her kindly over his pince-nez and urged her not to worry about work. In actual fact, he had already found a replacement. A large well known insurance company had recently been established in Muscat and the wife of one of the employees was a very well qualified and experienced TEFL teacher. She had approached the Institute looking for work and Thomas had jumped at the chance of employing someone of her calibre. Thomas handed Rosie her salary and told her that when she left the country, the PR from the Institute would accompany her to the airport and cancel her visa. Rosie was alarmed at the prospect.

"Does that mean I can't come back in?" she asked.

"Not with us, you can't," Thomas replied.

Tears welled up in her eyes and she sat down stiffly on the sofa and fiddled with a white Kleenex tissue.

"Oh now now, I'm so sorry, m'dear. I didna' mean to upset you," said Thomas jumping up when he realized the effect of his words.

"No it's alright, I'm sorry," said Rosie, wiping her eyes and blowing her nose, "I seem to cry at the slightest provocation these days." She looked up at him with red-rimmed eyes.

At that moment Penny came into the room holding two mugs of tea. She took one look at Rosie and asked what was wrong. When Rosie explained, Penny immediately put Rosie's mind at rest by suggesting she could return to Muscat on a visit visa.

"Anyway, I'm sure Shabib would be more than willing to have you on his sponsorship," she offered.

Rosie grinned. To show her gratitude she stood up and went over to Penny, kissing her on the cheek and giving Penny's enormous tummy a gentle stroke.

"Oh sweet baby," she said addressing Penny's bump, "you have such a beautiful mother!"

Two days later Rosie and Denise boarded the Emirates flight to Gatwick. Through the deep purple night sky Rosie looked down at the millions of tiny twinkling lights of Muscat city and thought about Salim, locked up in a prison cell somewhere below. There seemed to be no justice in the world. Salim had done nothing but act with great courage to save her life. *Why is he being punished for doing the right thing,* she thought grimly, *while others who have done great harm to others in this world, appear to get away with things scot-free?* She closed her eyes and prayed for him. She wondered how long it would be before they would be able to see each other again. No date had been set for the trial. She had been warned that it could take several months, if not years. *Meanwhile Salim rots in jail,* she thought sadly. She vowed to write to him regularly and hoped the authorities would allow him to receive her letters.

Later, while Denise tucked into the in-flight refreshments, Rosie reclined in her seat and tried to sleep. She was so looking forward to seeing her parents again, but she needed to decide what she would tell them. So far they knew very little about the recent events in her life. She and Denise had wanted to protect her parents from the full horror of her situation but Rosie knew she would find it difficult to hold things back once she saw her father. She had always told her dad the truth about everything. She remembered when she was a kid he had always said, 'Don't do anything you wouldn't like to tell me about.' But then she thought about her father's heart condition. It would not be fair to lumber him with all the gory details. She could tell them there had been some trouble at work. That would justify her leaving Oman before the end of her contract. They knew that she and Stuart were no longer an item, so that would add credence to her decision to leave. But how would she explain that she would have to return for a trial they knew nothing about?

Every cloud has a silver lining. She could see that at least one good thing had come out of this awful tragedy. This dreadful experience had taught her to realize the brevity of life. Life was just too short to bear a grudge. Rosie was determined to improve her relationship with her mother, recognizing at last, how hard her mother had always worked to please her. Her thoughts turned to poor Hannah, lying in the mortuary along with the man who claimed to be her father. Both waiting for post mortems to be performed on their bodies, as part of the requirements of this murder investigation. *Why had Hannah chosen to run away?* Rosie would never know. Hannah had carried her reasons to the grave. Rosie sighed, still feeling as if she was living through a nightmare and fervently wishing she could wake up and find that it had all been a terrible dream. It all seemed so unreal. She was constantly tormented by a recurring question: Why had she been stalked? Had she unwittingly sent the wrong signals? Did Roger think she was 'asking for it'? Would she attract another stalker in the same way? *Is there something wrong with me?* she thought.

Rosie groaned as the full weight of her circumstances came down and rested heavily on her shoulders. She pressed the button to bring her seat into the upright position and got up from her cramped seat. She stretched and walked up the aisle to the toilets. Looking in the mirror, she told herself to be positive and not to live in the past. *What is done is done and cannot be undone*, she thought. She knew she could not change what had happened, but she *could* change her perception of it. Now she must look to the future and get involved in life so that she would not dwell on past events. *I will have to get a job anyway, to pay my way at Denny's*, she thought, wondering if there was still a job for her at the Brink Institute. Again, she groaned. No way did she want to go back to her old job. So much had happened to her since she had left Brink. She felt she was now a completely different person.

Rosie remembered hearing her own sweet enthusiastic voice as she had described her hopes and dreams to Stuart when they first met on the beach in Brighton. Perhaps it was not too late to pursue her dreams. She could apply to art college and take a photography course. What was stopping her? She suddenly felt a spark of enthusiasm, a glimmer of hope for the future and was determined to nurture it in any way she could.

Chapter Forty-Four

Peter and Elizabeth did not know Rosie was coming home. The girls had decided to make it a surprise. As Rosie and Denise waited for touch-down, they talked about taking their parents out for lunch. Rosie found herself feeling eager to please her mother. Looking back, Rosie realized that their relationship had faltered when she was around fifteen or sixteen. Rosie had always equated being adult with being fiercely independent. Inevitably, she had pushed her mother away, no longer wanting to be treated like a child. Rosie understood now, why she had continually criticized and rejected her mother's efforts to help her. She had thought it implied her own inadequacy. She had misinterpreted the message. She no longer felt she had to prove to her mother that she was perfectly capable of managing her own affairs.

Rosie turned to Denise and said, "Denny, I've decided I'm going to treat Mum as if she's the best mother in the world from now on."

"That shouldn't be too difficult then," Denise replied smiling, "Mum *is* the best mum in the world, as far as I'm concerned!"

Rosie smiled. *Denise is always so nice. Why can't I be more like her? Why do I always find fault with everyone?* Rosie vowed to be less judgmental and more tolerant of others.

The plane landed and Rosie looked out of the window. It was raining hard in the dull early morning light. The girls reached up and took their hand luggage out of the overhead lockers and slowly made their way down the aisle with all the other passengers. Later, they loaded their suitcases onto two trolleys and wheeled them out towards the car park. Denise fed an enormous number of pounds into the ticket machine and they jumped into the car, feeling cold and shivery with the sudden change of climate.

Rosie thought of sunny Oman and of Salim. He seemed a million miles away, in a different world. When would she see him again? Tears filled her eyes again. Denise glanced at her as she put the windscreen wipers on and drove out of the car park, heading towards the M23. "Hey, come on now, Rosie, don't cry. Just think of Mum's face when she sees you. She's going to be ecstatic!"

Rosie smiled. Denise turned on Radio One and began singing along with Dido's 'White Flag'. "There will be no white flag upon my door!"

"Oh my god," Rosie moaned, in mock annoyance, "I hope you're not gonna sing all the way home!"

"Well, I *am* and you're just gonna have to put up with it!" Denise replied laughing.

The grey clouds were heavy and low in the sky. Rosie shivered. It looked as if it would rain all day. She turned on the car's heater and felt a blast of warm air on her face. But it soon became too stuffy and she wound down the window and inhaled the fresh smell of wet grass, amazed at all the vegetation on either side of the motorway. *I have been starved of greenery*. It did her heart good to see the lush green grass, tall trees and vibrant summer flowers everywhere. She had forgotten that England was such a 'green and pleasant land' and had to admit that, despite the rain, it felt good to be home. She adjusted her watch, winding it back three hours and said, "Hey, what are we going to do? It's a bit early to wake up Mum and Dad, isn't it? It's only seven thirty."

Denise nodded, keeping her eyes on the road and suggested they go straight to her flat to check the post, unpack and let Rosie settle in. She had hardly finished her sentence when the phone rang, with amazing synchronicity. Denise looked at the caller ID and realized it was her mother calling. She mouthed for Rosie to be quiet and answered the phone with her hands free mike.

"Hi, Mum! How are you? Yeah, I just got in." There was a pause. Rosie could hear Elizabeth asking questions at the other end of the line. Denise answered, "Yes, she's okay, don't worry. She sends her love. Oh yes, that would be lovely but listen don't cook anything, Mum. Let me take you and Dad out for lunch." Denise smiled at Rosie, her eyes alive with excitement. "I'll come and pick you both up then. Let's say half past twelve? Okay, look forward to seeing you. Bye for now."

Denise pressed the end call button and laughed out loud. Denise loved surprises and she was now in a state of delicious anticipation. Rosie smiled at her dear sister and thought Denise really had a childlike quality to her character. She hoped Denise would never lose her great love of life. Rosie fervently wished that she might develop a more fun-loving personality herself. She knew she took life far too seriously at the best of times. But recent events had been transformational. Realizing that life is brief and precious, she vowed to enjoy each moment. But her heart was weighted down with the knowledge of Salim's incarceration. The frustration of being unable to change his situation was unbearable. She felt contrasting emotions; vulnerable and sensitive, yet somehow dead inside. Nothing really touched the numbness. She wondered if these feeling would ever go away.

How different my life would have been if I had not gone to Oman. But then perhaps things might have turned out a good deal worse for her if she had stayed at home. If Roger had continued to stalk her in Brighton she might not have lived to tell the tale. She wondered what would happen to his body. Would it be flown back to England for burial? Had any next of kin come forward to claim Hannah's body?

Denise parked the car and told Rosie to wait while she dashed out in the rain, holding a bright green umbrella over her head. She disappeared into the supermarket and twenty minutes later, returned pushing a trolley full of groceries. Denise deposited them in the boot and jumped back in the car, shaking her short wet hair. She dumped a lovely bunch of yellow roses in Rosie's lap. "Oh Denise, you shouldn't have!" Rosie exclaimed.

"I didn't." Denise answered, giving her a quizzical look. "They're for you to give Mum."

Rosie blushed at her mistake and laughed.

When they arrived at the apartment Denise unlocked the door and they were immediately greeted by a mountain of post, lying on the blue carpet. The girls parked their suitcases in the hall with its canary yellow walls and Denise plodded into each room, opening windows and letting out the stale air, while Rosie went into the kitchen and turned on the electricity. The fridge light sprang to life and hummed as it started to cool. Soon the kitchen was filled with the rich aroma of fresh coffee and the girls worked together to put away the groceries. Fatigue, after a long night with insufficient sleep, suddenly overwhelmed them and they collapsed in a heap on the sofa and watched the news, slowly reviving, as they sipped steaming hot coffee and munched their way through a plate of biscuits.

At twelve-thirty sharp, Denise rang Peter and Elizabeth's door bell, while Rosie hid in the shadows at the side of the house. The door opened and Rosie watched Denise give her mother and father a hug. Then, unable to contain herself a moment longer, Rosie jumped out of the shadows and shouted "Hi, Mum! Hi, Dad!" in the loudest voice she could muster. Their mouths dropped open in surprise. Elizabeth hardly recognized her.

Peter was the first to react, grinning from ear to ear and stepping forward to plant a big kiss on Rosie's forehead. "Ah, Rosie what are you doing here? What a wonderful surprise! How are you, my love?" he asked, giving her an enormous hug.

Rosie broke free and offered her mother the bunch of yellow roses. Elizabeth was unable to speak. Eyes brimming with tears, she put her arms around her youngest daughter and rested her head on Rosie's shoulder. Rosie found her mother diminished and fragile and suddenly felt overwhelmingly protective towards her. Without voicing her concerns, Elizabeth, in turn, noted with dismay, the marked change in her daughter since January and vowed to build her up with plenty of good food and TLC.

She knew Rosie had been through some sort of major crisis while she was away, but she was still not aware of the details. She was convinced it had something to do with Stuart.

Laughing and crying simultaneously, they walked arm in arm down the hallway into the living room. The girls were soon giggling as Peter and Elizabeth moved the coffee table out of the way and danced around the room, demonstrating the latest steps from their sequence dancing class. Rosie was amazed to hear that her parents intended to go on a very energetic dancing holiday with friends from their dance class. It would involve learning new dance steps in the morning, hiking all afternoon and dancing every evening. It made Rosie feel tired just to think of it!

While Elizabeth went upstairs to get her coat, Peter stroked Rosie's hair and asked if everything was okay. Rosie could not look at her father's sympathetic eyes for fear of breaking down. She looked down and nodded, determined not to spoil the occasion by talking about her problems. For now, she was just happy to be back in good ol' England and she did not want to think beyond that. Her face clouded when she thought of Salim languishing in a jail thousands of miles away. He was there because of *her*. Denise caught her eye and lifted her eyebrows questioningly. Rosie stood up quickly and suggested they drive down to Market Square to have lunch at her father's favourite fish restaurant.

Peter rubbed his hands together in anticipation and they all piled into Denise's car for the short drive down to Brighton's town centre. In an enthusiastic tone, Peter started telling the girls corny jokes. Rosie and her mother, sitting in the back of the car, exchanged smiles and rolled their eyes. By the time they reached the restaurant in the Lanes, it had stopped raining and the sun was peeping through the clouds.

The waitress in the tight black miniskirt, white shirt and black tie, wiped the chairs so they could sit on the forecourt of the restaurant, under a cream and bamboo parasol in the lukewarm midday sun. While they ate, Denise told them all about her impressions of Muscat. Rosie listened quietly with a far-off look in her eye. Her father squeezed her hand and gently brought her back to the present by talking to her about Aunty Joyce. Unable to cope on her own, Joyce was now living in sheltered accommodation and loving every minute of it. She had made lots of new friends and was regularly taken on outings to the coast, or stately homes and gardens. Elizabeth was immensely relieved to know Joyce was getting professional support.

On their way home Elizabeth took the plunge by asking the loaded question that she and Peter had so far been avoiding. "So, Rosie, are you going back to Muscat, or are you staying home now?"

Rosie could sense they were both holding their breath, waiting for her reply.

"I don't know, Mum. I mean, I'll be staying here for the time being, but as for the future, I don't know." Tears pricked her eyes. How could she get on with her life? There was a stony silence.

"Well, perhaps we can help you decide," said her mother. "We'd love you to stay home. We've missed you so much, love."

Rosie shrugged. "I know, Mum. But it's just not as simple as that."

"Why not?" her mother asked.

"Oh I can't explain right now... I—"

Her father interrupted her. "It's alright love. We understand."

Her mother nodded. Denise pulled into the driveway, put the hand brake on and sat back in her seat, keeping the engine running. Rosie jumped out to help her dad get out of the car.

"Why don't you come in for a cup of tea?" her mother asked. "You've no need to rush off now, have you?"

Denise shook her head, catching Rosie's eye. She called out from the driver's seat. "No thanks, Mum, we're both really tired. I think we'll go home."

"Yeah, Mum, we need a siesta," Rosie added.

"What's that?"

"A sleep, Mum, an afternoon snooze."

"Oh, that sounds good. I think I'll have one of those too!" her mother laughed.

Rosie hugged her mother and promised to come over the following weekend. Rosie turned to climb back in the car but her mother grabbed her arm and said, "Rosie, I want you to know you can talk to me about it whenever you're ready."

Rosie looked dejected, her shoulders sagging. "I know that, Mum. We will talk, but just give me some time. I'll explain everything. Don't worry now, I'm fine. See you later," she said, waving goodbye.

"Enjoy your fiesta," said her mother, smiling.

That night, Rosie sat down at the desk in the tiny bedroom in Denise's apartment and wrote a long letter to Salim, telling him how much she missed him and encouraging him to be strong.

Chapter Forty-Five

It was early September and there was still no news from Muscat. Rosie was increasingly concerned about Salim. She had heard nothing from him since her return to UK, even though she had written him more than a dozen letters. Was he denied access to her letters? Or had Salim deliberately chosen not to reply? He would be perfectly justified in harbouring feelings of resentment towards her. After all, if he had never met her, he would not have been destined to a miserable life behind bars.

Now Rosie sat upstairs on the dark green double-decker bus clutching her rucksack. She pulled up the collar of her suede coat. The early morning September air was chilly. She opened the flap of her bag and checked that she had everything she would need for this important day. A new camera (from her parents) with automatic and manual settings and an enormous zoom lens sat in its black leather case, together with rolls of film, a notepad and some pens and pencils. Her portfolio of photographs, taken in Oman, lay on her lap. She had to admit she was excited. Today was the first day of the photographic course she had signed up for at the local art college. It was only a part-time course, but that suited her just fine because she was now teaching several English students, on a one-to-one basis, in order to make ends meet.

There were nine other students on the photography course. Five of them were school leavers. Rosie found them extremely young, naïve and spotty. One was a short grey-haired man named Stan, who was in his fifties and had recently taken early retirement.

There was also an extremely tall hippy guy with dreadlocks, ripped jeans and a beautiful smile. His name was Will. But Rosie was delighted to find there were two other girls in their late twenties. One called Amanda, who was extremely artistic, judging by her tie-dyed purple vest and the vast assortment of rings, necklaces and body piercings which adorned her body. A stripy green and white bandanna partially covered her short pink hair. The other girl, Kathrine, had startlingly blue eyes and shoulder-length black hair that seemed to be going prematurely grey. Her designer handbag and stylish, elegant clothes looked a little out of place in an art college, but Rosie immediately struck up a friendship with her.

Their lecturer was a suave man with obvious charisma. His name was Ozzie. Rosie listened intently as he outlined the course and his expectations, before taking them on a tour around the photo lab, dark room and lecture hall. He was a professional photographer and had exhibited his work in several galleries in Sussex. Later, Ozzie gave each one of them a private tutorial and Rosie came out from the tutorial feeling elated and enthusiastic. She was quickly able to come up with a theme for her course work. It was going to be called: 'Opposites Attract' and she planned to compose photographs of objects, people and animals out of context.

Over the next few weeks Rosie learnt about the workings of the camera and was taught how to develop her own film in the dark room. A week later the whole group went on a field trip down to Shoreham harbour to photograph boats, ropes and sailors etc. They had a great time and Rosie felt that the students were beginning to develop firm friendships with each other. Rosie also liked the way the group began to support each other, by showing encouragement and sparking ideas off one another.

It had been a glorious sunny day but now the sun had disappeared behind fast moving clouds. After the field trip,

Rosie was free to go home. But it was only three o'clock and Rosie was so fired up that she was eager to return to the college and develop her photographs. Kathrine had left her things at the college, so both girls took the bus back to Brighton. Kathrine chatted the whole way about her adventurous love life and what she hoped to achieve after the photography course. Kathrine's idea of heaven was to become a fashion photographer.

When they reached the college the girls said goodbye and Rosie headed to the dark room to remove the film from her camera. She became so totally absorbed, that she failed to hear her mobile phone ringing in her bag, outside the studio. At 6 p.m. Rosie emerged from the dark room, leaving her photos pegged up to dry. She picked up her bag and hurried down the steps of the college just as a bus came around the corner. She ran to the bus stop and jumped on, showing the driver her student pass. Her photographs had come out well, she was really pleased with the results. She walked hurriedly up the hill towards the block of flats, remembering that she was supposed to cook dinner. She and Denise normally took it in turns to shop and cook for each other. Whoever was not cooking, had to do the washing up. Rosie far preferred to cook than to wash dishes. Now Rosie checked her watch and realized she was running late. Denise usually arrived home at 6 p.m. and it was already 6.20 p.m. Luckily, Rosie had done the shopping that day before, but she realized dinner was going to be late. Denise hated to wait. She was always hungry when she came home from work. She would be cursing Rosie right now...

Rosie let herself into the flat quietly. But as soon as Denise heard the key in the door, she jumped up and came to meet Rosie in the hallway. Even before Denise could open her mouth, Rosie started apologizing. She threw her bag down on the chair and headed straight for the kitchen. But Denise grabbed her by the arm. "Stop a minute, will you! Listen to me!" Denise whispered.

Rosie stopped. She looked at Denise. Her sister looked different somehow. Denise's eyes were bright and shining.

"What is it, Denise? What's happened?" asked Rosie.

"It's *him*." Denise said, cocking her head towards the living room.

"What do you mean, 'him'? Who's 'him'?" asked Rosie, puzzled.

"You know," said Denise coming around behind Rosie and gently guiding her towards to the living room. "He's in *there*," Denise said, pointing.

"Who?" Rosie asked.

Denise rolled her eyes. "Just go, go and take a look," she grinned.

Rosie walked into the living room, frowning, thinking *whoever it is, I am in no mood for visitors. I have dinner to cook and...*

She stopped in the doorway and blinked. Sitting on the sofa, as completely out of context as one of her own bizarre photographs, was a man with extremely short dark hair and a beautiful smile. It was Salim, and Rosie was absolutely speechless.

Jane Jaffer, a primary school teacher from London, moved to Muscat in 1980. She is married to Redha and has three sons: Sami, Jass and Aymen. She is a counsellor, yoga teacher and Reiki healer. Scent of a Rose is Jane's first novel and her second book. Her first book, entitled Women on the Edge, was published in 2003 and is a book of poetry related to women's issues.